Full Figured 15:

Carl Weber Presents

Full Figured 15:

Carl Weber Presents

Anna J

and Honey

www.urbanbooks.net

Urban Books, LLC
300 Farmingdale Road, NY-Route 109
Farmingdale, NY 11735

ISBN 13: 978-1-64556-032-6
ISBN 10: 1-64556-032-5

First Trade Paperback Printing May 2020
Printed in the United States of America

10 9 8 7 6 5 4 3 2 1

Distributed by Kensington Publishing Corp.
Submit Orders to:
Customer Service
400 Hahn Road
Westminster, MD 21157-4627
Phone: 1-800-733-3000
Fax: 1-800-659-2436

Full Figured 15:

Carl Weber Presents

Anna J

and Honey

Other Women's Husbands

by

Anna J

Chapter One

Zaria

A secret can kill you in more ways than you may be willing to admit.

"I really hate that we even have to be in this situation right now," I spoke into the love of my life's ear as I walked circles around him and his wife. They were tied back-to-back in chairs in the middle of their gorgeous living room. I was irked that I even allowed him to pull me out of character like this. This was not usually how I acted, especially not over some dick. It was too readily available for me to be stuck on one, but he brought my heart into it. I just wasn't willing to tap out and take it on the chin. Not this time. No, this time, someone had to pay.

"Guess you didn't think I would find you, huh?" I asked, fully aware that he wasn't capable of answering. I had him bound and gagged because I didn't want that deep, sexy voice to convince me not to go forward with my plan. Just thinking about the things he did with his tongue caused an orgasmic jolt right to my clitoris. I had to squeeze my legs together and lean on the back of the couch for support to prevent collapse. This man had me open. I hated that about him. I hated that about me.

Here's the thing . . . or maybe a few things I'll make clear so that your judgmental ass can maybe see where

I was coming from. Yes, I knew Tariq was married. He made it very clear that he was unhappily married to Tracey, one of the CEOs in my division. No, he never, not one time, said that he would leave her for me, because it was "cheaper to keep her." His words, not mine. No, they were not fucking like that, but they didn't necessarily have an open relationship. They just kind of did them. Yes, I knew it was supposed to just be a fun thing, something to do, get this pussy worked out, and enjoy his company whenever he visited. No, I was not planning to fall in love with him, but I did.

Shit, love happens! It wasn't in the damn plan, but it happened. To me, of all people. I knew he had me when I cut off everyone else to be exclusively with him. This, knowing that he was only in town a few times a year. I'd have rather fucked my fingers until they fell off than given this juicy box to someone other than Tariq. Call me crazy, but it was my truth.

It wasn't like I didn't try, because believe me, I did. And more than once, but I couldn't concentrate on anyone else long enough, and the entire time I was with a different guy, I would be pretending it was Tariq who was responsible for the wonderful orgasms that were being dragged out of me. After a while, it just wasn't fair to any unsuspecting man I brought home. He consumed me, and my body wanted only him to touch it. So I waited for as long as it took until he came back to pleasure me again. This sometimes took weeks. Other times it was months, but no matter the duration, I always got mine until he rolled out again.

"I wasn't supposed to love you, Tariq," I said to him, stopping in front of his wife. I studied her face, her disheveled hair, the expensive sneakers on her feet, and the jewels around her neck. She was gorgeous. I could see why he chose her. She matched his fly. Her attitude, though . . . Oh, how I wanted to get a running start and dropkick this bitch in her esophagus the very first time I met her. Definitely not a people person. Not from what I could see. And I took extra pleasure in pleasing her man because I knew for certain she couldn't and wouldn't do the things to him that I was willing to do. Or would she?

"Wake up, princess," I said in a singsong voice as I lightly tapped her on the forehead with the butt of the gun. I didn't actually plan on killing them today. Not if they cooperated. I just had to get some shit off my chest. Maybe teach Tariq a lesson and Tracey too. Maybe this would bring their marriage closer together, and they would leave single people like me the fuck alone. Maybe, after this, they would see what they had in each other and not look to the outside. Make their bond stronger. Make him forget that he ever met me.

She stirred a little bit but didn't open her eyes. I guessed that punch to the face was a little harder than I thought. Tilting my head to the side, I examined her a little further before walking away, continuing to burn a circle in the carpet under my feet. Taking in my surroundings, I saw that it was clear they were rich in this bitch. By mogul standards, of course. From the Klipsch surround sound system attached to the seventy-five-inch wall-mounted Vizio, to the Vera Wang china in the cabinet near the Italian leather furniture, everything in this bitch looked expensive as fuck. I hated to get blood on any of it, so I was careful to place their bodies in the middle of the floor away from everything. Figured that was the least I could do considering the circumstances.

"Your wife is still sleeping," I informed Tariq when I got back around to him. Tear after tear escaped those caramel-colored eyes that pulled me in from the beginning. He was a head turner as well with caramel-colored skin, which was in excellent condition due to a strict skin-care regimen and plenty of water intake. I loved staring into his eyes while we made love. Well, we would have to be in love to make love, so clearly, it was just a deep fuck between one in love and one in lust. The thought was pissing me off all over again.

Grabbing the duct tape from the table, I propped up Tracey's head to the back of his and wrapped the tape around both of their heads down to the eyebrows, covering them with tape as well. Secretly, I hoped they would snatch both their damn eyebrows clean off when whoever found them removed the tape. If everything went as planned, I'd be long gone before anyone could find me. If he was as smart as I thought he was, he'd just let me go.

"Sorry I have to do this, but her head won't stay up. Maybe y'all can work as a team, because now is as good a time as any to give her support. Teamwork makes the dream work, right?" I asked him as I cut the tape and secured it in place, resisting the urge to slice both their damn throats.

I wanted to gut punch his ass for being so stupid. I had too much on my plate right now. My plane would be leaving in about two hours. I didn't have any bags to check in, so I pretty much just had to get through the security checkpoints, and then I would be on my way. I had a son to think about. Yes, I knew that before I did all this shit, but that was the single reason why I didn't kill both of them. Or maybe I should have, so as not to leave witnesses. It wasn't like anyone knew I was here.

I was confused, but I refused to cry in front of them. I had to be stronger than this, and since I was certain I would never see Tariq again after today, I had to make this shit memorable.

I was let go from the firm after word got out about our affair, and I had since relocated to another Fortune 500 company where I was actually getting paid more. I really didn't need the money, though. Tariq had my account crazy fat, and the job gave me a nice package upon my exit because they didn't want anything to tarnish their image as a company. Something like this could ruin everything. I kept it strictly professional at the new gig. No small talk, all business. I just had to see him one more time and get this, and him, out of my system.

Looking down at the gun, I picked it up, not concerned about fingerprints because of the white gloves that covered my hands. I saw that on an episode of *Snapped*. No evidence left behind. I walked up to the couple, trying to decide if killing them was indeed the best thing to do. He wouldn't say a word, but she would definitely want answers and repercussions. I didn't know if I was willing to roll the dice on her just yet.

"With the way this thing works," I said to Tariq, "all I have to do is pull the trigger, and it's over for both of you. One bullet, through your head and out of hers." I talked loud enough for him to hear me, but not so loud as to make anyone walking by outside aware of the situation. Paranoia was starting to set in, and I didn't want to fuck this up.

The look on his face was priceless, as a fresh stream of tears sprang from his already-bloodshot eyes, and he mumbled something inaudible through the gag. I wasn't crazy enough to remove it and risk him screaming for help. I wanted to kiss his lips one last time, but I resisted. I had to make a clean break. Raising the gun to his forehead, I looked him in the face before closing my eyes and putting my finger on the trigger.

Infidelity (noun): the action or state of being unfaithful to a spouse or other sexual partner.

Chapter Two

Tracey

The only way to keep a secret is to never tell it.

I walked into this house, and this fool was watching *What's Love Got to Do with It.* If you asked me, love hadn't had a damn thing to do with it in years. This was the kind of simple shit he would do instead of talking to me about whatever issue we were having at the time. Like usual, I was supposed to wait until the movie was over and let the theatrics begin. It was always the same thing, and tonight I just wasn't in the damn mood for this shit. Tariq was such a pussy sometimes, and it took everything in me not to go off on his ass. Sometimes a mofo needed to get punched in the face, but lucky for him, I was a lady, and it wasn't worth the broken nail or chipped polish. Deciding to speed things up, I didn't even bother to wait until the credits were rolling before our in-home show began.

Coming out of my Balenciaga Papier pumps, I grabbed the matching handbag and made my way to the bedroom. This was going to be one of those kinds of nights that I needed to be in some comfortable clothing. My Herve Leger Arabella dress with the matching jacket was not the proper attire for an all-night argument with old jackass. I needed to be down on the ground in a pair of sweats and a T-shirt, not standing in six-inch pumps and a $1,200 dress. I didn't think it would get physical this time (90 percent of the time, I initiated it by taking the first swing), but I needed to be ready just in case.

Stepping into my walk-in closet, which was the size of a master suite, I set my purse down on the oak chest closest to the door. Pressing the button on the wall near my vanity caused the wall to slide to the left, revealing endless pairs of designer shoes by Emilio Pucci, Jimmy Choo, Salvatore Ferragamo, and Badgley Mischka, just to name a few. I was a label whore, and I didn't give a flying rat's ass who didn't like it. I earned my chips and spent them where I felt like it as I saw fit.

Finding the spot where I took my current pair from this morning, I carefully placed them back in their spot in the black section, because you know I kept my shit organized and color-coded. It was the OCD in me, I guessed.

After pressing the button to close the door, I took a quick look in the mirror, remembering to call my stylist, Antonio, in the morning to see if he could fit me in on my lunch break for a quick touch-up and flat iron. Something had to be done about this gray that was popping up on my temples, no doubt caused by my crazy-ass husband, because I refused to believe it was due to aging. Moving farther into my closet, I pressed another button that produced several clothing rounds where I kept my dresses. Carefully stepping out of the soft, cream-colored material, I hung it back up on a silk-covered hanger, convinced that I could probably wear it again before I took it to be cleaned, but knowing I probably wouldn't.

Now standing in front of one of several full-length mirrors, I took a moment to admire the body I paid good money to get and worked even harder to maintain. With an intense workout regimen, a little nip/tuck here and there, and a high-protein, low-carb diet, my size-ten curves were simply the truth. I owned a nice, round booty that any sister would be proud of. It was firm and sat so high you could put a drink on it. Perky breasts the size of medium guava melons sat nicely in my Dirty Pretty Things bra, and a Brazilian-waxed kitty rested in the matching panties. Everything was toned and tight, just the way it was supposed to be. Milk chocolate skin that was softer than a baby's ass glistened a little from the diamond-sparkle body lotion I applied earlier in the day. To be hitting almost thirty-five, I looked damn good, and I would be even more on point once those stubborn grays were gone!

Brushing my mid-back-length tresses into a sloppy ponytail, I searched my bottom drawer for a pair of Victoria's Secret sweats and a T-shirt. I knew I should just stick to the script and eat the spinach salad I picked up on the way home for dinner, but walking in and seeing him in his bag worked my entire nerve, and I needed at least a scoop of ice cream to deal with this bullshit. I was an emotional eater, and at one point in my life, I had ballooned up to almost 250 pounds. I was so depressed it was crazy. I fought tooth and nail to get back down to a desirable size, but every so often my inner fat girl peeked her head out, and I had to fight like hell to drag her back in. This was one of those moments.

Stepping freshly pedicured feet into my favorite Ugg slippers, I took a deep breath and got ready to rumble. This was going to be a long-ass night, and if I was lucky, I could cut the time it would take to argue in half so that I could go to bed. Running a Fortune 500 company was a lot of work and long hours, and a d-i-v-a needed her sleep.

Dragging my feet, I made my way back downstairs only to find this man in the lotus position on the floor in front of the television. Oh, he was really working my set, and I had a few words for his ass. First, I had to get my ice cream, and then it would be on.

Entering the kitchen, I peered through the clear glass door of my refrigerator to see what goodies I had for the taking. I hated when people stood with the damn door open to look inside, so when General Electric came out with this model, I hopped right on it. I was a Frugal Franny in some areas, and PECO was not about to get dibs on extra money from wasting electricity when I had a love affair with Giuseppe Zanotti that I was not about to get help for.

Focused on getting just one scoop, I grabbed a little eight-ounce cup from the cabinet and dished out a small portion of Cherry Chocolate Chunk ice cream from Blue Bunny. This shit was like crack. Grabbing a bottle of Smartwater from the fridge, I sulked into the living room and took a seat on the couch. Enjoying my little snack, I sat in silence and waited until this fool was done with his little fake-ass meditation process. He worked my entire soul down to the bone, and just looking at him made me want to throw my cup at him. He was just so damn extra all the time, and it made me wonder what I ever saw in him.

I wouldn't lie and say that his gorgeous smile and the glint of his platinum American Express card didn't have me in the beginning, because it did. But nowadays, it wasn't enough. He was more of a nuisance than a knight in shining Armani, and I wasn't sure if I was sticking around to see how this drama played out. As of late, it just wasn't worth it to me like it used to be.

After about five minutes, he opened his eyes, and I got a good look at those pools of warm caramel that pulled me in five years ago but did absolutely nothing for me now. It just goes to show that you needed more than good looks to keep a sister around. Just throwing that out there for whoever needed to catch it.

"What's the problem, Tariq?" I asked in a strained voice that I hoped didn't sound angry from the gate. I didn't need the whining because he didn't like my tone, and I needed to get this over with as soon as possible. *Love & Hip Hop: Atlanta* was about to come on, and I needed my dose of trash TV before I called it a night.

"Why do you think there's a problem?" he responded as he unfolded his lean, muscular body and easily stood. I tried to control my face from contorting into an angry look, but he was already testing my patience, and I just wasn't beat for this shit tonight.

"Tariq, please don't try to play me short. You left the office early today, and when I get here, you're watching this depressing-ass movie. The same shit you do every time there's an issue I have to drag out of you. What is the problem now? Let's not drag it out this time."

"There isn't a problem," he said in an unbothered tone, which pissed me off even more. If nothing else, he knew exactly how to get me turned up. "I need to go out of town to check up on the flow of business in Houston, and I needed to get a head start."

Here we went with this bullshit. This was factor two of one million on the list of reasons why everything was so shady between us. In understanding that a part of our jobs caused us to be on the road a lot, Tariq spent more time out of town than in. It wasn't always this way, but now that I thought about it, the last year or so had this man on the move often. Every time I turned around, he had to jet some-damn-where, and then when he got home, he wanted to hit me off with a bullshit dick down that he could have kept to himself. Only sometimes, though. Lately, he hadn't even been trying when he got back, and I briefly wondered why. Honestly, I was better off finger popping my damn self. It took me less than a minute to bust off and be asleep, and I preferred that to faking it for five minutes with Mr. Quick Popper.

"Oh yeah?" I responded, deciding against dragging it out tonight and just letting it be what it was. He won this round simply on a technicality that I was dead tired, and my Ralph Lauren sheets were calling my name.

"Yeah," he responded nonchalantly like he didn't have a care in the world. Point well taken and noted.

"Okay, cool. I'm heading up. Make sure you set the alarm before coming up to bed," I responded just the same. Normally I would have started an argument, and I wondered if he noticed tonight that I just gave in or if he even cared. I had to admit the lack of response stung a little, but I wouldn't dare give him the satisfaction of knowing he put me in my feelings. He wouldn't get that victory.

"Will do. I love you, Tee," he said, calling me by the nickname he gave me when we first started dating. I didn't even bother to respond.

Lifting my body from the couch, I went and set my dirty dish in the sink, running water on it to keep it from getting sticky until I washed it. Then I placed my salad in the fridge to have for lunch the next day. I had to meet with some investors early in the morning to launch a new addition and business venture to the company. I was excited about it, and if I planned to get my workout in before I started my day, I would need to be asleep within the hour.

Turning the TV in the bedroom to VH1, I slipped out of my sweats and into bed, where I let the 3,000-thread-count sheets press against my body, not even concerned that I hadn't taken my evening shower. Once I set the DVR, I got comfortable, giggling every so often at the antics of Stevie J and Mimi as I drifted off to sleep.

I had a lot on my plate for the next day, and I need to work off some of this frustration. A small smile crept up on my face as I decided to replace my hair appointment with a quick session with my sidepiece. That was just what I needed to get my head on straight, and I could deal with this gray maybe later in the day. After all, it was about to be Wednesday, and I planned to take "hump day" to the next level . . . pun intended!

Chapter Three

Tariq

If you do tell your secret, tell it to a baby under the age of 1. They won't remember it long enough and can never repeat it.

I used to love Tracey, really love her. Like, my every thought was about when I would see her again, and when I did see her, thoughts of our next meeting after that would consume my mind. I loved her way before she loved me, and I knew that to be a fact. Tracey had a cockiness to her that wouldn't allow her to be too soft too early. I had to work on breaking that barrier, and when it felt like nothing could get through that "tough as nails" mentality, she finally gave in to me. It was the happiest day of my life, and I felt like I hit the jackpot.

The saddest day of my life was when I realized I didn't love her anymore. We were six years into our relationship, and truth be told, I had already invested too much to just walk away and lose everything. Tracey was a go-getter. That was the main reason why our company flourished the way it did. She didn't wait for others, and that was part of the problem. When you decide to go into business with someone, the decisions are supposed to be mutual among the group. Tracey had a habit of making decisions for both of us because it was convenient for her, regardless of how I felt about any of it. Yeah, she softened up in some aspects. She wasn't the twenty-four-seven/365 bitch anymore, but she definitely never let go of her bitch tendencies. I could list a million reasons why I loved Tracey, and I could also list twice as many reasons why I didn't.

The first and the last thing was that she got on my damn nerves. It was her mouth. It seemed like the only time she was quiet was when she had my dick in it, and lately that hadn't been working either. You ever meet a woman who was just too strong? Like, sit down with all that. She was just a nag. Complained about every-damn-thing. Nothing was ever good enough anymore. It didn't take much to please her in the beginning, but now I had to be a magician and a psychic at the same damn time to figure out how to make her happy, and I was tired of juggling both of those traits and a career. I chose work. It was easier and didn't talk back.

So I let the shit dwindle. Missed breakfast here and there turned into not showing up at all for both of us, which turned into missed lunch dates and eventually us merely seeing each other in passing. I saw her at the office every day, but I wasn't really seeing her. There, she was my colleague. Not the sexy VP all the men in the office drooled over when they thought I wasn't watching. Little did they know, I didn't even care. I had her when she was 300 pounds, and I watched the transformation. This new chick with this new body was a mess. They could have her ass. I was sure once the real her crept up, they wouldn't think she was so hot. I would gladly pass her ass off to one of them, and after a week, I was certain they'd be begging me to take her ass back. Sometimes I wanted us to get back to how it used to be, but I didn't think I was willing to put in the work.

I wondered sometimes if she missed me, missed us. We used to have a ball together before the other women, and other men on her part, came into play. Tracey loved to fuck, and she wasn't fucking me. I knew for sure she was giving it to someone else. She had a very large sexual appetite. At one point in our relationship, we would block out an hour and a half three days out of the workweek so that we could meet up at the hotel down the street from the job to get our midday freak on. This even after sex on most mornings and often times the night before. I barely made it through morning meetings just thinking about what we were about to get into. She loved it in every hole, too, and I loved that about her. I wondered who loved that about her now.

We both climbed the ladder fairly quickly in our company, and I questioned if that somehow played a part in our drifting apart. She said on more than one occasion that because she was a woman, she had to work twice as hard to get to the same level as me in the company. We were both one of ten VPs of Marketing, Inc., a company that specialized in information technologies and search engines, located in the Philadelphia office. There were seven locations nationwide. We were the face behind several large corporations that invested in getting their face global. There were two other women who held VP positions in our office, one Asian and one Caucasian.

In Tracey's head, she was convinced that in spite of her numerous degrees and years of expertise, she may have been given the position to make the company equally diverse. I'd told her plenty of times that if that was all they were looking for, they could have chosen anyone just to look pretty, but she wasn't trying to hear me. With that in mind, she was determined to not let them ever catch her slipping. Because of that, she had a cold-hearted attitude that made her more feared than respected, and I thought she preferred it that way. Honestly, it just turned the men on more. I was simply annoyed by it and her.

She even insinuated that I was given my position because I was one of the "boys." That pissed me off, because I was just as educated if not more so than any of the VPs there. That was the start of many arguments between us.

After turning the lights out and locking the house down, I went to the basement to make my nightly phone call before heading up to bed. We both had home offices with soundproof walls and private numbers, so even if she came downstairs, she wouldn't be able to hear what was going on in the office as long as the door was closed. I locked it just to be on the safe side, as well. As I dialed the numbers on the keypad, I wondered how long I would be able to keep this up before I went crazy. It was getting tiring, but it was something that had to be done. I made this bed, so I got comfortable in it. I really didn't have a choice.

"Tariq?" a soft voice came through on the line. I instantly got annoyed, because I hated stupidity. I called from this number every night. Who else would it be?

"Yes, baby. It's me," was my response in spite of my thoughts. I met this chick a few years ago while out on a business trip. It was supposed to be a one-hitter quitter, but I found myself hitting it every time I was in her neck of the woods. She made it so easy. That was until the slipup.

"Are you still flying in tomorrow?"

"Of course. I'll be there early. You'll be home alone, right?"

"Yes, it's already taken care of, but you promised—"

"I know what I promised," I cut her off immediately. I didn't feel like the nagging this evening, since I knew I would have to deal with the shit from my wife once I got upstairs and from her when I got to Texas. "It will be taken care of before I leave."

"Okay, but the last time—"

"Did you hear what I said?"

"Yes, daddy. Okay, see you tomorrow."

I didn't even bother with a response, damn near slamming the phone on the hook. Whoever said that leading a double life was easy needed to write the handbook, because this was all so nerve-wracking. I sat there for a few more minutes, mentally preparing for the bullshit that was due to rise once I entered the bedroom. Maybe tonight we could make it quick, because I really didn't have the energy to drag it out.

Once I got upstairs, it was quiet and dark in the bedroom. From the light shining through the hall, I could see that she was already asleep or pretending to be. Her hair was tied up tightly in a silk Coach scarf, and the covers were flipped back, revealing naked skin. The only thing she had on was a pair of French-cut panties that cupped her ass perfectly. My dick jumped in my pants, and for a second, I thought about pulling them to the side and sliding in. My wife had that good, tight pussy that any man would love and probably was in fact loving. The thought alone deflated my growth, and I instantly got an attitude.

Flipping the covers back on my side of the bed, I slid in without moving the bed too much and closed my eyes, rushing sleep. I would get my prize the minute the plane landed tomorrow. The thought alone put a huge smile on my face.

Chapter Four

Zaria

If someone insists that you can tell him or her your secret, that's full-blown proof that you need to bottle that shit up even tighter and really keep it to yourself. Trust me, if you don't, by morning, everyone on the planet will know.

My man would be here in a matter of minutes! You could never even fathom the level of happiness I was feeling right now. After all, it'd been six months since I'd seen him, and my boo always made me feel like I never missed a day when he came back. I was a little irked when he said I needed to find a sitter for Junior. He'd been waiting to see his dad just as long as I had, but Tariq did promise to spend more time with him this time around. Yeah, he promised that last time, too, and all my baby got was a thirty-minute hangout on the way to the airport.

We'd had this conversation before, Tariq and I, but he promised to be a better father when time allowed. It wasn't like I didn't know what I was getting myself into with him. I was fully aware. With him being stationed all the way in Philadelphia, it was hard for him to get home often, but I understood it. If I wanted to continue to live the life I had come accustomed to living, there were certain things I had to deal with. Him not always being here was one of them.

He made it so that I never had to want for anything. He paid my bills for months at a time and kept my bank account correct. I never had to touch my paychecks because he always deposited double what I made. It was like getting paid three times every week. As for our son, he had a separate account that was stacked, courtesy of his father, which I rarely touched. I didn't have to. Tariq took care of everything all the time. I would check periodically to see what was in there, and it was always more than what was there the last time I looked. Financially we were more than good, but we still needed improvement in other areas.

I raced through the house one last time to make sure that everything was where it was supposed to be, and in its proper place. Tariq hated disorder, and I didn't feel like allowing that to ruin the mood like it had in the past. That shit irked my nerves as well. All I had was a few pieces of dirty clothes—in the hamper, mind you—in the hallway! This dude went clean off, asking me what I was doing that I didn't have time to wash clothes before he got there. Shit, I had just taken them off the night before. It almost messed up the entire trip, but this time I was smart. I made sure all of the dirty clothes were in the basement in a trash bag in a dark corner where he wouldn't find them. That would save us both the attitude.

Eyeing the clock, I saw that he should be pulling up shortly. I ran my fingers up and down my legs and across my pussy to be sure there was no hair present. That was another thing he hated. My Brazilian wax was done a few days ago so that the swelling could go down, and I put Veet hair-removal lotion on everything else just to be sure that I was silky smooth and to give that perm smell time to go away. I was tired as hell, but I was wired at the same time. He would be arriving at six a.m., his normal arrival time, and just in time for me to put this good morning juice all over him.

At six on the nose, I heard the alarm beep and the door open. He punched his code in and set his bag on the hall table as he'd done so many times before. I stretched out on the top of the covers, naked with my back arched and facing the door, just like he liked it. He loved my plump ass, and that was the first thing he wanted to see when he walked into the bedroom. I faked like I was asleep as I listened to him remove his clothes. Soon, his weight shifted the bed a little as he climbed up and crawled up behind me.

A chill ran down the length of my body, and the hair on the back of my neck stood up as he began to trail kisses from my nape all the way down to the top of my ass. He leaned back and cupped it, bouncing it in his hands as if to check it for weight. I always kept it heavy back there, so I wasn't concerned. If I did nothing else, I made sure I got my squats in on a daily basis.

Spreading my cheeks apart, he pushed my body up, encouraging me to turn over. I quickly obliged, burying my head in the pillow so that my neighbors wouldn't hear the screams of pleasure that were sure to be coming from my mouth soon as I lay flat on my stomach.

Starting from the bottom, he dipped his tongue into my pussy opening, dragging his tongue up through the entire crack of my ass, stopping briefly to stuff it in my asshole before continuing his journey to the top of the crack of my ass. I exploded immediately. Taking the cue of him pushing my ass up, I swirled around a little and got up on my knees, bending in the doggie-style position to give him total access to all this juicy goodness. I was busting all over the place, and there was no shame in my game as guttural moans escaped my throat and filled the room. My man was home, fuck it. The neighbors would get over it eventually.

The feel of his full lips slurping me up was too much to handle, and I quickly reached another orgasm. Oh, he was showing off and showing out this morning. I guessed he missed me as much as I missed him. I wanted to feel him inside of me so bad, and no sooner than the thought popped in my head, I could feel him rising up behind me. I started pulsating immediately, anticipating his entry. My honey started to drip from my honey pot, just how he liked it.

He liked to tease me. I hated that shit, but I loved it just the same. He teased my clit with the head of his dick, and I dripped sticky honey on it. My pussy was clenching and pulsing ready to devour that beef stick, and I just wanted it in already! He parted me with the tip, stopping just at the opening. I clenched my walls around the head to try and pull him in, but he refused to cooperate. I knew from experience that he had a simple-ass smirk on his face that I wanted to knock right the hell off. I tried backing my ass up on him to push him inside, but he was stronger than me and wouldn't oblige. I was heated. Just at the moment when I thought I was going to go crazy and my head was going to spin on my shoulders like in *The Exorcist,* he slowly started to inch his way into the promised land. I damn near passed out.

"Yeah, you been waiting on daddy's dick, huh?" he spoke in a low, confident tone as if my response would be anything other than agreement. I wanted to answer, I really did, but he hit me with a quick pound that rattled my G-spot and shot me out into orbit. A bitch was drooling uncontrollably and everything. "I know you hear me talking to you, Za."

"Yes, daddy, I missed it," I managed to squeak out as he drilled into me once again, taking my breath in the process. This man was giving me life in more ways than one. I briefly tried to remember if I was caught up on my birth control as he smacked me on the ass and then gripped it tightly.

"Yeah, I missed you too. Show me how much you missed me, and I'll do the same."

That was all the encouragement I need to go buck fucking wild. Gripping him behind his legs with my feet, I bounced back on him until he was all the way in, milking and squeezing his length with my juicy walls. Somehow he ended up lying flat, and I was riding him in reverse. I made sure to give him a show as I eased up to just the tip and slammed back down on it like I was dunking a basketball.

"This what you wanted?" I moaned out as I handled my business. In the back of my mind, I couldn't help but wonder if his wife fucked him like this, and the shit started to make me mad.

Now before you go there, yes, I knew Tariq was married when I met him. Shit, Tariq knew he was married too, but if he didn't care, why should I? He wore a gorgeous wedding band that had to have been picked out by a woman: black onyx with embedded diamonds all the way around. Stunning, if a man's band could be. When he first came to the firm, I couldn't believe my eyes. Who the hell let him out by himself? If he were married to me, there was no way I would ever leave his side. He'd be in the shower, and I'd be right there on the other side with a towel waiting for him to come out.

Anyway, I was the secretary of the VP at the branch he was visiting in Houston. Part of my job was to prepare the boardroom for meetings and to greet visitors to the company on a higher level. Meaning, the people I saw were often higher-ups in the companies they represented, which meant they had money. There had been plenty of offers over the years by the men, and a few women, who wanted to show me a "good time" while they were in town, but I always declined. I wasn't into sleeping my way to the top, contrary to what rumors around the office said about us secretaries. I always maintained a professional stance, regardless of how much dick or pussy was thrown my way at all times.

Somehow that went out the window when Tariq showed up. He actually popped in a little earlier than expected, and he said it was because he wanted to see us in our natural habitat and not scripted behavior. That was genius in my eyes. Good thing we were always on point around here. We held light conversation as I continued to prepare the room and order lunch for the meeting. He had a great sense of humor, unlike most of the VPs who showed up all business, like it was a crime to crack a smile. That was until it was time for them to try to bag some pussy for the night. Their entire attitude changed then. He made me laugh, and I liked him. Not in an "Oh, I want to fuck" kind of way, but he was cool people. I could definitely see myself showing him the city and ending up at a bar and grill, drinking peach mojitos and eating Buffalo wings.

He didn't offer that time or the three times he showed up afterward. We just kept it friendly and familiar, always offering kudos when he was in town. I could never forget the one time he showed up with her.

I knew by the schedule that he was coming, so I made sure to order these Thanksgiving wraps that he raved about the last time he was here. It was carved turkey, stuffing, and cranberry sauce drizzled with gravy and wrapped in a tortilla. He said he could never find them in Philly, and he loved them, so I always made sure I had a few on the tray to pick from in case he wanted it. I was preparing the room as usual, and when I looked up, he still hadn't arrived. He always arrived an hour or so early, but I just chalked it up to maybe this time the flight was running late.

I was sitting at my desk, checking everyone in and finishing up notes, when they walked in. Gone was the smile that normally greeted me when he got off the elevator. His eyes even lost their sparkle, if that was at all possible. He had a straight face as he approached, giving me his name as if I didn't already know it. She didn't even bother to look up from her phone as she spat her name out and turned to walk into the boardroom without waiting for an escort. I kept my polished smile as I followed them to make sure they had all the materials for the meeting, his cologne wafting from him and invading my nose. Damn, he smelled delicious.

She was flawless! Her entire outfit screamed money. Designer everything, from the Diane von Furstenberg frames that covered her eyes all the way down to the Stuart Weitzman stilettos that covered her feet. And the rock! The diamond on her engagement ring was so sick my hand felt numb, and I wasn't even the one carrying it around. The band just sealed the deal. There wasn't a hair out of place on her perfectly executed feathered style, and her face was beat to the gawds. Gorgeous! But too damn serious for my taste. Everyone else in the meeting was light and breezy, but this chick was by the book, paying attention to every detail, calling you out on missed dictation, serious. You could tell no one particularly cared for her, but she knew her shit, so they had to listen. I hated her instantly.

That day they all left, him without even saying goodbye. It was unlike him, but I could clearly understand why. He lived with the warden. The next time he came, I treated him the same, ordering his favorite thing for lunch, but this time he asked me out. I immediately accepted. We didn't even have sex that night, opting for food and drinks at a spot not too far from the office. Every time he came to town, his visit got a little longer, and we spent more time after business hours, being sure not to hang out where we could possibly be spotted by others in the company. Before I knew what was happening, I loved him, and now look where we were.

"Yeah, this is what I wanted," he moaned back as I swirled on him and clenched him into a tight grip with my walls. I was getting even more pissed as time went on, getting more aggressive with each move. No, we never discussed being together permanently. Never even discussed entertaining a relationship of any sort, but wasn't I better than this?

"Am I the best?" I asked as I spun around to face him, keeping him inside the entire time. I was like the rapper Trina in the bedroom, doing all kinds of nasty shit to satisfy this man who didn't belong to me. This needed to change.

"Yes," he managed to moan out as I began to grind down on him, reaching back to cup his balls and squeeze slightly.

"Better than her?"

Instant deflation. It was like I said the code word for letting the air out of his dick. The little bit of sunshine that streamed through the cracks in the blinds gave me a slight view of his face, and clearly, he was irked. We agreed to never discuss her. I just had to take his word for it that he was making things right at home for both of us. Truth be told, it didn't feel like we were making any strides toward anything meaningful and were just sitting stagnant. I was over it.

"What did I tell you?" he asked, lifting me off of him in the process. His flaccid penis landed on his stomach in a juicy plop that echoed in the quiet room. I wanted to lean over and clean him off with my tongue, getting him back erect so that we could finish, but I knew better than that. Once he got in his bag, it took forever to get him out. Maybe I should have reached another orgasm before blowing it.

"Tariq," I began, but he cut me off.

"How many times do I have to tell you—"

"You won't, baby. It's just that . . ." I jumped in to avoid the long, drawn-out argument we were about to have. I should have just kept my damn mouth shut, but how long would my heart have to take this treatment?

"You knew what it was when we started out."

"I know I did," I replied as I moved back up and started tongue kissing his nipples. That always got him to calm down. Reaching down, I grabbed his sticky penis and started massaging it up and down, causing him to grow again. He was normally very adamant about wanting to finish an argument, but today I was finally taking control. Once he was fully erect, I climbed back on top to finish the job, taking the liberty of placing a nipple to his lips until he obliged and slurped me up. Barely avoiding a disruption, I went back in, giving him what I knew he wasn't getting at home. Before he went back, we would be discussing this issue. I couldn't keep lying to my son about where his father was and why he didn't love him. I just couldn't.

I gave it up until he fell asleep, and then I lay down beside him to do the same. I felt so horrible about what I was going to have to do, but Tariq didn't leave me a whole lot of choices. I did decide that I wasn't living how he wanted me to live anymore, and if he didn't want to cooperate, then I had to move forward with plan B. At the end of it all, regardless of how he and I moved, my son was more important. Tariq either had to be all the way in or all the way out. No in between.

Chapter Five

Tracey

But secrets are made to be told, contrary to popular belief. Whether you want them to be told or not. It's just the way of the world. What's done in the dark comes out shining bright like a diamond. The key is to prepare yourself. Always be ready to deny everything!

"Christopher, I'm not going to do this with you every time we hook up. You're really blowing me right now, and not in a good way."

My face was so tight I could barely see through the slits of my eyes. Why, oh, why could people never play their position? I chose Christopher because he was the complete opposite of my husband. Dark chocolate like a Hershey's bar with almond eyes that made me wet instantly. A bright white smile to match and a body that proved he worked out daily. I was horny at first sight. I could hardly pay attention in the meetings because I was staring at him so hard, not caring that, during the meetings, Tariq was sitting right next to me. Him being married was a bonus. That just ensured that he wouldn't be on my ass all the time, because he had a wife of his own, or so I thought. This dude seemed needier than the single guys I crept with, and it was disturbing.

That's the mistake that most married people make when cheating. Do not, I repeat, do not by any means cheat with someone single. Single people have way too much time on their hands and are not as understanding of your situation as they claim to be. In the beginning, they're cool because they're fucking someone else's property ("they're down with O.P.P."), but the minute those feelings that they are not supposed to be catching set in, they start acting up. Nobody has time for that.

His wife didn't have much going on either, which was surprising to me. Most of the VPs' wives were stay-at-home moms who shopped all day, took care of the kids, and had nothing but time to get ready to make an appearance. Top-of-the-line everything from head to toe, down to the dog. Like, their fucking dogs were walking around in Gucci raincoats and shit.

His wife, however, looked like she was having a hard time raising the kids or something. She never really had that polished look, and I wanted to offer her my stylist information. Her husband was a VP, so she could afford it. She was overly friendly, also, and very talkative at the company functions. One look at her and I knew why he wanted me. He didn't have this at home. Not that she was overweight or anything. She was just plain. No pizazz at all.

I had my eye on Christopher for months and decided to make my move at the company Christmas party one year. Tariq, along with a few of the other VPs in attendance, had been tossing back drinks all night. I stayed sober because I didn't want to forget anything that happened that night. I needed to remember everything. We had a designated driver so I could have gotten sloppy drunk as well, but I had my eye on the prize, and I needed to be on my game if I was going to pull it off properly.

I spotted Christopher at the bar looking at his phone. His wife had skipped out a while ago, stating that she had to get home to start the holiday cooking for their family's dinner the next night, as a few of the other wives began to leave as well to do the same thing. Or at least order catered cuisine. Tariq was in a wine cellar enjoying Cubans with some of the other guys. It was the perfect opportunity to set my plan into action.

Sneaking up next to him, I took the seat to the left of him at the bar and ordered a glass of pineapple juice. Eyeing him from the side, I could see that he was bored and ready to go as well but was probably just waiting for the right moment to dip on the festivities. I had to at least get a taste before he left, and he made it extra easy for me, and he didn't even know it.

"I know you're getting some vodka to top off that pineapple juice," he said jokingly, setting his phone down on the bar. Taking a good look at him, I could see that he was tired. I wasn't sure it if was from the party or home life, or both, but I knew I couldn't let him leave without at least trying to get a sample.

"Nope. This is it. I want to be fully aware of this entire night," I replied flirtatiously. I made sure to make eye contact so that he could see the fire in my eyes. I wanted him to know he could have it his way like Burger King. My walls were already quaking just thinking about the possibilities.

"Yeah?" he questioned, apparently catching on. I saw how he looked at me in meetings. Lust all in his eyes just like the other guys. The difference was that the rest of the men were cool with my husband, so I was kind of like a no-touch zone. With Christopher, although he was cool with Tariq, he really didn't play him too close. Always very professional. When they had guys' nights, he never came, even after being invited personally by my hus-

band. Not sure why, but that's how it was with them. It made it so much easier to push up on him, since he practically eliminated himself from the unspoken "look but don't touch" rule. His loyalty wasn't with Tariq, and that worked in my favor.

"Yeah," I replied sexily, playing with my straw with my tongue before sipping my drink. "I'm actually about to head out. I have a car parked out front. Need a ride?" I asked with an innocent look on my face.

"Sure. I sent my wife with our car. I'm sure she's probably in the kitchen preparing for tomorrow. I was just going to ask one of the partners for a lift. Since you're heading out, I might as well ride you . . . I mean, ride with you," he said with a slight smile while blushing.

Without any further words, I grabbed my fur from the coat check, sending Tariq a text that I would meet him at home. He didn't even respond, but the read receipt showed that he saw it. I knew he wouldn't be in for a while, but just to back up my story, I texted my best friend, Trisha, to let her know what might be happening. Just in case Tariq made it home before me, she was to instruct him that I was with her and had arrived at her place drunk and unable to find my house keys, or whatever lie she could think of. I kept the same secrets for her from her husband, so I knew she had my back.

I was a little nervous as I ordered the driver to race toward the Ritz-Carlton. I was almost afraid he would object, but when he sat back in the seat and sipped a ready-made drink from the car's bar, I knew it would be on, and I almost couldn't contain myself. My body wanted to climb on him and get it started right in the back seat, but I wanted to take all of him in, in more ways than one. Finally, grabbing a drink, I gave myself some liquid courage so that I could be ready for what was sure to come.

When we got to the hotel, I went inside first and checked in, texting him the room number and door code. I was smart enough to know there were cameras in the lobby, so I wouldn't just blatantly walk in with him on my hip. He obviously knew the deal too, both of us having way too much to lose. While I waited for him to come up, I took a quick minute to refresh my situation for him. I wanted this thing to taste yummy for him.

It actually took him a while to come up, and for a second, I thought maybe he had changed his mind. Just when I was getting discouraged, I heard the key code being pressed in, and the door swung open. I was laid out on the bed in B. Tempt'd by Wacoal, waiting to get this party started. Freshly sprayed Poppy Wildflower by Coach settled in the air, and he looked like he appreciated what was laid out for him. The condoms were on the table, in clear view, so that we were clear on everything. Nobody had time for slipups.

He smiled as he sauntered toward me, losing articles of clothing along the way. My mouth watered as his chiseled body became fully visible, not disappointing me at all. I was hoping he was toned. He wore his clothes well, but that didn't really mean a lot if you covered up your flaws. How you looked naked was what really mattered. He looked perfect.

No words were exchanged as he stepped in front of the bed completely naked, his excitement evident in his heavy, thick, long dick. I wanted to gulp him down whole, but I waited my turn. He leaned into me, licking my pussy through the sheer crotch of my panties. That shit put me on ten and had my entire body feeling like someone lit a match and put it on my skin. A low moan involuntarily escaped my throat, head digging in the pillow uncontrollably. Please don't let him be a quickie!

He licked me again, this time pulling the crotch of my panties to the side and using his fingers to spread me open. He inhaled my stickiness, his tongue darting out in between each intake of me while tasting my sweetness and scooping it out with his tongue. I resisted the urge to grind my pelvis into his face, allowing him to be in control for now.

He lapped and sucked and slurped me up, capturing my clit in his mouth and sucking it gently in between long strokes with his tongue. I thought I loved him. He had my legs spread so wide I thought they would snap at the hip, and if they did, I still wouldn't stop him. I wanted him to have full access to devour me completely. He licked and stroked and beat my pussy to death with his tongue until I exploded all over it, coating his tongue and lips with my juices. That alone had me ready to go to sleep, but it was only right I return the favor.

Motioning him to lie down on the bed, I crawled up toward him, planting kisses sporadically until I got to the prize. His stiffness stood strong and long, curving a little to the right. I loved a man with a right hook. I almost didn't want to touch it; it was so perfect. My mouth was watering in anticipation as I got closer to it.

Upon arrival, I first taste tested the thick vein that traveled up the underside of his thickness. I could feel it pulse like a heartbeat under my tongue, and that just excited me even more. I took my time, too, memorizing it along the way so that I would never forget it, knowing in that instant that I would do whatever it took to get it again. When I finally got to his thick mushroom head, I dipped my tongue in the pre-cum that puddled at the slit, before taking him into my mouth completely. He watched me through slits as I hungrily took him in, milking him as I tried to control his ejaculation.

His moans were so deep and sensual, filling my head like surround sound. I could listen to him forever. Pressing the space right underneath his heavy balls, I kept my finger on the pulse until it slowed down, and his semen backtracked until I was ready for it, temporarily mesmerized at how my Morgan Taylor Man of the Moment nail lacquer complemented his dark skin. I wanted to feel him.

Grabbing a condom from the table, I first tucked it into my mouth, and then I used my lips to apply it on him, savoring the feel of him in my mouth in the process. He seemed to have grown even thicker and stronger than before. Crawling up his body, I positioned myself on top of him, feeding him my nipples one by one then both at the same time. I took my time taking his length in, adjusting my tight walls to his girth until I was able to get all of him in comfortably, grinding my clit against his pelvis. I took that ride slow and long, taking life and giving life at the same time. I so needed this.

"You want to crack that nut inside of me, or you want me to suck it out?" I asked him low in his ear, grinding down on him slow and nasty. My pussy was making sopping sounds as I went up and down, it was so wet. I was enjoying this a little too much, and Tariq was never even a passing thought.

"Let me go deep and spit it out," he responded, lifting me from him and bending me over so that he could take me from the back. I thought he was going to pound me out, but he took his time getting back in and coasting with me right into home plate. With one leg draped over his strong arm as we switched to the side position, he played my clit like a guitar until we both screamed out in bliss. I felt bad immediately after he

pulled out. I couldn't believe I actually went through with it. I'd cheated before. Dozens of times actually. Never before this close to home, though. Work dick was off-limits, but this one I just had to have. Why was I so damn greedy?

We took our time catching our breath before getting up, finishing up in the shower, where he had me pressed against the wall giving it to me again. My feelings of guilt quickly diminished. I briefly wondered where the condom was, but I didn't think any more about it as he fucked me hard. By the time we were done I was spent.

Leaving the room after we were dressed, I waited for him in the car. He joined me shortly after, and when we got to his home, he quickly pecked me on the lips before leaving the car and slightly jogging up to his front door. I wondered what was going on in his head as I made my way home. When I got there, Tariq was still dressed, sprawled out on the couch in a drunken stupor. I left his ass right there as I quietly climbed the stairs and got into bed as if I'd been there the entire time. It was hard to wipe the smile off my face as I went to sleep, my body still pulsating to the feel of Christopher and the moment I had with him. I indeed was playing with fire, and I was ready to get burned.

This was one of the many nights we would hook up, and I just hoped I never regretted this. I hoped he didn't either. He was getting clingy on me all of a sudden, and that was definitely against the rules. Christopher came to play, though, and in his own way he was letting me know that he was making the rules tonight. We could have already fucked and been gone right now, but he just had to drag this thing out.

"Let's not pretend my feelings don't matter. I told you I wanted more, but you don't listen to me."

Blown.

Why couldn't this man just chill out and let shit be what the fuck it was? Sheesh. To say I was over it was an understatement.

Chapter Six

Tariq

It's almost impossible to hold a secret in. You just have to tell somebody so that you can say it out loud. Free your conscience of the guilt, if only for a little while.

Flashing back to four years ago, my head was still spinning with confusion. I was a father to a child I barely even knew. He looked just like me. Spitting damn image. Exactly how I looked at 4 years old. When she texted me the picture, it was like looking at myself. Tariq Jerome Mason Jr. That's what she named him without consulting me first. Last name and all. I wasn't even in the city when she gave birth, but I did make a half attempt to fly out to her. I may have seen her twice the entire pregnancy, both times in the company of Tracey. Not because I didn't want to outside of those moments, but my schedule just didn't work around an unplanned pregnancy. We were also in the midst of a huge merger, and I couldn't just leave without it being questionable. She said she understood. I let that lie put me to sleep every night.

"Tariq, I'm pregnant."

Silence.

"I know it wasn't in the plan, but I'm sixteen weeks. That's too far along to get a legal abortion."

More silence.

At that moment, she'd sounded like Charlie Brown's teacher, and my head felt like it was going to explode. I started questioning in my head if it was even mine, but I knew enough to know that if she was sleeping with another guy, she wasn't that stupid to get caught up like that. When the doctor confirmed how far along she was, it coincided with the last weekend visit I was there. Exact date, as we both counted it out on the calendar. She swore she hadn't been with anyone else, and I believed her. Not that I told her not to be. That was a decision she made on her own. Now I was somebody's dad. This shit sucked. Not being a dad, but not being able to be a dad. It was the worst feeling in the world.

Had she told me earlier in the pregnancy, I would have made her get an abortion. She was looking thicker than usual when I flew out a little over a month after the conception date, but it was all in the right places, and I loved it. Boobs bigger, ass fatter, thighs warmer, and pussy just gushy and juicy. I was in love! Not too long after that, while placing a call to her from my home office on a random night, she told me in a tearful voice that she was pregnant with my child and past the legal abortion stage. She had to keep it. I hung up the phone without a response and didn't call her back for almost three weeks. She didn't bother to contact me the entire time. That bothered me even more.

I had never met anyone in her family. Never. Not her mom, dad, siblings, aunts, no-damn-body. Even when I came out to meet my son for the first time, it was she and I alone at the house. Before showing up, I had been sending her money to get the nursery together and to keep her comfortable. She never asked me for anything, but for some reason, I felt obligated to do it. No one besides us knew I was the father. Even when we visited the company for meetings, we kept it regular, like there was nothing going on with us. She still ordered my favorite sandwiches for lunch, and we still met up on the low when Trace wasn't with me. She deserved the Side Jawn of the Year Award. She stayed in her place at all times.

One time, when Tracey joined us for a meeting, she commented that Zaria was letting herself go and gaining weight. When I told her I learned that she was expecting the last time I came out, she looked appalled.

"Is she married?" she had quizzed, face balled up like she smelled something rancid and already knew the answer.

"I don't know that much about her, Tracey. The last time I was here, they were giving her a baby shower. That's how I found out. I don't think it's really any of our business," I had concluded, trying not to sound too protective of her. After all, she was supposed to be a stranger I didn't know, not someone I had been intimate with for some time and who was now carrying my child.

"She's probably not. She looks like an easy lay," she'd quipped, refreshing her lipstick in a Donna Karan pocket mirror while making sure her hair was still on point. I was simmering on the low inside, but I just turned my attention to the meeting that was about to start, pretending that I was looking over the notes I was given. I wondered how many others looked at Zaria that way, and whether it was my fault that she was now subconsciously labeled someone's "baby mom." There wasn't anything I could do to protect her. This was our little secret.

I will admit, however, that when I saw my son in person for the first time, my heart melted instantly. He was 6 weeks old and just a little sleeping bundle that had the same face as me. He opened his eyes briefly while I held him to my chest, and he had my eye color also. *Look at what I created.* Zaria was still on maternity leave when I got into town, and the new girl they had temping in her position caught my eye immediately. She was curvy, just like Zaria, but a little younger. I avoided eye contact the entire time, afraid of what might happen if I didn't. Once my meeting was over, I'd jetted over to the house to see him. My first night there, I held him the entire time as I rocked gently in a Bananafish Benjamin rocking chair in his nursery. I couldn't believe this was even happening, and not with my wife.

During the wee hours of the morning, after finally putting his little body in the matching crib and making sure the baby monitor was on, I went and got in bed with Zaria cuddling up in the spoon position. Her body responded immediately, her pelvis grinding against mine as she stirred from her sleep. Mine responded, too, as I whispered in her ear, asking if it was okay to slide in. She assured me she was on birth control, and it was okay. The last thing I needed was for her to get pregnant again, and so soon.

She didn't have any panties on, and she was juicy just like I liked her. I pushed for her to arch her back a little, giving me full access to her box from the side. I slid in an inch at a time, gently, feeling her warmth around me as she tightened her walls to grip me up. I didn't know what to expect, but she felt even tighter and wetter than I remembered, if that was even possible. I held her as close as I could and stroked her so slowly it was almost painful. I held on to her thick hips as I dove in. Her moans were intoxicating. Tears slid from my eyes as I gave her my heart, unbeknownst to her. I wished I could be here with her and do the family thing, but Tracey wasn't having that shit. No, she didn't want me, but she'd be damned if someone else had me. Selfish bitch.

I spent the entire weekend bonding with my young son as I tried to figure out how to make this work. I gave Zaria free reign with my Black Card, allowing her to order anything she wanted for her and the baby, no limit. I thought she would go ham, but she was very conservative with her purchases, stating she got a lot of stuff from her family and coworkers at the baby showers and didn't really need much. I did, however, pay for a full-year gym membership with a personal trainer before I rolled out. She had to get that body back. I'd be damned if my son would be 3 and she's walking around talking about she's still carrying baby fat. I didn't accept it from Tracey, and she handled her shit quickly. Zaria wouldn't be the exception. I also paid for a personal chef to do her meal planning and prep for a year so that she wouldn't have any excuses as to why she couldn't eat right. I figured by then she should be snapped back in place fully.

When I boarded the plane back to Philly, I felt numb. I had many secrets, but this was the largest secret to date. I had a lot of thinking to do. I had to keep both of these women happy, even if it killed me.

Chapter Seven

Zaria

The guilt always comes back, though. Most times when you least expect it. Especially when the person you are holding the secret for is cuddled up under you, hearts in sync. That's when it becomes extra painful, and threatens to drive you insane.

"My homegirl will be dropping your son off here around one," I said to Tariq as we lay in bed watching television. He tensed up a little, but I wasn't letting him jet out like he had done in the past. TJ knew who his dad was. They did video chat sometimes, and he had pictures of him in his room, but he was at a very inquisitive age and kept asking questions. His friends at daycare had dads who came and picked them up. Why was his dad never around?

I couldn't possibly expect a 4-year-old to understand that his dad had a wife he couldn't leave to be with us and that he actually lived thousands of miles away in Philadelphia. He wouldn't understand that I was a jump off who caught feelings, and in today's terms, his mother was actually a THOT. He was a normal 4-year-old who didn't understand normalcy. He just knew a piece was missing, and he didn't know why. He just wanted his dad.

Tariq was really acting like he wasn't going to see his son before he left. I simply wasn't allowing it this time. Sometimes I didn't even tell my son his dad was coming because I didn't feel like the disappointment. As of late, he seemed less interested in seeing his dad. Not too long ago, I found the pictures of his dad that he had in his room in the trash. When I asked him why he threw them away, he said it didn't make sense to keep looking at a man who didn't want him. I didn't even think he could process his feelings that deeply. That shit hurt me to my core.

When I told him his dad was coming, he just said, "Okay." Usually, he was extra hype, jumping up and down and asking a million questions. I hated that this was starting to happen, but it was really out of my control. I almost regretted introducing him to his dad in the first place. I was basically a single mom, and I probably should have kept it that way.

When I first found out I was pregnant, I was devastated. *How did this happen?* Tariq and I always used protection. Whatever didn't end up in a condom was swallowed beforehand and washed off after. Even when we mutually decided to not use protection, I started birth control months before we go it in. We were extra careful, and he still pulled out sometimes just out of habit. His little spermies must have been determined that last time around, because sure enough, I was knocked up.

The thing was, I wasn't concerned with a missed period because since I started the pills, I was off track. I used to be able to pinpoint the exact date I was expected to bleed, but those last few months had been unpredictable. I just figured it was one of those off-track times when it didn't show up. One morning, I woke up feeling like trash. I felt like I was going to vomit every time I tried to get up out of bed. I immediately called out from work and called my doctor, thinking maybe I got a bad batch of pills this time around.

He gave me his earliest appointment, and I managed to get out of bed and crawl my way to the front door. This was after calling around to see which of my friends had the day off to take me because there was no way I could possibly drive myself. I'd never make it alive. My BFF Tony just happened to be off and happily took me. We almost didn't make it, having to stop several times for me to vomit on the side of the road while she held my hair back for me. This shit was crazy, and I was really getting concerned.

Imagine my concern when I finally got to the doctor, and he wheeled me back to the room because I couldn't walk. I managed to pee in a cup, although I didn't know why he was checking for pregnancy when I was taking these damn pills that were currently killing me. When he came back, he'd said with the straightest face ever, "Congrats! You're seven weeks pregnant!"

"How?" I'd questioned him. I had been taking the pills religiously like my life depended on it.

"Well, I see that you are on birth control. How soon did you have sex when you first started taking them?"

I had to think back for a second. Now I had been taking them for maybe a few months before Tariq came back in town. I may not have remembered every morning, but I did make sure to take the pill as soon as I remembered, sometimes doubling up the next day. No more than a missed day and a half went by until I was informed by a colleague to set a reminder for them. Ever since then, I'd been good. I explained all of that to the doctor.

"Sometimes, in the beginning when there is a lapse, you can still get pregnant. It takes your body some time to adjust to the new meds. It's also very likely the dosage you were prescribed wasn't strong enough, and sometimes if you consume alcohol, the pills won't work. With that being said, that could very well be the reason why you got pregnant. Before you go, we need to set up prenatal care, get blood work, and . . ."

He was going on and on, but I was stuck on the fact that I was almost two months pregnant by Tariq. He was going to flip! I had an instant headache and just wanted to lie down. He gave me a bunch of papers to follow up with, but I just needed to go back home and figure out life. When I got back out front, Tony had a ginger ale and some crackers for me to help settle my stomach. When she inquired, I just told her I had a stomach virus and I would be good in a few days. She took me home without question and instructed me to call her if I needed anything.

I cried like a baby for two days straight after calling out for the rest of the week. How was I going to explain this to everyone? I didn't tell Tony because I didn't want to have to lie again if I decided not to keep it. I didn't want to be anyone's baby mom. Especially not to a dude who lived a million miles away and I only saw a few times a year. My mind was going crazy. We used protection. Leaning over, I grabbed a condom from the drawer to check the expiration date. They were still good, so my next guess was that there was a hole in the one we used, or it was one of those times we went without. Hell, it happens to the best of us.

After about three days, I finally got myself together long enough to give Tony a call back. She never judged me no matter the situation, and I knew I could talk to her and it would stay between us. We were just as close, if not closer, than my identical twin sister and I. I knew if I told my sister, by the evening everyone in the family would know, and I just wasn't ready for that. Tony and I worked in the same office and had been tight from the beginning.

We'd kept plenty of secrets over the years, so I wasn't concerned. She knew about Tariq and me, and she was messing with one of the VPs herself. She would be the last one to place judgment.

"What do you want to do? You know I got a place that does the entire procedure in one day," she had said while cracking sunflower seeds in my ear. Tony was the abortion-clinic queen. Not that she'd been there a lot for herself, but she had no problem escorting others. Her motto stayed the same: "Three hundred dollars now or three million in a lifetime." We often laughed about it, but I never thought it would end up being me.

"I don't know. I mean, I'm getting up there in age, and I don't have any kids yet. He's definitely not going to want it, but I think I want my baby," I cried into the phone while contemplating my choices.

"I feel you, girl, and you know I will rock with you either way. Whether you decide to keep it or not, you know I got your back."

We stayed on the phone for a while, discussing the pros and cons, and by the time we hung up, I felt better about it mentally. I just had to figure out how to break the news to Tariq. For right then, I had decided I was just going to sit on that bit of information until it was the right time.

Chapter Eight

Tracey

You knew going in that a secret was in formation. You'd be crazy to spill the beans now . . . but it takes crazy to live this kind of lie, right?

As I said before, do not, I repeat, do not by any means cheat with someone single. One of the biggest tips of all times. Single people have way too much time on their hands. Nobody has time for that. By the way, the biggest mistake is cheating in the first place. I didn't necessarily have to spell that out, but I just wanted to make it clear that I knew the difference.

Christopher kept his cool for a minute, but I could feel that we were starting to hook up too much, and he was starting to catch feelings. He was always on my top, even at times when he shouldn't have been. Yeah, I enjoyed the naughty texts he would send me during meetings. Some were so steamy I would have to squeeze my legs together to keep my clit from pulsating. The things that he promised to do to my body he always delivered on. Always!

I kept it strictly sexual. We didn't really talk about anything at work but work, aside from the texts, and when we got together, we had sex. There was no in between. No date nights, and late dinners three states over to keep from getting caught. If we met at a hotel, it was when my husband was away, and we never ever stayed the entire night out. I was, in fact, married, and that was the most important thing to remember, no matter how unhappy or unsatisfied I was at home. I never accepted gifts from him, and I never gave him anything other than good pussy and bomb-ass head. I didn't need anything from him, and I didn't want anything to get misconstrued. I wasn't trying to take his wife's place, and I didn't want him in place of Tariq. We were supposed to be simply enjoying each other's company. This was sex, nothing more.

Lately, though, he'd been acting real needy. He wanted more time than I could give him, and it was starting to work my nerves just a little. After all, we did agree to keep it strictly sexual. No feelings involved. I wasn't about to be sneaking out of the house and showing up late and all the messiness. No, Tariq and I were no longer on the same page and no longer where we used to be, but I refused to blatantly disrespect him and what we'd built. Suspecting something and knowing something for sure are two entirely different things. We had a lot more to lose being apart than staying together. That was the bottom line, and Christopher would just have to get over it. It was cheaper to keep Tariq. Period.

"I'm blowing you? Really? I gave you an out, and you should have taken it. I told you months ago my feelings were changing and suggested that we should back off for a while," he practically yelled at me from across the room. This was so out of character for Christopher. He was always the levelheaded one, even in a crunch. We would all be in meetings losing our minds when things got out of whack, and he would be cool as a cucumber with a well thought-out solution that always saved us. His voice was so deep I didn't even think he could get loud, but here we were.

And walk away from all this good dick? I thought as I stood there and watched him rant and rave. I was so fucking selfish. That was no secret. There was no way I was letting him go without having a replacement, but honestly, I didn't feel like the hunt. Especially since he made it so easy to catch him.

"Christopher, do you really want to let all of this go?" I asked him seductively as I approached him, closing the space between us. I was so close, I inhaled his minty exhale, and that shit turned me on even more. Reaching to undo his Hermes button-up, I saw a glint of weakness in his eyes and knew I had him. *We should be in here making love like wild animals instead of fighting with each other. I should be in reverse cowgirl right now with him spreading my ass cheeks open so that he could watch himself go in and out of me. He should be preparing to lean up and reach around to play my clit like a flute with those satiny-soft fingertips he has on such strong hands.* There was no way I was letting him just walk away, and I could tell he wasn't really ready to either.

"We really need to figure out what we are doing here," he said weakly as he allowed me to undress him. I got more excited with the more skin that was revealed, and I couldn't wait for the prize as I trailed kisses down his back simultaneously.

"We're heading to paradise," I confirmed for him as I freed his erection from his Ralph Lauren boxer briefs.

I wanted to deep throat him immediately and greedily gobble him up until he exploded in the back of my throat, but I could tell today was one of those days that I needed to slowly walk him so that he felt appreciated. It'd happened before, more often than preferred. It was a good thing I always blocked out extra time on my schedule. You never knew what could happen on a lunch break.

Taking just the head of his dick into my mouth, I made sure to make it sloppy wet as I sucked it in and made my way down the thick vein that traveled the length of him on the underside of his joystick. It pulsed and jerked urgently as I lifted his heavy sac and teased him with my tongue underneath while slowly stroking him with my hand. He gave it his best shot and really tried hard to resist, but I was determined to break down that wall he so desperately wanted to build up. I just wasn't ready to end what we had, whatever it was.

"I wasn't supposed to love you, Tracey," he managed to voice as I led him to the bed, dick still in my mouth. He sat down on the edge and scooted back slowly until I was comfortable on the bed between his legs. I was going to work on him, pressing that spot underneath his balls to stop the cream from rising. I was going to torture him sweetly until he forgot all about leaving me. There was no one in the world who could do for him what I do, and I needed to remind him of that.

"You don't love me, Chris," I moaned out as I mounted him, squeezing him as tight as I could with my wet walls all the way down. "You just love what I do to you," I finished my thought, stuffing both of my nipples into his mouth, enjoying him sucking hungrily.

Tears escaped his eyes as he closed them and submitted. It was painful for him, I could tell, because he probably really loved his wife. Outside of her being frumpy and extra prudish, they really didn't have any issues. He said they had sex almost on the regular, but it was always that same straight missionary after some dry head, and then she was asleep. No riding, no legs over the shoulders, no doggie or froggy style, nothing. That's why he was fucking me. If she were more open, he wouldn't need me. Women need to get that and take that bit of information into consideration next time they deny their man something simple as a good dick suck. There's always someone out there willing to do what you won't.

They still had good times and actually enjoyed each other's company, so he said. They had date night set aside each week and often had weekend outings with the kids when he wasn't too busy at work. He splurged on them, but his wife was too down-to-earth to accept extravagant gifts. She often said she'd rather the money go into a trust fund for the kids than spend it frivolously on diamonds and the like. She wore labels, but real basic-type shit, like she got it from TJ Maxx or Marshalls. She still went to her same hair stylist from around the way, and she proudly drove her soccer-mom vehicle, although it was a BMW, with no complaints. Every time I saw her, she had a smile on her face, and let him tell it, she rarely complained. He had a hot meal every night, and if he had to stay out late, there was no fuss, and food was set aside for him for lunch the next day. He didn't make her feel the way Tariq made me feel, and to be honest, I was a little jealous.

To be even more honest, I probably started the entire cheating situation with Tariq and me. I got bored easily. Not that Tariq wasn't a monster in the bedroom, because this man was everything. Just keeping it real. I talked about him being a quick popper and said he ain't got it, but in reality, he was the man. I was just tired of those same old crackers. Saltines were cool, but every so often, you want a Ritz. Tariq was nasty as hell in bed and would have a regular chick turned all the way out. He wasn't always quick, though. I thought him wanting to get it over with quickly was what changed. When the heart changes for someone, your actions change as well.

I was the first to miss breakfast, then lunch, and eventually dinner. I had so much guilt in the beginning that I would start an argument just so we wouldn't have to have sex when he got in. I totally ignored him most days, and it didn't make a difference until he started leaving town more. At first, I didn't care, because that gave me more time to do me without him in the way. Every cheater thinks they are winning at that point. That's how stupid we are. I never thought he would be doing him as well with my simple ass. Just know that when you start pushing people away, eventually they will get the hint and stay away. I didn't know when I became so cold toward him, and what was even scarier was that I didn't even notice when I started to care again. All of these emotions were draining me.

I studied Christopher as I brought him to an orgasm so powerful he looked like he was going to stroke out. His seed felt extra hot as it coated my walls, and I squeezed and milked him until every drop was out. He didn't deserve this kind of pressure, and at that moment, I decided this would be our last round at the rodeo. If I were his wife, I would hope that whomever he cheated with would have this kind of compassion. Normally I didn't care, but this felt different. It was time to let Christopher go and try to figure out how to get my own shit back in order. I just had to hope Tariq was ready for the same thing, and if he wasn't, I'd have to figure out what I would need to do next.

Chapter Nine

Tariq

So you tuck that shit in even tighter, because you have no choice. That burning you feel is the heat from your lies starting to simmer.

"I wasn't supposed to love you, Za," I moaned in her ear as I hit it from the side. Our son was asleep in the other room, and we were quietly trying to get it in. I wasn't used to us having to prohibit our lovemaking and whisper. We usually went ham in this jawn, but we had someone in here with us, and he didn't need to hear us like this. Every other time I'd come to visit, I would see him briefly before he went away for the night or however long he was gone for. I usually only stayed for a night or two, and I guessed Zaria wanted her time because we didn't see each other often. As he started getting older, I didn't know him like that, and Zaria never forced him on me until recently. Maybe he was putting pressure on her to get to know me.

My mind was all over the place as I concentrated on not busting too early. Who else did she have around my son? Was she seeing other people? Did he call someone else Dad? Not being able to be here was killing me, but what could I do? I couldn't rightfully tell her that she wasn't allowed to love someone else or have my son around someone else if I wasn't here to do the damn job.

She couldn't teach him how to be a man, and apparently, neither could I.

This shit had me ready to fight, and I was getting madder with each stroke as I pounded her harder than the one before. She had her face buried in the pillow as she tried to hide her screams. I was killing the pussy and trying to fuck it up for anyone who dared come after me. This shit cut deep, but the reality of the situation was I would have to eventually just leave her alone.

Surprisingly, I was really entertaining rekindling the relationship I had with my wife. It was probably my fault shit was like this with us anyway. When I first laid eyes on Zaria, I was hooked. Tracey and I had already been spending less time with each other because we never bothered to manage our time correctly. In the beginning, we were inseparable. I thought her attitude was really what started pushing me away. When you have someone that strong, you have to learn how to deal with them accordingly. Tracey's issue was she wanted to be in charge of every-damn-thing. It just wasn't healthy for the relationship. There was an order of how things should go in a household, and when one thing was out of place, it caused disarray with everything else.

Zaria was like a breath of fresh air and a welcomed distraction. Thick in the waist and a smile always present on that beautiful face. She knew her place in the relationship and allowed me to be the man, as it was intended. There was never a power struggle, and she was submissive. That was a major issue for Tracey. Women needed to understand that being submissive did not mean giving up your power. It simply meant that you were allowing the man to lead. If you feel like you can't trust him to lead, then you picked the wrong man.

Zaria never gave me any trouble. In turn, I gave her everything she wanted. We never discussed being exclusive, and I kept it all the way one hundred with her with regard to Tracey. I had to, because it was very likely that Tracey would accompany me on meetings at her location. I was very honest with her about my marriage, and we made moves as we saw fit.

I should have backed off when feelings started getting involved, but she had me spoiled. When I came to town, it was like Christmas, and I was Santa. She was both naughty and nice, and that shit had me wide open. Even now it was hard to let go. I was being shallow with her pussy. I didn't want anyone else to have it. I was selfish, sue me. I knew before I left this weekend I had to just dead it. It was better to walk away while my son was young than to drag it out. The thought bothered me so much I couldn't even sleep on the plane ride over.

Hell, it ain't like he even knew me for real. When he pulled up to the crib yesterday, her friend practically had to drag him out of the car, and when he finally got out and in the house, he ran right up to his room and stayed there for the rest of the evening. He wasn't beat to see me like he was just months earlier, and I understood it because he didn't know me. I wasn't really sold on him either, so the feelings were mutual. This ain't TV. It's not like I was away at war and was back to stay for a while. He saw me in dribs and drabs and was completely disconnected. We both were. It was no one's fault but mine.

When he was around 2, I entertained telling Tracey about him just so I could make room for him in my schedule, but she never gave me the opportunity to broach the subject. We were growing further and further apart every day, and I just took those opportunities to come out here as much as I could. In all honesty, it wasn't fair to Zaria or TJ. I had to let them go.

"You got a few minutes before you go to the office?"

At this point, Tariq was coming up on his second birthday. I wanted to fly out to Texas to celebrate with him and Zaria and possibly meet her family, but we were in a lull at the company and didn't really have any business that needed attending to at that branch. The campaign we had running was going smoother than expected, and we were in a good place.

"For?" she said with so much attitude I wanted to put hands on her. She had a horrible attitude, and I hated even talking to her sometimes.

"Just wanted to catch up with you," I explained, trying to find a way to slide in the fact that I had a kid I needed to see on his birthday. She was not making this any easier.

"Does it have to be now? I have a hair appointment I need to get to soon."

Bitch.

It took everything in me not to burst her fucking bubble and just throw the shit out there, but I knew I needed to come at her better than that. If she was going to be someone's stepmom, the least I could do was pull her in slowly.

"It's fine. We can catch up another day."

She didn't even respond. She just turned around and grabbed one of her overpriced designer bags from the table and left to go do whatever she had planned for the day.

There were many moments like that when I'd tried to tell her, but it never worked out. Now here I was with a 4-year-old, and she still had no clue.

I fell asleep, but when I woke up, Zaria was coming into the room with a tray full of food, and little Mini-Me was carrying a bottle of orange juice. The shit almost brought tears to my eyes. This could be my life right now. Why wasn't I here for this? That thought was followed up with 1 million reasons why Tracey would kill me if she ever knew what was really going on. The guilt sitting on my chest made it almost impossible to sit up.

"Good morning, Daddy," TJ said with this tiny voice. My emotions were reeling out of control. This was my first time really hearing his voice in a long-ass time, and he called me Daddy! Like, I was his dad and shit for real.

"Good morning." I smiled at him as I sat up and took the orange juice from his little hands. Afterward, I pulled him up on the bed so that he could sit next to me. I was self-conscious because I was completely naked under the covers, and he didn't know me that well to see my balls hanging.

Zaria looked scrumptious in some little boy shorts that barely covered all that ass she was dragging and a wife beater that did nothing to hide her dark-chocolate nipples. My mouth started watering just looking at her. After setting the tray down, she slipped me a pair of boxers on the low that I shimmied into under the covers as she made herself comfortable on the other side of the bed.

"TJ, are you ready to say grace?" she asked him. He took her hand and mine, bowed his head, and said the cutest blessing for our food I had ever heard. She had really been raising him well, and I was impressed. I was seriously choking back tears, not wanting to believe I was missing out on all of this. I needed to be all in or all out. This just wasn't fair to them or me.

Truth was, it was painful. I had a great example of what a man should be to his son. My father was there for everything, and he and my mom worked well as a team. I saw what love was supposed to look like regularly, and I knew exactly what kind of dad I wanted to be. This wasn't it.

From the tray, Zaria made our plates as we conversed and watched cartoons. He was a lively little boy, but very respectful. He seemed genuinely happy for me to be here this time, which was a surprise since he totally avoided me yesterday, and it added to the guilt more. The more I looked at him, the more it hurt. He was a mirror image of me, and there was no denying him.

Halfway through one of his favorite shows, he dozed off with a full belly and a smile on his face. I lay down next to him, pulling him closer to me, and pretty soon I was asleep too. I knew, if nothing else, I had to make the best of the weekend, because after this, I had to walk away. It probably didn't seem like it now, but it was for the best. This way, he would have time to get over the hurt.

Chapter Ten

Zaria

And when it starts to burn, oh, baby! Shit just got real!

A picture is worth a thousand words.

I hate him. Like, with everything in me, I hate this man to the core. If I had known the last time I saw him would be the last time I'd see him, I wouldn't have bothered bringing my son into the picture.

TJ was really starting to get Tariq not being around. He really didn't even want to see him when he came in, but of course I had to force the issue. *Now look at us. I have this sad little boy who won't stop asking when his dad is coming back, and I don't have answers.*

I should have known, because the drive to the airport the next morning was weird. While they were sleeping, cuddled up, I took a picture. It was the cutest thing seeing them like that, and I wished it could always be this way. Why couldn't I have him to myself? It's not like his wife wanted him, and I knew for sure I would be a better woman to him than she was. I wanted to remember them like this, and I could only hope we would have more moments this way. After cleaning up our mess, I slid in bed with the guys, and we all took a nice nap together. My heart was so full of emotions from this.

After our nap, we cleaned up, Tariq getting both himself and TJ dressed for the day. They looked cute as we ran all over Legoland, doing every activity they had. We had so many pictures, continuous selfies and usies like we were a big, happy family. It was different seeing Tariq like this. The only capacities I'd ever seen him were either professional or during sex. Even past visits with his son were so brief I didn't think he could be a family man. Seeing him like this definitely changed the view and made me want him more. TJ was all in, holding Tariq's hand and not even wanting to be bothered with me. Tariq allowed his son to feed him fries when we stopped for lunch, and he rested his head on Tariq's shoulder as he carried him out, falling asleep before we even got to the car. I caught as many pics as I could so that TJ and I could look at them later, not really knowing when we would be like this again.

I wasn't expecting Tariq to just fall off the face of the earth, though. Later that night, after dinner, Tariq gave TJ a bath and put him to bed. Then he stayed in the room with him until he fell asleep. I stood outside of the door, taking it all in as father and son held a conversation until TJ dozed off. Tariq would make an excellent father. I wondered if he felt it too. When he came out of the room, we made eye contact. He looked confused and in disbelief. Taking him by the hand, I led him into the bedroom and closed the door.

Without words, I undressed him and fully took in his body as I showed him what he was missing out on. In my head, I was his wife, and his actual wife was the side mistress. Motioning for him to lie down on his stomach, I grabbed the warming oil from the top drawer and straddled him after stripping myself. Starting at his shoulders, I rubbed and kneaded and massaged his tense muscles until he started to relax. I ran well-oiled fingers over the muscles on his sides and down his arms. I could feel my juices starting to seep out as I ground my clit down on him as I slid down his body. I wanted to feel him inside of me so bad, but I waited. I wanted him to beg for it.

Now straddling him backward, I continued my massage down his thighs and calves, taking extra care to pay special attention to his pedicured feet. I wanted him to know what he would be missing when he was gone. I nudged him gently, and he flipped over, and I took my place back on top of him. My mouth was starting to water as I got closer to the thing I loved the most. It stood strong and long, with a cocky hook that went right and felt right when hitting the right spot.

Sticking my tongue out, I licked the underside of it. I wanted to touch it with my hands, but I knew he would want me to, so I didn't. Turning my head sideways, I created light suction with extra-wet lips as I went up and down on the thick vein that traveled his length until he started to pulsate. Every so often, I would take his balls into my mouth one at a time before going back to my original position. He was moaning and grabbing my head, pleading with me to just get on it. Instead, I swirled my tongue around the head, slurping at the pre-cum that had gathered there, swallowing greedily. I missed him so much when he was gone, and I felt like this time I really had to make it count.

With no hands, I bobbed up and down on him and swirled around like a tornado on his dick until he threatened to let one loose on my face, and I would have let him. I wanted him to love me, and I was so mad my feelings got involved. My feelings had been involved for years, and it was getting harder to ignore as more time went by. He should have been here with me, I needed him to understand that.

"Za, please," he pleaded with me, his breath getting lodged in his throat when I swirled around him again. He wanted me bad, but he would have to beg a little more.

"Please, what?" I asked him as I moved up and captured him between my legs but not allowing him to go inside. I was so slick and juicy I was pissing myself off, but he needed to learn a lesson.

Instead of answering, he grabbed my hips and tried to force himself in, and I just clamped down tighter, keeping him from doing so. He hated not being in control, but this was the only way I could control him. I wished I could see his face clearer. I would have loved to see him at his weakest.

A video is worth a million words.

Eyeing the blinking light from the camera lens I set up on top of the mirror on the dresser, I just hoped this thing could see everything. I did have the lamps in the room on low, so there was some light, because it would be all for nothing if it were completely dark in the room. I didn't think then that I would be using the tape as evidence later on, but when frustration strikes, you do whatever you need to do in a desperate situation. My plan was to show him the tape of us on maybe Valentine's Day. We could watch ourselves on film and hopefully make a new one. Something told me it wouldn't be used that way.

Tariq was going crazy under me as I sucked on one of his nipples while slightly pinching the other. I was driving myself crazy with anticipation, and just when I didn't think I could take it anymore, he said the words I needed to hear, words he had never said before. I was shocked.

"I love you, Za. I wasn't supposed to, but I do."

I melted. I had to control my tears as I finally let him inside of me. I was extra juicy as I took my time on top of him, never wanting the moment to end. I always felt like our hearts were in sync, but today more than ever, we were right on the same note. He gently flipped me over and deeply stroked me so slowly I thought I was going to die. This man loved me. This man wanted me, and I could tell he was torn about not being here. His strong hands lazily roamed my body like he was trying to glue it to his memory. We weren't nearly as loud as we usually were. It was an intense, sexy moment that mellowed us both out.

By the time we were done, hours had passed, and my body was completely spent. He fell asleep immediately once his head hit the pillow, and I did the same after turning the camera off and cutting the lights out completely. He pulled me close to him, and we were out like a light until the morning.

When morning came, it was like a different person was in the house. He had a serious attitude as he packed his stuff to go as if he didn't want to leave. I wanted to beg him to stay, but I knew he wouldn't, so I didn't waste my time. He always made sure he didn't leave anything behind, double- and triple-checking for accuracy. He was pretty quiet at breakfast as our son talked his head off about the other places he wanted to visit with his dad the next time he was in town. I ate tears for breakfast because my son didn't understand that his dad would be gone for a while again. He was too young to get that part.

Even once we got to the airport and TJ gave him the biggest hug he could, I had to turn away so that Tariq wouldn't see the pain on my face. This shit was not fair by any means. I couldn't believe I slipped up like this, but now someone had to pay. If he thought he was just going to step off and leave my boy dangling in the damn wind, he had another think coming.

I gave him time to get home, and even a day or so to get settled in. I didn't want to disrupt his home life, but the least he could have done was let me know he made it back alive. He wouldn't return my calls or texts, and he had me blocked from sending him emails to his personal account.

I wouldn't dare send anything on his corporate account, because if some shit happened, my ass was on the line also. It had now been four months since I'd seen or heard anything from Tariq, and he didn't come to the last meeting, sending the other VP, Christopher, in his place. If he thought he was going to duck me that easily, I had something for him that he was not going to like in the least. *Don't believe me? Just watch! By the time I get done, he's going to wish he never met me in his entire life.*

Chapter Eleven

Tracey

The most important thing to remember is every lie starts with some form of truth. It's the covering up of the truth that starts a downward spiral, and that's how secrets are born.

When your heart changes for someone, your actions change as well.

My husband was home, and my sidepiece was ignoring me. He was so damn petty, and to say I was irked was an understatement. He avoided me like the plague at the office, and even at times when we needed to meet for actual business purposes, he always had a third party in the room with us as if it were needed. We always kept it very professional at the office, so he was really playing himself with this behavior. We never discussed the shit fully. Like, he did say that his heart wouldn't allow him to keep cheating on her, but damn. I guessed some people could handle guilt better than others.

I kept it all the way professional as always. Shit, I was the best to ever do it. I acted like all we had was an office relationship, and I treated him just like I treated the others who wanted so badly to get with me. I forced him to make eye contact with me when we had meetings, all the while my body aching to make contact with his.

I wouldn't dare give him the satisfaction of letting him know he had me open. I was so far open I was surprised Tariq couldn't see right through me.

When he came back home, he was different this time around. Quieter than usual. Tariq is always pretty low-key, never really saying much. Especially since our relationship had become so strained, but this was weird even for him. He unpacked his bags, throwing dirty clothes from the weekend into the washing machine because his OCD wouldn't allow him to let them sit for a day or so. When he saw me, he actually spoke and didn't just walk by like we'd been doing for months.

"Are you hungry?" he inquired while looking through a few menus, and I was speechless for a split second because we hadn't shared a meal in ages. Was Tariq having a change of heart as well? I was afraid to broach the subject, because Tariq and I were like strangers now. What if he was over us? The thought alone almost brought me to tears, but I held it together. I knew if we were going to be us again, it was going to take work. I was ready to do whatever it took to get my man back.

"Yeah, I could use a bite. What do you have in mind?" I asked while getting closer and peering over his shoulder. Normally he would flinch, but this time it was almost like he welcomed me into his space. It didn't feel foreign like it used to.

"Let's go out. Maybe we could sit and catch up," he suggested, finally looking at me in the eyes. Those caramel pools that I first fell in love with had me open. I wanted to wrap around him and be like we used to be.

"I'd like that."

For the first time in a long time, I smiled at my husband and it was genuine. I was actually looking forward to spending time with him. Grabbing my jacket, I met him outside, and we both drove in his car. My first instinct was to grab my car keys, but I wanted to be close to him for some reason. I didn't ask where we were going, I just enjoyed the music as we zoomed through the city to a restaurant of his choice. It felt good being chauffeured for once and not having to take the wheel.

We pulled up in front of a diner that we used to frequent years before we would only eat in five-star restaurants. It'd been ages since I'd eaten at a greasy spoon for fear of gaining my weight back, but tonight wasn't a night for me to be worried about my figure. Clearly, we were getting back to basics, so I went along with it without fussing. He held the door for me, but that was nothing new. Tariq has always been a gentleman, even at our worst moments. Regardless of what went on at home, we never let others know we had beef. It wasn't their business. The minute a chick thinks there is room to slide in, she will try it, men too.

We grabbed a booth near the window, and for the first few minutes, we just sat and looked at each other.

"Can we start over?" I blurted out, tears stinging my eyes. What if he said no? What if he was bringing me here to break it off for good? What if he replaced me? The thought alone made it hard to breathe, but if he did, it was no one's fault but mine. For years, I took for granted that Tariq had too much to lose by losing me. Maybe walking away would be better for him after all. He did spend a lot of time away. Maybe he was setting up his situation so that he could survive the blow if we parted. All this time, he may have been getting his shit together, and I was just taking for granted that he would always stay. I felt so stupid.

"How do we do that?" he responded in a voice full of hurt. It'd been so long, and we should have been done this before it got so far out of control. It was like we were on a yacht in the middle of the ocean surrounded by nothing but water with no land in sight. We were just drifting along, no land for miles, and no map for direction. I wouldn't say it was all on me, because Tariq did his dirt as well, but more than likely, I pushed him to do it. He wasn't even the cheating type.

"Maybe let's just start with the truth. The very least we can do is air out any dirt we have so that we can start fresh. I've done shit, and you've done shit. Let's just get it out and over so that we can get back to us," I suggested, going through my thought process on how much to divulge. Yeah, we could speak the truth, but there's just some shit that shouldn't be said no matter how truthful you were trying to be.

Like, I knew for sure I could never ever tell him about Christopher. Just in case I could get that again. It's a shame to say, but a small part of me believed that Christopher would come back once the guilt died down. Sex with him was phenomenal. He knew it, too. I just had to give him some time. That, and I knew Tariq wouldn't be able to handle that kind of situation. We had to work with Christopher, and Tariq wasn't capable of being the bigger person knowing one of the guys at work knew what his wife looked like naked. He would never be able to get past the fact that Christopher knew what I tasted like, knew what I felt like, and the favor I returned was for the records. He wouldn't be able to get over it, so that secret would have to stay tucked tight and be taken to my grave.

"Maybe let's start with dinner first and some casual convo. You know, just to break the ice?" he asked, a slight smile on his sexy lips.

Taking him in, it was like looking at him for the first time in ages. He'd aged a little since our first date, but it looked damn good on him. Made him look more distinguished. My clit throbbed a little as I thought about how we used to get it in and could barely make it through dinner without him fingering me under the table or me crawling under there to give him head. I would stuff my own fingers into my dripping wet pussy, and once I came from under the table, I would offer them to him, and he would lick them clean. We would overpay the bill and jet out, trying to find the first dark spot we could on the road so that we could get it in before the food even came out.

So many nights, I climbed on top of him in the back seat and rode down on him in a parking lot like a trashy whore he had just picked up on the side of the road. We would be loud with this shit, no care given to whoever walked or drove by. I loved how he would palm my ass and drive himself in deeper, tapping the hell out of my G-spot until I exploded all over him. He would shoot a hot, thick load soon after, and we would lay there spent until we could catch our breath. Those were the days I wanted back, and tonight would be one of those nights if I had it my way.

In between light conversation, we managed to order our food, both of us opting for a fat-filled meal instead of a salad. Tariq was just as conscious about keeping his body fit as I was about I mine. That's another reason why we made such a good team. In the beginning when I first started my weight-loss journey, we were actually in the gym together, and somehow that drifted apart too. Maybe we spent too much time together in the beginning, but it's never too much when love is involved. I knew that now, and I hoped my realization wasn't too late.

"I slept with two people in the last two years." I started the conversation off just to really get a feel of how deep we would go with our reveal. I definitely wouldn't be dropping names, and I for sure wasn't going to tell him more than I thought he could handle.

"I slept with one other person," he replied. For some reason, I was still shocked by his reveal, but I couldn't be mad at it. *Multiply that by three, and that's the real number of people.*

I told him some dirt, and he told me some dirt throughout our meal, both of us looking at each other like we couldn't believe what the other had done. We also decided that maybe a therapist should be involved to keep things peaceful. Some of the stuff we laughed at, and other stuff brought us to tears from both having to say it and having to listen to it. It was a cleansing experience, and by the time we got done, I actually felt like just maybe we could move forward with becoming one again.

By the time we got home, we took a nice, long shower together, and surprisingly didn't try any freaky shit. He washed me thoroughly from top to bottom, and I did the same for him. When we were done, he wrapped a fluffy towel around my body, afterward wrapping himself before he led me into the room by my hand. Once there, he applied lotion to my body, and I returned the favor for him. We didn't bother to put on pajamas, we just crawled into bed and held each other until we fell asleep. I remembered hoping it would always be like this, and I prayed that God would take the need for other men away from me. I wanted to focus on getting us back, and I felt like Tariq was in. We were both strong enough to make it happen, we just had to consciously put forth the effort to do it. This was day one of forever. I was ready for him. *Hopefully, he's ready for me.*

Chapter Twelve

Tariq

Always, no matter what, stick to your guns.
Unless, of course, you have nothing to lose.

I couldn't tell her I had a child. My whole intent was to just put the shit out there to get it off my back for a second. For the entire plane ride, I went over the scenarios, and none of them had a good outcome. I concluded that just telling her would be the best thing to do. Somehow all of that changed when I saw her. For the first time in a very long time, she actually looked like she needed me. No longer did I see the look of disgust in her eyes when she looked at me. Dared I say there was actually some love there? Like, did Tracey care about me again?

I wanted to hold her so tight that she would be breathless, but guilt wouldn't allow it. I was afraid she would smell Zaria's perfume on me. She gave me the longest hug at the airport, and my son was holding on to me for dear life as well. It was like they knew they would never see me again. The tears that formed in his eyes were huge, and I wondered how such a tiny body could produce such big tears. I felt like shit. My father didn't do this to us. He would be ashamed if he knew how I was treating his grandson. If I could help it, a grandson he would never get the chance to meet. I grew up in a two-parent household, and they were still happily married for forty-plus years. I wouldn't dare introduce them to a child who didn't come from my wife and who was not conceived out of love.

I loved Zaria eventually. Definitely not in the beginning, and damn sure not when she told me she was pregnant. Well, I loved things about her, but I wasn't necessarily in love with her. Mistakes like this had a domino effect. It wasn't just about Tracey, Zaria, and me. It was about all of her family, and all of my family who didn't even know this shit was happening. We were doing a whole lot of people dirty, and I just couldn't live in filth anymore.

At one point, I felt like she strapped me. Who the fuck gets pregnant and keeps a secret for four whole months? That shit had me looking at her extra crazy, and my first instinct was to fly out and make her get the abortion anyway. My feelings changed for her majorly at that moment. It was like I hated her, but somehow love snuck in there and got me. She made things complicated for no reason and was supposed to stick to the damn script. Know your position as the sideline chick. Regardless of how much protection I provided, always at all costs make sure you are cool first. That's rule number one in the side-chick handbook. Rule number two: if you get pregnant, get rid of it. Not every man is going to leave his wife for his side woman like Peter Gunz did. Do not allow reality TV to fuck up your shit, because in reality, that shit is not realistic. Regular people don't live like that, regardless of how entertaining you think it may be.

When I finally got back to Texas, my wife and a few other colleagues accompanied me on the trip. I had to ignore her completely because Tracey was there, although I had a million questions. Partly because if Tracey sensed in the slightest that we had more going on than casual conversation, she would have turned into a beast. Zaria would have been out of a job for sure, and our marriage would have been a wrap. Yeah, at times I wanted our marriage to be over. I'd be the first to admit it. I simply wasn't interested in Tracey like that anymore, nor was I willing to end in on those terms. We always agreed to a mutual breakup when we thought we would never break it off. Nowadays, it seemed more likely than not.

When I saw her belly, I almost lost it. My child was in there. She carried motherhood well, too. She had definitely gotten thicker but was more belly than anything. Her coworkers had given her a baby shower that day, and I could see all of her gifts piled up in the corner behind her desk. She was all smiles as we came in, even with Tracey being totally disrespectful, but the smile stayed put. At that point, we hadn't talked since the reveal conversation. Oh, how I wanted to press my ear to her belly and see if I could hear my baby in there. I actually had to blink back fucking tears because I couldn't even believe this shit was happening. To this day, I couldn't even tell you what happened in the meeting. Thank God Tracey was always on point.

I was supposed to come home and tell my wife I had a son out of wedlock with a woman she'd seen before but didn't know personally. I was supposed to sit and let her rant and rave and go clean the fuck off about how stupid I was to get caught up like that, and how that made her look to our colleagues and as the face of the company. I was supposed to let her tell me how I made our marriage another statistic, and that I was the reason why black power couples couldn't last. Men like me were the reason why women like her marred white, and vice versa. How dare I embarrass her in front of her family and friends! How could I give someone else her life? I was supposed to let her get that shit off her chest and not say a damn word. Not even "I'm sorry," even though I was.

Tracey was supposed to not be speaking to me, and maybe even in the process of moving some of her things from out of the house, even though we both knew she couldn't live without that custom closet she had built. She was supposed to be staying at her friend's house, letting her diet go out the window as she crammed junk food down her throat and cried into tissue after tissue to her BFF about how unfair all of this was. Her friend would agree but eventually tell her to come home and work it out. At that point, we would argue more and become so distant it would just end. One of us would come home and find the other gone completely, no trace of them as if they never lived there. Drawers and shit empty. That would be the sacrifice we would make all because of my mistake.

This is the kind of shit that happens when you are with an independent woman. Beyoncé and Iyanla got y'all thinking you can do it by yourself. You don't need a man. You are independent. What folks need to be clear on is the difference between being independent and being self-sufficient. When you speak into existence that you are independent, you are letting the world know that you don't need anything or anybody but you. You don't need help from a man, family, or friends. You are able to run efficiently without the likes or help of anyone. You have it all under control. That has to be the loneliest existence ever.

Now being self-sufficient is an entirely different ball game. While you are able to maintain and roll with the big boys or girls, you have the aptitude to allow a man to lead as it is intended. You are capable of submitting without feeling like you are losing your power or yourself. You are allowing the flow of energy in your life to go in the direction it's supposed to, and in turn, you are at peace in your confidence and what you bring to the relationship.

That shit is sexy. That was the difference between Tracey and Zaria.

I loved Tracey because she had drive, but have you ever met a woman that was too strong? Like damn, bitch, relax. She had nothing to prove to me. I could clearly see that she was brilliant and way ahead of her time. We were not in competition with each other as far as I was concerned. It rightfully should have been us against the world. The problem with Tracey was she saw everyone as a potential threat to her making it to the top, me included. It drew a clear line as to who was the lead in our relationship, and in her eyes, it was her. She was climbing the ladder in designer stilettos with blades attached to the heels so that you couldn't latch on. There was no way you were dragging her down without getting cut.

I tried to chalk it up to her being hurt in that past. Maybe someone really fucked her over once or twice, maybe even three times, but I would have respected her more had she just told me she wasn't ready for the kind of man I was. When I met her, she was in the process of slimming down, and I was there for the journey. This new skinny bitch was mean. I wasn't a nut by any means, and I didn't necessarily need a totally submissive woman. I did, however, need a woman who was not in constant competition with me. It was tiring trying to keep up with a woman who pretended she wanted to be caught but really didn't. We all like a good chase, but I'd be damned if I wanted to keep running forever. Eventually, a man will look to hunt someone who's moving a little slower. No, it may not be his ideal choice, but he's appreciated. That's all that matters in the end. I wanted a woman who showed me she loved me and not just said it to shut me up. Mean it with all of your heart and it comes out naturally.

I felt bad for Zaria. She would have to raise that boy by herself. There was no way I could be a part of it without hurting him and her in the process. Was it fair? Hell no! Did I care? Maybe a little, but not enough to risk what I had here. Rule number three in the side-chick handbook: if you keep the mistake, it's now yours to deal with alone. Do not involve anyone else since you knew you were supposed to handle it early on in the first place. I wanted to hate her for what she did, but in retrospect, she had to do what she had to do for her. Maybe this was her only shot at having a child. Who knew? You'd think she would have chosen someone more stable than me, but in reality, I didn't think she chose me on purpose. It just kind of happened that way.

We had been doing this for over four years! I'd never made a commitment. The dynamics changed once the child came, and my trips out west became fewer and farther apart. Not because I was working shit out with Tracey, but because I didn't want to deal with Zaria's shit. She was forcing the child on me. I didn't want him. Once he was old enough to know who I was, I would have been cool with her eliminating that fact from the equation all together. Shit, she could have told him I was killed when he was just born, because technically I was dead to them both. That would have been a nice, believable lie that would have satisfied his curiosity. I was not about to have fatherhood forced on me before my time. Yeah, it was wrong, but fuck it.

She forced this heartbreak on us. All of this was her fault. I knew eventually I'd have to say something to her . . . or maybe not. Right now, I was going to lie here in the dark, hold my wife, and hope for normalcy or some form thereof to come to us. I was speaking it into existence. I just hoped someone was listening.

Chapter Thirteen

Zaria

But let's be real. There's always a loss. Otherwise, we wouldn't be keeping secrets in the first place.

"I wasn't supposed to love you, Tariq," I practically screamed at him as I circled him and his wife for what felt like the 800th time. Taking things back to the present for a moment, I need you to know that if you're thinking I was crazy, you are absolutely fucking right. He did this to me. Crazy was what he wanted, so crazy was what he got.

She did not fucking deserve him. Oh, he was a low-down, dirty motherfucker who played us both. That's what she deserved to know. She earned the right to know that I had been doing her gotdamn job for years now. I was sucking and fucking all over this delicious-ass man she married because her simple ass wouldn't please him the way she vowed to. She pushed him into my bed. It was her fucking fault, if we all wanted to keep it 100 percent real. She did this to all of us. Had she played her position, we wouldn't be here right now. I fucking hated her.

All this "tentative husband" bullshit that he pulled out of no-damn-where was not the real him, or at least not the him I'd gotten to know over the last four years. Like, where the fuck did that shit come from? He showed no interest at all in her ever. At least not in my presence. I guessed he wasn't supposed to. I was merely there for entertainment purposes, right? This was just a sex thing, right? He was supposed to get in and get the hell out. He didn't know he had to learn a lesson.

There's always a loss. Al-the-fuck-ways a loss! Don't ever believe you can get out of dirt clean as a whistle. There's always a smudge left somewhere. He did give it a good try, though. I had to give him that. He really tried to skate off like I wouldn't board a gotdamn plane and come right down this bitch. He had me fucked up. *Don't hurt my son.* I could deal with hurt. I had my entire life. My son was innocent.

I stopped to take a look at his wife again. Tracey. This dizzy bitch. Besides good looks, what the hell did he see in her? Her attitude was the worst I'd encountered in years. She had to be like that all the time. There was no way possible to turn that shit on and off. She was like that twenty-four-seven/365, and there was no one in the world who could convince me otherwise. I wondered how many other women were there before me, or was I the first? I was shocked that he even let it get this far. He just didn't seem like the type to step out of the marriage. Most guys who stepped out of their marriage didn't. Who in hell was I fooling?

I had no business being here. I should have stayed my simple ass in Texas. Was it worth all of this in the end? Me killing his ass wouldn't make him mine, and after this, he damn sure wouldn't want to see me again. *Zaria, what are you doing?* Catching a glimpse of my face in the wall mirror, I stopped in shock. Gone was the always-smiling, always-pleasant woman who was living her best life. What I saw looking back at me was a tear streaked, sad-in-the-eyes, crazy-looking woman I did not recognize. Was I really about to throw away everything I had for him? I had to get the hell out of here.

Maybe after that third date I should have walked away. Maybe I should have not introduced TJ to his dad. Maybe once TJ stopped showing interest, I should have let it go. *Maybe I should just off my fucking self and let them live with the guilt.* I should have just not come here.

"Mommy, do I have to see my dad?" my son had asked as I got him ready to go with my best friend. She was TJ's godmother and totally disagreed with what I was trying to do. It was her idea to take him for the first part of the weekend, because she already knew Tariq would not be happy about him just being there when he showed up. I shared a lot with her about him, and she tried to warn me that this wouldn't go over well. I should have listened.

"You don't want to see him? You've been asking about him," I had responded as I continued to pack his bag for the night.

"Mom, I really don't want to see him."

He'd had a straight face. The same face his dad had when he meant business, when he was trying to get his point across in a meeting, and was determined to make his view known, he had that face. I should have taken his feelings into consideration. I didn't. I was so damn stupid.

"Maybe you'll change your mind once you see him."

"I won't," he'd said, the beginning of tears pooling in his eyes. Why was I putting my baby through this kind of pain? Did it make me a bad mom? I was really trying to give him a fair chance at getting to know his father, but my dumb ass didn't realize that the tactic only worked when they both wanted it. Tariq Sr. damn sure wasn't feeling it, and Jr. wasn't beat on it either. My selfish ass just had to force the issue. Silly of me.

"TJ, we'll discuss this later," I'd said to him sternly once my friend pulled up. I walked him out to the car, and he hopped inside and didn't even return my hug when I took him into my arms. I kissed his cheeks, and he wiped them off. I told him I love him, and he didn't say a word. I thanked my homegirl for everything and went inside to prepare for the bullshit. Tariq was not going to be happy, but I concluded that it was not about him being totally happy. We had a child. When did only his happiness start to matter? I felt like he needed to meet the person who gave him his face.

Lost in thought, I almost didn't hear the phone ringing, bringing me back to the present. Walking back into the living room, I circled the body lying on the floor, unconscious and oblivious to what was happening. Christopher was taped at the hands and feet like the others. Reaching down into his pocket, I pulled out his cell phone and glanced at the screen. It was his wife. It was a shame she wasn't in on this shit. She was probably just wondering where her loving husband was. I'd let him deal with his poison on his own. Once the phone stopped ringing, I turned it on silent and set it on the table next to the other two phones. I felt bad for him because he was caught up just like I was. I didn't feel too bad, though, because he was just like Tariq: a fucking cheater.

Removing the gag from Tariq's mouth, I decided to let him plead his case, warning him that if he made the wrong move, I would take him out after gently throwing in the reminder that their heads were taped together.

"In through yours, out through hers. Understand?" I asked him before removing it. He nodded. I removed the gag but stayed close. I was not in the mood to play with him.

"Speak. You have one minute to convince me why I shouldn't take y'all asses out."

"What does Christopher have to do with this?" he asked, trying to put the pieces of the puzzle together.

"Oh, your queen never told you, huh? You weren't the only fool running around the castle. Maybe I should wake her up so that she can tell you herself."

Chapter Fourteen

Tracey

So you might as well ride that shit out until the end.

I had my husband back! How lucky was I? We actually came to a mutual agreement to work things out so that we could be one again. I didn't even realize how much I missed us until I had it again. He made me remember why I chose him in the first place. I must have been crazy to think that I had to step out and risk losing this. Thank God I finally came to my senses.

We saw a couples therapist. I'd be the first to admit that therapy was my go-to thing. I wasn't one of those black women who felt like seeing a therapist was admitting you were crazy. There wasn't shit wrong with involving a mutual, unbiased party who had no ties to either of us. It kept it fair and made us see things as they were. We were both dead-ass wrong for how we handled our issues with each other.

"It's okay to be afraid, Tracey," the therapist spoke to me like an adult. I didn't feel like she was talking down to me like a child or like I couldn't comprehend. We had a very open adult conversation among the three of us that put the blame right where it should be. "Showing your fear to your husband lets him know that you trust him to be your protector. You can be vulnerable in front of each other without feeling weak. You also have to allow him the same emotion."

A lot of the things she brought up made sense, and once I actually began to listen to Tariq's issues with me, I realized that over the years, I had belittled him. I made him feel like the woman in the relationship, and he felt unwanted. He gave up the fight once he realized I wasn't interested in him staying. I pushed him away.

"How did it feel for you to admit to your husband that you shared your body with other men?" she asked, peering over her Michael Kors frames at me. I could see his eyes twitching from the corner of my eye as we both shuffled in our seats. This shit made us both uncomfortable, but we agreed that we would be uncomfortable to get back to a better place if that's what it took.

"Once it was out, I felt relief," I answered honestly. It was like a weight was lifted. "I will admit that immediately after the relief came the pain of betrayal. We took vows. I shouldn't have done it."

"How many was it?" Tariq asked, burning a hole through my face with his piercing eyes. I wanted to look away, but he had me locked in. Looking away would admit guilt.

"Does it matter?" I asked, irritated. Hell, I had already told him that at dinner. Why was he asking me again?

"How many was it, Tracey?" he asked again more sternly, his hand clenching into tight fists at his sides. He was pissed, but this was a part of the healing process. He needed to hear the truth.

"Tariq, before she answers, do you really want specifics?" the therapist interjected, giving me a moment to think. I would tell him as much truth as I could without telling a total lie. Hell, at this point, the number wasn't really the issue. The deed was what caused the trouble. "If you do, I'll respect your decision to know."

"How many, Tracey?" he repeated, completely ignoring her.

"Two."

He blinked.

Closed his eyes for ten seconds.

Blinked again.

He hated me.

"How many from the office?"

What the fuck was he talking about? Did he know something I didn't know? Did someone spill the fucking beans? Usually when people asked pointed questions, they already knew the answer. Or they were fishing to see if you would blurt out some real tea. He caught me off guard with this one, but I wasn't that damn slow. He was dragging me for filth today. I deserved it.

"None."

Silence.

Some relief, although short-lived. I could tell he wasn't sure if he could believe me, but at this point, we were trying to heal. If we were going to move forward and start fresh, we had to clear out as many skeletons as we could so that we could, in fact, move forward. Bones take up a lot of room, folks, no matter how big a house you build. Shit, sometimes they just fell the hell out unexpectedly. You never know when some old shit might pop up. Always be ready to never stop fighting for what you want. Love or otherwise.

"Let's just end the session here for now. I'll see you both next week, and I want you to think about who you are as people," she requested, looking at us to be sure we understood what she meant. "When I say that, I mean, who are the real Tariq and Tracey? Not your pedigrees and your accomplishments. If you were stripped of all of your worldly possessions, what would you have left?"

We thanked her for her time and made our way to Tariq's car. I wished for a second I had driven myself this time. I needed a minute to think. Today's session was heavy, and I just needed some time to process it all. I could see in his face that he wanted the same thing. We got in the car and just sat in silence for a while before he started it. I didn't really know what to expect from him at this point, but I wasn't about to poke a sleeping bear. I just really hoped he felt that I wanted us to work. I was even willing to take the blame for his shit, too, if that meant he would stay.

"Thanks for your honesty," he said, still looking forward, but taking my hand in his.

This shit was hard, and I appreciated him acknowledging my effort. If I told Tariq that I had, in fact, slept with more like six men and two women, he would have been sick. Him knowing that Christopher was one of them would have made it worse. Regardless of what we did, work relations were off-limits and a definite deal breaker. I knew we were supposed to be honest, but that just could never come to light.

Finally, we pulled off. I just needed a damn nap. When we got back home, I sifted through the mail, separating the bills from his personal mail and mine. He had an envelope from our Texas office and some other stuff. I put his mail on the island in the kitchen so that he could grab it before heading to the shower, and I dropped mine in the basket in my office upstairs. I was beat to death at the moment, and although I felt like we were making progress, we still had a lot of shit with us. This was just the beginning. Who was I without everything I had? I hadn't the slightest idea, and that shit was scary. I couldn't even think about it right now, but I knew I had to talk to my husband . . . after my nap.

But as I stood in the bathroom door, I watched his silhouette through the steamed glass of the shower door. The body on this man was ridiculous. He certainly hadn't let himself go over the years. If anything, he looked more toned and in shape than I could remember. My nipples perked up and my pussy began to stir. I wanted my husband, but I was afraid of being rejected. We still hadn't had sex since he'd been home. Every time we tried to, we lost the moment somehow. I was afraid he wouldn't want me, especially after today's session, but I was even more afraid of a missed opportunity.

Stripping out of my clothes, I walked toward the shower, standing naked outside the glass, waiting for him to acknowledge me. I wanted him to want me. I stood there for what felt like forever, watching him lather his muscular body. I wanted him to feel me in the room, to feel our connection. Just when I was about to give up, he turned around. My heartbeat found his, and we connected. He looked at me through the steam, and I saw the struggle.

Let me in, I pleaded in my head as we stared each other down. *God, please tell me he still wants me.*

Finally, after what felt like an eternity, he slid the door back and invited me inside. Tears streaked my face as my man took me in and held me under the twin shower heads in our custom shower. I closed my eyes, not caring that my freshly pressed-out hair was getting wet and would definitely revert to its naturally curly state. I was so vulnerable at the moment, and I just wanted him to make me feel whole again. He grabbed the loofah and soaped it up with my favorite shower gel. With my back pressed against his chest, he took his time with my body, like he was washing a baby. With his free hand, he traced my body parts like he was committing them to memory for the first time.

I cried softly at first, and then uncontrollable sobs filled my throat as I leaned on him for support. To think I had almost given all of this up. What the heck was I thinking? He held me up and gave me time to cleanse my soul from the inside. He never missed a beat as he rinsed my front and turned me around, cradling me in his arms as he continued to cleanse my body, covering my back.

I cried, "Honey." Watching myself cry in the mirror, it was one of those types that was ugly, like Janet Jackson in *Poetic Justice*. I had to let it all out. He rinsed my back off and then moved behind me, pressing my body against the glass. I felt him lean into me, his muscular frame fitting perfectly into mine as he dipped down a little and slid smoothly inside of me. My cry caught in my throat, turning into a guttural moan as he stroked me so slowly it was killing me. Why was this man torturing me like this? I took it, because I deserved to be punished in any way he saw fit.

I didn't protest as he took a fistful of my hair in his powerful fist and gently pulled my hair back, biting my neck, sure to leave a mark. His stroke remained slow but became more forceful as if he were testing to see if he still had a snug fit. He pulled back and bent me over, making me grab my ankles, water falling all around me like I was standing under a waterfall. He was killing my pussy with each stroke, and I took the beating because I warranted it, and I liked it.

It felt like he had me in there forever, not letting up until the water became ice cold. Picking me up like a caveman, he threw me over his shoulder and carried me into the room. He wanted to finish his assault on my body and make up for lost time. He was staking his claim. I knew what it was about, and I took that shit for the team because I didn't have a choice.

"You better love me, Tee," he growled into my ear. I couldn't even respond, because he was fucking me so hard he seemingly knocked my voice out of me. He stayed in me for hours, and when he finally gave in, he pushed himself in as deep as he could and let out a nut so hot it felt like he scorched my insides. This was frustration and love wrapped up in one. I was not letting my man go, and this was a small step back toward us. We were going to get that old thing back, and we were ready to fight for it. I wanted it back, I thought.

Chapter Fifteen

Tariq

Don't worry, you'll find new ways to cover your ass. It's just like packing for a trip. You figure out how to fit everything in your suitcase before you close it. You'll also find a way to pack those skeletons in your closet nice and neat so that they don't keep spilling out.

So maybe I wouldn't tell her. Fuck it. What good would it do? She wasn't going to be happy either way, and just like all the shit we were still hiding, it would come out eventually. It probably wasn't fair to let her find out that way, but at that point, I was feeling backed in a corner. I made an appointment to see the therapist without my wife a few weeks after we had been going, and while sitting out here in the waiting area, I wondered if I was doing the right thing. We agreed to keep everything up front, but I had questions. We had been there twice a week in the beginning for about two and a half months straight, and for the last three weeks, we had been meeting once a week every Wednesday. I couldn't wait until Wednesday because this shit was really burning a hole in my chest, and I couldn't sleep at night. I needed to see her today. That's all there was to it. There was some shit I needed help figuring out.

For instance, Zaria didn't "technically" work for the company, but was having sex with her considered an on-the-job offense? Of course it was. Who was I kidding? She didn't work in the Philadelphia office, but she was on the damn payroll of Marketing, Inc., a company my wife and I partially owned. I just had to talk to someone who wouldn't tell on me. Sounded crazy, I knew, but that's pretty much how I was feeling nowadays.

It felt like I was sitting out there for an eternity before she called me to come back. I changed my mind about staying a million times before the couple emerged, and I took that as a sign that maybe I was in the right place after all. When I saw the couple who had come out, I wondered if Tracey and I looked as defeated as them. The husband just looked lost, and the wife had obviously been crying. I wondered who had started the cycle of cheating in their relationship. Tracey did hold her tears until we got in the car most times, but it was the same bullshit across the board. Somebody had fucked up somewhere along the line, and now it was time to put the pieces back together.

"What brings you here today, Mr. Mason?" she asked as I entered her office.

Just walking in, I noticed a million things I didn't see the few times I came to see her with Tracey. For one, her office was huge and very stylishly decorated. From the modern paintings to the futuristic style of her desk and pale pink walls with a light gray border, you could see she was paid well in her profession. When my gaze came back to her, I had to blink. She was gorgeous. All kinds of impure thoughts ran through my mind in a matter of seconds. Surprisingly, I didn't even feel ashamed.

Today she looked different. Instead of the tight bun and glasses, her hair was down, flowing past her shoulders and cascading over her breasts a little. She had highlights and lowlights that played beautifully with each other as the little slices of sun that crept in between the blinds danced on her soft tresses. And her eyes, those almond-shaped eyes surrounded dark brown pupils that pierced right through you. Eyebrows on fleek, and although her face was beat, it looked natural, like not much effort had to go into enhancing her beauty. Why wasn't she married? Looking around at the photos, it looked like she had family, but there were none that said she was involved or had a kid. She had to be dating someone at least. Who would let this beauty walk around single?

"Mr. Mason? Are you okay?

"Oh yeah, I'm fine. Sorry, I was distracted," I apologized as I finally took a seat. I wanted to see her naked. I was here seeing her about issues with my wife, and all I could think about was stripping her naked and standing her before me so that I could take it all in. What kind of monster was I?

"What brings you here today? I wasn't expecting to see you and Mrs. Mason until your next scheduled appointment."

"I know, but there was an issue that I needed to discuss with you in private. I know my wife and I agreed to be up front about our mutual discretions, but there is a thing or two that I don't think she'll be able to digest," I began, trying to zone back into the reason why I came in the first place and not the thoughts of bending her over the desk and exposing her pussy. In my mind, she didn't have on any panties under that tight, little pencil skirt she was wearing, and her nipples were just waiting to be kissed. *I'm such a fucking dog.*

"Okay, but before we get into the issue, let me ask you this," she replied, licking her lips, unaware of the thoughts in my head. Oh, how I wanted her tongue to be tracing the head of my dick before it got lost between her lips. Controlling my erection was getting harder to do the longer I sat here, and I knew for certain I could never come to see her without Tracey present again. "Would Mrs. Mason appreciate you discussing this with me without her present?"

"Probably not, but to be fully honest, I really don't have the courage to tell her."

"Then don't tell her."

Silence.

Did this chick, the therapist, just tell me to keep a secret from my wife? Where they do that at? Hell, I think I love her! I had to be sure I heard what I heard before I played myself. She had me a little hype in this jawn, and I needed to make sure I should be.

"You're telling me to keep a secret from my wife?"

"Not exactly," she said while adjusting in her seat. Now I was confused. *This bitch just said don't tell her, and now she's saying that's not what she said.* What the fuck was I supposed to be doing? My face was nice and tight, and I was ready to roll. She was making an already-confusing and difficult situation worse. *Thanks for the help, Doc!*

"What I'm trying to say, Mr. Mason, is you don't have to spill the whole pot of beans at one time. Ladle it out a little at a time so that it's easier to digest. You will eventually have to tell your wife everything, even the deep, dark things that we would love to forget but can't because they happened. She's going to be hurt and in disbelief, but in all actuality, that's a part of the healing process. You also have to understand that there's a possibility that she may hit you with something you can't handle as well. Are you ready for that?"

Speechless yet again.

I never even thought that just maybe Tracey was holding her ace like we were in a spades game as well. What if she told me something I just could not get past?

Would it really be a deal breaker for real this time? So many thoughts consumed me, but I still needed to tell her my deepest, darkest secret. I had to get it out before it came out at the wrong time.

"I have a son."

She didn't flinch. Didn't change her facial expression or anything. That scared me even more.

"He was not conceived with my wife," I continued, and she sat in silence, never breaking eye contact. I wanted her to interject. *Damn, say something*. She didn't. I hated her.

"He's four years old, and his mother is the secretary at one of our branch offices."

You could hear a mouse piss on cotton, that's how quiet is was in there. She was good. Did they teach you to detach like this in psych class? She had no facial expression or change of emotion. She would just periodically jot down a note or two on her pad.

"Say something," I practically begged as tears surfaced and fell. I wanted her to tell me how stupid I was and that I deserved everything that happened to me. I wanted her to tell me what to expect from Tracey when I told her so that I could be prepared. *Say the fuck something besides just sitting there looking at me.*

"Do you want your wife to know that information right now?" she asked.

"No."

"Then don't tell her. Tell her when you are ready to receive the consequences."

"But what would you do if you were her?" I asked. I needed more than that. This wasn't a fucking game. This was real "life without my wife" shit. I didn't know how to handle it. I wasn't ready.

"I'm not at liberty to say, because I'm not your wife. You want me to tell you that I would probably try to fight you or even kill you, and how I could probably never speak to you again after such a reveal. That's what you want to hear, right, Mr. Mason?" she quizzed. I just put my head down, no longer able to make eye contact.

"In our minds, that's the most logical reaction because it satisfies the wrong and somehow justifies what you did because you got a reaction somewhat of what you expected. It changes the game because she fed you what you wanted to feel. The thing you need to realize is your hurt may not affect her in that way. How do you know the secret she's holding is not deeper than what you just revealed? I could tell you how I would react today because it's not happening to me. I can't, however, tell you what my reaction would be if I were in the moment because that would depend on what was happening in my life at the time. Do you understand what I'm saying, Mr. Mason?"

I nodded. She just opened my eyes even more. What if my having a son wasn't shit compared to something Tracey had done? I never even thought about it that way, and I knew that I would eventually have to tell her. Just not right now, definitely not at our next session, and maybe not even this year.

I thanked her for her time and made my way to my car. I needed to talk to Zaria at least to clear the air. It'd been months since we'd communicated correctly, and that was some dirty shit I did to her as well. I was actually surprised she stayed quiet this long.

Pulling up to the house, I was relieved that Tracey wasn't home yet, but I did briefly wonder where she was. Was she really at the office working on our next campaign, or was she somewhere getting fucked all kinds of crazy by one of her side pieces? I really needed to pull myself together before my thoughts drove me crazy. Going down to the basement, I grabbed the stack of mail that had been piling up for the last few weeks off the island before taking the stairs. Out of respect, we never entered each other's office when we were not home. If I had a package for her, I would leave it in the basket at the door, and she would leave my stuff in the kitchen. Well, at least I never went into her office as agreed. I didn't know if she'd ever come down here.

I went through the stack, not really looking for anything in particular. There was the basic shuffle of credit card bills that were already paid online and brochures from companies I wasn't interested in. When I got to the bottom, there was a thick package from the Texas branch of our company. When did they start sending mail to the house? I was confused as I grabbed the twenty-four-karat gold letter opener to slice open the package. I immediately dropped it once the contents fell out. I guessed I wasn't the only one who was willing to get burned in the fire, but if nothing else, I knew this had to be stopped before it spread. Grabbing the desk phone, I dialed the one number I was trying so desperately to forget as the skeletons started forcing the damn door open again.

Chapter Sixteen

Zaria

You'll get tired of shuffling eventually, because let's face it, skeletons take up a lot of room!

When you poke a sleeping bear, you have to get ready to run or fight. A split-second decision is the difference between life or death. You know that once that bear is awake, it's going to come out fighting and ready to draw blood until the fight is over. But you have to decide who will be defeated: you or the bear?

It took Tariq longer to call than I thought it would. Knowing him, he might not have opened his mail right away. I was hoping his wife would be the one to open the envelope since it was sent from the company, but she probably wasn't even home enough to look at the mail. I should have addressed it directly to her. It did have his name on it. *The next one will be addressed to her if he doesn't give me the answer I'm looking for*.

My son cried for days once he realized his dad wouldn't be coming back. This after a few unanswered and unreturned calls. TJ even left a message himself for his dad to call back. Every time the phone rang, TJ would jump up to see if it was his dad, and once he realized it wasn't, he would be in his bag for the rest of the day. As his mother, this shit was hard to watch, and it killed me.

It was horrible watching my son hurt like this, and the more days that went by, the more I wanted Tariq to pay. All I wanted was a phone call. *Just pick up the phone and tell me to leave you the fuck alone.* He was being a real coward, and I was sick of his actions. He knew it, too. That's why he hadn't been to our division since the last time he was here. He didn't want to face me.

I was in the midst of a much-needed nap when my phone rang. TJ was with my sister and her kids at Sky Zone, and I welcomed the break. He needed to take his mind off of his father as much as I did, and this was a nice distraction for him. He loved being around his cousins, and my sister was more than happy to take him along. She knew I was having a rough time dealing with this issue with TJ's father, and she had been very supportive.

At first I thought I was dreaming, until Tariq's ringtone broke the silence again. I started not to answer it and do the same shit he did to me for months on end. The only reason why he wanted to talk now was because I sent his ass that package. If I wouldn't have taken the initiative to send it, he wouldn't even be checking for me right now. I should have let his ass go to voicemail, but the fire that was burning in me was so deep I couldn't allow it to happen. I had to give him a few choice words for both me and my son. I was not about to let him know how much we were bothered by his absence, though. Oh, I was about to piss him off.

"Hello?" I spoke into the phone like I was really half asleep when, in reality, I woke right the fuck up when I saw that it was him calling.

"Are you seriously trying to ruin my life?" Tariq asked, surprisingly rather calmly from the other end. He was trying to control his anger, just like I was.

"Excuse me?" I responded, still keeping my voice in check. He wanted me to go off so he'd have a reason to not be bothered. I'd be damned if I was giving him that satisfaction.

"Zaria, let's not play. You know why I'm calling."

"Your son is not here. Maybe call back tomorrow when he's available to talk."

Silence.

Figured that would shut his arrogant ass up for a second. If only he could feel what my son was feeling now. Abandoned. Or maybe he had. I didn't know anything about his family. Maybe his dad did the same thing to him, and that's why he was acting like this.

"Zaria, stop being petty. Pictures to my house using company mail? Really? What if my wife had opened the package? You really took it there."

"Man, fuck that bitch and fuck you too. I was hoping she would open it so that she could see the truth. Ain't like you gonna tell her," I managed to say without raising my voice. I was shocked myself how calm I remained on the phone in direct contrast to how pissed off I really was. Did he think I gave a flying rat's ass about his wife? *The next package will have her name on it. That's a guarantee.*

"Don't disrespect my wife," he responded weakly, obviously caught off guard by my response. I clearly had the upper hand in this situation now.

"You already did," I threw back at him so fast his breath caught in his throat. Gone was the submissive mistress who was obedient to him. He hurt my son. All that docile shit was a wrap. "What was the purpose of this call, Tariq?"

I was done playing with him. He was going to regret ever meeting me if it was the last thing I did. I'd already transferred all the money he had given me for our son to my private account. He was not about to take that back. There was over $300,000 just sitting there. No way would I allow him to backtrack on that much money. That's the first thing dudes try to do when shit goes sour. I was already two steps ahead of his cheating ass. Every time he made a deposit, it transferred to my private account.

"What do you want from me? You knew going in that we would never be together. You did this to us!" he shouted, catching me off guard. Maybe I did, but if that was the case, he should have just stayed away from the very beginning and let me be a single mom. He should have never gotten involved.

"It's really not about me, Tariq. It's about what you did to your son that caused this. You hurt him. You should have stayed away."

"You act like I had a choice. You already know that I can't be there with him like you want me to. I didn't even want him there the last time I came. You forced it on both of us. You should have gotten an abortion years ago."

Click.

I didn't even bother to respond. Maybe I should have gotten an abortion, but I didn't, and it ain't like I could put him back in my pussy and start over again. He was 4 now, and he knew who his dad was. Since he wanted to play hardball, it was time to turn up the heat. I knew shit about both him and his wife that he didn't know I had a clue about. His wife's assistant was a very good friend of mine, and she hated her just as much as I did. Came to find out she was mean to every-damn-body. We'd been talking about her for years before I actually put a face to the name. I'd admit she was a lot prettier than my friend made her out to be, but she was all of the bitch I ever heard she was.

I hated even to go there, but I really didn't give a fuck at this point. It was time to put my plan into motion. I was going to let Tariq be great, but not until after I had the last word. *After me, I promise he will never ever think about stepping out again. Not if he cherishes his life.* I had to teach this bastard a lesson he would never forget. It was time he learned to not fuck over people like he did me and his son, and I was the perfect person to teach his ass what was real.

Picking up my phone, I sent my homegirl a text for her to call me at the gig in the morning. Oftentimes, when I had to come there for company business or she had to come here, we would stay at each other's house even though the company paid for a hotel. We had been doing it for years once we met in person after our internet/phone relationship blossomed. I knew I had to make a trip to Philly soon, so I just wanted to let her know I was coming. I wouldn't involve her in this because I didn't want her job on the line as well, but I definitely needed the updated scoop on the Masons before I touched down. I also wanted it to be a surprise when I got there to shake things up a bit. She hated Tracey just as much as I did, so I knew it wouldn't be hard to get her help. I just hated that I had to lie to her to get it.

Turning over, I thought about my plan and how to move forward, and I knew for certain that I had to make this a clean shot. Hopefully, things didn't get out of hand, and if they did, oh well. Tariq rightfully deserved whatever happened to him, so just maybe he'd cooperate. We'd see once I got there. For the first time in months, I slept without being sad or angry, and it felt good. My revenge was coming soon. I just had to wait for it.

Chapter Seventeen

Tracey

And what do you do when there's no more room? You find another damn closet! Duh!

Who am I?

I'd been sitting in front of this mirror, trying to come up with an answer I could live with. The last thing the therapist requested was for us to figure out who we really were. I was a lot of things. College graduate, wife, mogul, beauty, and brains. I made the world stop at the snap of a finger like Beyoncé, and folks moved with just a look. I made shit happen. I was every business owner's dream. I built corporations from the ground up that were run so solid that CEOs passed my name to others with word that I was a sure thing. Bet on me and win every time. I was dependable, and I got most things right the first time. *I am reliable. I am loyal to those who are loyal to me, kind of.* This cheating shit might have put a smudge or two on my suit of armor, but I wasn't claiming it just yet. Inside, I was a good person. I just got lost along the way.

But hypothetically, of course, what if I lost everything? Like, what if I lost my job and husband all in one swoop? Could I maintain? I had a loving heart. I really did. I just needed folks to understand that in the male-dominated business that I was in, I had to come out with claws showing, ready to scratch and draw blood until I made it to the top. Damn that glass ceiling. I made sure I rode a bulldozer up the ladder so that when I got to the top, I could knock down boulders with ease. It made me come off as a real bitch, but no one successful was nice. Every female worth mentioning from our past was trouble. They didn't give up without a fight, if at all.

Who am I?

I got out a notepad and wrote down everything that made me worth being with. My list was short as shit. Outside of being financially sound, what else did I bring in? Beauty and brains were givens, but what did I have to offer to make my husband feel safe and secure with me? I'd be the first to admit that our relationship was getting better since therapy. We actually came home at night. No, we were not back at the stage where we snuck off for lunch-break sex, but we were getting it in more than before. We rode in to work together most mornings, rotating cars, and days like today, when we went to work on a Saturday, we had sex before he left. Could I be a good wife to him, though? Could I make him feel secure again? Could trust be rebuilt? I was so confused and frustrated. Putting my pen down, I decided to walk off and clear my head. Maybe I needed a breather before proceeding.

Deciding to work off some frustration, I went upstairs and put on some gym clothes. Maybe I could take a quick Zumba class or something to let off some steam. I had a membership at LA Fitness, and they always had a class going on. Of course I stayed away from anything near water because I was not about to be getting my hair wet again. Sweat was one thing, but chlorine was a whole other poison I wasn't willing to deal with.

Once I was dressed, I called my husband to communicate with him. That was another thing the therapist suggested we work on. "It's not about checking in. It's about being aware."

"Hey, babe," he answered on the second ring in that voice that gave me chills in a good way. After last night, I was surprised that he was even able to work. We got that shit in for what felt like hours before we finally went to sleep. Every time I thought I had tamed the beast, he was right back inside of me, driving me to the edge and dangling me in midair until I submitted to him. I was finally in love again, and it felt wonderful. Unfortunately, there was always a little sprinkle of doubt resting in the back of my mind that I was having a hard time shaking off. Mostly that was due to my own infidelity. Since I couldn't fully trust myself, I couldn't find it in my heart to trust him as much as I should.

"Good morning. How is your day going?" I asked. To think my simple ass almost lost him. I must have bumped my head thinking I could do better than Tariq. *What's wrong with me?* Any woman would gladly take him if I was done. Even before Tariq, every man I had always ended up leaving because of my fucked-up attitude and domineering personality. *How did I get like this?* The thought alone almost brought me to tears.

"Not bad, got a lot done. Was thinking movies and dinner tonight. You in?" he asked, inviting me on a date.

I took the phone from my face and looked at it before placing it back to my ear. We hadn't done that in years. I guessed he was really trying to get that old thing back. "Uh, sure," I responded, caught off guard. "What's out right now?"

While Tariq went through the current movie listings, I busied myself getting ready for the gym. I definitely wanted to at least get a spin class or something in before he got back home. Maybe we could even get in a quickie before we went out tonight. Loving this man really had me on fire lately, and it felt nice to be getting back to us.

"Babe, you pick the movie. It doesn't matter as long as it's not scary," I said. We both chuckled into the phone at my fear of horror films. Yes, I was too old to be having nightmares, but it never failed after watching something spooky, and I couldn't afford to lose any sleep tonight with having to prepare for my presentation on Monday.

While he talked, I searched all over for my favorite workout shoes. Yeah, I had plenty, but I needed the lime green, yellow, and pink grapefruit New Balances I had to match my workout outfit. Just as I started to go check outside to see if I left them in my car, I remembered I tossed them in the wash the last time Tariq and I went to the gym. That's where they had to be. If not, then I'd check the trunk.

"Okay, love, I'm going to jet down to LA Fitness to catch the early afternoon spin class. You know I want a seat up front before it gets crowded. "

"Yeah, I know you do. I should be meeting you home by then, and maybe we could spin in the shower before we go?"

"Yeah? That's how you feel?" I responded flirtatiously as my clit jumped against the crotch of my panties. He was so fucking nasty. I loved that shit. "I'll be ready for you, daddy."

Disconnecting the call, I continued my hunt for my gym shoes in the basement. When I got downstairs, the first thing that I noticed was that Tariq's office door was slightly cracked open. I walked past it to see if my shoes were either in the washer or dryer, hoping for the latter. If they were moldy in the washer, I'd have to change my clothes and find different shoes to match, and I'd have to rewash the stuff that was left in there.

Thankfully, they were in the dryer with the rest of the workout stuff that we neglected to come back for. Sitting in the chair next to the dryer, I busied myself looking for matching socks, but my mind kept wandering. I'd never invaded Tariq's space. Never. Honestly, I rarely came down to the basement, as the majority of my clothes were dry clean only, and I had enough underclothes to put a pair of panties on every female in Philadelphia. The fact that I was too lazy to wash clothes added to that, and when I started to get low on undergarments, I would just go buy more. So the basement rarely saw me. Tariq would wash our unmentionables and bring mine up when he brought his, so that saved me a trip as well.

Something in that office was calling me, though. Like, I couldn't go upstairs until I at least had a look. I knew I was wrong, but curiosity got the best of me, and I just had to see what he did in there. After securing my sneakers on my feet, I walked over to his office door and pushed it open. I stood outside the door battling with myself for longer than I should have before just stepping in. To my surprise, he'd totally remodeled it from what I remembered it looking like.

It was very masculine. All black everything from the onyx desk to the Italian leather chair that sat behind it. A sixteen-by-twenty portrait of himself hung on the wall behind the chair, surrounded by his many accolades and achievements for a job well done. A few heavy marbled pieces in black and white were mixed in, down to the stunning paperweight that sat on top of a few papers on his desk shaped like a gorgeous letter Z. The twenty-four-karat-gold fountain pen that I gave him for his birthday a few years ago rested in its engraved holder in the corner, and a five-by-seven photo of us from years ago sat next to a landline phone. He had a sexy four-foot-tall vase with black, white, and granite plumage spilling from it, and there wasn't an ounce of dust in sight, due to his OCD, I was sure.

I glanced at the few papers he had on his desk, and everything looked related to work. I briefly wondered again why he was getting work-related packages sent to the house, thinking maybe it was brochures for our newest company that recently came on board. Curiosity was still getting the best of me as I reached for the envelope to see what was inside. Before I could open it, my phone rang, scaring the shit out of me. I freaked out for five seconds, carefully placing the envelope back where I'd gotten it from, hoping that it was where I'd found it. Tiptoeing out of the office, I eased the door back to where I remembered it being, and I answered the phone once I got upstairs. Did he know I was in his office? Maybe he had cameras installed down there that I didn't know about. I became so paranoid I couldn't breathe.

"Baby, are you okay?" Tariq asked with a concern-laced voice. My dumb ass almost got caught, and I felt so guilty.

"Yes. I went to the basement to get my sneakers out of the dryer, and a spider jumped out at me," I lied, acting like that was the real reason why I was acting crazy at the moment.

"Oh, baby, I know you're not scared of some silly spider," he laughed, and it eased my mind. Thank God he didn't suspect me of snooping in his stuff. "On your way back from the gym, do you mind grabbing my suits from the cleaner? That would really save me a trip all the way across town, and I can just head straight home to get ready for you."

"Sure, love, anything for you," I responded. We chatted a little more as I headed to the car, and once I got in, we disconnected the call. As petrified as I was that I just got caught, something was still bugging at me, and I knew I had to look around his office the next chance I got. Something about that company mail envelope didn't sit all the way right with me, and just to satisfy my own corrupted behavior, I needed to see what it was. When I first saw the envelope, I thought maybe it was a project he was working on, but I was too busy with my own shit to be worried about some mess coming to the house from work for my husband. Not sure why it was bothering me so much now. Call me crazy, but until we got back to 100 percent, that's just how it had to be.

Chapter Eighteen

Tariq

But who feels like the shuffle? "When you tell one lie, it leads to another/So you tell two lies to cover each other." You know the song.

That's one sneaky bitch right there. I took the liberty of installing cameras in the basement when we first started therapy. At that point in our lives, there was no trust to be found with us, and I just wanted to be sure that she wasn't snooping around in my shit while I was gone. Never before today had I been so sloppy as to leave my door open, so I guessed she was baited somehow.

I could sign in from any device to monitor the live feed, and I rarely looked because lately we'd been together all the time. It was a rare occurrence that I worked at the office on the weekend, but some of the things I needed to do for our presentation on Monday I couldn't do from home. The cameras were only installed in the basement, although I contemplated putting them in other places like the hall upstairs to see if she was bringing people to our bedroom. We had an entirely separate set of surveillance for the perimeter of the house. I just never got around to adding more, and I didn't want her questioning the cameras in my office. She didn't need to know I didn't trust her just yet.

I really wasn't even thinking about it until she told me she was going to the gym. Mind you, we both had plenty of workout clothes to choose from, but I knew my wife. Everything had to match all the way down to the ground. It had been a few weeks since we both were at the gym at the same time, and I kept forgetting to take the clothes I had washed and dried upstairs. She'd been to the basement a few times but never even paused for a slight second by my office door. It was like it wasn't even there. Today though, when I zoomed in and noticed that the door was open, I freaked out. I did not need her finding that envelope from Zaria. Not right now when we were doing so good.

I didn't call at first, because I wanted to give her the benefit of maybe just walking by, but who was I fooling? If I were in her shoes, I probably would have done the same thing. I watched the pained expression on her face as she battled with herself about going in, but I guessed she couldn't fight it off. Switching the view, I could now see inside my office where she was. She was just looking around, not really touching anything, but when she spotted the envelope, I knew she would reach for it. I was surprised she didn't open it when it first arrived. I couldn't dial her number fast enough, and I just hoped that she would answer it instead of going with her gut. She ran out of the office so fast I almost laughed, and she didn't answer the phone until she was out of breath upstairs. I barely missed it, but I knew I needed to get home and get rid of the contents of that envelope.

Grabbing the stuff that I was working on, I raced to my car and drove like a madman through the city until I got home. Heading down to my office, I set down the things that I was working on and grabbed the envelope. I had to be smart about this, so I knew exactly what I had to do. Removing the picture of me from the wall, I revealed a safe that I had built years before. I'd had a few hundred thousand dollars stacked in there, most of which I'd deposited into my son's account, and other valuables like life insurance policies and jewels.

I took the envelope from the desk and took the photos out. Flipping through them quickly, I got choked up as I flashed back to the last time I spent time with my son and Zaria. We had a ball that day, and I hadn't been back since. I couldn't lie. I missed Zaria more than I wanted to admit. Her softness, those curves, that extra-wet box that she gave up so willingly . . . I was feeling like I needed to take a trip to Texas one last time just to at least get some proper closure and maybe one last round at the rodeo. Placing the pictures in the safe, I closed it, securing it with my son's birthdate code, 0827.

Sitting at my desk, I took out the brochures that I had been working on at work and set them on top of the now-empty envelope as if they were the contents all along. If I knew my wife as well as I thought, she would be back to look again. It's not on purpose. It's human nature to be curious. I'd appease her with the brochures, so that way she could be at peace.

Pulling up my bank info, I took a peek into the savings that I had for my son and was floored. The balance in the account said $0.13. In disbelief, I logged out and logged back in to be sure I was reading it properly. *What the heck happened to all the money I put in there?* There was well over $300,000 that had stacked up over the years, and Zaria rarely touched it. I always made sure any daycare, karate classes, or whatever he needed was taken care of in addition to the money that I put in there on a biweekly basis just for Zaria to have. Someone had to have hacked into this account.

I wasn't worried at first. My bank was good at recovering funds lost due to fraudulent activity. I never even bothered to look at the activity, but had I taken that step, I could have saved myself a phone call. The bank teller explained that the money was withdrawn by Zaria Banks, an authorized user on the account. I was so irked. *What kind of low-down ghetto shit is this?* I was livid, and my first instinct was to call and curse her ass out. Why would she do something so shady? It was definitely to get back at me, but I needed to talk to her.

Just as I was reaching for the phone, I heard the door beep, indicating someone was coming in. My wife was home. I closed the screen and pulled up my work documents to look busy. I was steaming on the inside. Zaria had never shown she was grimy like this, but it was cool. The last money she got would be the last money she'd get for a while. She had more than enough to take care of TJ as far as I was concerned. I'd just have to show her what happened when you bit the hand that was feeding you. Although very irritated, I managed to straighten my face a little as my wife came down the stairs and knocked on my partially open office door.

"Come in, love," I said to her as I typed in a few lines on my presentation like I was busy. I could see her eyes bouncing around the office, trying to look like she wasn't just in here earlier.

"This is nice," she complimented it while taking a seat on one of the overstuffed chairs I had in the corner. I believed the last time she came in here, besides earlier, was when I first moved into this office after having it built. I'd made a lot of changes since then, and she looked like she was impressed.

"I try," I laughed as I saved my file and signaled her over to me, leaving it up so that she could see what I was doing. I wanted her to get a clear view of that envelope before we left so that she'd stay away. Nobody had time to keep being paranoid about dirt they'd done in the past.

She sauntered over to me, looking extra sexy in her workout gear. One thing I did not like was a fat chick. You could be thick, but damn that fat shit. Tracey did well with her weight loss, not that she was ever huge, and she stayed on top of her health now. I just had to make sure Zaria didn't let herself go while we were doing us. Nobody had time for that shit.

As she straddled me, I leaned in so that I could kiss her lips. She gave the best head with those lips, and I began to lengthen just thinking about it. She tried to back off a little because she had just come in from the gym, but I wanted it. She tried halfheartedly to put up a fight, but when I pressed on her clit through her clothes, she almost lost it. Watching her eyes close and her head drop back took me to the next level, and I knew I had to have it now.

Making her stand up, I pulled her clothes off from her waist down. She wanted to fight me so bad on this. She couldn't handle having any kind of bodily contact straight from the gym, but it didn't matter to me. It's not like she smelled like garbage. A little sweat never hurt anyone. Removing my own pants, I moved to the cushioned seat on the side and sat down, signaling for her to come get on it. That shit was killing her, but we had to learn to be more open and spontaneous. It's not like we were confined to the bedroom or shower for sexual activity. Hell, we had an entire house to get freaky in.

She approached me slowly like she was going to ask to shower real quick, but I guessed she figured if I didn't mind the sweat, why should she? Straddling me, she eased down on it a little at a time until it was all in. She felt extra warm and gushy, getting wetter with each up-and-down motion. Grabbing her hips, I held her steady as I thrust upward to tap her G-spot just how she liked it. I couldn't believe I almost fucked things up with her.

When she reached up to remove her clothes from her top half, I was in love all over again. Perfect breasts, smooth stomach, her hair was wild and down her back . . . I had my very own porn star right at home.

"You gonna bend over the desk so I can get it from the back?" I asked her, trying to keep from cracking this nut too early. Although the thought of her being with other men pissed me off, I had to say that old girl still had it. I know whoever had her definitely enjoyed it.

Without a word, she eased off of me and graciously bent over the desk, waiting for me to join her. I wanted her to see the envelope with the brochures spilling out of it before we left here today. That way, she would keep from wanting to come back in this room, hopefully.

By the time we were done, we were all over the desk, and all the papers ended up on the floor. We did end up in the shower eventually, where we slowed it down and really go into each other. Needless to say, we never made that movie date, but I did not forget to hit Zaria up to discuss her foolishness. I saw I was going to have to show her what kind of pull I had better than I'd ever told her. I really didn't want to go there, but I had no choice. These women were going to drive me crazy, but I'd be the first to admit that cheating was not for me. This was a definite lesson well learned.

Chapter Nineteen

Zaria

Skeletons are tricky, though. They'll stay quiet for a while having you think you've won. Years will go by, and then one day, boom! Skeleton just waving around in the air for everyone to see at the most inopportune time.

"Miss Banks, can I see you in my office?" My boss called down for me not even an hour after I'd gotten settled into my workday. He really irked me when he called at these odd times, knowing that I had a full schedule and plenty of stuff he needed me to do. This man had more flights out of the city than I could count, and I knew it wasn't all business. I was a little naive in the beginning, but after dealing with Tariq for years, I clearly saw how they got down. 90 percent of men high on the corporate ladder have a mistress. Some in several cities. I wondered if he had secret love children in other places, too.

Maybe I should have been alarmed when he called me by my last name. We were on a first-name basis on a regular basis unless there was someone in the office from one of the other locations and he wanted to present a more professional front. Otherwise, I was called by my first name or the nickname they gave me, Miss Z. My mind raced as I made my way to his office, trying to remember if I dotted all of my I's and crossed every T. I was very thorough with my work, but every so often, things slipped through the cracks.

As I approached his office door, I could hear voices from the other side. One in particular made me stop dead in my tracks. Was that Tariq in there? I hadn't seen this man in almost a year, and he had the nerve to show up here unannounced! I definitely didn't remember seeing him on the schedule for today, so what was this about? Taking a moment to gather myself, I put my best smile on my face as I entered the room. This fool was not about to think he was going to rattle me on my own turf. I played harder than that, and he of all people should know.

"Good morning, Mr. Reynolds and Mr. Mason. To what do I owe the pleasure of speaking with you gentlemen this morning?" I asked, standing at the desk, hoping that if I stood, we could make it quick. I was boiling inside, trying to keep myself from grabbing Tariq by the neck and choking him out. Like, I wanted to literally get a running start from down the hall so that I could dropkick him in the esophagus like I was a character in that *Street Fighter* game. I hated this man, and I didn't even realize how much until now.

"Well, Miss Banks, an interesting situation has been brought to my attention that has caused some alarm," he stated while shuffling through some papers on his desk. Now the alarms were going off for real. What did he have on his desk that had any connection between me and Tariq? Like, we had our beef, but none of it was related to work.

"Okay, what exactly?" I questioned, wishing he would just get to the damn point. He dragged out every damn thing, and now just wasn't the time.

"It appears that you have been having an extramarital affair with Mr. Mason," he began, still not looking up from his desk.

A bitch was shocked! Like, what did he just say? "Excuse me?" I managed to spit out. He had to be kidding me right now. "Do you mind repeating that?" I asked, looking back and forth between both of them. Neither would make eye contact. My boss was shuffling papers on his desk, and Tariq was on his damn cell phone.

Instead of answering, he got up and walked around his desk, handing me a folder when he got close. I couldn't breathe for a second, and I almost didn't want to open it. This fool was really playing in my face.

"Now, Miss Banks, we both are well aware of how important discretion is in this business. Any extracurricular affairs with our associates are frowned upon," he droned on as I took a seat and tried to concentrate on the contents of the folder. There was a photocopy of the packaging envelope I sent Tariq, along with a few pictures of us together. I did notice that there were no photos of him and TJ inside, so he was definitely trying to keep that secret in spite of everything else, and I appreciated him not dragging our son into this bullshit, but he was a low-down, dirty dog. I definitely underestimated him.

Further flipping through the papers, I saw a bank statement that read the $0.13 balance and a statement from Tariq saying I extorted him for over a hundred grand to keep quiet about what had been going on. At the very bottom, there was a letter of recommendation from Mr. Reynolds singing praises of my work for him, and how I would be an excellent candidate for any said position. He really flipped the script on me, and honestly, I was more hurt and disappointed than anything. He took it all the way there, and I was not prepared.

"So as not to draw attention, I'll give you fifteen minutes to clean out your desk. All of your files have been forwarded by my new assistant during this meeting, and you have already been logged out of your accounts.

I contacted an associate of mine to place you in a new position in his company. His information is included in your exit packaging. Are there any questions?"

"I'm fired?" I asked. I missed everything he said before because I couldn't believe the bullshit Tariq had pulled, and by the time I tuned back in, it sounded like he was letting me go.

"You'll be contacted by human resources to aid in dissolving any 401k and other money market accounts you may have. Your insurance will still be good for six months from today, and your last check will include one year's severance pay for your troubles. So as to not tarnish your image, this will be recorded as a voluntary resignation, and you have the option to start with the company in your packet if you wish to move in that direction," he continued. My damn mouth was wide open. "I'm a little disheartened that after all of these years, this is how it ends with us, Zaria, but through it all we have to protect the company."

"But how could he—"

"Zaria, just sign the paper," Tariq finally spoke, looking me in the eye for the first time since I walked into the room. This motherfucker got me fired but with benefits. At least he looked out for his son. Mr. Reynolds needed me to hold his secrets, too, and that was probably why he set me up the way he did.

Scanning the paper, I finally signed my name at the bottom and took a copy as well as the folder I was given and left the room. When I got back to my desk, the same assistant who covered me when I was out on maternity leave was posted up at my desk like she belonged there. The contents of my desk and my locker were stacked neatly in a company box, and my jacket rested on top. I could not believe this shit.

Instead of causing a scene, I gathered my things and rolled out quietly. I could not believe this was even fucking happening. I kept feeling like I was about to cry, but I refused to give them the satisfaction. I made it all the way to the parking lot and home without spazzing out. Things were not supposed to end this way, and I actually lost my job in the process. I was seriously thinking about just letting Tariq be, but he crossed the line today. The only respectable thing for me to do was to get his ass back. It wouldn't be right if I didn't.

Chapter Twenty

Tracey

At some point, you just have to own your shit, though. You can't keep hiding behind secrets forever. Live in your truth for once.

I wasn't letting it go that easy. Although Tariq didn't say anything, something was telling me that he wanted me to see what was in his office on purpose. Once he got home and realized his office door was open, he had to think that I looked around. Come on now, let's not play stupid. I saw the envelope in plain view on the desk with brochures spilling out of it, but my gut was telling me that those brochures were not the original contents of the envelope. If it were that simple, they would have sent them to the office like they always did. And if I remembered correctly, the envelope didn't feel heavy enough to contain that many. He was hiding something. I just had to figure out what.

It'd been a few weeks since the incident, and do know your girl was getting a plan in action. One morning, after some bomb-ass sex, Tariq decided to go back to sleep while I ran to the store to get a few things for a late breakfast. I took his car just to see what keys he had on his key ring. Running in the basement while he was sleeping, of course I tested the keys to see which one fit the office door. Once that was figured out, I got a copy made while

I was out and tucked that in the top drawer in my closet for safekeeping. I needed to get a really good look around his office while he wasn't here to see what was going on in there.

Lo and behold, just when I almost forgot about it, he informed me that he was taking a trip to our Texas branch to start their next move-up phase within the company. It was only going to be a day trip, so he would be flying out early and getting back late the same day. Texas has a huge oil industry, and we were beginning to partner with a few people out there to cash in on that cow as well. Of course, they needed us for marketing so that we could get a nice running start on the competition. He asked if I wanted to go, and I started to jump on it, just for the sake of us spending time together. Then I remembered I had the key and some inspecting to do. This was the perfect opportunity to get some real solid answers.

"You sure you don't want to go? We can hit that restaurant we saw on *Diners, Drive-Ins and Dives,*" he asked, trying to convince me to travel along. Anyone who knew me knew that the way to my heart was through my belly. I loved a good meal, but that wouldn't be enough this time around.

"I'm already up ten pounds fooling with you the last few months. I'm back in the gym, honey, going hard," I responded playfully as I lay on the bed in front of him in my newest Pretty Dirty Things two-piece cami set. I knew I was looking delicious, and red was his favorite color. My hair was fanned out over the pillow like I was just waiting for someone to take my picture and put me in a lingerie catalog. I could see in his eyes that he liked what he saw, and it turned me on. At one point, he couldn't stand the sight of me. Now he couldn't get enough of me.

He moved to the edge of the bed, grabbed my ankles, and slid me down to the edge, placing my legs over his shoulders. He set his mouth on the crotch of my panties, inhaled through his nose, and exhaled hot breath out of his mouth, causing my clit to stiffen. My body actually craved him when he wasn't around, and I was hoping I would get a little loving from him to hold me over until he got back. Lucky me.

I could feel him suctioning my clit through my panties as it pulsed wildly under his tongue. I wanted to reach down and pull my panties off so that he would have full access, but I knew better than to interrupt Mr. Mason's flow. He would get to it when he was ready. Teasing was a part of the game with him, and I promised I would let him be in control for now on. He never disappointed me, ever.

By the time he was done devouring me, I was four orgasms in, and he still wasn't finished. Pushing me back on the bed, he climbed in behind me and pushed in from the gate. It felt like he had gotten even bigger than the last time, it that was at all possible. Tariq was the man when it came to putting it down in bed, and I refused to give any opportunity to share him again. He belonged to me, forever and always.

"So about that trip to Texas," he growled real low in my ear as he hit me with the longest strokes I'd ever felt. Oh, he was going in for the kill, but I had to stay focused. I needed him to go so that I could do what I needed to do.

"I'm . . . I can't go, Tariq," I moaned out, breath catching in the middle of another explosion. He was really trying hard, but I refused to let him get me that easily.

"But I want you to," he replied, cutting me off by pressing my clit between his thumb and forefinger. If I weren't already lying down, I would have passed out. He was not playing fair at all.

"I have work to finish," I managed to spit out before flames engulfed my body again in another wave of scrumptious orgasm. "I'll come down on Sunday if you decide to stay the weekend. We . . . we can have dinner."

I was acting like a stuttering fool, and he was enjoying that shit. He went in and drilled up in me, talking his time speeding back up only to slow down again until he finally let a hot, sticky load off inside of me. It was so much it spilled out and left a creamy puddle under me on the sheets. Damn, that was good.

Once we caught our breath, he gently lifted me from the bed and carried me into the shower. It was a good thing he did because my legs felt wobbly for a second. He cleaned us both, and we ended up with a quick nap before he was waking me to tell me his car was here to take him to the airport. I was grateful he called a car and I didn't have to drive him myself.

Once he was gone, I lay in bed a little while longer before I got up to investigate. I figured if he did have surveillance down there, he wouldn't be able to check it while he was in the air. I never found a camera, but that didn't mean it wasn't there. My sweet, dear husband was hiding something, and I had to know what it was.

Chapter Twenty-one

Tariq

They say the truth will set you free. The truth will also get your fronts knocked out, so be prepared for the worst.

Did I feel bad about Zaria getting fired? A little. She had to learn how to shake and move in this business, though, and she really didn't leave me any choice. It was an unspoken rule that the secretary's position was to keep the boss's secrets, especially from the wife. Her job was to book the flights and make it all look related to business. If she would betray me by sending pictures to my house, what would she do to her own superior? That was exactly how I kicked it to him, and he was devastated and afraid. We all had shit to lose, and we just couldn't chance it with her. She had to learn how to operate in corporate America if she was going to maintain this type of job. He really looked out for her in the end, and I really hoped she saw how lucky she was.

It was a good thing her boss and I were very close and I could go to him with half-truths, because I definitely wasn't crazy enough to tell him everything. He was appalled by her actions and instantly felt like his own shit would be exposed next. Hell, he had three kids outside of his marriage who his wife knew absolutely nothing about. His wife had been trying to get pregnant for years unsuccessfully, so that info would have been way too messy to clean up if leaked. He was pissed at Zaria's actions and decided to fire her on the spot. I had to talk him into at least giving her a nice severance pay and something for her troubles, because she was a great employee to him in spite of this little slipup. I even let her keep the money she took out of the account, but I wanted her to know I saw what she did and she wouldn't be getting any more for a long-ass time. Because he was so afraid, he readily obliged, hooking up the new gig for her to keep the peace. That was the least I could do for someone who was trying to wreck my flow. I didn't play all the time. Especially when it came to my livelihood. I'd just as soon dead your career and have you back on food stamps before I allowed you to fuck up my shit.

She handled it way better than I thought she would. I'd admit I was surprised. I just knew she would protest, but she bowed out gracefully. At first, I was relieved, but the more I thought about it, it started to make me nervous. Was she going to try to get me back? She walked away with a husky amount of money. Just thinking about it gave me a headache, and after I finished with business at the company, I grabbed a hotel room and took a much-needed nap. I was so used to going to Zaria's house when I was here that I felt weird checking into a hotel and actually staying here. His new assistant handled everything and put me up in something nice. I felt too guilty to enjoy it. Originally I was going to head back out tonight, but I decided to stay and let my wife meet me down here. That way I could formally introduce her to the new girl and catch her up on operations. Before long, I was fast asleep and having one of the craziest dreams ever.

I was in this hotel room, but both my wife and Zaria were all over me and enjoying each other. I didn't even know Tracey got down like that, but these ladies were really enjoying each other's company. Of course, I was enjoying myself. Tracey had a firm grip on my dick with the majority of it stuffed in her mouth, while Zaria slurped and gulped at my balls, making them super wet. I was handcuffed to the bed by my arms and legs and was shocked that I even agreed to something like that.

Zaria climbed on top of me and slid down on my erection ever so gently. Tracey moved between my legs, and through the mirror on the ceiling, I could see her lapping at Zaria's clit while she rode on top of me. I wanted to moan out loud, but for some reason, I couldn't hear myself say anything. I was clearly having the best time of my life, but my moans fell on death ears. Not one sound came out of my mouth.

At that moment, I started to panic. Did these bitches drug me? And why was it so hot in this damn room all of a sudden? I could see them laughing and carrying on as they took turns taking pleasure from me, and as bad as I wanted to bust a nut so that they could get off of me, I couldn't ejaculate. Tears started streaming from my eyes as these women, dare I say, raped me. I wanted it to be over, but they wouldn't stop. I was yelling at the top of my lungs for help, but no one could hear me. This shit was getting crazier by the second.

Next thing I knew, Zaria knelt next to me on one side of the bed and Tracey on the other. They leaned in over me and started to kiss, their breasts touching each other's in the process. I couldn't help but think about how beautiful they were together. Milk-chocolate Tracey and butter-pecan Zaria. Despite my efforts, I began to stiffen again, and there was nothing I could do about it. I wanted one of the to get on top of me again, but then again, I wanted them to untie me and set me free. I closed my eyes briefly, hoping this was just a horrible yet tantalizing nightmare that I would wake up from any second. Before I could open them again, I felt a piercing pain in my chest.

My eyes flew open, and I couldn't believe what I saw. Both Zaria and Tracey were taking turns stabbing me with these huge-ass knives. Blood splattered all over their gorgeous, naked bodies, and the looks on their faces were scary as hell. It was like the devil took over both of them, and there were horns growing from their scalps. The sexiest devils I'd ever seen. Just when I thought I couldn't take any more, Tracey got up from the bed and grabbed my still-stick dick and raised a machete. I begged her not to do it, and her arm swung down to dismember me.

I jumped up out of my sleep to the sound of my phone going off. I was drenched in sweat and shaking uncontrollably. Was I being warned that some craziness was about to happen? It felt so real. Looking down at my shirt, I was relieved not to see any blood, but my shirt was so sweaty I had to take it off. It took me a while to get myself together, and once my heart rate came down to normal, I felt safe to go grab a shower. I was going to stick around until Sunday, but I would be grabbing the first thing smoking. I had to get the hell out of Texas.

Grabbing my phone to check for notifications, I scrolled through. I had the typical update emails from my secretary and a message from Tracey checking to see if my flight landed okay. At the bottom, there was a message from Zaria that made my hair stand up on the back of my neck. It was a short, simple message, but it packed so much heat it took my breath away. My victory was definitely short-lived as I read the words that would change my life: Check mate.

I didn't necessarily know what that meant, but I wasn't about to stick around to find out. Calling the airline, I was relieved to be able to grab the red-eye flight leaving at midnight tonight. I texted Tracey back, letting her know everything went well and that I would be leaving by midnight. Of course she asked questions, but I just told her that I missed her and didn't want to be away from her for longer than I had to be. She didn't need to know all of the bullshit that was going on and didn't have to waste her time traveling this far.

I had showered in record time and had all of my belongings packed and ready to go. Just as I was putting the last of my stuff in my bag, I got a knock at the door. No one knew I was here except my wife, so I didn't think much about the disturbance. She could have sent me a surprise or shown up to surprise me. I went to the door to see who it was, but no one was standing out there from what I could see through the peephole. I figured maybe they rang the wrong bell, but I opened the door anyway to make sure. On the floor sat a black rose and a card with lips on it as if someone had kissed it with bright red lipstick. I didn't even bother to pick the shit up.

Closing the door, I sped up my packing and took the steps down instead of waiting for the elevator to get to the lobby. Once I was done checking out, luckily, there was a cab that had just let someone out, so I hopped in and headed to the airport. I didn't really know what Zaria was capable of, although we shared a kid. We never discussed who we were as people. We basically just met and had sex. We didn't know much about each other except for the basics. Who was to say she wasn't a stalking loony tune who wouldn't hesitate to cut me up into a million pieces and hide my body in a deep freezer in the basement? No one would ever find me. I didn't even know what the damn basement looked like. Either way, if she was trying to scare me, it was definitely working. I had to get back home to my wife as soon as possible, and I wouldn't be stepping foot back in Texas unless it was absolutely necessary.

Chapter Twenty-two

Zaria

And what you think may be the worst thing that could happen to you don't even be the worst! It can get horrible if you're not ready, and it always does.

My homegirl gave me the information about his hotel. She couldn't believe they did me like this after all the years I put in, and she was even more pissed off about it than I was. The only thing about this job was we all used the same database to coordinate flight information and keep accurate records. Once they terminated me, all of my access was gone. I hit her up once I got home and told her the bad news. I was the best assistant they had in the Texas branch, and one incident got me booted? I didn't even get a chance to explain myself.

Was I wrong for harassing Tariq? Probably, but he had it coming. The way he did me and my son was so unnecessary. A woman scorned is one to watch out for. I guessed he didn't know that, but I was about to clue his dumb ass in. I was definitely taking pleasure in torturing his ass for real. I was already fired with a new position lined up. There was nothing they could do to me now.

Surprisingly, I still hadn't really cried like I probably should have. Honestly, I was still in disbelief. Once I got home, I took out the paperwork that was given to me to look over it. They definitely hooked me up. My severance was double my salary, and my 401k investments had been taken care of for more than a year. I would still be receiving my biweekly stipend for six months, and my travel was taken care of for a year. I wasn't even sure how they managed to pull it off, but I wasn't about to ask. At first, I didn't think I would even need the travel. Everyone I knew lived in Texas, but then a brilliant idea came to mind. Maybe I did need the travel after all.

I asked my sister to keep my son overnight because I needed to get my head on right. I told her that I had been let go but didn't give her a lot of detail because she was a low-key hater. The last thing I needed was to give her ammunition for the rest of her squad. They had been waiting for me to fall for as long as I could remember. Even fired, I wasn't down, but they didn't need to know that.

I went and got a single black rose from this little flower shop that was near my house, accompanied by a blank card. I was going to play with his head a little before he left until I sat and decided how I was really going to get revenge. Most say revenge isn't really worth it in the end, but for me, I knew getting him back would make me feel better, at least for a little while, and I was willing to take that short-lived victory. I refused to let him walk away from this without a good lesson learned. After me, he would never have to think twice about cheating on his wife again. He wasn't even going to have the urge. Not after what I would do to him.

Surprisingly, I wasn't nervous as I approached the hotel room door. I wanted to kick the shit to the floor and bang his head against the wall, but I maintained my composure as I knelt down to leave the rose shortly after knocking on the door and fleeing the scene. It was late, so I knew he wouldn't answer the door quickly, and that would give me plenty of time to hop back on the elevator or take the stairs. I really hated this man. Hate was such a strong word, but there was no other word in the English language that could describe these emotions.

Like, I wanted him dead. I didn't want anyone else to get a chance at enjoying that good dick again. Not even his wife. If I couldn't have it, I didn't want anyone to have it. By the time I got home, I looked up the information that I was given, and I couldn't help but laugh out loud when I saw that he changed his flight to leave tonight. I definitely scared him, but I wasn't finished. Not by a long shot. As good as the sex was, that didn't change that he was a lying-ass dog. I was a way better woman than his wife, and Tariq knew that. He knew he was better off with me.

Once comfortable, I took out the information I had on his wife, including the pictures that her assistant sent me. No one liked her, so when I said I was having an issue, she was more than happy to spill the tea. I made sure I had a big cup, too, ready to blow and sip on every ounce of it whether it was piping hot or ice cold. Come to find out little Mrs. Perfect had some shit she wanted to hide as well. I took the liberty a while back to have her followed when I felt like there was a chance that Tariq and I could actually be something. I was glad I did.

So his wife wasn't perfect. Who really cared? Hell, none of us are. The thing was, did he know it? Men can cheat for years on end, and once they apologize, they feel like that's the end of the conversation. It's not over unless they say it's over. After all, he chose to stay at home so she should be happy, right? We cheat, and it's like the end of the damn world. They can't believe we would actually let someone else hit what they already laid claim to. How dare she be a cheating-ass whore just like them? I was sure Tariq was a model husband. They seemed like the perfect power couple. *Let's just see how she feels once I send her this nice little package.*

I scrolled through all the pictures my private detective sent me, and I was bursting at the seams with pure hate for both of them. It appeared that she was seeing one of the CEOs I'd seen come to visit with Tariq. There were close-up pics of them entering and exiting hotels, but never none of them out and about like Tariq and I did. She was smart. She kept it strictly professional and didn't appear to blur the lines between what they had going on between them. I should have kept our shit that way, and the thought just made me even more upset. I was so stupid to fall for him.

Getting up to turn on my printer, I put in the picture paper that I had purchased and prepared to print the evidence. As each page printed out, my chest got tighter and I got angrier. I couldn't believe things ended this way with Tariq and me. I was livid by the time I was done, but I did not allow that to cloud my judgment. After carefully wrapping the pictures so that they wouldn't smudge in transport, I grabbed a sheet of the address labels I kept at home for office use and used one as the return address. I was sending his wife a little gift to the office, but I didn't want her to know it came from me. Setting it by the door, I made a mental note to get to the post office first thing in the morning, using the company's account so that it would arrive same-day air. I didn't want my name or credit card information on anything, just in case they tried to trace it back.

As I lay in bed that night, I couldn't settle down even though I was dead tired. My soul was restless just thinking about what had become of my life. I had to get Tariq back. That was the only thing I could think of that would make me feel better, at least in my head. Grabbing my laptop, I scrolled the airlines to see what was available to Philadelphia on short notice. I needed to pay Tariq a visit. I wasn't sure what would happen once I got there, but I did know he'd be glad when I was gone.

Chapter Twenty-three

Tracey

It's in those horrible moments when you have to stop and think for a second. One irrational move not thought out and acting in haste could really throw you under the bus. Always think logically and move carefully under any circumstance.

Boom! There it was in plain sight for me to see, but so easy to miss if I had been the average Joanne. A fucking wall safe. This shit made me almost need a cigarette if I were a smoker. What was in that safe? I sat on the edge of his desk and studied it. What would a man be trying to hide that he would need to keep locked away from his wife?

When I first got to the office, I just stood in the doorway and looked around. It was like I was playing *Clue* and had to figure out who was the murderer. Everything looked like it was where it should have been, but what secrets were hiding only God would know. Now the wall safe wasn't an odd thing to have. Don't get me wrong. I had a safe in my closet, but it had jewelry and other things that probably only I found valuable. A thief would only be interested in selling my items, not wearing them. So for the record, the having of the safe wasn't what bothered me. Not knowing what it contained was what really ruffled my feathers.

I first walked over to the file cabinet, which was surprisingly not locked. Of course I took the liberty of looking to see what he had on file. That was the entire purpose of me being here, correct? I randomly pulled out files and moved things around to see if there was anything hidden, but it was regular job stuff, bills, the deed to the house that we both signed, and tax documents from previous years. Nothing that shouldn't have been there.

In his actual desk, I did find a gun I had no idea he owned, and my first thought was, why in hell was it in the basement? If something were to happen upstairs, his locked office would be the farthest away from safety for either of us. As I moved to close the drawer, I knocked some papers from his desk that scattered everywhere. Hoping the pages were numbered, I bent down to pick them up, and as I stood, my head hit the portrait, shifting it dramatically. I was already irritated, and I knew I couldn't just leave it that way.

As I grabbed it to return it to its original position, something told me to look behind it. You know, just to be sure it was just a plain wall and nothing else. I almost dropped the portrait when what looked back at me was nothing other than a wall safe. Carefully propping the portrait on the floor, I sat down and stared at it. The bright green numbers of the keypad appeared to be glowing, angry that I found their hiding place. What was inside?

I sat and studied the safe for what felt like forever, going back and forth on whether I should try to crack the code. Was I ready for what was inside? What if it was something that would damage our marriage even more? After all, I was the only one in the world who only kept jewelry and money in a safe. Everyone else had to be hiding something, right? Did I really want to know? All of this stuff was dizzying, and I just needed to lie down for a second. After hanging the portrait in its proper place, I locked his office back up and made my way upstairs.

My feet felt like I was dragging twenty-pound weights by my ankles as I slowly ascended to the top. So many thoughts ran through my head that I needed answers to. By the time I got upstairs, I was confused, angry, hurt, disappointed, all of the above, but I didn't know why. What did I do to us that had us keeping secrets? Did I damage Tariq for the next woman if we were to ever part? Why wasn't he a stronger man? Why had he never put me in my place? Did he still love me? All of these emotions were too much at one time, and I really wasn't ready to deal with them just yet. All of this because I didn't know how to mind my damn business.

By the time Tariq got in from Texas, I was so confused as to how I felt about us as a unit. I tried to act like nothing was wrong, but my body language said it all. There was trouble in paradise again. I felt bad because he was all over me and I just wasn't feeling him. He asked repeatedly what was going on with me, but how could I tell him without telling on myself? They say when you look for dirt, you get dirt, and I wasn't even clear on what kind of dirt I had found. I could be in here in a funk for nothing, or it could be a very valid reason. I knew I needed to pick a side, but I was in my feelings at the moment and didn't feel like coming out of them just yet. *Just open the fucking safe, Tariq*. I was aware it wasn't fair to him, but at the moment, I didn't care.

"What happened since I've been gone that has you acting like this now that I'm back?" he asked as we lay in bed in the dark. He caught the red-eye out of Texas so that we could spend more time together, something he had never done before. I should have taken that as a sign that he was really trying hard to bring us close, but why was I feeling like he still wasn't telling me what I needed to know?

"Tariq, I'm sorry. I'm just confused about how we got to be so dysfunctional in the first place. It's really disheartening," I answered him, moving closer to him and allowing him to wrap me in his arms. Thoughts of Christopher flooded my mind, and that made me angry as well. Truth be told, I missed sex with him. Both men were excellent lovers, but Christopher just gave me something different that Tariq couldn't.

"I know it is, Tee. I promise you I will do whatever I need to do to keep us moving forward. I just need you to believe in me again. Believe in us. Believe we can make it work."

Tears instantly sprang from my eyes. I had to learn to trust this man again. I wanted to, regardless of how we got here or whose fault it was. As I ran my hand down his body to stroke his length, Christopher's face kept flashing before my eyes. He was really playing hard to get, and it was pissing me off like you wouldn't believe. My husband moaned, but it sounded like Christopher's voice in my ears as I moved down to take him into my mouth. I needed to taste Christopher one last time, and as I closed my eyes, I pretended that it was him in my mouth instead of Tariq.

Was Christopher really happy with his home life? Just looking at his wife, I would have had to say he was. Looks and designer clothes aren't everything. Regardless of how raggedy she appeared in my eyes, that woman always had a huge smile on her face whenever I saw her. The love was undeniable when they looked at each other, and I could tell that Christopher really cared about her. So why did he cheat on her? That was the question of the century. Like most men, he probably just took advantage of a once-in-a-lifetime opportunity, I was sure. Hell, I sat the pussy right in his face. All he had to do was stick his tongue out and lick it.

Trying to forget that it was my real husband in the bed, I made sure to touch all the spots that Christopher liked, surprised that Tariq liked them too. That just made me even hotter as I began my journey to pleasing Christopher in my mind. Getting between his legs the way he liked, I gently massaged the full length of him before taking him into my mouth. Christopher used to love that shit. The moan that escaped his mouth found its way to my clit and had me wetter than ever.

Traveling up. I made sure to pay special attention to the spot just under his rib cage that I knew for sure drove him crazy when I kissed him there. He could hardly take it as I created suction and breathed hot breaths on his nipples, all while trapping him between my legs. I was so slick and juicy as I slid up and down him, only allowing entry after he begged me for it. I rode the head like I was a champ at it, squeezing him as I went with my juices running down him. Finally taking it all in, I reached back and gave his balls a light squeeze that drove him crazy.

I went from taking him in deep to taking just the head then deep again until he grabbed ahold of me to try to keep me still. It was so good I almost called out the wrong name and had to catch myself and come out of fantasy land. Somehow he managed to grab me in a bear hug and scoot all the way up the bed to a sitting position. He was holding me close to his chest and drilling into my G-spot like crazy. I knew the neighbors had to hear us as loud as we were. This shit was really getting out of control.

He lifted me up off of him and flipped me over, dunking back inside like he was slamming on a basketball court. He must have really missed me while he was gone, even though I gave him some before he left. It was like a tug of war as we fought to be on top until we exploded. As I lay next to my husband, trying to catch my breath, I knew I had to forget about Christopher and just move on if I wanted our marriage to have a chance. He had clearly moved on with his wife and seemed content. I needed to get on board and do the same.

"I love you, Tee," he whispered in my ear as he slid back in for round two.

"I love you more," I responded as I prepared for the ride, hoping that love would be enough.

Chapter Twenty-four

Tariq

Every. Single. Thing. You. Do. In. The. Dark. Comes. Out. In. The. Light. Never forget that.

We were moving forward finally. Therapy was doing what it was supposed to be doing for us as a couple. Tracey and I were closer than we'd ever been, and I hadn't heard from Zaria in a while. I continued to put money in my son's account as promised, because despite his mom being a nutcase, he didn't ask to be here. Since I wasn't in his life, the least I could do was make sure he was financially stable.

I really only thought about him sometimes, mostly when I had to go to Texas on business. I never stayed long enough for anything other than business to happen, unlike before, when I would get a hotel room but never use it because I was at Zaria's house. When my assistant asked if I needed to book a room, I always declined, opting to take the next flight back to Philly to be with my wife no matter how late it was. I only stayed if I absolutely could not get a trip back, and at those times, I would stay on the phone with Tracey all night until we both fell asleep. As soon as I woke up in the morning, I was back on the phone with her as I made my way to the airport. It was easier that way and pushed aside any trust issues she may have had with me in the past.

The happiest and saddest day of my life happened at once. Usually, when things are going great, those skeletons start getting restless and want to show they damn face. That's what skeletons do, just bust out and ruin a good thing whenever they felt like it. They do not live by the rules like those of us among the living. I should have known, because things were just going too good.

My day started off regular. I had my wife spread out on the island in the kitchen before breakfast, giving her that work that had you skipping around all day. I wasn't sure what it was, but I just couldn't get enough of her lately. She was getting thick in all the right places, and the pussy was extra damn juicy. I wanted to be in it all the time. This is how I felt when we first met, and I was glad the feeling was back again. She would bust it open for me with no problem, and it made me love her even more.

By the time we were done, we both had to hurry up so that we wouldn't be late for work. We were meeting new clients today and wanted to make a great impression. We took separate cars because she had a doctor's appointment right after the meeting and I had to go to our northeast branch to pick up documents before the end of the week. I was truly happy, but that shit is always short-lived when you have a shady past.

By the time I got to the office, I had a few minutes to check my emails and go over today's accounts to make sure I knew what I should know before the meeting started. I was sifting through the mail that had accumulated on my desk over the last week or so and came across an envelope that I didn't remember seeing before from the Texas branch. Grabbing the letter opener, I sliced into the envelope, curious as to what they had sent me through the mail, given that I was there not too long ago and most correspondence was sent electronically. Upon opening the letter, I found a picture of my son and was angry immediately.

Here she goes with this bullshit again. Zaria was up to her dumb shit, and I just wasn't in the mood. *What's wrong with this chick?* If this was ever a lesson on what not to do in a marriage, I'd definitely learned it. I would never, for as long as I was married, cheat on my spouse again. In the end, it wasn't really worth it, no matter how good the smash was. Deciding not to even entertain her shenanigans, I popped the picture and the envelope in the shredder and went on to my meeting. I gave my wife a quick hug from the side when I arrived, thinking I couldn't wait for us to get home so that I could get back inside of her again.

We had a very productive meeting, and my wife and I went back to my office to chat really quickly before she left for her appointment. I was ready to spread her out on my desk and give it to her right there, but she promised to let me in when I got home later in the day. Once she left her doctor's appointment, she would be going to get her hair and nails done, so I was expecting to see her home around six.

I was thinking it would be nice to set up a little dinner for us and just make it a romantic night in. After composing a list, I sent my assistant out for groceries while I finished up so that I could go home and prepare our meal. That was one of the things she loved when we first got together. My father was a chef, and I learned a lot of the tricks of the trade being in the kitchen growing up, so I knew how to put together a gourmet meal of restaurant quality. Sending my assistant a quick text to pick up pink roses as well, I dove into my work so that I could be done in time to get home and get dinner ready for my queen.

About an hour or more later, I got a text from Tracey telling me she had some news she couldn't wait to share with me once we got home. That made me smile as I texted her back that I couldn't wait to hear what it was and I loved her. Finally, things were really looking up.

Just as I was finishing up, I got a call from security telling me I needed to come down to my car. Still not thinking much of it, I saved the information that I needed on my computer, shooting myself an email with it attached so that I could look at it once I got home. I figured I probably had a flat tire, and they might have needed my rim key to unlock the wheel to change it. I quickly wished that was the only thing wrong once I got there.

Upon getting out of the elevator, I saw my assistant standing there with a look of shock on her face. My car was a mess! Deep scratches across the hood and down the sides, broken sideview mirrors, three flat tires, and what smelled like paint covering all the windows minus a small circle on the driver side that no one could see through while driving. I already knew who was responsible for it without even having to say it. What was she doing in Philly?

"I've already called for a replacement car for you, sir, and a tow truck will be here shortly," the guard explained just as a driver was pulling up with a rental car. My assistant loaded the items I asked for in the passenger seat, and I numbly walked around to the driver's side, forgetting to thank them both for their assistance.

I was beyond pissed! Zaria was crazier than I thought, and I felt like choking her. I was screaming on the inside all the way home and was trying to decide how I would tell Tracey what happened before she found out at the office. When I pulled up to the house, I saw Tracey's car was already there. She must have been planning a surprise for me as well that I was about to ruin with bad news. I felt like shit. Gathering the groceries, I made my way into the house.

I wasn't sure what I was expecting when I got in, but it was very quiet considering I felt like Tracey was planning a surprise for me. I didn't smell any food cooking or anything. All I remembered when I stepped inside was a flashing pain in the back of my head before everything went black. I felt myself going down but couldn't stop myself from falling. It was lights out before I even hit the ground. What did I do to deserve this?

Chapter Twenty-five

Zaria

Above all things, be careful what you wish for. You may just get it, and it may not be exactly what you thought you wanted. This is just a warning.

Maybe I took a little too much pleasure in destroying Tariq's car. I wasn't concerned about him being able to get it fixed, because if nothing else, Tariq had money and at the very least great car insurance. Those damages were a drop in the bucket for him. I was actually humming as I emptied four bags of sugar and an entire box of full-sized candy bars into his gas tank. Who knew I could find such joy in a thing so simple?

I thought about what I should do for months before I actually made a move and came here, ditching the idea to send his wife the photos. All she would do was hide them or trash them the same way I was sure Tariq was doing his. It was like, the more I thought about how he did us, and the more I thought about my son not having a father, the madder I got as the days went on. Some days I could hardly get out of the bed because I was filled with so much rage it was crippling me. Junior was moving along just fine and seemed to have forgotten about Tariq. I, on the other hand, was livid that I had gotten played in the worst way imaginable.

I booked the flight before I could change my mind. I had to show this man what he did wasn't cool, and neither was how he hurt us in the process. Everybody always says how men cheat all the time, but that doesn't make it acceptable. They cheat, and it's like, "Oh, that's what men do." We cheat, and it's like, "This whore-ass bitch cheated on me, and she got my son in the house? I have to kill her tonight!" The stigma is unfair, but for Tariq, I planned to make sure there was one less man willing to step out on his wife in this world. Ladies, you can thank me later.

I hugged my son extra tight before I left him that morning, glad that my mom offered to take him for me while I handled some "business" in Philly. I made sure to travel light, just my large MK purse with a pair of panties and what was required to board the plane. My plan was to be in and out of Philly before I was missed.

All sorts of scenarios ran through my head as the plane flew through the clouds. What if I got caught? Honestly, I just wanted to talk to him and let him know he wasn't untouchable, but I didn't think it would happen this way. He made it very clear that he wanted nothing to do with me. Halfway through the flight, I got the bright idea to talk to his wife instead. You can Google anything these days, and how lucky was I to find that his phone number was listed in the white pages? A picture of the front of their house, as well as the address including the zip code, popped right up. I had never even been to Philadelphia before, so all of that information came in handy once I had my rented car and GPS ready.

When I got to their block—this after visiting the job and looking for the car with the license plate number that my friend gave me—I was not surprised to see that they lived in a nice, upscale neighborhood. They looked like the type who only wanted the finest things in life. I parked at the end of the block and walked down so that they wouldn't know what car I had when it was time for me to roll out. I made sure my wig and my hat covered my face good, just in case there were cameras on the houses in the neighborhood.

Upon approaching the house, I saw that a beautiful cherry BMW sat parked in their driveway. Searching through my bag as I got closer, my hand grazed the butt of the gun I obtained upon arrival courtesy of my cousin Monica. Her sister, Yolanda, was back in Philadelphia after a horrible time in Los Angeles, and she gave me the drop on everything I needed. I searched for something to scratch the car up with but came up empty. I was completely irritated that I couldn't find anything, but I quickly realized that most rentals have a tire-changing kit, and the handle to the jack would work just fine. I was ready to write my name on the hood of this bitch, but just digging into it was just as satisfying.

Scouting the house, I walked a complete circle around the single home, spotting his wife in the kitchen occupied with something on what looked like an island in the center of the kitchen floor. I really came for Tariq and wasn't thinking about her, but when I flashed back to how she treated me when they came for a meeting once, I decided to shatter her world too. Double fucking bubble.

Creeping back around the front, I boldly walked up and rang the bell. Depending on how this played out, just dealing with her may be enough, and I wouldn't have to even deal with Tariq's trifling ass. It didn't take long for her to come to the door, and for a second, I was stunned by her beauty. I couldn't remember her being this pretty when we first met. Maybe because she was being such a bitch. It pissed me off just looking at her.

"Hi, how may I help you?" she asked with a bright smile on her face that I had no idea she possessed, since every time I encountered her, her face was always balled up extra tight.

"Tracey?" I questioned, knowing exactly who she was.

"Yes, how may I help you?" she asked again, still smiling. I wanted to punch her in the throat.

"My name is Zaria, Mr. Mason's assistant. He sent me here to drop some files off for him later," I replied, digging in my bag for the manila envelope I had with the pictures of her, Christopher, Tariq's son, and captures of us from the sex tape he didn't know I recorded the last time he was there. I was carrying the truth with me today, whether they wanted to see it or not.

"Okay. Come on in," she replied, not even questioning it. *This the dumb shit that gets people killed in movies.* She just let the killer right in.

She walked away like I knew where to put the envelope that I had. I took the liberty of looking around, and the place was stunning. Bright white furniture, multicolored paintings with bursts of solid color in the form of decorative pillows, and odd-shaped lamps completed the decor. Everything looked top-of-the-line and in its proper place. No wonder he was so anal about not having things out of place when he came to visit.

"Looks like you're preparing for a celebration," I commented as I caught up with her in the kitchen. She was whipping up a nice spread of all the stuff I assumed Tariq liked. When he came to visit me, it wasn't because I was a good cook, if you get what I mean.

"Yes, I just found out I'm finally pregnant! He is going to be excited when he hears the news. I saw this idea on Pinterest . . ." She rambled on and on while I was stuck on a daze. TJ was going to have a little brother or sister he would never get the chance to meet. They would be treating this child as if it was his first. I started boiling on the inside.

"Here, let me show you his office. You can set everything in there for him, and I'll let him know you came by. What's your name again?" she asked as she walked in front of me, turning to hear my response.

I didn't know what came over me, but before I could stop myself, I had reached out and punched her square in the fucking face. I obviously caught her off guard as she fell back, and I wasted no time pouncing on her. I kept punching her until she stopped moving, and that was when I stopped to catch my breath.

Moving quickly, I grabbed the duct tape that I stopped to get from my pocketbook. Dragging her body across the floor, I propped her up in one of the dining chairs and taped her arms and legs to it so that she couldn't move once she woke up. I wrapped some tape just under her breasts to keep her back to the chair because she was slumped over, and I made sure not to go anywhere near her stomach. Her unborn child had nothing to do with its father's idiocy.

Walking around the house, I found a bat in the basement, among other things. There was a door down there, but it was locked. Honestly I really didn't care what was behind it. I wasn't here to steal. I was here to give out lessons. Sitting in the living room, I got comfortable and waited for Tariq to get here. Hopefully it would be soon. I had a flight to catch.

Just as I was starting to get comfortable, I heard a sound coming from her phone. It was from someone named Christopher asking if they could talk. I was surprised she didn't have a lock code on her phone. I went ahead and scrolled through the messages to see who he was, wondering if he was the same guy who was in the photos. She and Tariq deserved each other. From what I could see, both of their asses were scum.

I heard a car pulling up in the driveway, so I quickly typed in for him to come over, letting him know to come right in and the door would be open. Then I grabbed the bat and hid behind the door. My heart was beating so fast it felt like it was going to jump out of my chest. I had a good, tight grip on the bat, and as I heard his keys go in the lock, I raised it, ready to strike. As soon as he came into view, I took the hardest swing I could take, connecting right on the side of his head, causing him to drop like a sack of potatoes. Rushing, I dragged him to the next chair, taping him down and propping him up the same as I did Tracey. Now all I had to do was wait for Christopher to show up and we could begin. This was going way better than I originally planned, and it scared me to death.

Sooner than expected, who showed up but the one and only Christopher. He was handsome in a different way than Tariq was. I could see how she fell for him. I wasted no time cracking his ass in the head early on, but I just left him duct taped on the floor by the door with his ankles secured and his hands behind his back. It was a shame he had to be involved, but they needed to know the truth.

Walking up to Tariq, I began to wake him so that we could get this party started. It was time to play truth or dare, and I was making up the rules.

Chapter Twenty-six

Zaria

So you learn a lesson hopefully, and pray that you never get the urge to step out again… or at least be smarter about it the next time you do.

"What does Christopher have to do with this? Why is he here?" Tariq questioned me with tears in his eyes. Apparently, he had no idea that his wife was just as much a whore as he was. I wasn't surprised. That's usually how it was. When he finally came to, he was stunned to find himself taped and tied to his wife. I still had the bat present and had since then pulled out the weapon I brought along with me just in case I needed it.

"Well, let's ask her. I'm sure you would rather hear it from the bitch's, I mean, right from the horse's mouth," I replied, venom dripping from every word. I walked around to her. "Wake up, princess," I said in a singsong voice, but she still wouldn't open her eyes. I tapped her on her forehead first. She hadn't come to in a while, and the only thing that reassured me she was still alive was because I kept checking her pulse, and I could see her chest move up and down with each breath. By this point, their heads were taped together, so I could see her clearly.

Thinking quickly, I ran into the kitchen and rummaged through the cabinets until I found a bottle of vinegar. I was thinking bleach at first or something that smelled strong, but I didn't want to bring harm to her baby with her sniffing cleaning products, and I figured vinegar was the best way to go. Opening the cap, I held the bottle right under her nose and was thankful when she started to blink her eyes and try to move her head back and forth. Thank God I hadn't killed her. I stood there until she was able to focus, and when she finally came to, tears filled her eyes immediately. I didn't feel sorry for her in the least.

"Glad you could finally join us," I said to her as we made eye contact. She had tape over her mouth so that she couldn't talk, and I knew I would have to move it in order for her to answer her husband's question. "Let me introduce myself to you, although I wish we could have met under better circumstances. My name is Zaria. I'm Tariq's baby mom."

Her eyes got as wide as fifty-cent pieces. Of course she didn't know he had a fucking kid. Why would he have told her that? That was why he and I were having so many issues. He was keeping secrets from her that she shouldn't have been keeping. Today they were all going to come out.

"His son is about to turn five in a week. This is him," I said, pulling a picture from the last time he spent the weekend with us. I made sure I held it there so that she could get a good look at it and have no doubt in her mind that TJ was her husband's son. They looked exactly alike.

"Your husband has known about him since I was pregnant. I've been sleeping with him for years. Now," I continued as I pulled a chair up and sat down in front of her, "I'm here because your husband hurt my son by walking out of his life. Before we get to that, your husband has a question. What did you want to know, Tariq?"

He sat quiet for a minute, and I was really hoping I wouldn't have to bust this dude in the head again. Time was winding down, and I needed to wrap this up so that I could get to the airport. Today was truth-telling day, and I wasn't leaving until she knew everything.

"Why is Christopher here?" he repeated, sounding like he was crying. His wife's gaze finally moved to the man lying on the floor. He hadn't moved an inch since I hit him with the bat, so I knew I had to check his pulse to be sure he was alive as well.

"Your husband asked you a question," I said to her with a menacing look on my face. Tears fell from his eyes before she answered. I wasn't leaving until everything was exposed, so she might as well serve her tea hot while our cups were ready.

Chapter Twenty-seven

Tracey

You pray, pray that no matter what you say, you can make it work once it's over.

I looked at Christopher, regretting that I had ever reeled him in. He was innocent in all of this, honestly. No, I didn't detach his dick and force him inside of me repeatedly, but I knew he was weak, and I went in for the kill. He didn't stand a chance denying me, and had I never approached him, he would have continued to lust from the sidelines just like everyone else. He deserved better, and I just hoped he'd make it out alive after all of this.

"I'm not sure why he's here. I didn't invite him," I replied, which was the truth. I didn't invite him. I had texted him earlier to let him know the good news about being pregnant, and that I was sorry I had ever taken him out of his comfort zone. I wanted to apologize to him face-to-face before Tariq got home, but I never got around to it.

The strange woman, who was starting to look oddly familiar, stood up and looked at me like I had two heads. I was scared for my life at the moment. I didn't know what she was going to do. I could clearly see what she was capable of. *I can't believe I just let her in my damn house!* This baby must have had my mind in a fog, because under normal circumstances I would have never done that.

She walked away and grabbed my phone, bringing it back over to where we were. I kicked myself again because why didn't I have a lock on it? I was truly slipping lately. She hit several spots on the screen until she came up to what I assumed were the messages to Christopher. I was trying to remember all of what I had left in there, because I made sure to delete everything from our affair months ago. I didn't want Tariq to be able to find anything. Even the videos had to go.

"Do you really want me to read this out loud? I'm trying to give you a chance to redeem yourself," she asked. I looked at her, and to be honest, I could see the hurt. She really didn't want to be here holding us hostage. She was acting on pure emotion. She was hurt. I promised myself that if we made it out alive, I would let her just go and live her life.

"What does the message say, Tracey?" my husband asked me from the other side. She had our heads taped together somehow, and we were sitting stiff as a board. I wanted to turn to him and look him in his eyes, but that was out of the question. I just had to blurt it out.

"I was telling him," I began in a shaky voice, not wanting to deliver the news this way. "I was letting him know that I was pregnant, and I wanted it to be a surprise for you."

"And what else?" the woman asked. She was looking defeated at this point, and I could tell she just wanted it to be over. So did I.

"And I apologized to him for us having an affair."

Silence.

When he asked me months ago if I had ever slept with anyone on the job, I told him no to spare his feelings. The truth always comes out. There was an underlying rule that we never had to discuss once we started drifting apart. We did what we wanted to do within reason, but never with anyone we both knew and never ever a coworker. This just pushed us back to the beginning.

"You're pregnant?" he asked again. If only I could just see his face. If he could have looked into my eyes, he would have seen that I genuinely wanted him and only him.

"Yes. I'm three months pregnant. I just found out today. I left the office after the meeting to see the doctor for a follow-up. I was planning a surprise dinner before all of this happened. I texted Christopher earlier because I wanted to apologize to him for almost destroying his life. I pursued him. I just wanted a clean start for this next chapter in our life."

"I'm going to be a dad?" he asked in disbelief, but before I could answer, homegirl jumped right in.

"You're already a damn dad! Did you forget that your son is in Texas right now with the same face you have? Are you fucking kidding me?"

"That's not what I meant, Zaria. I was—"

"What the fuck did you mean then? You've been a dad for almost five fucking years. You have a child!" she yelled at him, but all I could do was take it all in.

"You forced him on me. I never wanted a child with you, and you purposely waited to tell me so that you wouldn't have to abort. You know that's the truth, just like I know."

"I will kill everybody up in this bitch! Are you fucking kidding me?"

She went off on a tangent calling him all kinds of scum. I let her go because I didn't want to upset her even more, but the more I thought about it, the more it all made sense. *She's the pregnant secretary from the Texas office!* This man of mine had slept with a coworker too. I just closed my eyes and let it all sink in. We were both some jacked-up individuals. Maybe we deserved each other. Once she quieted down, I felt more comfortable talking to her. I clearly understood her stance on this entire situation. Maybe she would have sympathy for my unborn child and just let us be.

"I'm sorry. I can't remember your name. Please tell me what I can do to help you," I begged her. I got that she was upset, but was it worth possible jail time? Tariq was good in bed, but not worth dying for. At least, I didn't think he was. I just needed to know what she was trying to accomplish here today.

"Thanks to your husband, I'm straight financially. He made sure of that, right, Tariq?" she asked over my shoulder. "I just needed you to know what kind of person you had on your hands, and he needed to be taught a lesson."

"I truly understand. We both have a lot of work to do. What is it that you want from us?" I asked her again.

She looked like she wanted to die at the moment. She was probably just starting to realize that she made a huge mistake. She had to have been in love with Tariq to even do all of this. I never loved Christopher. I just loved how he made me feel in bed. That was probably why it was so easy for me to just walk away from him. I was hoping she would just go.

"Listen, I understand why you are feeling how you feel. I really do. You look like you have a lot on your shoulders, and you don't really want to leave your son without a mother. He already doesn't have a father who's willing to step in, and it's a horrible feeling. If you leave now, I promise we will just let you go. No calling the cops to report you or anything. Just go be with your son. You will never hear from us again. However Tariq has been compensating you financially, he will continue to do so. You have my word."

She stood there and looked at me as tears fell from her eyes. I was sure she couldn't believe she allowed herself to even go this far. Love will have you out here looking crazy in these streets, and surprisingly I felt bad for her. I couldn't imagine being in her shoes and having to feel like she felt at the moment. She had this child who was a daily reminder of a man she would never have. She stared at me, and I never broke eye contact, hoping that she would take it that I was being sincere. I didn't need this kind of news getting out and possibly ruining our reputation at the company. I was upset with Tariq for dragging this situation out with this girl for this long, but shit happens. We would just have to find a way to get past it. For the moment, I just wanted her to be on her merry way. We would figure out the rest after she was gone.

To my surprise, she turned, grabbed her purse, and walked out. I thought for sure she was going to make one last move like they did in the movies, but she didn't. She just walked away. We sat in silence for what felt like forever before moving just to be sure she wouldn't change her mind and come back to kill our asses. Christopher still hadn't budged from his position on the floor, and I was hoping he was okay. I wasn't sure how he did it, but Tariq somehow got his hands free and worked quickly to free me afterward. I checked on Christopher while Tariq went and got something to cut his ties loose. This shit was crazy, and I knew it would be a long time before we were back to normal again. Hopefully Tariq would stick it out with me.

We eventually got Christopher to wake up, and we all took a trip to the hospital after getting our story together that we got jumped by some crazy person. Christopher never even saw the girl, from what I understood, because both he and Tariq got hit from behind. As I lay in the hospital bed while the nurse did the ultrasound, assuring me that the baby was okay, I just thanked God that I made it out alive. Hopefully we all learned from this and could eventually heal.

Chapter Twenty-eight

Zaria

And you take your loss like a champ and heal. This isn't your first time dealing with heartbreak. Hopefully you learn enough this time around to hurt a little less the next time it happens.

I made it to the plane, surprisingly in one piece. I wiped the gun clean and returned it to Yolanda, and I made sure the rental was in good shape as well. I was shaking so badly while I was driving I thought I was going to crash several times. What the hell made me do this? I just prayed that she kept her word and didn't call the police on me. I just wanted to go home, get my son, and move forward with my life.

The entire time I was in line entering the airport, I kept looking to make sure I wasn't being followed. I didn't want to get pulled out of line for looking suspicious, especially in this day and age of terrorism. Thankfully by the time I got done checking in, there wasn't a long wait and I could get right on board. I found my seat and ordered a drink immediately when the stewardess started taking orders. My damn nerves where shot, and I could hardly breathe. Once the plane actually took off, I felt a little better knowing the cops couldn't just pop up in midair and drag me off to jail. That did help me relax a little until I started to think that maybe they would be waiting for me when I landed in Texas. This was all just too much, so I kept the drinks coming until I passed out and went to sleep.

I woke up as we were landing, and the anxiety started again. *I must have been crazy to do what I just did. I could be under the jail right now for this mess.* Moving quickly, I got my car out of parking and raced through the city all the way home. I was too much of a mess to deal with my son today, so I left him with my family another night. They didn't know when I was getting back, so I didn't need to even alert them that I was back in the city. I simply parked my car inside the garage so that they wouldn't see it parked if they happened to drive by. After popping two Benadryl, I lay down and eventually drifted off to sleep. I had a lot to reevaluate, and I needed to clear my head.

As the days went by, it got easier to accept my position. I was a single mom, and my baby's father wasn't getting me locked up for assault. His wife kept her promise. That alone gave me a different view of what type of person she was, and just maybe she wasn't as much of a bitch as I thought she was. So what did I learn from this whole ordeal?

1: Married men are off-limits. Do not, by any means, engage in encounters with a man who already belongs to someone else. It's truly not worth it in the end.

2: Refer to number one.

I was just so glad this mess was over. I would admit that I immediately sought out the help of a therapist when I got back. My mindset was warped, and I was really having a hard time getting it together. It wasn't fair to my son. At work, I kept my head down and focused, and at the end of the day, I went and got my son, and we went home. A few of the men who came in, of course, tried to holler, but I cut that shit shorter than a midget's dick before they could even get started. I wasn't entertaining anyone married, single, or in between. Right now, I had to get me together, and maybe down the line I could possibly look into the dating scene. Until then . . . vibrators and fingertips only, and not necessarily in that order!

Chapter Twenty-nine

Tariq

Remove your skeletons one by one, and don't give them a reason to start multiplying again. They double and quadruple right before your eyes, and before you know it, it's out of control. Learn, take heed, stay in control of your life.

Six months and four days later, my daughter entered the world. It was truly a rough road to recovery, one we were still treading. The pile of lies was difficult to sift through, but luckily we started to see the light sooner than expected. We had trust issues still. But we were working on it. It wasn't about us being around each other all the time. It was trusting that in those moments when we were not together, we felt safe in knowing we were doing what we said we were doing and not something sneaky. We deserved to be at ease regardless of the situations we put ourselves in.

I had a daughter. A girly version of my son. They looked alike when he was her age. Apparently I had strong genes. It was a shame they would never know each other. After all the mess with Zaria, we felt it was best to never reach out to her. At first, we were thinking to keep my son in the loop at least, but we came to find out she was a lunatic and not worth the hassle. My wife needed peace, so we just left that situation alone. Maybe once he got older and reached out on his own we could build a bond.

It was hard to keep myself on a straight path. Once a cheater, always a cheater. It's in your blood. My eyes wandered so much I had to wear shades. It was horrible, but with the help from a second therapist outside of couples therapy, I was getting better control of my cravings. *My wife is all I need.* I said it to myself every day as a reminder not to forget.

Word of advice: don't get married for love alone. It's not enough to make you stay. You need more than love to stay focused, though they say love is the most powerful force on earth. Don't believe that bullshit for a second. Lust is way more powerful and will fuck around and have you dead. Keep business and pleasure separate. Work booty is off-limits at all costs! It's too close to home to keep it a secret. Trust me, I know.

You not only need love. You need to be able to see yourself for who you really are. Stop trying to be someone you can't keep up. It takes way too much work, and you will lose in the end. You need understanding for the past of your spouse, and you need to understand that whatever happened in your respective journeys led you to each other. Do not go to sleep mad at each other, talk out your problems, work together, stay committed, and get ready for the fight of your life.

While I was sitting here rocking my daughter in my arms and watching my wife sleep, all I could think about was how lucky I was to have gotten a second chance. Poor Christopher had no idea of what happened that crazy afternoon, and it was better that way. I didn't even bring up his situation with my wife because he apparently cut that short. He cherished what he had at home. All we could do was move forward one day at a time.

Just as I was putting my daughter down in her crib to sleep, my phone vibrated in the pocket of my pajama pants. I thought it might have been an email, but it was actually a text from this young lady I had on my top for a while now. She was a temp at the firm who was willing to do anything to get a permanent position, *anything*. I knew we had no business talking outside of work hours, and after Zaria, you would think I had learned. I ignored the text and made a mental note to contact the agency, let them know I would no longer need her services, and request a male replacement. No one knew how to be discreet anymore, and I refused to be the victim of a Snapchat video. Blocking her number, then turning the phone completely off, I snuggled up next to my wife and called it a night. We had a future together, and that was all that needed my focus right now. I prayed it stayed that way.

A Whole Lotta Lovin'

A Full-figured Short Romance

by

Honey

Chapter One

And I've come to pour
My praise on Him like oil
from Mary's Alabaster Box
Don't be angry if I wash His feet with my tears
And I dry them with my hair . . .

There were only a few things in the world that impressed Dorian Hendrix more than a skillful Hammond B3 organist and an angelic voice. A big, beautiful, bubble booty was one of them. The sight of the phat, perfectly round ass jiggling up and down the rows of chairs in the empty choir stand made him forget all about the rich, velvety voice. That ass was an amazing abstract work of art, priceless perfection. It could restore sight to every one of the Blind Boys of Alabama and Stevie Wonder too. Dorian's hands began to sweat and itch, just imagining what all that ass would feel like as he squeezed it in a full, two-palm grip while hitting the voluptuous woman's pus—

The young lady dropped one of the hymn books she was placing in each chair in the choir stand. It landed on the floor with a loud thud, yanking Dorian's nasty mind back from the gutter.

Lord, please forgive me for lusting after this woman's booty in your house, he silently prayed, figuring the fallen book was a warning sign from heaven. Yeah, somebody up there had sent him a reminder that, not so long ago, another donkey butt and a set of perky double-D breasts had landed him in one of the messiest church sex scandals in the history of the Windy City. And that was exactly why he had been terminated as director of the music department and senior organist at the second largest Baptist church in Chicago, disgraced and despised. Getting caught in mid-stroke smashing the assistant pastor's fiancée three weeks before what had been forecast to be Chi-Town's black wedding of the century had surely come with serious consequences. Therefore, a big butt should've been the furthest thing from Dorian's mind, but it wasn't, and that was a damn shame.

Fighting back a slow-mounting erection, Dorian willed his mind to focus on the voice of the woman instead of her ass. Her tone was flawless and crystal clear. A genuine alto with an incredible range, she had unbelievable control. And although her runs were tricky, they landed smoothly at the end of her phrases and not on top of the song's powerful lyrics. Dorian couldn't recall hearing a prettier or more passionate voice in all the years he'd played for choirs and various types of bands. This girl was phenomenal.

And you don't know the cost
Of the oil in my Alabaster box!

"Amen!" Dorian couldn't hold back his applause and verbal approval after the young lady belted out the ending of the CeCe Winans' classic. "Amen!"

However, he regretted it within seconds when she spun around quickly, shrieking in obvious horror with her hand patting her hefty bosom. The sound of a whole stack of hymn books crashing to the floor could've easily been mistaken for a cattle stampede the way it bounced off the walls in the spacious sanctuary.

"I'm so sorry, sweetheart," Dorian apologized, rushing toward the terrified woman.

A quick jog up the short staircase that led to the pulpit and a few giant steps placed him by her side in the choir stand in no time. He reached out and rubbed her back in a smooth, circular motion. A sneaky combination of her heavenly scent, which made him think of citrus fruits and wild flowers, and her chocolate eyes was slowly luring him into a trance. The woman was exotically gorgeous. Her natural beauty wrapped around a brotha's heart and made him feel born again. It also made a brotha want to see her thick body butt-ass naked.

"Mister, you scared the crap out of me," she blurted out over heavy panting. "Who are you, and why were you spying on me?"

Damn, her Southern drawl is making my dick hard! It's sexy as hell!

Dorian closed his eyes and shook his head to clear his thoughts. This butterscotch babe was giving him a natural high, and he was about to get caught up if he wasn't careful. "Please forgive me for scaring you, sweetie. I wasn't spying on you at all." He extended his right hand. "I'm Dorian Hendrix, the new director of music and lead organist."

"Oooh. Hey. I'm Harmony Baxter, one of your choir members. I sing alto." She shook his offered hand.

Watching her eyelids flutter shut, clearly in shyness, as she bit down on her bottom lip was more arousing than porn. Her curvy lashes were so long that they brushed against her high cheekbones. Dorian had always been a sucker for long, God-given hair. So her thick, sandy-brown mane secured in a neat, loose ponytail that fell to rest in the middle of her back was a major turn-on. And her plump, heart-shaped lips gave him visions that had no business flashing through his head while he stood in the church. But her shapely thickness and pretty face were working against him. The total package of Harmony Baxter was messing with his head and making him weak.

Dude was so trapped at the moment that he didn't even realize he was still holding her hand in his possessive grasp until he felt her subtly easing it away, freeing herself. Totally embarrassed, Dorian took a backward step and slid a palm down the length of his face.

Harmony didn't know whether she should run away from the handsome hunk of male chocolate towering over her or stick out her tongue and lick him. Until she could figure out the appropriate thing to do without making a fool of herself, she decided to just look at him, drinking him in like a tall triple mocha latte with two shots of fudge. He was a daydream for tired Thursday-night eyes. Those thick lips of his looked so soft and succulent. Harmony wondered what they would feel like and taste like pressed against hers as she sucked his tongue. Mmmm, his mustache would probably tickle her nose at some point, and shit like that gave her life.

And that wild and crazy hair, she loved it. His natural coils styled in a high, curly-top fade gave him that retro Eric Benét 2006 look. Yeah, he was a pretty boy for sure. And he was tall, very tall. Harmony was certain the new music director stood well over six feet because he appeared to be around the same height as her second oldest brother, Otis. That meant he was in the six foot four to six foot six range. But he wasn't big and bulky like her brother or the rest of the Baxter men. Dorian Hendrix rocked a medium build with a few muscles in the right places. He was a solid teddy bear. The man was fit and ripped raw to her approving eyes, with straight, pearly white teeth and slanted, midnight eyes.

Dorian cleared his throat and flashed a pussy-dripping smile that forced Harmony to fight for her sanity. His pretty lips had resurrected some old, familiar feelings she'd thought were dead and gone forever. Miss Kitty was smacking her juicy lips, feenin' for some manly attention down there after an unfortunate two-year hiatus.

"You got serious vocal skills, Harmony. Girl, you blew me away."

She pressed the back of her hand against her lips just in case she was drooling, before she smiled and said, "Thank you."

"Come on over to the organ with me." He grabbed her hand and gently tugged. "I wrote a song that fits your voice down to the final note. You'll kill the verses and the ad-libs."

Harmony stood her ground, not even leaning in his direction. She shook her head. "I don't sing solo. I'm just a faithful choir member who arrives early and sets up the choir stand and—"

"Whoooa! What do you mean you don't sing solo? Sweetheart, that's criminal. I should call the cops to press charges against you for robbing the world of your voice."

"Call them. I'll let you use my phone." Harmony laughed from deep in her gut. "I love to sing, but I have sense enough to stay in my lane."

"Girl, with pipes and skills like yours, your lane should be front and center before a hot microphone."

"I'm flattered. Believe me, I am. But I can't compete with the other singers in the choir. This is Atlanta, the country's African American mecca. Most black folk here are crazy talented." She leaned in close and whispered, "A lot of the female singers in the choir and quite a few males are professionals. Some sing backup for well-known recording artists, or they're holding down standing gigs with their own bands at popular hot spots. Jerron is on the road right now, traveling nationwide, starring in one of Tyler Perry's stage plays. And Amari's single made it to the top twenty on the iTunes chart. That girl is bad. She's the one who'll do your song justice."

"I can't imagine this Amari chick singing better than you."

"Well, she does. Amari Simmons is Light of the World Missionary Baptist Church's darling diva. She sings lead on lots of songs in the Voices of Victory, our adult choir. Rashad, our former director of music, used to write songs especially for her voice, just so she could shine. And she always thanked him quite generously." Harmony raised and lowered her eyebrows suggestively a few times.

"That was how things *used* to go down around here. I, Dorian Hendrix, am the new sheriff in town, baby, and I'm about to shake things up. My first order of business is to teach you the solo part to 'Flowing Favor,' the beautiful song I wrote, and put your golden voice on showcase for the entire congregation. Come on." He took hold of her hand again and attempted to lead her to the organ.

"No, Dorian. Amari is the singer you need for your song. And if she can't give you the sound you're looking for, Sister Julia Mae can. She's getting up there in age, but she can still tear the church up if you put a mic in her hand."

He shook his head emphatically. "I'm sure the other ladies are great, but I want *you*."

An involuntary tremor took over Harmony's body, followed by a sneaky hot flash. She knew Dorian only wanted her to sing his song, but hearing a man say he wanted her after two years of singleness and celibacy still felt like a fairy tale.

For the third time, Dorian gave her hand a gentle tug, and determined as ever, she maintained her stance. Harmony was adamant that she wasn't going anywhere near that organ.

"Fine. I'll just announce to the choir that you're going to sing solo on the song, and you and I can practice your part privately later on. That way, Amari will know she will not get the spotlight this time."

"Please don't do that, Dorian. I'll faint." Harmony pulled on his muscular arm in desperation. The defined grooves in the sinewy limb under her fingertips ignited a spark in her feminine core, but it didn't stop her from pleading her case. "You'll become my enemy if you embarrass me like that. I swear I'll quit the choir and never speak to you again."

His grin seemed mischievous and taunting, but it was oozing with sex appeal. "Okay. Then I guess you'll have to meet me tomorrow evening for a private vocal session. If you agree to that, I'll let you slide this evening. But get permission from your hubby first."

Before Harmony could clap back, the front doors of the church swung open and choir members started trickling in. Leading the pack was Noni, her sister-in-law. An organic beauty with a magnetic personality, he was the wife of Harmony's eldest brother, Nat.

"Meet you where tomorrow evening and what time?" she hissed under her breath, narrowing her eyes.

Without a word, Dorian removed his cell phone from the pocket of his sweatpants and handed it to Harmony. "Dial your number and let it ring a few times and then hang up. I'll lock your number in and text you all the info you need to know after rehearsal."

"Okay." She reached for his phone. "And I'm not married."

"Cool. I'm not married either," he announced. He suddenly pulled the cell phone back before Harmony could take possession of it. "Don't try me, sweetheart. Just because you're beautiful doesn't mean I'll be a fool for you."

Harmony nodded, too shaken up and aroused by his bass-bottom voice and compliment to speak. She took the phone and followed Dorian's directions step-by-step. Then she quickly shoved it in his direction, and once she felt his grip, she released it and scurried away to join Noni on the second row in the alto section of the choir stand.

Chapter Two

Noni took a long swig from her water bottle before she followed Harmony down the stairs. “Girl, I’m about to pass out. Rashad never made us sing that hard. And we never sounded that good, either. Brother Dorian ain’t no joke.”

“Yeah, he’s pretty good.”

“Pretty good, huh? That’s it? Girl, bye! He plays that organ way better than Rashad ever could, he has a silky voice, and he teaches parts like a pro.”

When Harmony didn’t reply, Noni looked at her out of the corner of her eye and followed her line of vision over to the organ, where Dorian was still sitting with a group of female choir members huddled around him. Amari was sitting right next to him on the bench, smiling like a toothpaste model as he played some complex composition.

“I saw you and Brother Dorian talking when I first walked in. Girl, you were showing all thirty-two of your teeth. What was he saying to you that had you blushing and squirming so much?”

“He caught me singing before rehearsal, and he asked me to sing lead on the first song he taught us this evening.”

“What? Oh my God, that’s great, Puddin’! It’s about time you blessed the church with that pretty voice!”

Harmony clamped her hand over Noni’s mouth and pulled her out into the vestibule. “Girl, bite your tongue.

I'm not about to sing solo. I just made him believe I would."

"So, you lied to the man? Did you give him a fake phone number, too? I saw you saving your number in his phone. Yeah, I caught you."

Harmony's jaw nearly dropped to her chest, but not a single word came forth. She just stood in place, shocked speechless, looking at her sister-in-law with wide eyes. Noni knew her too well. They had become inseparable twenty years ago in New York City the day before the NFL Draft. Harmony had been an impressionable 10-year-old little girl back then who'd instantly accepted her oldest brother's girlfriend as the big sister she'd never had in a house full of brothers. The two had bonded over their shared love for future Super Bowl Champion Nathaniel "Nat" Baxter and good music. They had been down like four flats on a Cadillac ever since.

Dropping her eyes to stare at her feet, Harmony shyly mumbled, "I didn't give Dorian a fake number. I couldn't. I had to give him my real number so he wouldn't call me out in front of the whole choir. I've got to meet him somewhere tomorrow evening for a vocal session. He's going to teach me the verse and ad-libs to 'Flowing Favor.' He kinda twisted my arm."

Noni reached out and pulled Harmony into a warm embrace. "Oh, Puddin', he must really want you to sing that song to have pressed you that hard. Do you want to sing lead for him?"

Harmony stepped back, looked into Noni's eyes, and nodded. "Yes."

"All right now! The *real* singing sensation is about to make her mark."

"Ssshhh. Noni, lower your voice. I don't want Amari or anyone in her crew to hear us. And please don't say a word to Nat. Otherwise, the other two O'Jays and Luther will know all about it before the eleven o'clock news. I don't need them ringing my phone off the hook and giving me a bunch of unsolicited advice for nothing. It's just about singing and nothing else. Okay?"

"I won't say a word, Puddin'. I promise. But you better call me and pour the tea as soon as your little la-la session with Mr. Sexual Chocolate is over."

Harmony giggled. "I promise."

Harmony reached for her glass of red wine and took a sip after she graded the last food-prep safety exam from her sixth-period class. Overall, most of the students had scored well, but Kemi Wilson had once again done the minimum and made a C- by the skin of his teeth. That boy truly believed football was all that mattered in life. Unfortunately, he would soon learn differently. Harmony had lectured Kemi about his lack of interest in academics and his obsession with football many times. She knew the deal for real since all four of her brothers had excelled in football and received scholarships to play on the collegiate level.

After graduating from Auburn University, Nat, her eldest brother, had been drafted into the NFL, where he'd spent fourteen years with three different teams. Because of his hard work and passion for the game, he'd won a Super Bowl ring and set a record for the number of man-on-man tackles in a single game. Now, the retired defensive tackle was enjoying a gravy job as an athletic recruiter for Georgia Tech.

Otis, brother number two, had become a physical education teacher and high school head coach of the game he loved after graduating from Grambling State University. His team, the Innovation Academy Mustangs, had captured two triple-A division state championships under his leadership so far. With Otis's football IQ and insane tenacity, Harmony believed that, by the end of his career, his team would stack on many more state titles.

A severely broken tibia and a torn anterior cruciate ligament during his senior year at Florida A&M University had robbed Marvin, the third Baxter brother, of his NFL dreams. But his master's degree in physical therapy had kept him close to football over the years as a freelance trainer in NCAA football and the NFL.

Luther Baxter, the baby boy, was only two years older than Harmony. They were very close and had always been since they were little children growing up in Gray, Georgia. In fact, they had attended the University of Georgia together, always swapped their deepest secrets, and were currently sharing a fabulous mansion in the suburb of Berkeley Lake just north of the city limits. The superstar center of the Atlanta Falcons was very protective of his baby sister, as were his older brothers. But because Luther and Harmony were roommates, he sometimes used their living arrangement as a license to stick his nose in her business. Well, at least he would have stuck his nose in her business if she had some. But she didn't. Harmony lived a pretty uneventful life, and her brothers were her best friends.

Outside of teaching home economics and fashion design at Benjamin E. Mays High School, hanging with her brothers and their families, and singing in the choir at church, Harmony Baxter, aka Puddin', was a certified homebody. And she was cool with that, but she wouldn't protest if a little bit of excitement were to come her way, especially if it included a man in the mix.

A quick glance at the huge diamond engagement ring sparkling on her finger caused tears to pool in Harmony's eyes, but she sniffed and willed them not to fall. The memories of love lost and romance vanished replayed in her psyche like a movie—the good times as well as the few bad times. The depth of her grief and the tenderness of her heart amazed her after two years. It still hurt like hell.

When will my heart mend and allow me to finally move on?

Just then, Harmony's cell phone rang, rescuing her from her moment of sadness. After snatching it up, she checked the screen and saw a number she didn't recognize. Nosy, she swiped the phone icon to answer anyway.

"Hello?"

"Hey, beautiful."

The strong pounding of her heart filled in the silent seconds that ticked by. Harmony had only been in his presence once, but his hypnotic voice had been engrained in her memory since the first damn syllable that floated from his luscious-looking lips to her ears.

"Harmony, are you still there, baby?"

"Um, yeah. Yeah, I'm here." She drew in a deep breath and released it slowly. "I thought you were going to send me a text message. I wasn't expecting a phone call."

Dorian chuckled, and his deep timbre sent shockwaves throughout Harmony's body. "I called hoping I'd be able to persuade you to sing for me. What's your key?"

A soulful piano chord sounded in the background followed by a smooth, floating melody that Harmony wasn't familiar with. Clearly, Dorian was playing a keyboard or piano as they spoke.

"I'm an E-flat chick all day, every day."

Without hesitation, Dorian's fingers struck another flawless chord and made a skillful sweep over the keys that caused the fine hairs on Harmony's nape to bristle. "Sing this for me."

"What song is that?"

"It's Tamar Braxton's 'Love and War.' Go ahead and jump in. I know you know it."

Yes, she knew the song all right. She had rocked a whole damn ship and almost tipped it over when she sang it off the coast of Mahé two years ago during the Baxter family cruise to the East African islands of Seychelles. Although it had only been a fun karaoke performance she'd done strictly on a dare from Noni, lots of passengers aboard the luxury liner started treating her like an award-winning recording artist after hearing her sing. Harmony became the karaoke queen, and everywhere she went on the boat, random shipmates asked for her autograph and begged her to sing on the spot.

Clearly impatient, Dorian banged out a short version of the song's intro. "I'm waiting, sweetheart."

Somebody said every day was gon' be sunny skies
Only Marvin Gaye and lingerie

Harmony surprised her-damn-self when she eased into the song without any further hesitation. She felt free and very much alive as she put her vocal spin on Tamar's Grammy-nominated hit. She wondered what was it about this cool, slick-talking musician from Chicago that made her want to sing her heart out. If he had her crooning for him over the phone after a simple request, there was no telling what else he could sweet talk her into doing if he touched her the right way. Just the thought of Dorian's huge hands caressing her body while he kissed her passionately caused Harmony to almost stumble over her favorite part of the song. But she did a nasty run to smooth over it and kept flowing like a seasoned songstress.

Sometimes you're my general, you quarterback all these plays
Sometimes you're my enemy, and I'm throwing grenades

"Yeah! Sing, girl! Wooo!"

Laughter Harmony had tried like hell to suppress came bubbling out, ending her impromptu over-the-phone performance. Dorian stopped playing abruptly, too, and laughed as well.

"That was fun. I've never sung over the phone with accompaniment before. It was kind of weird, but it was cool, too."

"You could sing a cappella in front of a rib shack in a clown suit on Groundhog Day and you'd still blow my mind. Your voice is solid gold, baby. I can't wait to teach you the song tomorrow and hear you kill it live."

Harmony had been so engrossed in singing "Love and War" that she'd forgotten all about their upcoming vocal session.

"Don't you start having second thoughts, sweetheart. Where I come from, a deal is a deal. A man or a woman's word should always be their bond."

How did he know I was about to try to wriggle out of our little agreement?

"I can feel your nervousness through the phone line. You can't even deny it, because it's true. But I just want you to know you have no reason to be on edge in my presence. You'll always be in good hands with me, baby. So no worries, okay?"

"Okay."

"Great. What time do you get off work?"

"I usually leave campus around three o'clock or a little bit after."

"Campus?"

Harmony chuckled softly. "I'm a high school teacher. I teach home economics and fashion design slash sewing."

"Damn, girl, you're multitalented."

"Yes, I guess you could say that."

"Okay, musicians' rehearsal will be over around four, so you and I can meet at the spot at five sharp. I'll text you the address as soon as we hang up. Is that cool?"

"Yeah, it sounds like a plan."

"Word. I'll see you tomorrow. Be ready to sing, baby."

"I'll be ready."

"You better be. Good night, Harmony. Sleep well."

"Good night."

Chapter Three

"Okay, so is everybody clear on what I want this time?"

"Yeah, I'm clear," J. Breeze, the drummer, mumbled, returning Dorian's glare with an ice grill.

The bass player nodded. "I got it."

"Yeah, we know what to do," the trumpet player offered on behalf of the brass trio.

Everyone else simply nodded their heads.

Dorian did a visual sweep of the men who were now under his authority since he'd become director of music at Light of the World. His eyes lingered on J. Breeze for a few seconds longer than the other guys. The dude was a cold piece of work. He had challenged Dorian three times during rehearsal and had had the audacity to make a few slick remarks comparing his new boss to Rashad, his old boss.

"Okay, let's take it from the vamp one more time, fellas. One, two, three . . ."

The nine-man band ripped into Ricky Dillard's "Best Day of My Life" for what seemed like the hundredth time. Dorian had been drilling them on the popular song for over an hour mainly because J. Breeze had continuously refused to stay in the pocket and basically keep the beat. Instead, he had gone on a roll, doing all kinds of crazy cadences and beat acrobatics that kept throwing the other musicians off.

Dorian despised a showboat, especially one who wasn't that great in his respective musical craft. J. Breeze had been all over the place on this particular song like an inexperienced drummer trying his damnedest to get noticed. His failure to follow new leadership and lack of musicianship was about to get his ass fired.

In fact, Dorian was so pissed right now that if J. Breeze didn't get his shit together this time around, he was going to get his first citation from the new director of music. It would only take two more before he'd be served a pink slip, and Dorian didn't have a problem with that. He needed the music for this song to be perfect in order to complement Harmony's voice on the lead. He was excited about hearing her rendition of the song that gospel recording artist Tiffany Boone had made a mega hit. Harmony didn't know it yet, but this song would be another one of many she would sing lead on in the near future.

Thoughts of Harmony caused Dorian to smile as he and the musicians approached the ending of the song. Finally, J. Breeze had kept his hyperactive ass in the pocket instead of attacking the drums and crashing the cymbals like a damn maniac. One glance at the clock and Dorian knew it was time to wrap the rehearsal up. It was a quarter 'til four, so he needed to leave soon so he could go and prepare for his little one-on-one with Harmony.

Dude wanted everything to be perfect for some reason, although it would be all about music for him and the pretty lady with the golden voice. As soon as the song ended, he rushed the other musicians out the door, set the alarm, and locked up the church. Then with a smile on his face and extra pep in his step, Dorian hopped in his white Lexus LX570 and tore out of the parking lot.

"Of course he was checking me out!" Amari popped her lips with a hard neck roll. "I ain't met a man who can ignore all of this." Her quick twerk move, clapping her ass cheeks together, earned her a round of applause and catcalls from the client in her chair and the other ladies waiting for her to style their hair.

"What's his status?" a pregnant chick asked. "Is he married, engaged, single, or what?"

Joette, a fellow soprano in the choir and Amari's BFF, threw her hands up in the air. "Fuck that! Is the nigga straight? That's what you need to be trying to find out. These days you can't tell. Niggas be walking around here all ripped with muscles every damn where and covered with gangsta tattoos. But when they take off their clothes, they have on a lace thong and want another man to bend them over!"

"She's right!"

"Facts!"

"Hell yeah!" Joette gave the pregnant chick a high five.

Amari slid the ceramic flat iron through her client's long hair and bent it under. "This man ain't hardly gay or bisexual. If them thirsty heifers hadn't circled him on the organ like a pack of wolves last night, I could've taken his fine ass home and let him sample my goodies. But it's Gucci. I called him this morning, and he's coming over to the crib tomorrow night for dinner and *dessert*."

"You invited the new director of music to dinner, Mari?" Joette asked, smirking. "Your ass can't even boil water."

"That's how come my cousin Alikah and her friend are gonna come over and make a deep-dish lasagna, some garlic bread, and a seven-layer salad. And I'm gonna pick up a sweet potato pie from my grandma in the morning. He ain't gonna know I can't cook." She laughed. "Li'l V will be with his trifling-ass daddy, so Mr. Hendrix and I should be butt-ass naked and fucking like rabbits by midnight."

All of the ladies burst into a fit of laughter. High fives sounded all around Amari's small but chic salon. Her regular clients knew her well. Whenever she cast her eyes on a man and set out to lure him into her sex trap, she never failed. Dorian Hendrix would get his first taste of a real Georgia peach tomorrow night.

"What does his place look like? Is it a house or an apartment?"

Harmony killed her engine and shrugged as if Noni could see her through the dashboard connection. "It's not a house, but it ain't really an apartment, either. The sign says SOUND KINGDOM, and there's a giant microphone on it."

"I think it's a studio."

"Why the hell would he want me to meet him at a studio?"

Noni laughed. "Maybe because you're supposed to be working on music. Remember? Where did you want the session to take place, huh? His bedroom?"

"Shut up, heifer! Only a sexaholic woman with six children would say some nasty crap like that."

"I can't help it that your big brother puts it down so good that now all I can think about is sex."

"Uggghhh! That was too much information, Noni, way too much. Goodbye!"

Harmony sat for a few seconds, staring at the front door of the building after hanging up on her sister-in-law's annoying snickering. Clueless about what awaited her inside, she entertained a couple of possibilities. Maybe Dorian's intentions were legit and this meeting would be strictly about music. But what if his interest in her went beyond music? Could a sexy-ass man like him be attracted to her?

"Oh shit!"

Harmony's heart went from zero to a thousand when the door suddenly opened and Dorian stepped outside the building smiling. He was a sinful sight of pleasure in a pair of loose-fitting, ripped jeans and a black V-neck tee that gripped his broad chest just right. His fluid, confident gait was worth a million bucks and some change. Harmony watched in awe as he approached her SUV. She released the locks, and he opened her door.

"Are you going to sit out here all night?"

"No." She shook her head. "I'm coming inside," she said softly, reaching for her purse in the passenger's seat.

Like a cool gentleman, Dorian extended his hand to assist her from the truck and closed the door.

"Thanks," Harmony whispered. The feel of his huge hand on the small of her back caused air to swoosh from her lungs as he escorted her toward the building.

Lawd, his touch is making me want to act like a bald-headed ho! And he smells sooo damn good.

Dorian opened the door and stepped aside to allow Harmony to enter the unfamiliar space first. "I hope you like stir-fry. I ordered a few entrées because I had no idea what type of meat you would prefer. So you have options. A brotha should always give a woman options, right?"

"Sure." Harmony walked farther into the massive sitting area boasting modern African decor. The artwork and tribal masks adorning the walls screamed authenticity, and the silk palm trees added lots of flair to the atmosphere.

Dorian waved his arm toward the taupe leather sectional. "Have a seat, and make yourself comfortable until the food arrives. You seem like a red-wine type of lady. Can I interest you in a glass of Shiraz? Penfolds St. Henri has a nice one. It's semisweet, so I think you'll like it."

"How did you know I prefer red wine over white wine?" Harmony sat down on the far-left end of the sofa.

"Because you're sweet and mysterious." He licked his lips and winked before he left the room.

Dear Jesus, this man is flirting with me! I came here to sing, not smash.

Harmony crossed her legs to suppress the tingling sensation between her thick thighs. What the hell had she gotten herself into? If Dorian thought he was about to sing and play her out of her drawers, his confidence was about to take a beat down. She was not going to give a man she knew very little about her cookie no matter how handsome and swaggerlicious he was. She didn't give a damn how hard he had her clit thumping all through her coochie, either. It had taken her sweet Ham sixteen years, weekly ice cream cones, and a million kisses for her to finally trust him with her virginity. She'd be damned if Dorian or any other dude was going to enjoy her goodies after a glass of wine and some damn stir-fry. Oh, hell nah!

Dorian returned with the uncorked bottle of Shiraz in one hand and two crystal wineglasses in the other. When he sat down next to Harmony, his closeness caused an electrical current to shoot up her spine, and she was helpless to control the way her body trembled in response.

"Are you cold, sweetheart?" He placed the glasses on the coffee table in front of them and began to pour wine into one.

"There's a slight chill in the air," she lied.

"Should I turn off the air conditioner and open a few windows instead?"

"No. I'll be fine."

Dorian smiled and handed Harmony the glass of wine. "For the beautiful lady with the magical voice."

"Thank you." She accepted the offered wineglass and took a quick sip. "Mmm, this is good."

The doorbell rang just as Dorian lifted his glass to his lips for a taste. He stood up and stared down at Harmony. "That should be our grub. Let me handle that, and I'll be right back."

Harmony took two deep gulps of wine to calm her nerves as she watched Dorian glide like he was floating on air to the door. He was one smooth operator, and his swag number was off the chart. Only a deranged woman would find him unattractive. And his voice could hypnotize a sista right out of her panties if she wasn't careful. Harmony smiled when he returned to the sitting area clutching a large brown takeout bag. The aroma of delicious food immediately infiltrated the air.

"Are you one of those divas who can only sing on an empty stomach, or can you chow down and still perform a full concert like Beyoncé?"

With a shy smile, Harmony told him, "I can sing on a full stomach or an empty stomach. Hell, I can even sing while I'm eating."

"Oh yeah? See, you're my kind of girl. That's why I like you. Let's eat, baby. Then we'll make some music magic. Will that work for you?"

"Yeah, that'll work."

Dorian sat down next to Harmony again and opened the bag. "I ordered veggie stir-fry just in case you don't meat. Your other three entrée choices include one with chicken, the other one is shrimp, and there's one with beef. Please feel free to try all of them if you'd like. I'm going to work on the one with chicken while I get all up in your business."

"I'll take shrimp and a little bit of the one with beef."

"Anything for you, gorgeous." Dorian removed all four containers from the bag and placed them on the coffee table. As he arranged the condiments and cutlery before them, he began his probe. "You made it clear that you're not married, but you forgot to mention you have a fiancé. I see that big block of ice on your left ring finger. Tell me about your man."

Chapter Four

"I had a fiancé, but I don't anymore."

Dorian cocked his head to the side and looked into Harmony's eyes. The day before, her chocolate orbs had held a bright sparkle and lots of passion. Now they appeared empty and sad. Had he said something wrong?

"The cat must've really screwed up bad if he let you keep the ring after you called off the engagement. That's what his ass deserved. A buster."

Harmony shook her head slowly with her eyes focused on the brilliant oval-shaped diamond set in white gold. "I didn't call off the engagement."

"You didn't? Damn, what the hell happened then?"

"He died, Dorian. Six months before our wedding, my fiancé was killed in a terrible car accident, and his death changed my life forever. I haven't dated anyone since he died."

"I'm so sorry, sweetheart." He squeezed her knee tenderly. "I had no idea. Do you want to talk about it?"

"Nah, I'd rather not. Let's just eat and play Twenty Questions. That way, you can learn everything you want to know about me, and I can discover the mystery behind the music man from Chicago named Dorian Hendrix. After that, you can give me a tour of the studio, and we can work on the song."

"I like the way you think, gorgeous." Dorian raised his wineglass and smiled. "Cheers. This is a toast to a budding friendship and future music collaborations."

His words brought a smile to Harmony's face, and it warmed his heart. Thankfully, the sparkle in her eyes had returned. She looked more beautiful than the day before, if that was even possible.

"I'll drink to that, sir." Harmony picked up her wine-glass from the coffee table and tapped it against Dorian's, creating a soft clink. "Cheers."

"All right, pretty lady, let's start from the beginning. Were you born in Atlanta? How many siblings do you have? And what type of firearm does your daddy use to scare off no-good niggas who try to run game on you?"

Harmony threw her head back and laughed. "No, I wasn't born in Atlanta. I'm from Gray, Georgia, a small city south of here that's close to Macon, which is the home of music legends Little Richard and Otis Redding."

"Okay. Thanks for that music history lesson with that Georgia geography twist. Now tell me about your family."

"Well, I'm the baby and only girl of five children born to a truck-driving deacon and his seamstress wife. Everybody in the Baxter family sings, including our dog, Wilbur, and our brood of chickens. So music and football . . ."

Her velvety voice dripping with that seductive Southern drawl was pushing all of Dorian's masculine-heat buttons. He could listen to her talk or sing all night long. He wondered if she sang in perfect pitch during an orgasm or if she just moaned and chanted her lover's name. Either way, Dorian loved being in Harmony's presence, and although he wasn't ready to make an open confession at the moment, he was definitely attracted to her. And that incredible voice of hers had nothing to do with it.

Dorian left the control room and made his way into the soundproof live room, where Harmony sat on a barstool in front of a state-of-the-art mic. He saw dark circles of fatigue underneath her eyes, and stress lines from a full day at work and a long recording session had begun to crease her face. He stood behind her and massaged her drooping shoulders.

"I know it's late and you're tired, sweetheart, but can we take it from the top one more time? Please?"

"Yeah, I think I've got one more bullet in my chamber, like my granny used to say. I just hope it'll hit the bull's-eye this time. I'm sorry, Dorian, but this is all so new to me. I've never even stepped inside a recording studio before."

"Oh, nah, sweetheart, you've hit the bull's-eye every time you laid your vocals. I just want you to destroy the damn thing on this final run like I know you can. And I thought if you actually heard your voice on my song, you'd be able to capture the purest essence of the melody and the lyrics and truly make 'Flowing Favor' Harmony Baxter's musical masterpiece."

She gave him a half smile. "Okay, let's do this."

"Nah, baby, we're about to kill it this time."

Dorian quickly returned to the control room and took a seat. Through the glass partition, he watched Harmony place the earphones over her ears before he pressed the button to start the instrumental track from the beginning. She closed her eyes and rocked from side to side as the introduction sounded in her ears. Dorian's heartbeat accelerated in anticipation of what he believed would be an epic performance. Harmony's vocal cords were hot and relaxed after vigorous scale exercises and singing for over an hour. His gut told him she was about to turn up.

No, I don't deserve it, yet you pour it upon me so generously

I'm so imperfect, yet your grace covers me sufficiently

He was supposed to have given her a thumbs-up for laying the first verse impeccably, but for some reason he couldn't explain, Dorian had blown Harmony a kiss instead. He didn't know what was happening to him. No other woman had ever had this kind of effect on him, no matter how phat her ass was or regardless of her beauty. Shit, truth be told, he had never been attracted to a full-figured sista before. But damn it, Harmony was tempting him to taste her. She was every-damn-thing every brotha wanted in a woman. In addition to being sweet, she was more than easy on the eyes with a thick hourglass figure. Plus, she could sing any man out of a month's worth of paychecks. Hell, the way she was going hard in the studio at the moment had Dorian mentally counting his coins.

He leaned back in his chair and just let Harmony do her thing. She was in a zone. He could tell it. Her eyes were closed, and her tone, diction, and breathing were as smooth as country gravy. She didn't need any assistance from Dorian. So he closed his eyes and allowed himself to get lost in her rich and soulful timbre as she gave his lyrics and composition life.

Harmony ran out of the bathroom wrapped in a towel, soaking wet. Luckily, she reached her cell phone before it stopped ringing. "Hello?"

"You were supposed to call me when you reached the crib."

"Oh, I'm sorry, Dorian. I forgot."

"Cool. You get a pass this time, but don't let it happen again."

A swift and spicy comeback was shattered because the bass in Dorian's voice, combined with alpha-male confidence at two o'clock in the morning, was intoxicating. Harmony couldn't formulate a single intelligible sentence, and she had problems breathing.

"Anyway, I've heard about the delicious soul food Georgia is known for, but I haven't tasted any yet. So a brotha was wondering if you could join me for lunch after church Sunday. This is your town, so I want you to choose the spot as long as soul food is its specialty."

Harmony sat down on her king-sized sleigh bed. "I'm sorry, but I can't have lunch with you on Sunday. I'm cooking an early dinner for my entire family at my house so we can watch the game together. It's like a tradition. But what about tomorrow? We could go to the Busy Bee Cafe. Their soul food is always on point."

"Um, I kinda already made plans for tomorrow evening," Dorian confessed with a vision of Amari's fine ass floating through his head.

"Well, I have an idea, but I'm not sure if you'll be down with it."

"Try me."

"You're more than welcome to have dinner with my family and me Sunday. I always cook way too much, and the O'Jays always say I'm the best cook ever next to Mama."

"Hold up. Did you say the O'Jays?"

Harmony couldn't contain her laughter, imagining the look of confusion on Dorian's face. "It's a long story, a family thing. But I'm sure my brothers will fill you in if you show up for dinner Sunday."

"I'll be there."

"All right, I'll text you the directions to my place early Sunday morning before Sunday school."

"Ah, man, you go to Sunday school, girl?"

"Nope. I teach the Kiddie Kingdom's Klass, ages four through six. I love my babies."

"I don't know why I'm surprised. You're a woman of many gifts and talents."

"Thank you."

"Well, I'll see you Sunday, beautiful. You need to rest now because you put in work at the studio tonight. It's a damn shame how you committed murder on my song."

"You really think I did a decent job?"

"Do I? Girl, you're going to bring the house down when you make your solo debut at church."

"I hope so."

"No worries, baby. You will. I'm thinking Sunday after next should be the day. How do you feel about that?"

"I hope I'll be ready."

"I'll make sure you're more than ready. Get some rest, sweetheart. Until Sunday."

"Until Sunday."

Chapter Five

Dorian's eyes almost sprang from their sockets when Amari's front door opened. Ol' girl was dressed in an extremely short, form-fitting, strapless dress. Clearly, she wasn't wearing panties or a bra. The thin lavender fabric was telling all her business with her hard nipples pressing against it, screaming for his attention. He couldn't lie. She was looking fine as hell in a slutty-ghetto-cheap kinda way. Bang! Bang! Bang! Dorian was pretty sure that was how the evening would end.

"Stop drooling and come on in," Amari purred seductively, stepping aside. "Welcome to my humble abode."

"Oh yeah, thank you." Dorian entered the townhouse and got a whiff her Estée Lauder Chance perfume as she closed the door behind him. It smelled real good on her cinnamon skin. "I brought this to go along with dinner." He raised the bottle of wine. "Chardonnay is appropriate for all occasions, right?"

"I guess so, but I got a whole twelve-pack of Bud Light Straw-Ber-Rita back there chilling in the fridge. That's my drink," she made clear as she accepted the bottle of wine.

"O . . . kay."

"Have a seat while I check on the food. It's almost ready. I cooked something special for you, boo."

Dorian walked farther into the wide-open den and looked around. The mauve and antique gold color scheme accentuated the black leather furniture nicely. There were pictures of Amari on every wall and available surface. An enormous portrait of her and a cute little boy in a black baroque frame hung above the gas fireplace. Dorian decided to relax on the leather recliner facing another one just like it on the other side of the coffee table.

"Dinner will be served in about seven minutes. We're just waiting on the rolls."

Dorian looked up and smiled politely at Amari when she reentered the room. "That's cool."

"You want me to pour you a glass of that fancy wine you brought?"

"Nah. I can wait until dinner. I don't like to consume alcohol on an empty stomach."

"All right. Well, tell me all about you. What brought your good-looking ass all the way from Chicago to the Dirty South?"

I got caught banging a trick like you and was fired from my former congregation.

"Um, it was time for me to move on. I was born, raised, and educated in Chicago. I'd been on the music scene up there since I was a thirteen-year-old shorty. At thirty-six, I needed a change of scenery. And since the A is considered the black people's paradise, it was my first choice to put down new roots." He leaned forward and looked at her head-on. "What's your story, Amari? Why, after meeting me for the very first time, did you invite me into your personal space for dinner? Did I look like I was starving?"

"Hell nah! You looked very healthy to me."

"So why am I here?"

"Look, I'm a grown-ass woman, so I'ma just shoot it to you straight." Licking her cherry red lips, Amari crossed her right leg over the left one, exposing her pussy and then a whole ass cheek in the process. "I wanted to let you know that *I* am the premier soloist in Voices of Victory, and I wanna fuck you. That's all."

"Aaah shit, girl!

Amari slurped and released a throaty grunt when Dorian's entire dick disappeared down her throat. Standing at his full six foot four stature, he watched her nose smash against his bushy pubic hairs each time she swallowed him whole. There was something mind-blowing about watching a chick suck his dick on her knees while he yanked and twisted his fingers in her real hair. The shit was multi-orgasmic. It could make a nigga cum so hard that he'd pass out from shock. Or so he had heard.

"Uggghhh! Girl, you . . . you're about to make my god-damn dick explode. Fuck!" Dorian couldn't stop himself from screaming that corny shit when Amari pressed her middle finger into the meaty bridge of flesh between his balls and his asshole and slid it back and forth.

The broad was an expert multitasker, working her mouth, throat, and finger in coordination to his freakish pleasure. She had a deep throat, too. That was probably why she was such a good singer. Her larynx, tonsils, vocal cords, and everything else down there obviously got plenty of exercise. Those muscles, tissues, and ligaments must've been lean and tender as hell. He would bet his Steinway baby grand piano that Amari's range was over five octaves.

As she continued to suck Dorian's brains out, his body stiffened. His oncoming nut made him hiss and yank her hair until she screamed. It was creeping through his body in slow motion en route to his dick, but the turbulence that came along with it was heavy. A nigga was twitching and cussing loud, and his eyes had rolled to the back of his damn head.

"Fuck! Fuck! Fuck!" Dorian shoved Amari's forehead back and released her hair, which caused her to lose her oral lock on his dick.

She kept that finger-massage thing going behind his jewels even as he stroked his dick wildly until warm semen splattered all over her face. The stream was so strong and plentiful that beads of cum scattered all through her wavy hair. And like a veteran porn-show personality, Amari opened her mouth, stuck out her tongue, and caught as much of his dick milk as she could. The girl was licking, swallowing, and moaning like it was the most delicious shit she'd ever tasted.

Amari stood up and pushed Dorian forcefully, and he landed on his back on her bed. He bounced a few times on the semi-firm mattress before she hopped on top of his naked body and smiled. Straddling his torso, she lifted the hem of her dress over her head and snatched it off as he watched. Then she let it fall freely to the floor. When she leaned in low for a kiss, Dorian avoided her lips by quickly changing their positions.

Now on top, he covered her left nipple with his mouth and sucked hard with no mercy.

"Damn, nigga, you trying to eat my tittie." She smiled. "But Amari likes that kinda shit."

Still torturing that nipple, Dorian reach down and slid two fingers inside her pussy and discovered it was sloppy wet just the way he liked it. Amari started grinding against his fingers as he strummed her clit. She was growling and bucking her hips violently.

"Fuck me, Dorian. Come on, baby. Ram that big dick up in me right now."

Just for the hell of it, Dorian decided to tease her and make her wait on the dick a little while longer. He started finger fucking her hard, going deep into her wetness. Her hip action became more aggressive, and she went into a cussing fit the closer he pushed her to an orgasm.

"Goddamn it, Dorian, fuck me! Stop teasing this good pussy with your fingers and get up in it!"

When Amari's thighs began to tremble, he knew it was time to fuck her before she got off on his finger action. The chick wanted some dick, and he was about to let her have it. So, he withdrew his fingers and sat up to rest all 255 pounds of his body weight on his knees. He leaned over the side of the bed in search of his pants with his fingers glistening with pussy juice. And that's when it hit him like a stray bullet.

What the fuck?

A foul odor that reminded him of greasy mullet fish attacked his nostrils. Hesitantly, he brought his fingers to his nose and inhaled. His stomach churned and rumbled in response to the awful scent of stank-ass pussy. How could a woman so attractive and curvy with an abundance of talent fail to take care of her feminine hygiene before she spread her legs for a nigga? Amari smelled like Estée Lauder up high and expired, maggot-infested tuna fish down below.

Dorian swung his legs over the side of the bed and rested on his ass with his belly rebelling against him. He was fighting like hell not to throw on his clothes and haul ass back to the crib so he could shower. The disgusting stench of crab coochie on his fingers had him so nauseous that he was about to throw up all that delicious lasagna and sweet potato pie she'd served him.

"What's wrong, big papa?" Amari sat up too and raked the tips of her stiletto-shaped fingernails down Dorian's bare back.

Refusing to give her eye contact, he maintained his focus on the half moon glowing through the window. "You know what? I think we're moving too fast. We don't know each other well enough to be getting it in after only one dinner. You deserve better than that, girl."

"Say what? I didn't hear you talking that shit when I was giving you nuclear head a few minutes ago! We weren't moving too fast then! You must be still on that Chicago shit." She jumped off the bed and snatched up her dress from the floor. "You may be fine and all, but you got a lot to learn about women from the A. As cute as I am with all these curves, I could have any man I want. And I'm paid, too. Nigga, please! Get your ass outta my house!"

Amari stormed inside her en suite bathroom and slammed the door shut behind her.

Dorian rushed around the bedroom, gathering his clothes, and quickly got dressed. *Yeah, take your ass in the bathroom and douche that toxic pussy out with some goddamn Pine-Sol.*

"Didn't our choir sound like heaven's angels this morning, church?" Reverend Holloway asked with the biggest grin on his face. As usual, his bald head was glowing under the pulpit's chandelier.

The congregation erupted with boisterous applause and amens.

"Yes, God sent us a super dynamic director of music all the way from Chicago, Illinois! Hallelujah!" He turned and waved his open palm in the direction of the musicians' pit. "Take a bow, Brother Hendrix."

Dorian stood and waved to the capacity crowd of 2,000 worshippers occupying the pews. Satan must've told him to sneak a peek at the choir, because when he turned his head, the first person in his line of vision was Amari, and she looked none too happy. Of the fifty-plus choir members, she was the only one sitting on her ass with her arms folded and rolling her eyes while the others gave him a standing ovation.

So over her ass, his eyes skidded across the choir stand to the alto section and landed on his music crush. It was second Sunday at Light of the World, and out of tradition, all of the female choir members were decked out in black dresses accessorized with single strands of pearls and matching pearl stud earrings. Harmony's smile alone set her apart from the other ladies, especially Amari. Yeah, Ms. Baxter was looking sixteen kinds of sexy with her thick self. When she suddenly cast her eyes on Dorian, their orbs locked, and something unfamiliar stirred deep down in his soul. It was an unsettling feeling he couldn't explain. Thrown completely off his game, he broke eye contact and retook his seat on the organ bench.

Chapter Six

Dorian closed Harmony's door and leaned into her truck's lowered window. "Put your seat belt on and go ahead, baby. I'll be right behind you as soon as I stop by the store."

"What do you need to go to the store for?"

He chuckled. "Girl, I can't pull up on you and your family for Sunday dinner empty-handed. I ain't from the South, but I know basic etiquette. Hell, my mama raised me and my sister right."

"I understand, but we really don't need anything. But if you—"

"Hey, Hillary, girl! How're you doing?"

Dorian did a swift about-face at the sound of Amari's voice. He glared at her, Joette, and their crew.

Harmony flashed a smile and waved. "It's Harmony, not Hillary, Amari. Anyway, I'm blessed. How are you ladies today?"

"Oh, we're fine. Do you wanna roll with us to Club Rhapsody for Sunday brunch? Girl, the food is amazing, and that's where all the ballers and real niggas hang out in VIP. We're all 'bout to try to snag us a bae apiece. You in?"

"No, thank you. I spent all day yesterday and this morning before church preparing a big dinner for my family, so I'll pass this time. But thanks for inviting me."

"Okay, girl, we'll see you at choir rehearsal Thursday."

"All right. You ladies have fun."

Dorian had remained quiet throughout Harmony's brief exchange with Amari. The shade had been real, but he didn't give a damn. He mean-mugged her ass when she threw a smirk his way before she walked off with her posse. He made a mental memo to stay clear of Amari and her girls and to keep Harmony as far away from them as possible.

Amari was pissed the hell off as she cruised toward Club Rhapsody in her midnight Cadillac Escalade. Her girls were spilling all flavors of tea and kee-keeing nonstop on full blast, but she wasn't hearing any of it. Amari was still stuck on Dorian's buster ass standing in the church parking lot talking to that fat chick in the choir and ignoring her like his dick hadn't just been down her throat last night. If that motherfucker thought he could get sucked and then duck, he was on some bad crack. No nigga dipped on Amari Liliana Simmons after getting his rocks off unless she said so. Fuck nah! It didn't matter if he was from Chicago or L.A. or fucking Mozambique. He wasn't gonna get away with disrespecting her like Rashad had. Amari couldn't allow that shit to happen again.

Rashad had damn near fucked her pussy dry and been on the receiving of her million-dollar blowjobs for seven years before he hopped up out of the blue and eloped with some bitch he had met at the Gospel Music Workshop of America in Houston, Texas earlier this year. Now that low-down motherfucker was somewhere in Seattle with his wifey, living his best life, while she was stuck in place being disrespected by another music director. But Dorian Hendrix wasn't about to get away with his lame-ass bullshit. Uh-uh. Amari had a lesson or two to teach that slick, Chicago, two-stepping nigga.

Humph, he must not know 'bout me.

***

"Argggghhh!" Harmony patted her chest and spun around from the keypad on the wall. "What the hell, Nat? What made you sneak up on me like that?"

"I'm trying to figure out who you're buzzing through the gate." He laughed and shook his head.

"I haven't buzzed anybody through yet, but we are going to have a dinner guest, so I expect y'all to act like you have some home training. Okay?"

"Maybe we will and maybe we won't. Is it one of your teacher girlfriends or some dude?"

"What difference does it make, Nat, huh?"

"You know the deal, Puddin'. I don't want some no-good nigga running up through here trying to get inside your head or your panties and then leave you heartbroken."

"I guess you think I'm real stupid. Or is it hard to believe a man can take a fat girl from the country like me serious?"

"Nah, baby girl, it ain't that." Nat reached for his sister and wrapped his arms around her. "Any man would be glad to have a woman like you. Since you were a little girl, you had the biggest heart, so I know you got a whole lotta love to give. You're prettier than a butterfly in flight, can't nobody except Mama cook better than you, and you've got three degrees. And name me one female singer dead or alive with a voice purer and more powerful than yours."

Harmony didn't answer him with words. She smiled and squeezed her big brother's bulky body tight. "I love you, Nathaniel Baxter."

"You know I love you too, Puddin'."

"You better love me." She shoved him away and looked way up high until their eyes connected. "I swear if you or the other two O'Jays start acting a fool in front of my guest, I'll call Mama. Try me."

"Whatever." Nat waved his hand and walked off in the direction of the sunken great room.

Harmony sucked her teeth and watched him until he disappeared. He had gone to join his brothers, Otis and Marvin, his sons, and his nephews in front of the ninety-two-inch HDTV wall theater unit. That was where the Baxters watched all of the Atlanta Falcons road games. But whenever the Dirty Birds played at home, the whole troop, children and all, were in a luxury skybox at Mercedes-Benz Stadium. When the baby boy of the family was the starting center for the team and a four-time Pro Bowler, raking in $10.6 million a year—not including his Irish Spring and Krispy Kreme Doughnuts endorsement deals—it was the only way to roll.

"Hey, Puddin', the timer on the small oven just went off!" Rhema, Otis's wife, yelled from the kitchen. "Do you want me to check the spare ribs for you?"

"Hell nah, heifer! You know you can't cook nothing but breakfast food! Leave my spare ribs alone! I'm coming!" Harmony power walked to the kitchen to finish cooking.

When Dorian saw the crystal waterfall at the entrance of a red brick and iron-rail gate, it reminded him of a scene from a medieval fairy tale. It was the kind of wall that protected a castle where a princess lay in waiting, dreaming about her knight in shining armor. Confused, he immediately pulled over and parked to check the address Harmony had texted him that morning.

"Yep, this is it, 10 Sahara Chase." He ran his thumb over his mustache. "How the hell can she afford to live like this on a teacher's salary?"

With curiosity gnawing at him, Dorian shifted his whip into drive and cruised toward the gate. When he reached the security shack, he rolled down his window to speak to the young cat in uniform grinning at him

"Good afternoon, Mr. Hendrix. Ms. Baxter is expecting you. Just let me check your ID for verification and you can be on your way, sir."

Damn! Harmony and her family must be balling out. She's on some high-security shit. This toy cop already knows my name.

"Cool." Dorian removed his wallet from the glove compartment and slid his brand-new Georgia license out. "Here you go, my man."

The security guard took the license and looked it over before handing it back. "Enjoy your visit, sir," he said and then pushed a green button on the control panel to open the gate.

"Thanks."

The only word that came to mind at first glimpse was "grand." Dorian released a sharp whistle when the massive structure and its immaculate landscaping came into full view. A granite three-tier fountain that essentially served as a birdbath was an appealing centerpiece in the plush grass surrounded by the circular driveway filled with an array of luxury vehicles. Dorian peeped Harmony's platinum Lincoln Navigator among the impressive fleet. The mansion, an ecru stucco architectural masterpiece, had been designed with a hint of contemporary Arabian influence. Dorian had never seen a more magnificent home.

It was a good thing he'd had the instinct to pick up a bottle of Pahlmeyer Merlot for his gracious hostess and a twelve-pack of Corona for the men in her family. Otherwise, he would have looked like a moocher. The dozen yellow roses were for Harmony too. Pretty flowers for a pretty woman always earned a guy points.

Beads of sweat formed on Dorian's brow as he made his way to the front door. The early October weather was very pleasant and not hot at all, but he was nervous and feeling some imaginary heat. He stepped back after pressing the doorbell. A ripple of chimes rang out loud enough to be heard outside on the stoop. Dorian pasted a smile on his face when the door locks clicked, disengaging. A husky giant of a man with a scowl on his face opened the door.

"Good afternoon. I'm Dorian Hendrix. Harmony invited me to Sunday dinner."

"Puddin'!" Nat yelled from the front door.

"He's here." Harmony rubbed her palms down the skirt of her UGA Bulldogs apron a few times.

"What are you waiting for?" Rhema asked. "Girl, go get your man."

"He ain't my man."

Rhema cracked the hell up, laughing. "Well, you want him to be."

Noni closed the refrigerator with her hip before she carried the big bowl of Harmony's famous potato salad over to the center island and set it down. "Please go and rescue poor Brother Dorian before my husband eats him alive. We can't afford to lose our new music director so soon. We just got him."

"Okay." Harmony removed her favorite apron and handed it to her sister-in-law before she left the kitchen. Her stomach muscles contracted when she saw Dorian standing tall and handsome in the foyer with a bouquet of yellow roses in one hand and a bottle of red wine in the other.

Nat turned around with a twelve-pack of beer in the crook of his right arm. Harmony's smile turned upside down when she noticed the unpleasant expression on her big brother's face. She was going to have to tattle to her mama before dinner was over for sure.

"Hey." Dorian presented Harmony with the roses. "These are for you."

"They're so pretty." She took them and inhaled their heavenly fragrance. "Thank you."

Nat's fake coughing reminded Harmony he was still standing their mean mugging Dorian without a legitimate cause.

"Nat, meet Dorian Hendrix, Light of the World's new director of music and lead organist. If you had made it to church this morning, you would already know that. Anyway, Dorian, this is my oldest brother—"

"Nat 'Bone Crusher' Baxter! It's a pleasure to meet you, man." He grabbed his free hand and shook it firmly. "I had no idea you were Harmony's brother."

Nat was cheesing now. "How come you didn't tell the man you were the baby sister of a Super Bowl Champion, Puddin'?"

"Grrrr! Oh my God! I didn't think it was important." She tilted her head toward the kitchen. "Come on and meet the rest of the family, Dorian."

Chapter Seven

"Sweet Jesus! What a spread!" Dorian felt like he was in soul food heaven. He discreetly hooked his pinky around Harmony's and smiled at her. "Did you cook all this good food?"

"Yep, I prepared everything by myself."

The fourteen-seat dining room table had enough food on it to feed a church choir. The aroma of down-home soul food wafting in the air made Dorian's stomach growl. The fine china and sterling silver flatware were fabulous, but he could eat this kind of food from a cheap-ass paper plate with his fingers.

"Let me tell you what each dish is before the others come in here acting like starving crackheads." She started pointing with her index finger as she announced, "We have beef short ribs in brown onion gravy, garlic-roasted chicken, collard greens with cured jowls, crackling bread, black-eyed peas, chitterlings, baked macaroni and cheese, yellow rice, candied yams, corn on the cob, and my famous potato salad. The whipping-cream pound cake is still in the small oven, and two deep-dish blueberry cobblers are in the big one. We've got some French vanilla ice cream, too."

"Damn, girl, you're going to make a cat marry you just so you can cook for me and serenade me every day."

Harmony secretly squeezed his pinky with hers and smiled.

"Nope. That ain't gonna work. My baby sister is gonna marry a man who'll love her just because. Damn all that cooking and singing. You need to hire a private singer and a maid, bruh."

Harmony rolled her eyes hard at Otis when he entered the dining room. "He really didn't mean it like that. It was just a cute way of complimenting me, O. Damn."

"That's not how it sounded to me." He folded his beefy arms across his chest and frowned.

Otis's imposing killer stance and bigger-than-life presence would've intimidated most men, but not Dorian. No way. Not even a little bit. Brothas from the south side of the Chi didn't punk out very easily. He quickly sized up his potential adversary and left Harmony's side to step to him toe-to-toe. The two men were even in height, but Dorian had the weight advantage because Otis had evidently overindulged in a few too many of Harmony's Sunday-afternoon soul-food spreads. Bruh was at least fifty pounds past plump and, more than likely, slower than the coming of Christ. Dorian wasn't about to let this dude disrespect him, or Harmony either, even if he was her older brother.

"Man, I meant no shade or game toward your baby sister. Like she said, my words were simply a playful way of giving her props on her singing and cooking skills. No harm. No foul. I'm sorry you misinterpreted me." He offered his hand in a goodwill gesture. "Are we good?"

Dorian felt Harmony's eyes all over him and Otis, taking in their little standoff. He could also sense her vibe. He would bet a G she was on the brink of losing her mind over some petty bullshit her big brother and his mountain-size ego had started.

"Auntie Puddin', is it time to eat yet? We hawngry."

All three adults turned around at the sound of a child's voice. The boy and four more little Baxters had marched into the dining room on a food mission.

Harmony rushed over to the children and placed a hand on the little spokesman's shoulder. Ignoring Otis, Dorian watched her with a smile.

"Go wash your hands and tell everybody dinner is ready, Li'l Nat. All of you wash your hands. Go!"

"Yes, ma'am!" He turned and broke out into a speedy sprint with his followers on his heels. "It's time to eat, everybody! It's time to eat!"

Dorian faced Otis again. "Are we good, man?" He offered his hand in a shake for the second time.

Otis turned and left the dining room quietly. No handshake and no truce.

"Let me help you, sweetheart." Dorian grabbed a pair of empty serving dishes, one in each hand, and placed both on the hostess cart Harmony was pushing around the table.

She shook her head. "You don't have to do that. I'm just clearing the table for Ritza, the housekeeper. She'll be here shortly to clean up everything." Reaching out, she touched Dorian's arm. "I'm sorry for how Nat treated you when he answered the door. I apologize for Otis too. He really showed his ass in here before dinner for no reason. And I don't know what was wrong with Marvin. He could've let you have that last chicken wing. You're our guest."

"Nah, baby, I'm *your* guest. The three older Baxter brothers ain't feeling your boy."

"But Noni, Rhema, and all of the kids like you."

Dorian placed the empty chicken platter on the cart. "Maybe, but I kinda think they don't hold too much weight in this situation. Thor, the Hulk, and Black Panther want a nigga dead. I can dig it, though. Your brothers don't know me, so they think I'm some fool trying to push up on their baby sister."

"Are you?"

"Am I what?"

Harmony blew air from her cheeks and planted her fists on her ample hips. "Are you trying to push up on me, or is all your shameless flirting with me innocent and strictly about me singing your song?"

"I can't lie to you, Harmony. I'm in love with your voice, and I need it on my song. But there's something magnetic about you that pulls me closer to you every time I'm in your presence. No other woman has ever made me feel this way before."

"Stop it, Dorian! Just stop it! You don't have to say all that! It ain't necessary for you to butter me up just so I can sing lead on 'Flowing Favor.' I'm going to sing the damn song for you, so please save your weak, wack-ass lines for some thirsty chick." She left the cart and stomped off, but she didn't get very far because Dorian reached out and took hold of her wrist.

An adrenaline rush caused him to lose touch with his strength. One tug brought Harmony's body fully against his in a forceful collision, feminine softness meeting a wall of solid masculinity. They were so close that he could see his reflection in her shocked eyes, smell the subtle floral scent of her perfume, and feel her breasts pressing into his upper abdomen. His accelerated heart-beat made him dizzy, but it was that same heart that was driving him to speak his truth, bear his soul.

"My attraction to you ain't got nothing to do with my song, girl. I could get Amari or the older lady you told me about to sing lead for me. Shit, my girl Tiffany Boone would be more than happy to come through and knock it out the park. But I want you to sing it, Harmony, because you've got a special gift you need to share with the world, and the world deserves to hear it."

When Harmony lowered her gaze and remained quiet, Dorian felt his heart squeeze. This stunning, talented woman didn't even realize what a priceless jewel she was. Why was she so unaware of her beauty and the impact of her amazing vocal ability? Surely, her late fiancé had told her how great a catch she was. And if he hadn't, that was a damn shame.

"Look at me, Harmony." He released her wrist and cupped her chin to lift her face. He needed her to look into his eyes so she could see his sincerity. "I am very, very attracted to you. Even if you didn't know E-flat from a can of spinach, I would want to spend time with you and taste those pretty lips of yours."

Dorian thought it was cute how she blushed and shuddered at his confession.

"It's true. Music may have drawn me to you initially, but your spirit and every damn thing that makes you a woman keeps me hanging around."

When he lowered his head and took possession of her lips with his, he was glad she didn't resist. In fact, she moaned and allowed his tongue to have its way with hers, tasting, tickling, and teasing it until she swayed with what he assumed was passion, and he had to grip her hips to keep her from falling. He went in for the kill then, wrapping his arms around her waist tightly and drawing her closer until she gasped at the feel of his erection thumping against her belly.

Harmony pulled back slowly with her eyelids fluttering open. "The pre-game show is about to start. Mama and Daddy will be calling soon. They always call before every road game so we can pray for Knee Ba . . . I mean, Luther's safety on the field."

Dorian nodded. "All right, baby, but I'm going to hang around after the game because we need to talk." He leaned in and gave her a soft forehead kiss. "Is that okay with you?"

Harmony nodded.

"What about your brothers? Do you think they'll have a problem leaving me here with you alone?"

"They might, but Noni and Rhema can handle Nat and Otis. And Marvin will be rushing to get Marvin Junior and Ilyssia home to their mother so she won't call the police on him again."

Laughing, Dorian mumbled, "That's good. That'll give us privacy and time to talk so we can figure out what's going on between us."

"Go! Go! Go! He's gooone! Touchdown!"

Noni jumped up from her screaming husband's lap and hit everybody with an X-rated version of the snake. "Yeah, baby! Yasss!"

"Whoop! Whoop!" Otis punched his fist in the air.

Every Baxter in the great room, with the exception of Harmony, was up jumping and screaming wildly after the Falcons star running back ran out the clock to score a touchdown at the very end of the second quarter. Even the babies were dancing and cheering out of control. The sound of heavy hands slapping high fives filled the air.

Dorian leaned over and touched Harmony's sensitive earlobe with his lips. "Where's the bathroom, baby? Those three beers got your boy's bladder full to the max."

His warm breath and the leathery-spicy scent of his cologne caused her thighs to quiver while she basked in his nearness. His hard thigh was kissing her softer one, and he'd draped his arm around her shoulders the moment he sat down next to her on the love seat.

"It's down the hall opposite from the kitchen, all the way down on the left side."

"I'll be back way before halftime is over. Okay?"

"Okay."

A gush of air left Harmony's lungs at the sight of Dorian's fluid and measured gait. Everything about him exuded confidence and finesse. Watching him walk out of the room was like foreplay. Harmony instantly started craving another kiss from him. Lawd, if he did kiss her again, she was sure her panties would drop to her ankles on their own. Refusing to further entertain the thought of being kissed out of her lace boy shorts, Harmony sat back and anticipated Dorian's return. She already missed his scent and body heat. Damn it, she just missed *him*.

Chapter Eight

The sound of youthful voices singing hit Dorian head-on when he exited the bathroom. He heard someone playing a piano, too. He was sure it wasn't a keyboard. The heavy acoustics told his acute ear for all things musical as much. Curious, he followed the music to an elaborately decorated room where a Bösendorfer grand piano sat facing an enormous picture window. A breathtaking view of the setting sun bidding farewell to another Sunday created a generous glimmer over a nature pool with a rolling waterfall. It was the ideal location for a piano. A music fanatic like him could draw unlimited inspiration to write some boss compositions and meaningful lyrics every day from such a beautiful vision.

There was a full drum set in one corner and a bass guitar on a stand next to it. Dorian noticed two mics secured on stands across the room. He wondered who owned all of this music equipment and if they ever used it. The piano was well tuned, so someone was taking care of it, but who?

"You're off-key, O2!"

The other children laughed at the pianist's open criticism of the lead singer of the group of four, and she laughed with them. There were three stocky boys, presumably between the ages of 9 and 12, standing behind O2.

He cleared his throat dramatically. "Okay, I'll get it right this time. Play it again," he instructed. "I'm about to bust it wide open like Auntie Puddin' taught me. Tap them keys, Purity."

To Dorian's surprise, the girl, who couldn't have been a day over 13, strummed into Jodeci's "All My Life." She had hella skills. This time, when O2 began to sing, she offered him the "okay" finger signal. He really did sound good. His tone and control were quite impressive. When his three background vocalists joined him on the chorus, Dorian closed his eyes and closely scrutinized their harmony. These kids had awesome voices. With some intense training, they could be ready to record.

And I thank God that I, that I finally found you
All my life I've prayed for someone like you
And I hope that you feel the same way too

"Man, you guys sound better than Jodeci!" Dorian's compliment and clapping interrupted the song.

O2, Purity, and all the other little Baxters seemed embarrassed when he walked all the way into the room, but Dorian didn't miss the slight smiles on their faces. They appreciated his praise for their music.

"We would sound better if we could practice more, but it's football season, and the boys practice every day and play games on Saturdays," Purity explained. "And I'm in the gifted program at my school, so I have to study a lot. That's why we keep messing up."

"Maybe I can help y'all. Slide over, baby girl."

Purity shifted to her right to give Dorian room to sit with her on the piano bench.

"Okay, we're going to work on the harmony on the chorus first. Then I'll go back and help O2 bust the verse wide open. Are y'all ready?"

"Yeah!" the boys said, dapping each other up like 40-year-old men.

"Cool. One, two, three, four . . ."

Dorian eased into the chorus, and the young Baxter boys started crooning with full voices. He stopped playing abruptly. "First, we've got to polish up your collective tone and balance."

"I told y'all!" Purity pointed a chastising finger at the group and rolled her neck.

"Don't worry about it, baby girl. Mr. Dorian is about to whip their voices into shape. In one hour, these dudes will be performance ready."

Harmony was having a nervous breakdown because Dorian hadn't returned from the bathroom yet. Halftime had ended, and the game was deep into the third quarter. She hoped he hadn't eaten something that didn't agree with his stomach. Three helpings of her mac and cheese and all of those damn chicken wings on top of everything else he'd wolfed down may have been too heavy for his Chicago palate. Worried, Harmony stood to go and look for him.

"Auntie Puddin'! Auntie Puddin'!" Purity ran into the great room. "You gotta come to the music room quick. We got a surprise for you!"

Harmony power walked out of the room behind her oldest niece, who was running. Noni and Rhema jumped up and followed them. When the women reached the music room, they found Purity and Dorian sitting on the piano bench. O2 had a cordless mic in his hand, and his background vocalists were huddled around a mic on a stand.

"Dorian, what's going on?" Harmony asked. "I thought you were in the bathroom sick, puking your damn liver out."

"Nah, baby, I ain't sick. I'm back here rehearsing with my new group. Why don't you ladies relax over there and let them entertain you?"

After Harmony, Noni, and Rhema sat down on the sofa across the room, Dorian leaned over and whispered something in Purity's ear. She tucked both her lips inside her mouth with a serious expression on her face and nodded her head. Then she placed her fingertips on the piano keys and began to play.

Harmony's jaw damn near dropped to her boobs when O2 slid into the first verse of Jodeci's "All My Life." His pitch was impeccable, and he had unbelievable control she'd never heard from him before.

"Oh my God, listen to my baby!" Rhema gushed with tears in her eyes.

When O2's brother and two cousins joined him on the chorus, his mama and aunties lost their damn minds. They started clapping and screaming like they were at an eighties R&B concert. All they needed were some flashlights in their hands so they could wave them in the air. Dorian grinned and shook his head at the women's shenanigans. The smiles on the children's faces were priceless as they continued singing their little hearts out. By the time they hit the final note, all three women were bawling all over each other.

Booming applause from the doorway scared the shit out of everybody. Harmony looked up and smiled at the O'Jays through her tears. Rhema stood and walked over to her husband and wrapped her arms around him. Nat took her place on the sofa next to Noni when Harmony hurried over and embraced O2. She kissed the boy on his cheek and then hugged Purity and her other three nephews. Unabashed pride was oozing from their smiles.

"Y'all rocked the house! I am so proud of y'all." She turned and looked at her brothers and sisters-in-law. "Didn't they sound like cash money, y'all?"

Rhema was still crying. "I can't believe how great they sounded."

"We need to call Baby Face! We got a hot singing group in the family!"

Harmony laughed at Nat's excitement.

"They sound almost as good as we did when we were their ages and singing O'Jays hits in all the school talent shows."

Marvin shook his head, laughing. "Don't even try it, O. You know damn well we never even came close to that kind of harmony, so quit lying, bruh."

"How did you do it?" Harmony asked, gazing into Dorian's eyes like they were the only two souls in the room. She placed her hand on his shoulder. "What did you do to make them sing like that?"

"Not much. I really didn't have to. They were born with that raw Baxter talent like another awesome singer I know." He winked and swiped his tongue over his plump bottom lip.

Harmony lowered her eyes and smiled bashfully with her heart racing full throttle. Sudden deafening silence made her check her surroundings. Everywhere she looked, there was a pair of accusing eyes penetrating straight through her. Or at least that's how it felt. Even the children seemed to have been judging her.

"Oh my goodness! We better get back to the game," Noni rushed to suggest in what Harmony recognized as an attempt to divert everyone's attention from her and Dorian. "Y'all know the home team will blow a lead in the twinkling of an eye." She stood up from the sofa.

Without another word, the Baxter men and their wives filed out of the music room, heading back to the great room to finish watching the game. The children lingered behind with their auntie and the man who had pushed their music to the next level in less than an hour.

"Thank you for helping us, Mr. Dorian." Purity smiled with a sparkle in her eyes. "When can we practice with you again?"

His gaze connected with Harmony's. "It'll be soon, baby girl. Your auntie and I will work out a practice schedule for you guys so I can teach y'all a few more fundamentals and get the group ready for the studio."

"The studio?" O2 repeated.

"Are we gonna record a CD?"

Dorian chuckled at Li'l Nat's enthusiasm. "Let's start off with a hit single first, okay?"

"Okay. We're gonna be football players *and* singing stars!"

"All the girls are gonna be jocking us!"

"I bet I get more girls than you."

"Well, I'm still going to be the first black female supreme court justice while I play for y'all on the side."

The voices of Harmony's niece and nephews faded out when Dorian stood from the piano bench and discreetly hooked his pinky around hers. A soft forehead kiss almost pushed her over the edge. He had cast some kind of spell on her with his Chicago charm, love for music, good looks, and swag. And that kiss . . . Lawd, have mercy! The way he'd made love to her mouth with his earlier had left Harmony wanting more—a helluva lot more.

Damn, I want this man! But I've got to guard my heart. I cannot survive another broken heart.

"Let's go catch the rest of the game, *Puddin'*."

"Oh, you want to tease me about my nickname, huh?"

"Nah, I think it's cute. I just hope one day I'll get to find out if you really live up to that nickname."

"Huh?" Harmony was genuinely confused.

Dorian placed his wide palm on her hip and leaned down to whisper in her ear. "All of the flavors of pudding I like—vanilla, chocolate, and butterscotch—are sweet and delicate on my tongue. Are you?"

Harmony's brain immediately went on strike, but her body tingled all over with full awareness. Dorian was coming for her hard and fast with no detours or breaks, and she didn't know how to handle his aggression. Her sweet Ham, God rest his soul, had been her first, last, and only. He had never spoken to her with such brashness or sexually charged language. It hadn't been his style. Although Harmony had appreciated Ham's mild and slow approach, Dorian's straightforwardness made her pussy drip with need, and she liked it.

Somehow Harmony's mind won its battle with lust and pulled her back to her current situation. She audibly exhaled. "The game . . ." she whispered.

"Come on, baby." Dorian laced his fingers through hers and escorted her from the room. "Let's go finish watching your brother play."

Chapter Nine

After literally pushing her brothers out the door, Harmony decided to take Dorian for a walk around the perimeter of the house and through her slice of the secluded neighborhood where five of the most luxurious mansions were tucked away from the rest of the world. Hand in hand, they walked under a starry, moonlit sky. With the exception of a few crickets chirping and an occasional croak from a frog, the sounds of nature had retired for the night. Peace and tranquility enveloped them until Dorian decided to dive a little deeper into the conversation the Baxter siblings had indulged in over blackberry cobbler and French vanilla ice cream after the Falcons victory.

"Nat was named after Nat King Cole and Otis was named after Otis Redding?"

Harmony nodded. "Yep. And Mama loved Marvin Gaye to death, so she named Marvin after him. Daddy named Knee . . . um, Luther after Luther Vandross."

"But y'all call his big, mean, four-hundre-pound, chitterling-eating ass Knee Baby!" Dorian doubled over, laughing his ass off.

Harmony punched him softly on the shoulder. "Who told you that? Did those bad-ass kids run their mouths?"

"Yo, lay off my new artists. They didn't tell me anything about you, your brothers, or all of them country-ass nicknames y'all call each other." Still laughing, Dorian explained, "I heard Marvin call Luther Knee Baby a couple of times and Noni too. But you're good. Each time you almost slipped, you caught yourself. I didn't miss it, though."

Harmony and Dorian shared a laugh over Luther's secret nickname and the family's failure to keep it on lock. Then their moonlight stroll fell silent again for some time. But once again, Dorian felt like talking. He had so many questions about Harmony and her family. His fascination with her was over the top. She was like no other woman he'd ever met, and he had met too many to count. The woman was drop-dead gorgeous with the most voluptuous body and unlimited curves. And he loved the way she stood back on her thick bow legs. It was so damn sexy. Her voice was phenomenal, and she knew her way around the kitchen. Harmony could sew, design clothes, and she'd taught herself how to play the piano by ear at a very early age. For some reason, it hadn't surprised him at all when Noni had poured that little bit of tea. But it just wasn't enough. Dorian wanted to know more about Harmony. No, he wanted to know everything about her.

"Who was Harmony named after?"

When she looked up into Dorian's eyes, he heard heaven's angels sing. The glimmer in her orbs under the light of the stars made his heart do an energetic two-step in his chest. Even though they were outside roaming God's green earth in the fresh air, he found it hard to breathe.

"Daddy said he named me Harmony because my birth completed the family. I was the missing link, the harmony my brothers had needed to sing and play football better. Daddy and Mama had prayed for a little girl, but they accepted that I wasn't meant to be after having three boys straight. But after a six-year wait, they agreed to give it one more shot."

"And that's when Luther came along, right?"

"Nope." Harmony shook her head. "Mama had a miscarriage when she was five months pregnant the year before Luther was born. It was a girl. They named her Ella Diana in honor of Ella Fitzgerald and Diana Ross. Then a little over nine months after Luther came along, I made my debut to the world."

"And now you're the reigning princess of the family."

"I guess you could say that. But sometimes Princess Harmony gets tired of being smothered by four overprotective brothers, especially Luther. He's the meanest one of all."

"Say what?" Dorian stopped walking, but he maintained his hold on Harmony's hand. "Are you trying to tell me that Knee Baby is going give me more grief than the O'Jays did?"

"I'm sorry, Dorian, but Luther can be a pain in the ass when it comes to me. He acts more like my daddy and less like my brother, who's barely nine months my senior."

They resumed their stroll around the nature pool with the sound of the waterfall playing pitter-pat with the wall of large stones on its descent. The break in conversation gave Dorian a moment to think about this new revelation. After initially being treated like shit by the oldest three Baxter brothers, he'd finally won them over by helping their sons sharpen their music skills with a promise over dessert to continue to mentor them. What the hell was it going to take to get Knee Baby to accept him into the fold?

"I like you a lot, Harmony, and I want to get to know you better. So I'm willing to put in the work to win Luther's approval. But I ain't about to kiss his big ass."

"When you say you like me and want to get to know me better, what exactly does that mean, Dorian?"

He stood still again and faced Harmony with both of her hands possessively secured inside his. "I want to date you, spend time with you. Let me court you and wine and dine your pretty self while we learn all we need to know about each other. Does that sound like something you want?"

"Yes."

This time when he kissed her, his hands snaked around her waist and drew her in close. She returned his embrace by reaching up and resting her palms on the tops of his broad shoulders. This kiss was more urgent and passionate than the earlier one. Their mating tongues seemed greedier. Dorian loved the taste of Harmony and the sound of her lust-filled moans each time he sucked her tongue, pulling it farther into his hungry mouth. He suppressed his laughter when she gasped in response to him palming her ass with both hands, something he'd been imagining doing since day one. It was Sunday, the Lord's day, but he couldn't resist the temptation to take possession of that big booty he'd dreamed and daydreamed about since he'd first laid eyes on it. He would ask God for forgiveness for getting frisky on the Sabbath tonight during his bedtime prayers.

Dorian couldn't breathe. He needed air, but the kiss was much too delicious to end it now. So he eased up just a little. In an effort to breathe and allow Harmony to do the same, he withdrew his lips from the kiss and rested his forehead against hers. Then, after his second wind, he took command of her mouth again with a series of soft pecks before he sought out her sweet tongue again. His erection grew stiffer and bigger, thumping against her belly.

Dorian's cell phone vibrating and playing Tupac's "Dear Mama" in his pocket couldn't have come at a worse time. Reluctant as hell, he ended the kiss and watched Harmony's eyelids flit and flit until they opened.

"This is my mama. Let me see what she wants. It'll only take a minute. I promise."

A quick nod from Harmony was her answer.

"What's up, Mama?" he greeted her after removing the phone from his pocket, pressing the power button, and raising it to her ear.

"Aaahhh! Oh my God, Puddin'! That man is so damn fine! You think you can handle all of that without getting strung out on the dick?"

"Damn, Noni, you act like she's gonna give the man some coochie tomorrow. All he did was kiss her." Rhema laughed hysterically. "Let Dorian take the scenic route before he lands that big Boeing 747 in Puddin's hangar. You know it's been two years since she parted them juicy thighs for a man."

Harmony rolled her eyes to the ceiling and wrapped a thick section of her hair around one of those jumbo satin rollers while her sisters-in-law kept discussing her new friendship with Dorian like she wasn't even a part of their three-way call. They sounded like a pair of clucking ducks over the speaker phone.

Harmony searched her bed for her organic hair moisturizer until she found it and poured some into her hand. As she applied it over her loose tresses, she thought about how much she'd enjoyed spending time with Dorian today. A smile crept up on her face, and she was glad that neither Rhema nor Noni was there to see it. They didn't need to know she was falling fast and hard for him.

“When are you going to tell Knee Baby you’ve got a new boyfriend, Puddin’?”

“Oooh, he’s going to pitch a thousand fits!” Noni chimed in before Harmony had a chance to answer Rhema’s question.

“I’ll have that conversation with him when the time is right.”

“Never!” Noni and Rhema screamed in unison and burst into another round of giggles.

“On a serious note, Dorian and I are just two friends getting to know each other. I want us to take it slow and easy, so I don’t see a need to say anything to Papa Luther yet.”

“My husband is going to mention Dorian to Knee Baby as soon as they talk later on tonight.”

“And y’all think Otis is going to keep his big mouth? Girl, bye. Y’all know my man can’t hold water.”

“Marvin can’t either,” Harmony added softly. “But I ain’t worried about him, O, or Nat. I’m a grown-ass woman, and I can date whoever I want, and my brothers can kiss my ass, crack and all, if they don’t like.”

“Good for you, Puddin’.”

“That’s right, Rhema. Puddin’ deserves to be happy with a hot stud after all she’s been through, and as her sisters, we’ll make it easy for her by keeping our husbands’ overbearing asses out of her business.”

“Hell yeah, we will. Just concentrate on building an honest, open, and strong friendship with that man, Puddin’. Take your time and enjoy the ride, girl.”

“I will. Thanks, you two. I don’t know what I would do without y’all. I can always count on my Noni Boloney and Rainbow Rhema. I love y’all crazy heifers.”

“Awww, Puddin’, we love you too.”

"Since you were ten years old," Noni reminded her. "Go to bed, Puddin'. You've got to deal with your students tomorrow. And I know you want to go to sleep and dream about your new bae. Good night, ladies."

"Good night."

"I'll talk to y'all tomorrow." Harmony ended the call and finished rolling her hair with visions of Dorian dancing through her head.

Chapter Ten

"Wow! Another bouquet of roses? That's the second one this week, isn't it, Ms. Baxter?"

Harmony couldn't help but smile as she picked up the crystal vase and admired the dozen lavender roses sprinkled with baby's breath. Their fragrance was heavenly. Out of the corner of her eye, she noticed her principal/boss, Dr. Pennington, still standing at the counter in the main office with an expectant look in her eyes.

"Yeah, Dr. P., this is my second vase of roses this week. I got balloons and a teddy bear yesterday."

"Oh, my. Some beau must be terribly smitten with a certain home ec teacher."

"I guess so."

Harmony hurried out of the office and down the hall because she had no desire to discuss her new friendship with Dorian with anyone except Noni and Rhema. She didn't want to jinx it by tossing it out into the atmosphere too early and all willy-nilly. Their special situation was blossoming beautifully, and she wanted to nurture and protect it like a delicate flower until it was strong enough to endure anything life could possibly throw its way. And that included the wrath of Luther Baxter, whom she still hadn't told she was dating Dorian.

However, Harmony knew he'd picked up on the clues that someone new had entered her life by her late-night phone chats and the humongous anthurium plant with pretty pink petals he'd helped her drag into the house the day before. If she hadn't moved fast enough, Luther would've intercepted the card attached and read Dorian's sweet message to her, and then all hell would've broken loose.

"Ah, snap, Ms. Baxter got some more flowers! Some OG must really be feelin' her!"

Harmony shook her head at Kemi's nonsense when she entered her classroom carrying the vase of roses. "Boy, sit down and finish the straight stitch on your quilt."

He smirked. "I finished already. Ask Ms. Tina. She said I sew better than every female in this class."

Harmony glanced over at her trusted teaching intern, who nodded her confirmation with a smile. Out of spite, she refused to give Kemi's cocky ass the satisfaction of eye contact, so she continued to her desk and placed the roses on top of it next to the other ones.

"Okay, class, I'm about to come around and grade your straight stitches. Who wants to be first? I'll start with anybody but Kemi."

The classroom exploded with laughter and teasing, and Ms. Baxter was the ring leader.

Let it keep flowing! Lord, let it keep flowiiing!

Just let your flowing favor fall down on meee!

"Yeah! That's what I'm talking about! Y'all killed it, choir!" Dorian looked at Carrie, the choir director, with approval. "You did your thing, girl. Didn't she, y'all? And how about these super bad musicians? Didn't they rock it out?"

"Yesss!"

"Amen!"

In the midst of the claps and cheers from the choir members after a flawless take four on "Flowing Favor," Amari, the one bad apple, was trying like hell to spoil the whole damn bunch. The sour scowl on her face was evidence of her funky attitude. Dorian wondered why the hell she'd even shown up for choir rehearsal, but it really didn't matter. Regardless of her hate, he was a happy man because of how well Voices of Victory had just performed his song, and an attractive alto named Harmony, who was slowly making him fall for her. Life was golden.

"Okay, y'all, that will be the sermonic selection next Sunday. Of course, this coming Sunday is youth day, so you guys will get a well-deserved break."

"Hold up!"

As if she were a queen or someone important, the choir fell silent when Amari jumped up all dramatically, waving her hand in the air. Dorian's eyes sought out Harmony, who was on chill as usual. He gave her a faint smile and a wink, and she returned his smile and looked away.

"We sound good and all, but what about the lead? Who's gonna sing the verses and do the ad-libs? We're tired of listening to you falsetto your way through the lead parts. You wrote the song in a key for a female soloist, so where is she? We wanna hear her."

"Don't worry about that. One of the most extraordinary voices I've ever heard in my life will grace us on the song, and she sounded great during our last rehearsal. So no worries, y'all. Everything is under control." Dorian looked at his watch. "I think I'll let you guys go home early tonight since y'all blew me away on all three songs we practiced. Let us stand for our closing prayer. Sister Julia Mae, can you lead us, please?"

"I sure can. Let's join hands and close our eyes."

Amari finished off her watermelon margarita and placed the glass on the table. "Did y'all hear that slick-tongue nigga? Talking 'bout some surprise singer is gonna sing solo on his song. What kinda shit is that? The choir is full of some of the baddest singers in town. Any one of us can snatch the teeth outta that damn song. We don't need one of his celebrity friends to come and sing for us. He makes me sick." She sucked her teeth.

"He didn't make you sick the other night when y'all were fucking. I know you gave that pretty, chocolate nigga some pussy even though you didn't give us the scoop. How was the dick? I bet it was good. As tall and thick as he is, I know he's got a telephone pole."

The other two female choir members snickered at Joette's joke and slapped hands.

"Bitch, I don't know if his shit is big and good or li'l and weak, 'cause I did *not* fuck him. Ol' lame-ass nigga."

Joette looked around the restaurant and smirked. "I don't hardly believe that shit. Since when did you start acting like the Virgin Mary and holding back on the pussy?"

"That nigga is a twisted freak! He wanted to nut all in my face and hair, but I wasn't down with that shit. I did let him eat my pussy, though. I made that giant 'Jack and the Beanstalk' motherfucker get down on his knees and eat my pussy while I yanked on his good, curly hair and clawed up his neck."

"What happened after he ate you out?"

"I sent his freaky ass home with the blue balls 'cause I wasn't 'bout to let that nigga skeet cum all over me. Amari has fucked ballers from every pro sports team in the A—the Braves, Hawks, Falcons, and even Atlanta United, the hometown soccer squad. Okay? Not one of them dudes tried to drown me with cum. Dorian Hendrix is just a nasty pervert, and I don't like him."

"Well, I still think he's cute, and I love his tall, stocky body. He can sing and play the hell out of that organ, too.

And I don't care if he brings Whoopi Goldberg to church to sing the lead on his song. I bet you we're going to bring the house down."

The other two girls nodded their heads in agreement with Joette, but Amari rolled her eyes at her crew and waved her hand at them dismissively.

"Whatever, bitches."

"Mmmm." Harmony tore her lips away from Dorian's and wriggled out of his embrace. She wiped the window to clear away some of the thick fog so she could sneak a peek at her front door. Luther was home, and the last thing she needed was for him to come outside and catch her making out with Dorian in his truck like a silly 16-year-old slut.

"What's wrong, baby? How come you keep watching the front door?"

"My brother is somewhere in the house, and I don't want him to come out here and start some shit."

"You're an adult, Harmony." He traced her chin with his fingertip. "Luther is your brother, not your daddy. You're too damn old to let him bully you. Come on. Let's go inside so I can meet him."

"Nooo! Tonight is not a good time for an introduction between you two."

"Cool. Will I meet him Sunday after the game? That is why you invited me, right? You want me to meet your youngest brother and your parents."

"That's the plan, but I'm so nervous about you meeting Luther. Mama and Daddy will be cool, but the very thought of me introducing you to Luther makes my nerves bad."

"Why, baby? Tell me why you're nervous about me meeting Luther."

Harmony swallowed the lump in her throat and looked at the front door again. "Knee Baby and Ham, my late fiancé, were best friends from the sandbox until the day he died. We grew up down the street from each other. The three of us attended college together. We were thick as thieves. Knee Baby trusted Ham with my heart because he had loved me all his life. He knew he would never do anything to hurt me."

"I understand. But maybe after Luther and I meet and he gets to know what kind of man I am, he'll feel the same way about me."

"Exactly what kind of man are you, Dorian?" She searched his eyes for honesty.

"I like you too much to lie to you, baby. I ain't no altar boy. I've had more than my share of women and then some. I'm not proud of it, but that's my truth. There're some things in my past that I'm ashamed of and I wish I could take back, but I can't. Moving to Atlanta was my first step toward my new beginning."

"And how do I fit into that?"

His smile, even in the dark interior of his truck, was appealing enough to make Harmony's clit jump. "You represent a new, fresh, and exciting stage in my personal life. I've never dated a woman like you before. Actually, I've never really given exclusive dating a fair shot. I could never commit to a monogamous relationship in all my thirty-six years."

"What about now?"

"I'm all the way in, baby. So let's just go with the flow and see where it'll lead us. I won't make you any promises, but right now, you're the only woman I'm interested in."

"If that changes, I want to be the first to know. Don't hide it from me or tell me lies. Always be truthful with me no matter what. That's all I'm asking of you. Just be honest."

"I can do that." Dorian leaned over the console and pecked Harmony's lips. "Let me walk you to the door."

"No, that's okay. I'll be fine." She opened the passenger door. "Good night."

"Good night. I'll call you when I reach the crib."

"Okay. I'll be waiting."

Chapter Eleven

Luther jogged to the foyer and planted all 388 pounds of his six foot three inch physique front and center when he heard Harmony entering the security code to release the front door. Dressed in a pair of UGA basketball shorts, a wife beater, and a pair of Jordan sports slides, he crossed his arms over his chest, prepared for battle.

He was in his feelings because he'd seen Harmony sitting outside in a Lexus SUV with some dude. The windows were tinted, and it was after eleven o'clock at night, so he couldn't see inside the truck, but he knew his sister was inside with some nigga. He'd watched her pull into the driveway on the security camera with the guy trailing her in his whip. Then she got out of her ride and hopped in his. They had been sitting in his truck doing only God knew what for two hours. Now that she'd decided to bring her ass in the house, Luther wanted his face to be the first thing she saw.

"Hey," she mumbled when she turned around and saw him.

"Who is that nigga you were sitting in that Lexus with, Puddin'?"

"His name is Dorian, and he's the new director of music at the church. But don't pretend like you didn't know who he was. I'm sure Nat, O, and Marvin have already given you a heads-up."

"Wrong. Them niggas ain't said nothing to me. I guess you told Noni and Rhema to handle Nat and O with bedroom magic or something so they wouldn't snitch. And I don't know what's up with Marvin. Maybe his pending divorce and custody battle are messing with his head more than we thought, because he's slipping. I need to have a talk with him and the O'Jays because they're keeping secrets from me."

Harmony smiled. "So you're salty because your boys didn't tell you my business? Boy, bye. Quit worrying about what's going on in my life and concentrate on yours. You're the one walking around here with twenty different women claiming you as their man. "

"And how is that your concern, Puddin'?"

"It's not. Just like my friendship with Dorian shouldn't be your concern. Good night, Knee Baby. Sleep tight."

"I gotta potty, Auntie Puddin'!" Ilyssia whined, jumping and twisting. "I gotta pee!"

Dorian squeezed Harmony's hand as her eyes darted around the crowded area just outside the Falcons media room. The entire Baxter family was present and accounted for, the patriarch and matriarch included.

Everyone was on a natural high over the home team's narrow win over the Tennessee Titans. The game had been a nail-biter right down to the final seconds, when the Falcons barely made it down the field through the opposition's stonewall defense to field goal range. And even then, the wind almost swept the football away, which would've forced them into overtime. Thankfully, the kicker had aligned his kick perfectly with the goal post and put the right amount of force behind it to secure the three-point win.

Now the family was patiently waiting for Luther, his teammates, and head coach to wrap up post-game interviews so they could congratulate him before Cousin Zeke drove Mr. and Mrs. Baxter back home to Gray. Dorian thought the Baxters were a cute older couple. They were funny as hell, too. Their deep Southern drawls and shameless honesty had kept him laughing throughout the game. He'd even acted as Mr. Baxter's personal bartender every time the good deacon wanted a Wild Turkey and Coke until Mama Baxter caught on around drink number three. That's when she'd threatened Dorian and her husband with bodily harm if either one of them took another sip of alcohol.

"Uh-oh, Auntie Puddin', I'm 'bout to wet my pants!" Ilyssia was in full animation mode, dancing and hopping around.

"Take her to the restroom, baby," Dorian finally said.

"But what about—"

"If he comes out before you get back, I can introduce myself. Just take this baby to the restroom before you have a mess on your hands."

"Okay. We'll be right back."

A minute after Harmony and Ilyssia vanished down the jam-packed hallway, Luther emerged from the media room with two of his teammates. The cat was dapper to death in a custom-designed bronze three-piece suit accessorized with a paisley tie and matching handkerchief made up of the rich earth-tone colors of sienna, ash, and gold. A pair of two-carat diamond studs flashed blinding light like the sun from his earlobes. The sweet diamond-cluster ring on his left pinky was stiff competition for the studs, but the humongous diamonds in the tennis bracelet on his right wrist refused to be ignored. That baby was the beast of bling. Dorian believed it cost more than the solid yellow gold Rolly splattered with diamonds he was rocking on his left wrist. His bronze Versace wingtips completed his big-baller appearance. Dorian was impressed.

He watched Luther as he hugged and kissed his mother and kept her close with his arm around her shoulders as he dapped it up with his dad. It gave photographers the ideal chance for a memorable photo op with the superstar and his parents. After posing for a few shots, Luther hugged his brothers and talked smack with them before he kissed and wrapped Noni and Rhema in bear hugs. His nieces and nephews got all of his attention after that. He showered them with hugs, kisses, and high fives and listened to their rambling. Although he was a tough and vicious-looking mountain of a man, the love shining in his eyes for his brothers' children showed his true heart. He wasn't the mean monster Harmony had described he could be. Nah, that was a front, a role he played to control the people in his circle, especially Harmony.

"Knee Baby! You won the game for me!"

Dorian and the Baxter brood looked up and laughed at little Ilyssia when she called out to her uncle. She was in her auntie's arms, giggling and waving excitedly. When they reached the family, she extended her little chubby arms to Luther, and he reached down and scooped her up. Ilyssia's squeaky laughter rose above the bustle of conversations, laughter, and flashing cameras when he kissed her face all over and growled like a grizzly bear.

"I want a new baby doll and some ice cream for winning the game."

Luther tickled his niece. "I won the game for you, but you want gifts from me?"

"Yeah!"

"Okay, Unc is gonna make it happen for his pretty princess."

"Yay!" She pumped her fists in the air.

"You played a good game, Luther," Harmony spoke slightly above a whisper with her arm looped through Dorian's. "Congrats on those four big blocks. Daddy almost broke out in the mashed potato when you threw the Titans nose guard out of your path like a ragdoll."

"Oh yeah?" He allowed a half smile to slip through his hard countenance.

"Yeah."

"Who is this?" Luther tilted his head toward Dorian and then handed Ilyssia to Marvin.

"This is Dorian Hendrix, my new friend. Dorian, meet my brother Luther Baxter, the Falcons starting four-time Pro Bowler center."

Dorian extended his hand for a shake. "What's good, man? You were a beast on the field today."

"Thanks." He gave Dorian a firm shake while staring directly into his eyes like he was trying to read him. Then he dropped his hand and snaked his arm around his mama again. "Let's go, y'all. I'm sore and tired as hell."

The introduction Harmony had dreaded was over fast and without incident, and everyone seemed relieved. But Dorian was nobody's fool. Luther didn't like him. That ice grill he'd hit him with that was supposed to have intimidated him but failed told him as much. There would be no ass kissing from Dorian, though. Whatever issues big-ass Knee Baby had with him would be worked out between them man-to-man, and he would not allow the situation to affect his relationship with Harmony or cause her grief with her brother. He cared too much about her to create drama in her life.

Dorian snaked his arm around Harmony's waist before they followed Luther and his family out of the stadium.

By the middle of the week, Harmony started feeling anxious about her upcoming solo debut. No matter how much Rhema and Noni had encouraged her and assured her she was going to sing down fire from heaven, she still couldn't shake the feeling that she was going to flop Sunday morning and embarrass herself and her family. Dorian would be so disappointed. Lawd, have mercy, that man had been amazing all week, rehearsing extensively with her and encouraging her to keep the faith. Unfortunately, nothing he'd said to her had made her feel better.

So Wednesday, Dorian came up with the idea to put music aside and pamper Harmony instead. He'd asked her to come to his midtown loft directly after work, disregarding all other business. To her surprise, he had even promised to help her grade papers if necessary. All he wanted was her in his presence in the privacy of his place so she could relax while he took care of her. And, boy, did he take care of her.

Harmony's evening of pampering had started off with a glass of merlot and a foot massage ten seconds after crossing Dorian's threshold. After that, he'd fed her white seedless grapes and the sweetest Rainier cherries while they waited for the dinner he was preparing to finish cooking. The aroma of blackened colossal shrimp, crab-stuffed portobello mushrooms topped with parmesan cheese, sautéed kale, and garlic-roasted russet potatoes had damn near tortured Harmony while they waited for the food. However, Dorian relieved her of her misery fifteen minutes later when he served her like a queen at his candlelit bistro table.

"I may have to marry you just so you can cook for me and give me foot massages every day. Everything is delicious, Dorian. Thank you."

He washed down a mouthful of potatoes with a big gulp of wine. "You ain't got to thank me, baby. You deserved to be pampered every day. What do you want me to cook for you tomorrow?"

"Nothing. I'll start back eating salads and fruit in the evenings tomorrow like I've been doing all semester. My ass is thick enough, so I'm not about to let you pack extra pounds on me. You can cook for me every Wednesday, but that's it."

"Shit, I like your thickness. That's the first thing I noticed about you the day we met. Of course, then your voice rocked my world. And I've been stuck on you ever since."

"Have you always been attracted to full-figured chicks, or am I the first?"

"Honestly?"

"Always."

"You're the first."

Harmony placed her fork on the edge of her plate. "I hope I'm not an experiment."

"Believe me, you're not. The feelings I've caught for you are real."

"I hope so."

"I wouldn't lie to you."

"Are you sure about that?"

"I promise I'll always be honest with you. I already told you that."

"Thank you."

Dorian laughed. "I ain't crazy, girl. I promise to keep it real with you because I'm scared of your brothers. Can you imagine what those big niggas would do to me if I made their baby sister cry over some bullshit? They would kick my ass, throw me on the grill with some BBQ sauce, and then eat me down to the bone."

"Oooh, I'm going to tell them what you said!" Harmony laughed and threw her cloth napkin across the table at Dorian.

He hopped off his stool, rushed around the table, and threw his arms around Harmony. "Don't tell them. You better not snitch on me and have your brothers hunting me down. Say you won't tell them." He tickled her. "Promise me you won't snitch."

"Okay! Okay! I won't snitch!"

He kissed her lips. "That's my girl."

Their lips connected again, and a passionate flame of pure lust caused Harmony's heart to skip a beat. Dorian had seeped into her pores, infiltrated her blood, and was now on his way to her heart, and there wasn't a damn thing she could do about it.

Chapter Twelve

"Her ass just walked in the house." Luther looked out the window and spotted Harmony's SUV parked behind his Bentley. He switched the phone to his other ear. "I got some words for her for rolling up in my house at five o'clock in the morning like some loose trick. I ain't with it."

"Chill out, man. She's grown. I keep telling your ass that. And she ain't gotta live in your house," Marvin reminded him in a groggy voice. "Puddin' can cash out on a crib right now if she wanted to with the money from that million-dollar insurance policy Ham made her beneficiary over. You know she ain't touched one dime of it yet. Daddy talked her into investing it, so it's somewhere stacking up and getting fat."

"I don't give a damn about that. I'm concerned about her running around with that lame-ass musician. She don't know shit about that nigga, Marvin. Puddin' don't need to be entertaining that buster until all hours of the morning. He might hurt her, man. Then I'll have to kill him."

Marvin laughed, and it only fueled Luther's anger. "Take it easy on her, and watch your words. She don't deserve to be dogged out, bruh. As a matter of fact, you shouldn't say anything to her at all. Dorian seems like a cool dude so far, and your nieces and nephews like him a lot. Mama and Daddy do too."

"Well, I don't like his ass, and I'm gonna let Puddin' know how I feel."

"Cool. But remember, if you try to steer her away from ol' dude, it'll only make her want him more."

"I'll take my chances."

"So you're lying up all night with random niggas now, Puddin'? I thought you were better than that."

Harmony reached way back and followed through with a sharp, backhanded blow to the right side of Luther's face. "Was that a code phrase for calling me a slut?"

He rubbed his jaw and glared at her as their early morning standoff on the staircase began. Harmony wasn't surprised that Luther had come out of his room to confront her on her trek up the stairs. He'd had every right to question her about staying out all night out of concern. But what he didn't have the right to do was imply that she had been "lying up" with Dorian or any other man for that matter.

"Damn, girl, you're so in love with that dude already that you're swinging on me?"

Harmony was so angry and emotionally wounded that her whole body was shaking. She wanted to cry. That's how bad Luther had hurt her feelings. But she was ready to fight his ass at the same time for believing she was so thirsty and whorish that she'd put her good home training aside and stay out all night long during the workweek just to fuck a man. Hell, she could've invited Dorian to her bed if dick was all she'd wanted.

"Get out of my way!" she screamed with tears threatening to spill from her eyes.

Luther shifted his massive body, blocking her from clearing the next step. "I don't like that guy, Puddin'. Something about him gives me a bad vibe."

"You don't even know him!"

"And you don't either."

Harmony gave up on holding back her tears. Her brother's words had hit their mark—her heart. "I'm trying to get to know him. And for your information, he has been nothing but a gentleman to me."

"Humph, let's see if he'll continue to be a gentleman now that he done popped them panties last night."

Harmony balled up her right hand into a tight fist and drew it back, ready to pound Luther like she'd done many times when they were kids and teenagers. Then she changed her mind when she suddenly realized kicking his ass wouldn't solve anything. Luther believed what he believed.

"Not that it's any of your business, but Dorian didn't *pop my panties* last night or any other night. He hasn't even tried to because he respects me. I fell asleep on his couch, watching a movie. I ain't like those easy, sleazy tramps you fool around with. I'm still the lady Bobby and Corrine Baxter raised me to be. But when I feel like letting Dorian or Tom, Dick, or Harry *pop my panties*, oh, baby, I will! You know why? Because I'm a grown-ass woman, and I can screw whoever the hell I want to screw! Go to hell, Knee Baby!"

This time, Harmony pushed past Luther with all her might, almost sending his big ass tumbling down the stairs. She was livid, and her heart was broken because of his lack of trust in her and his blatant disrespect. Yes, he was her brother and best friend, and he had always taken care of her, but now it was time for him to cut her some slack so she could spread her wings and start enjoying life again.

Of course, Luther was still mourning Ham's death, just like Harmony, but it was time that he embraced the fact that his best friend wasn't coming back. No amount of love, grief, or tears could raise his life-long buddy and college roommate from the dead. Besides, Ham was in a better place, and he wouldn't want to come back to this cruel world. He no longer had to take blood-pressure and high-cholesterol medications or endure insulin injections to control his diabetes. Harmony would never have to prepare another bland, low-sodium, high-protein meal to help him lose weight. The constant headaches and back pains were over. God had called His good and faithful servant home and healed him from all sickness. It was tragic that Ham had lost his life in a one-car accident after suffering a heart attack while driving, but the Lord worked in mysterious ways.

Harmony had finally wrapped her mind around the fact that the only man she'd ever loved, her fiancé and number-one fan, was gone forever. And knowing Henry James "Ham" Perry better than anyone else, she believed deep down in her heart he would want her to move on and live her best life even if it included a new chance at love and happiness with Dorian.

Dorian was on his way out of his church office when his desk phone rang. After checking his watch, he realized he had about thirty minutes to spare, so he dropped his jacket and briefcase on his desk, sat back down, and pushed the button to connect the call via speaker phone.

"This is Dorian Hendrix. How may I help you?"

"Dorian, it's Reverend Cleveland. How are you, young man?"

"I'm well, Rev. How about you?"

"I'm blessed and have no complaints. How's it going at Light of the World? Do you have the choir making a joyful noise?"

The rev's question put a smile on Dorian's face. "Yeah, I've got them rocking. I'm working with a group of exceptionally talented people. The choir members and musicians down here take the Lord's business seriously. They're truly committed to their calling."

"I'm glad to hear that. Um, how are you faring with the, uh, sisters? I hope you're on your best behavior. You promised me you—"

"Rev, it's cool. I'm behaving with the ladies as promised."

"Thank God, because I told Reverend Holloway you were a decent young man who just got caught up with the wrong woman. And because of the solid friendship we established during our days at the Morehouse School of Religion many years ago, he took me at my word and gave you a chance despite the scandal you'd been involved in up here."

"I'm aware of that, and I'll always be grateful to you for making the recommendation to Reverend Holloway on my behalf and to him for accepting me in light of my circumstances."

"There's no need to get sappy and sentimental on me, son. Just make me proud and do the right thing. Serve Reverend Holloway and Light of the World with honor in Jesus' name. Then find you a nice, wholesome girl to settle down with. Marry her and have a tribe of babies. Georgia has some mighty fine women. They're usually pretty and curvaceous and can cook like nobody's business. I should know, because First Lady Valeria is a sweet Georgia peach, and she has thoroughly satisfied my emotional and physical needs for forty-one years."

"I'll keep that in mind, sir." A vision of Harmony sleeping peacefully on his sofa this morning popped up in his mind's eye, and his heart started beating double time.

"Yes, you do that, son." The reverend chuckled. "Please give my regards to Reverend Holloway and First Lady Patricia Anne."

"Will do, sir."

"Thank you. Well, enjoy the rest of your day, Dorian."

"I'll try, Reverend Cleveland. You do the same. Goodbye."

After disconnecting the call, Dorian leaned back in his chair, thinking about the circumstances that had caused him to flee Chicago and seek refuge in Atlanta. Although he and Harmony weren't officially a couple, it was the one thing in his past he didn't want her to know about, at least not now while their courtship was still so new and promising. If they became more serious in the future, he wouldn't hesitate to confide in her about his worst transgression ever. He would owe her that much. Honesty was all she had asked of him, and he'd be damned if he would deny her that one simple request. No matter what, he would tell her everything when the time was right. Until then, it would remain the dreaded secret that haunted him more often than not.

"Did you hear that, Jade?" Dorian raised his head and looked around the dark bedroom.

Jade squeezed her long dancer's legs tighter around his waist and palmed his ass to pull him farther into her body. "No, I didn't hear a damn thing, bae."

Another series of thuds sounded from downstairs, and Dorian distinctly heard them, but he couldn't stop to check them out even if he'd wanted to. He was balls deep in some sweet pussy that had a monster grip on his dick. It was borrowed pussy, but it was his at the moment. Dude was deep stroking on a hundred, hitting sensitive nooks and crannies and turning corners like a madman. He was fucking Jade so good that she was digging her nails in his back and screaming all kinds of crazy shit at the top of her lungs.

"Damn it, I'm cumming, bae! Oh shit, I'm about to cum!"

"Ah, fuck!" Dorian's face contorted when his balls grew tight. His nut was stirring around in the pit of his stomach, causing every damn muscle in his anatomy to contract. He couldn't slow down, and pulling out wasn't an option.

"Oh, Doriaaaaan!" The headboard slammed like crazy against the wall when Jade began to buck her hips aggressively through her climax. "Goddamn it, Doriaaaaan!"

"What the hell is going on here?" The roaring male voice was followed by several pounding footsteps. Flashing lights from a cell phone camera sliced through the darkness repeatedly. "Jade, baby, how could you do this to me? Why, girl? You know I love you!"

Dorian rolled off the bed and dropped to the floor when the man he now realized was Reverend Jackson, the assistant pastor of his church, flew through the air and dove toward him.

"J.P., what are you doing here? You were supposed to be in Indianapolis." Jade threw her hand up, apparently to block the video and cell phone camera from capturing direct images of her face. But her breasts and the rest of her naked body were on full display.

The good reverend snatched his fiancée by her bleach blond hair and started punching her in the face. His adrenaline-induced rage seemed almost impossible to contain for a now-partially dressed Dorian, who was trying to pull him off of Jade. Then the sound of a gun cocking decelerated the whole chaotic scene into a blur of slow motion.

Dorian jumped in his seat at the sound of the echoing bang. With beads of perspiration covering his forehead, he looked at his closed office door as his unexpected visitor continued to knock hard and nonstop.

Grateful to escape his trudge down memory lane, he called out, "Come in!"

Chapter Thirteen

Luther entered Dorian's office and closed the door. "We need to talk." Without waiting for an invitation or even asking permission, he crossed the room and lowered his towering frame into the chair facing the desk.

Dorian just eyeballed Luther's cocky ass and waited for him to state his business.

"I ain't got a lot of time to waste talking because I need to get to practice. So I'm just gonna speak my piece and be out."

Dorian wasn't with that shit. "Nah, man, if you had the balls to roll up in my office unannounced, then after you say whatever you came to say, you will hear me out. It's called respect, my man."

"Are you respecting my sister? Did you show her any respect last night when she was at your crib?"

"Absolutely."

Luther narrowed his eyes. "Then how come she didn't make it home until five o'clock this morning?"

"She was exhausted from work. So when she fell asleep while we were watching *The Equalizer 2,* I covered her with a blanket and allowed her to rest. How would you have handled the situation, Luther? Would you have woken her up and sent her home anyway, knowing she was tired?"

"I just wanna make sure your intentions toward my baby sister are legit. She's been through hell and back over the past two years after losing her fiancé in a car accident. Her sanity was on the line because of her guilt and the way Ham's family turned on her over the insurance money. That's why I moved her up here with me." Luther swiped his hand through the air. "I'm sure she already told you the story."

Wrong. No, she didn't.

"Luther, my intentions concerning Harmony are legit. I would never do anything intentionally to hurt her. We're in the very early stages of building our relationship, and we may hit a bump or a pothole every now and then. But we care enough about each other to work through our issues if possible or cut our losses and walk away in order to save the friendship if we find ourselves facing the impossible."

Luther nodded his head as if he understood where Dorian was coming from. "Why my sister, though, nigga? Out of all these exotic-looking, fine chicks at the church and all over Atlanta and the surrounding areas, why did you have to pick her? You're an okay-looking dude, and women love musicians. You could have any hottie you want, so why did you decide to shoot your shot at Harmony?"

"Would you prefer a collection of cubic zirconias over a single flawless diamond, my man? If given the choice between a fleet of brand-new Toyotas and Hondas and a fully loaded, top-of-the-line Rolls-Royce Cullinan with all the best features available and in your favorite color, which prize would you claim?"

Luther's blank stare and silence screamed his truth, his real issue with Dorian dating Harmony. The revealing silence was bouncing off all four walls. Luther's unspoken concern was loud and crystal clear, and it pissed Dorian off down to his core. The protective big brother didn't believe a decent-looking, upstanding guy with swag and his own money could have a genuine romantic interest in his baby sister because she was a full-figured sista. Luther couldn't look beyond Harmony's weight and see her beauty, grace, and feminine charm. He was obviously blind to how sexy she was, too. All Luther saw when he looked at his baby sister was a fat girl who no man in his right man except his late buddy, Ham, could ever love.

"No matter what you see when you look at your sister, my view of her is altogether different. Harmony Baxter is feminine flawlessness, and I'm happy she's in my life."

"So you'll do right by her?"

"Absolutely."

"And you won't break her heart?"

Dorian shook his head. "Never. Not intentionally anyway."

"You better not." Luther stood up. "'Cause if you do, I'll destroy you."

"You would have every right to, my man."

Harmony jerked in her seat when her cell phone buzzed inside her purse out of the blue. Everyone who really knew her knew she was in choir rehearsal every Thursday evening, so she had no idea who had texted her. She reached down and picked up her phone to check the message.

Dorian: Meet me at the Waffle House around the corner as soon as rehearsal is over.

Harmony covered her smile with her hand before allowing her eyes to float over to the organ. Dorian was too damn good-looking to be winking and licking his lips at her in church. Something about the way it made her feel seemed sinful.

Harmony: Can't. Promised Luther I would cook him a roast & potatoes. Need 2 finish crocheting a poncho 4 a display model 4 my last class 2.

Dorian: Put all that on hold for 1 hour. I need 2 see u.

Harmony: Why?

Dorian: Cuz if I can't hold u and kiss u tonight I will die.

If Harmony were anywhere close to being the ho Luther thought she was, she would say damn his roast and those freaking potatoes, and she would forget all about the poncho for her sixth-period class and meet Dorian at his house instead of the Waffle House. And she would let him do a helluva lot more than hold and kiss her. The brotha would be all up in her, tapping her spot with that big ol' dick of his that always got cast-iron hard whenever they kissed and held each other close. But she was nobody's ho, and she never had been. However, she was going to be the ultimate ho for her husband if the Lord would be so kind to bless her with one.

Could Dorian be the one?

Harmony's phoned buzzed again during Sister Mazie Brown's long, drawn-out speech about Voices of Victory's upcoming fundraiser, which would be another bake sale/fish fry. Per usual, it would go down in the empty lot across the street from her raggedy-ass house in the Bluff, one of Atlanta's roughest and most crime-infested neighborhoods.

The alto to Harmony's left, a makeup artist named Epiphany, shot her a side-eye and kissed her teeth. Harmony wasn't thinking about that bony heifer. She ignored her and peeped at her phone.

Dorian: U coming baby? Please.

Harmony: Yeah but I can only stay 15 mins.

Dorian: I'll take whatever I can get.

Just a few more steps, Harmony mentally encouraged herself every time she lifted one of her aching feet and placed it back down. Her little secret meeting with Dorian had lasted way past the designated fifteen minutes, which meant she didn't get home until after midnight. Unfortunately, that prime-choice roast she'd seasoned like a gourmet chef Tuesday night, and the russet potatoes Ritza had peeled, diced, and dropped into a bowl of water, were waiting for her in the fridge when she arrived. The incomplete poncho she had been working on all week was chilling in her work area in the laundry room, too. But the modern-day superwoman had easily knocked out both tasks and was now ready for a long, hot shower and her bed.

Harmony didn't expect sleep to come easy, though. Her mind would be too busy sifting through the pros and cons of accepting Dorian's invitation to a weekend getaway to Savannah a week from tomorrow. He'd definitely stolen a few kisses and squeezed her body tight in his muscular arms when they'd met at the Waffle House, but his main purpose for asking Harmony to see him tonight had been to drop his bombshell invitation on her. It had turned out to be the most romantic moment they had shared so far. And Harmony was still reeling from the thrill of it as well as the shock.

Just as she reached the landing and started her slow creep past the master suite, the door opened, and Luther appeared in a pair of flannel Falcons pajama bottoms and a wife beater. Their eyes connected, but neither of them uttered a word. His unexpected emergence was supposed to have intimidated Harmony, but it didn't. She didn't have head space for Luther and his antics. The only things worthy of her time and contemplation were her solo debut at church Sunday morning and her answer to Dorian's invitation.

I know I'm not worthy, Lord,
But please let it fall down on me!

"Sing, girl! Hallelujah!"
"Let the Lord use you, honey!"

Yeah, yeah, yeah
Let Your flowing favor fall down on meee!

"Glory to God!"
"Thank you, Jesus!"
"Hallelujah!"

Like lightning, the praise break popped off. Shouting, clapping, dancing, and stomping spread throughout the sanctuary like a California wildfire. The Holy Ghost was in the building pouring out blessings all over Light of the World Missionary Baptist Church. The musicians, led by Dorian, were jamming some fiery praise music, and the saints caught up in the Spirit were giving God irrational praise. But the woman, Christ's vessel, who'd sung the anointing down from glory, had returned to her seat on the second row of the alto section virtually unnoticed.

One person had noticed her, though, and he couldn't snatch his eyes away from her. Even as his fingers floated skillfully up and down the organ keys, Dorian's gaze drank in the essence of the woman whose voice was God's gift to the world, and she had used it this morning to bless His people. Now while her fellow church members were getting their praise on, Harmony was smiling at them and waving her hand like she hadn't just brought them face-to-face with the Creator. Dorian was awestruck by her humility.

As the praise break started to dwindle down, Harmony caught Dorian staring at her, and she quickly shifted her eyes away from his. That one brief look was all it took to raise his body temperature. Something weird was going on inside of Dorian, and he couldn't identify it. He was having thoughts he'd never entertained before, and if he went more than three hours without texting Harmony or hearing her voice, his world seemed to pause. They hadn't even been intimate, yet he was already stuck on her. He hated it, and he would not voice his feelings to anyone, not even his mother or his sister, but he was definitely stuck on Harmony.

Reverend Holloway stood and took his place behind the podium immediately after the praise break ended. He beamed with pride and asked Harmony to stand up and take a bow. The congregation gave her a standing ovation, and in return, she offered them a pretty smile. Still in awe, Dorian blew her a kiss and joined everyone else in applause.

That's my baby. She doesn't know it yet, but she is.

Chapter Fourteen

Amari snatched off her strappy stiletto sandals and threw them across her bedroom.

Li'l V came running into her room. "Mama, what's wrong?"

"Boy, get your ass outta here and leave me alone! And close my goddamn door!"

The child left the room without a word and closed the door behind him, which was a very smart move because his mama was furious. Dorian and that big-booty Hillary or Heavenly or whatever the hell her name was had pulled a fast one on Amari and the choir. How dare she hide that she had an average voice and soloist goals? And how the hell did that nigga even know her fat ass could sing in the first place? He had probably let her audition for him after she'd sucked his dick.

Amari stripped out of her floral maxi dress and left it on the floor. Her phone was chiming off the rails with text message notifications. More than likely, Joette and the crew wanted to gossip about the big solo shakeup, but Amari was too pissed to discuss it right now. Her girls on the usher board were probably reaching out too, being nosy. No doubt the whole church was talking about the new director of music and his surprise soloist.

It was *sooo* embarrassing that she, Amari Simmons, the best singer in the choir, had been overlooked by the new director of music in favor of some overweight, mediocre-singing bitch. What kinda shit was that? And what was up with the secrecy behind Miss Piggy's solo debut? Amari couldn't understand it. She didn't understand Dorian either. How could he prefer fucking some chunky-ass trick over her? Maybe he was gay.

Maybach, Amari's cousin's baby daddy, paid her brain a quick visit. He was a club and concert promoter in Chicago, so she was pretty sure he had to deal with musicians from time to time. Maybe he and Dorian had crossed paths. If not, Maybach could find somebody who knew the nigga. Amari hoped so, because there was something shady about Mr. Hendrix, and she wanted to know all about it. Never a girl to waste time, she crossed the room, grabbed her phone, and scrolled her contacts for her cousin's number. Amari was now on a mission.

"What about these?" Harmony held up a pair of red lace boy shorts. "There's a matching bra in one of these bags."

"Girrrl, you're going to make that man lose his mind in those."

"Mmm-hmmm, listen to Noni, Puddin'. You know she's the sex doctor in the family with her nasty ass."

Noni threw a ball of yarn at Rhema and stuck out her tongue.

Harmony dangled a silk fuchsia thong from her index finger. "I don't know what possessed me to buy these when I know my ass is too big to wear stuff like this."

"Oooh!" Noni and Rhema screeched in a duet.

Harmony jumped up from her bed and rushed over to close the door. "Have y'all heifers lost your minds? Do y'all want Knee Baby running up in here acting a fool? He's right down the hall in his room."

"We're sorry, girl. Me and Rhema are just happy Dorian is about to re-pop that cherry. Chile, you're a virgin all over again."

"I am not!" Harmony cracked up. "You two think y'all know everything. What if Dorian isn't interested in 'doing it' this weekend? He may just want to visit Savannah. Y'all know it's a historical city. I might've bought all of this lingerie and that cocktail dress for nothing."

"Aw, Puddin', I know you've been off the meat market for a while, but nothing has changed. Men are still the same as they've been since caves. Dorian invited you to Savannah because y'all have been kicking it for a few weeks, and he likes you. Ain't that right, Noni?"

"Yep. He's feeling you, girl, and he wants to show you just how much. That means he wants to make love to you, boo. And a romantic getaway on the Savannah Riverwalk seems like the right time and place to make it happen. You're going to enjoy having that man all to yourself, even if it's just for a mini vay-cay. It ain't how much time you got to get it. It's how good you get it in the time you got."

"Well, I hope I remember how to *get it in* when the time comes. It's not like I'm rolling in experience. Y'all know Ham was the only one. We had a decent love life, but I always felt like something was missing. We did the same thing the same way every time."

"What?" Noni looked at her sister-in-law and shook her head. "You poor thing."

"Ham was pretty basic, y'all. I swear. No tricks or toys or kinky stuff."

"Did you ever cum?"

"No. Not during actual intercourse. I only had an orgasm when he played with it and whenever he went down on me."

Rhema sat down on the bed next to Harmony and placed a hand on her shoulder. "You'll be fine. It's just like riding a bi—"

"Don't tell her that bullshit!" Noni walked over and stood in front of them. "Yes, you will be fine, Puddin', but I want you to give that man something he can feel. Let him introduce you to his world of pleasure, and don't be shy about it. Get in touch with your inner freak. She's down in there somewhere. Ain't nothing wrong with letting a man smack it, flip it, and rub it down."

The three Baxter sisters-in-law shared a laugh.

"I'm just so nervous and worried."

"Why?" Rhema pressed.

"Dorian ain't ever been with a big girl before. I hope he'll like the way I look in lingerie."

"He'll like it for two whole minutes before he rips it off your ass just like Nat always does."

"I hope so." Harmony spotted her phone on the dresser. "I've bought all of this new stuff and told y'all I'm going to Savannah with Dorian, but I haven't told him yet. I guess I better call him with my answer."

"Put him on speaker phone so Rhema and I can hear the excitement in his voice when you tell him."

Harmony went to the dresser and picked up her phone. After dialing Dorian's number, she pressed the speaker phone icon and waited for him to answer. She chewed her thumbnail and stared at the phone anxiously while it rang.

"What's up, beautiful? I was just thinking about you."

"Really?"

"Yeah, girl. I'm always thinking about you."

"That's sweet."

"What's up, baby?"

"I decided to go to Savannah with you Friday. I've already made arrangements for a substitute teacher, so we can leave around noon like you planned."

"I'm happy you decided to come with me. I wouldn't have made the trip without you," he confessed with a hint of a smile in his voice. "Expect a good time, girl. I'm going to give you the world on a silver platter in one weekend. By the time I bring you back home, you'll be in love with me."

Speechless and aroused, Harmony cut her eyes at Noni and Rhema. They were giggling silently and rolling all over the bed like a pair of silly toddlers. She swallowed hard and continued listening to Dorian talk about their upcoming getaway.

"Keep the change, ma'am." Dorian handed the bag of caramel popcorn to Harmony with a smile and curved his arm around her waist again.

"Thank you."

Dorian did a visual sweep of their surroundings, taking in the hundreds of people exploring the many shops, attractions, and restaurants along Savannah's famous River Street. The bite from the chilly, early November weather didn't take away from the beauty of the river. The view of the sun slowly making its descent over the lazy current was evidence of God's handiwork. Entertainment boats and industrial vessels shared the water equally as tourists and workers aboard each barely acknowledged each other.

With the crook of his arm resting in the arch of Harmony's back, Dorian asked, "What do you want to do now?"

"I don't know. What do you want to do?"

"Remember the jazz singer we saw on that poster in front of the French bistro?"

Harmony swallowed a mouthful of caramel popcorn and licked the excess of gooey drizzle from her fingers. "Yeah, I remember."

"I wouldn't mind checking out his first set. It starts in about an hour."

"I think I'd like to see him too."

"Come on, baby! The boy is bad! Did you hear him scatting? Ella Fitzgerald was smiling down from heaven. I swear!"

"His performance was just okay for me, Dorian. It was very safe and robotic. He couldn't have gone off on a freestyle tangent in his wildest dream because he would've lost his rehearsed groove. No showmanship. How is that impressive?"

Dorian looked up into Harmony's eyes from his comfortable slouch on his back on the sofa. He had been relaxing with his head on her lap since returning to their riverfront hotel suite after the jazz show. "You really studied his performance, huh?"

"Yep." Harmony smiled.

"And what grade did you give the poor cat?"

"Overall, he earned a firm B. His repertoire was nice. It told a cute love story for those of us who were able to connect the dots. In my opinion, his tone trumped his vocal skills, and his stage presentation, including his good looks, hid his lack of spontaneity. I was waiting for him to let go and bust it wide open just one time during his performance."

"Damn, girl, you're more ruthless than Simon Cowell. Remind me to never ask you to critique me."

Harmony thumped Dorian playfully on the forehead before she stifled a yawn with the back of her hand.

"You're tired, baby. Why don't you take a shower, slip into something more comfortable, and relax? I can hop in when you're done. Then we can chill and watch a movie over that bottle of Shiraz chilling in the fridge."

"A long, hot shower sounds like a dream."

"Go ahead then. I'm about to check my email and the choir's social media pages."

"Oh my God!" Harmony buried her face in Dorian's chest when the pickup truck driven by the good guy in the movie in chase of his nemesis careened over a cliff.

She couldn't see the many times the truck flipped and slammed against boulders and trees, but she heard the sounds of each impact. The crunch of the metal grated her nerves, causing her body to jerk. Her nails' sharp edges sank into the flesh on Dorian's forearm when the truck exploded into flames. The bang and its echoes ripped through her and ushered in memories she'd been running from for two years. Harmony had not been in the truck with Ham or anywhere near the scene of the crash the night he was killed, but she knew the horrifying details, and they broke her heart into a million pieces.

Harmony didn't even realize she was crying until her soft whimpers began to resound in her own ears. She lifted her head and wiped her tears away with her fingertips. Harmony was ashamed of crying her eyes out over her deceased lover when Dorian had gone through so much trouble to show her a good time on their getaway. "I'm sorry."

Dorian aimed the remote control at the TV and turned it off. "You owe me no apology, baby." He tightened his arm around her shoulders and kissed her temple. "Talk to me. Tell me about the accident that killed your fiancé."

"Who told you he died in an accident?"

"Luther."

"When?"

"He came to see me the other day at the church to warn me about respecting you."

"Why didn't you tell me?"

"I didn't think it was important. Now tell me about the accident."

Chapter Fifteen

"He had taken three of his senior football players to Atlanta to meet with college recruiters and members of the coaching staff from University of Georgia, Georgia Tech, and Clemson. The boys looked up to Ham, my fiancé, as a father figure because their dads were nowhere to be found."

"Football coaches usually play the surrogate-father role to many boys on their teams. Ham sounds like he was a stand-up guy."

"He was." Harmony wiped away a lone tear trickling down her cheek. "That's why he decided to do something so damn foolish."

"It's okay, baby. It's okay."

"No, it's not, Dorian. Ham had no business on the road. I told him I would be fine if he couldn't make it to my . . . my performance. I told him not to come. I knew it was too much for him."

"Where did you have to perform?"

"It was the first time in history the city of Gray had asked an African American to sing for the lighting of the Christmas tree in the town square. For years, the committee had overlooked awesome black singers for white singers who couldn't even hold a tune. Lots of people of all races had complained about it, but nothing had changed. And then, unexpectedly, it happened. I was totally floored. The mayor called me personally and asked me to sing, and I said yes. But there was a conflict."

"I'm still listening."

"The tree lighting ceremony fell on the same day Ham's boys would be working out with some collegiate football players. Then they were supposed to attend a Falcons game the following day, thanks to Luther." Harmony sniffled and closed her eyes tight, and Dorian could see the pain in her features. "Daddy was going to record me, and Ham knew it. Why he chose to rush down from Atlanta to surprise me still drives me insane even today. I told him not to come, Dorian. I specifically told him, and he said he wouldn't make the drive."

"But he tried to surprise you anyway."

Harmony nodded with tears flowing heavily down both cheeks now.

"It wasn't your fault, sweetheart." Dorian wiped her face with his palm and pulled her closer to him with his free arm. "The man wanted to hear his woman sing so badly that he risked making the trip and lost his life because of it. It was his choice, Harmony. There wasn't anything you could've done about it. Again, it wasn't your fault."

"I hear you, and I know you're telling me the truth, but it still hurts like hell. The coroner said Ham had a massive heart attack that caused him to lose control of his SUV. He ran off a long country road into a heavily wooded area twelve miles away from the town square. The truck didn't stop rolling until it crashed into a gigantic oak tree. I'll never know if the heart attack killed him or if it was his injuries from the crash. All I know is he's gone forever."

Dorian hugged Harmony and allowed her to cry out her pain and unmerited guilt against his chest. She was no more responsible for her late fiancé's death than Barack Obama was. Ham had died honorably trying to please his woman. She was the same woman who had Dorian acting sprung, although he hadn't even sampled her goodies yet. And she had him making road trips so he could selfishly isolate her from the rest of the world if only for a weekend. After carefully assessing the tragic situation, Dorian could relate to Ham. Harmony was like an addictive drug. Just being in her presence made a man want to hang around for eternity.

Dorian didn't know how things would pan out between him and Harmony because he didn't have a plan. However, there were a few things he knew for sure. For starters, he would help her heal from her pain no matter what he had to do. Their weekend getaway was still going be a special time she would always remember. Dorian refused to let her past ruin her present with him. And most important of all, he would keep his promise to Luther. Never, ever, would he intentionally disrespect her or break her heart.

"Let me hit that."

Joette rolled her eyes before she passed the blunt to Amari.

"Can you believe Maybach ain't called Alikah with the scoop on that nigga Dorian yet?" Amari took a long pull on the blunt and inhaled the smoke from the potent herb. She didn't hold it in very long because the Kush was so strong that it almost made her cough up a lung.

"That man is up in Chi-Town grinding for coins. The mission you got him on don't pay him shit. You need to hire a private investigator if it's that important to you."

Joette and her girls laughed at her shade, but Amari didn't find the humor in it.

"That's easy for you to say, Joette, because you're used to being Jermaine and never Michael. Bitch, you don't even know how it feels to be Tito. Has your hand ever held a mic?"

This time, Amari's shade got the laughs, and Joette joined in like it didn't even faze her.

"Fuck you, Mari. I don't care about leading a song in the choir. This sinner is just proud to be up there giving God some praise. That's why I lift my voice." She pointed her finger at Amari. "I don't give a damn about fucking a musician who wouldn't piss on me if I was on fire. You need to leave that man alone. He don't want your ass, and he don't need you to sing for him, either. He's got Harmony to sing his songs and do anything else his sexy ass wants. Oh, and by the way, that girl can sing her face off. The Spirit ain't ever fell in our church like that in all the thirteen years I've been a member there. Everybody was talking about how beautiful Harmony's voice is. Ain't that right, LeLe and Yim?"

Both ladies quietly looked away when Amari narrowed her eyes to thin slits at them.

Sensing their guilt, she exhaled smoke from her flaring nostrils and smashed the blunt out in an ashtray on the coffee table. "How 'bout all three of you bitches get up out my house? It seems like y'all been lip flipping on me. Y'all shady as fuck. Get out!" She hopped off the sofa, ran to her front door, and snatched it open. "I bet y'all gonna miss me Friday after them edges backslide and that glue starts losing its grip. Low-down heifers."

"Uh-oh! Uh-oh! She can't handle it! My baby can't handle that Bankhead Bounce!"

Harmony threw her head back and laughed from her gut, but she kept wiggling her hips and snapping her fingers to the rhythm of the music. Dorian had some smooth moves, but she couldn't take him seriously on the dance floor because all he wanted to do was compete with her. So far, they were even on the scoreboard. Harmony had aced him when they'd joined a group of other dancers in the Wobble, but he had a nasty turn on the Cupid Shuffle that had blown her away. Now they were free styling, and he was still trying to score points.

Dorian hit Harmony with an old-school, Jackson 5 spin and started thrusting his lower body in the middle of "Jungle Boogie" by Kool & The Gang. "What you know about that, baby? What you know about that?"

Harmony didn't clap back with words. Instead, she did a graceful twirl on her stilettos and started twerking on him. She felt her ass cheeks jiggling and clapping together rhythmically. She rolled her hips to add a little more spice to it. Then the devil told her to drop it. She didn't want to hurt Dorian like that, but she couldn't resist the temptation.

"Whoooa!" He enfolded her in his arms from behind and kissed the side of her neck. "You can't be doing that kind of shit in public. You're gonna have me kicking every nigga's ass on the boat for trying to get at you. Let's go take a moonlight stroll on the upper deck before the captain heads back to the port."

Arm in arm, they left the dance floor and headed up the stairs. Harmony felt confident in her black, beaded cocktail dress. The low sweetheart neckline was giving everyone generous cleavage. She had swept her hair into a curly up-do with soft tendrils framing her face. In her opinion, she and Dorian made a fabulous couple because his black suit and his silk black dress shirt complemented her look perfectly. Neither had known the other would be dressed in black, but the universe had coordinated their fashion selections.

"I can't remember the last time I went dancing."

"Did you have a good time?" Dorian leaned over the safety rail, looking out on the river.

"It was the best night of my life. Thank you for bringing me here."

"It was my pleasure."

The hum of the riverboat's engine and the subtle rocking motion over the waves kept them company during the silence. Harmony didn't know what was on Dorian's mind, but she had love on hers. He had been the perfect gentleman, totally respecting her since the first moment they'd met. Not once had he made her feel uncomfortable or unwanted. Harmony had enjoyed every moment they had shared, whether they'd been working on music or just sipping wine while watching a movie. His kisses were always sweet but fiery, and he could work her big toe during a foot massage like he'd been born to do it. All the time they had spent in each other's presence had been great, but Harmony wanted to take things to the next level. But she couldn't dare tell him that.

As if he'd read her mind, he pulled her to him and pecked her lips lightly. Then he stepped back, allowing her to study his gaze. The combustible passion flickering in his orbs gave her a hot flash in the midst of the breeze rising over the river. Noni and Rhema sure did know about the ways of men. Dorian wanted her. He'd brought her to Savannah to escape their everyday lives, but there was definitely another part to his agenda. As Harmony lived and breathed, she knew beyond a shadow of a doubt he would make love to her tonight.

They were so caught up in the magic of the moment that they didn't realize the boat had reached the port until the dull, bass squeak of the horn sounded, startling them. No words were necessary at this point because Dorian's eyes had conveyed the message clearly. Harmony placed her hand in his open palm and allowed him to escort her across the deck to the extended platform and onto the dock.

"We could stop and have a nightcap in the hotel lounge before we turn in if you'd like."

"No, thank you. I'm fine."

"Are you sure, baby?"

Harmony nodded.

"Cool. Well, to the room . . ."

Yeah, to the room . . .

Chapter Sixteen

Harmony stepped out of the bathroom and added life to Dorian's most desired fantasy. He'd been waiting patiently for this moment, and now that it had finally arrived, he intended to give her all of him so she would forever cherish the memory of this night in her heart. He removed a remote control from the pocket of his pajama bottoms and aimed at the smart TV.

Let me hold you tight
If only for one night
Let me keep you near
To ease away your fear

He stood from the bed and opened his arms to Harmony. "Dance with me."

She walked into his embrace without hesitation, and he felt like the luckiest man alive. Her scent and softness instantly ignited a fire in his loins that threatened his resolve, but he fought it off. This would not be a rushed experience for Harmony. She deserved so much better than that. Only thorough and methodical loving would do. If there was one woman in the world who needed to be reintroduced to romance and sexual pleasure, it was the gorgeous woman in his arms. Two years had been long enough for her to live without a man's intimate touch, and he felt blessed that he would be the man touching her intimately tonight.

They were a perfect fit in each other's arms, like a bolt and screw. Dorian explored her curves with roaming hands caressing her shoulders, down to her waist and hips, and eventually her ass. He palmed it and squeezed gently, and she released a faint sigh in his ear. Her skin was smooth and silky and smelled like a bouquet of fresh wildflowers. The longer Dorian held Harmony and led her body in an easy sway with the real Luther serenading them, the harder it was for him to will his erection away. But some acts of human nature, especially those between a man and a woman, are beyond our control.

A slow, wet kiss broke the ice, and the lust in the air shot straight through the roof. Their hungry tongues licked and latched on to one another feverishly. Dorian's deep groans and Harmony's soft purrs created an erotic melody, a sultry duet mating call.

He took a backward step, now holding her in a loose embrace. He wanted to see her eyes. No, he needed to see her eyes for a sign of confirmation that she was ready to give herself completely over to him. The instant their gazes came together, Dorian knew all he needed to know. Harmony's eyes had darkened in hue, and her pupils were shimmering with pure lust. He released her and took another step back.

"You're so damn beautiful. Just let me look at you." Dorian retook his seat on the bed and scooted back for a better view. "Model your sexy lingerie for me."

Shyness covered Harmony's face. She lowered her eyes as she stood before Dorian.

"Take off your robe. I want to see you, baby. Don't be shy."

With coy and timid movements, Harmony removed her short, lavender kimono and placed it on the edge of the bed. Dorian released a low growl and stroked his dick through his flannel pajama bottoms as his eyes crept over her well-defined curves. Her lavender lace negligee with spaghetti straps teased his libido beyond the limit, but he wanted to see more of her delicate butterscotch skin.

"Turn around."

Harmony gave Dorian two 360-degree twirls and faced him again.

"I want to see all of you."

"Dorian, I—"

"Come on, baby, take it off for me."

"But—"

Dorian left the bed and approached Harmony. He felt her body tremble when he took her in his arms. "You are the most gorgeous woman on the planet, and I love everything about you, including your body. You don't ever have to be shy or feel insecure with me. I want you to feel comfortable and free in my presence at all times. Do you understand?"

"Yeah."

Dorian slid the thin straps over Harmony's shoulders and down her arms. When they reached her fingertips, the negligee fell and pooled around her ankles. Dorian sensed her uneasiness over being fully exposed, but he wished she could see what his eyes saw when he looked at her. Her body was exquisite in every way. There were no flaws, insufficiencies, or excesses. Harmony was pretty well stacked, and Dorian's dick appreciated her thickness.

He lowered his head and made love to her mouth with his until he felt her body sway in his arms after her knees buckled. He leaned down and wrapped his arms around her hips and lifted her in the air. Harmony's legs encircled his waist right before he turned around and walked toward the bed. He placed her in the middle of the mattress and stepped back to gaze at her voluptuous body again. Dorian made haste removing his pajama bottoms as he watched Harmony watching him with ravenous eyes that doubled in size when she saw his big, hard dick pointing in her direction. She blinked several times with her bottom lip pinched between her teeth.

When Dorian joined Harmony on the bed, he reached for her, and she rolled over into his arms. Their kisses were spicier this time, and the sweet aroma of hot sexual desire wafted in the air. Dorian positioned his body on top of Harmony's and began a trail of kisses that soon moved lower to her breasts. The tip of his tongue teased one nipple, circling it slowly, and then paid equal attention to the other stiff peak. Greedy, he pulled one nipple fully into his warm mouth and suckled it, causing Harmony to coo and toss her head from side to side.

While Dorian continued to shift his oral pleasure from one tit to the other, his hand slid between their bodies. He inserted his middle finger between the hairy lips of her pussy and entered her deep wetness. It was extremely tight and hotter than boiling water. When he started sliding his finger in and out of her honey, she rocked her hips against his strokes in response. Harmony's thrusts became stronger and faster as Dorian plunged deeper and with more force. He withdrew his finger suddenly and brought it to his mouth with her liquid lust dripping down his palm. He licked his finger and then sucked it bone dry.

He rained kisses all over her belly and thighs and buried his face in her pubic hair. He inhaled deeply and exhaled warm air. Harmony's natural scent was uniquely hers. It was a potent incense that made another stream of warm blood rush to his already-swollen dick. He kissed the lips of her pussy and teased her juicy slit with his tongue before finally covering her clit with his mouth. He sucked the stiff bud and licked it from top to bottom repeatedly. Harmony ground her pussy against his face and rolled her hips. He licked, and she ground. His mouth worked its magic on her pussy, and it caused more of her nectar to coat his tongue. Dorian couldn't believe how wet and tight she was.

Harmony's thighs started to shake and tighten around Dorian's head. "Oooh, it feels so good! Please don't stop."

"Cum for me, baby." He pressed his tongue against the sensitive tip of her clit and held it briefly. "Let it go and cum for me. Go ahead, baby. Cum."

Dorian sat up and rested his body on his knees just as Harmony began to jerk and kick through her first climax of the night. He fingered her clit, and she ground her hips as the orgasm continued to rock her body. Dorian watched her facial expression, noticing that only the whites of her eyes could be seen. Beads of perspiration covered her face and neck as she continued to buck until she returned from the stars.

"Sing for me, Harmony," Dorian requested, positioning his body between her thighs.

"Huh?"

"The music ended. Sing for me while I make love to you. I don't care what you sing. I just want to hear your pretty voice."

"Ummm . . . um, I . . ."

"Sing anything." Dorian massaged Harmony's clit with the head of his penis, teasing it. "Just sing."

Looking out on the morning rain
I used to feel so inspired

Dorian penetrated Harmony a few inches, and she stopped singing. He pushed, attempting to sink farther into her depth, but he met resistance. Her pussy was flash flood wet, but her walls were tighter than tight. Dorian ran his tongue across Harmony's bottom lip and thrust on a raspy grunt. It earned him another inch or two of access to her juicy warmth, but he was a long way from where he wanted to be.

With his lips still pressed against Harmony's open mouth and their eyes fused, he whispered, "Sing."

Before the day I met you, life was so unkind
But you're the key to my peace of mind

The soulful lyrics got lost in an electrifying kiss with mating tongues devouring one another. Dorian had buried his dick within Harmony's butterscotch walls to the hilt while she was serenading him, and now he was dicking her down with fluid and deliberate strokes. He couldn't tear his eyes away from hers because the flashes of passion he saw in them each time he entered her and retreated held him prisoner. Nothing was more fascinating than watching her features as he gave her body the pleasure it deserved.

Dorian's thrusts grew more intense, and his pace quickened. The rhythm of their lovemaking was strong and consistent. Harmony gyrated and pumped her hips to match Dorian's deep grinds. The snugness of her walls hugging his dick was milking him of every ounce of energy he had. His hands were holding on to her hips tightly as he pounded in and out of her with the sound of juicy pussy smacking through the strokes.

"Fuck!"

Harmony's body trembled underneath his, and her walls contracted around his dick with no mercy. His heart beat fast and furiously in his chest, and he could actually hear his pulse thumping in his ears. Harmony was on the threshold of an orgasm. Dorian could see it in her glazed eyes, hear it in her ragged breathing, and feel it in the way her inner muscles were now choking his dick as her honey flowed continuously.

When Harmony finally unraveled, her wide, bucking hips lifted Dorian's body an inch in the air, but he maintained his hold on them and gave it right back to her by pounding her pussy aggressively until he exploded inside of her. The rush of his seed entering her body was powerful, and it weakened him, sending him into a state of dizziness. Dorian felt like he was floating in the air.

He rolled off of Harmony and cuddled her from behind with his arms encircling her waist. He inhaled the heady scent of their lovemaking lingering in the air, feeling like the king of the world. Then in a flash, he sobered from his post-orgasmic high when reality sank in. Before making love to Harmony, Dorian had felt she was the kind of woman any man would be happy to claim as his own. Now that he had experienced her good loving, he knew she was indeed a treasure. But he wanted her to be his treasure and his alone.

Dorian had never been the one-chick-at-a-time, commitment type of guy. He hadn't come across a woman who made him think about settling down like Reverend Cleveland had suggested until now. As much as he wanted to fight those feelings and deny them, the truth was whispering in his ear, and those words were flowing right to his heart. Harmony was the one. No woman in his past could compare to her, and he seriously doubted there was some chick around the corner waiting for the opportunity to satisfy his every desire. And if such a chick did exist, she was already at a disadvantage because Harmony was a woman of many talents in and outside the bedroom.

Dorian pulled the warm, damp body in his embrace closer to his chest. Sleep was calling out to him as he listened to Harmony snoring lightly. The faint rumble was a telling sign. Only a satiated woman could slip into a peaceful sleep before her lover right after such rigorous lovemaking. He smiled with pride, knowing he had pleased her. He wanted the chance to please her over and over again. And the only way a respectable woman like Harmony would be willing to give him an open invitation to her body was if he were her man.

Dorian hadn't been any woman's "man" since college. God had created too many fine black beauties for a brotha to limit himself to just one. But when there was a special one who outshined all the others you've known, being her "man" didn't seem like such a bad thing. There were advantages to being involved in an exclusive relationship, yet there were some disadvantages, too. Dorian didn't know if the good outweighed the bad or vice versa, and he was too damn exhausted to sort it all out. Right now, he was content with his friendship with Harmony, and he wanted to keep the music between them playing until it stopped or changed keys.

Chapter Seventeen

Amari realized she wasn't the only one late for church when she saw Dorian's truck speed recklessly through the parking lot and whip into his designated spot. Through her rearview mirror, she watched him exit his vehicle and jog around to the passenger's side and open the door. This motherfucker was supposed to have had his ass on that Hammond B3 organ ten minutes ago, but he was wasting precious time playing Mr. Swag to Harmony. Hell yeah, Amari knew her name now because she'd been hearing it all week whenever she ran into somebody from the church. Everybody was talking about Harmony this and Harmony that. Harmony! Harmony! Harmony! If one more person mentioned how awesome Harmony Baxter's voice was, Amari swore she'd smoke crack and shave her head bald.

"Uggggghhhhh!"

She lost it when Dorian kissed Harmony's lips and squeezed a handful of her big ass before sprinting toward the side entrance to the sanctuary. She banged both fists on the steering wheel and roared out her frustrations. What did he see in Harmony that he didn't see in her? He had given her fat ass the solo part on his original song without auditioning her or any other singers. And his shady ass was definitely fucking big girl. Amari knew that dreamy look a woman gave a man when he was standing up in that pussy and walking around in it barefoot. She had just witnessed it clearly with her own two eyes. Harmony was literally glowing.

Yes, Mr. Shady was humping her, but he had outright refused to fuck Amari even after she'd fed him and sucked his dick good. What was up with him? Maybach was moving too damn slowly digging into Dorian's past life in Chicago. A weird feeling deep down in Amari's gut told her the nigga wasn't legit. Something about him wasn't right, and she wanted to know what the hell it was. At this point, she was willing to do anything to get the scoop, even if she had to take a secret trip to the Windy City and do some digging around herself. No matter what, Amari would get the tea on Dorian Hendrix if it was the last thing she ever did.

With that settled, Amari gathered her choir robe and purse and exited her truck just as Harmony started walking toward the church.

"Hey, Harmony! How are you doing this morning?"

Harmony turned around so fast when she heard a female voice call her name that she dropped her clutch bag and spilled most of its contents. She smiled anyway when she saw Amari rushing toward her. "Good morning."

"Girl, let me help you." Amari bent over and started picking up the items Harmony had dropped. "I hate running late. It makes me nervous, and I go to dropping shit too."

"I usually don't run late for anything." Harmony reached for the three-by-four picture she and Dorian had taken with the captain aboard the R&B riverboat dinner cruise last night.

Amari reached out for the picture at the same time. Their hands actually touched. Fast and discreetly, Harmony snatched the picture up from the ground and stuffed it back inside her purse. She couldn't be too sure, but she didn't think Amari had had enough time to really focus on the picture so her brain could capture the images. Harmony whispered a prayer, hoping she was right. The last thing she wanted was a bunch of church folk gossiping about her and Dorian. She wanted to keep their relationship on the low as long as she could. Things were flowing smoothly between them, and Harmony didn't want to jinx it.

"I think that's everything." Amari stood up. "Let's go sing and get our praise on."

"I've got to stop by the choir lounge and get my robe first. You go ahead. Thanks for helping me."

"No problem, girl. You wanna hang out with me and my clique after service? We're going to Club Rhapsody for their Sunday brunch again."

"I can't. Maybe next time, okay?"

"Damn, girl, you gotta cook for your family again?"

"Nah, I won't be in anybody's kitchen today. I'm going to sleep the afternoon away."

"Uh-oh! You must've had a long night." Amari cocked her head to the side with a smirk on her face.

Harmony couldn't hide her smile when memories of her time in Savannah with Dorian began to replay in her head like scenes from a romantic movie. She had to swallow a moan when a vision of them making love in the shower this morning flashed in slow motion.

Amari cupped her shoulder. "Harmony, are you all right? You're blushing and breathing all hard and shit. It seems like you had one helluva night."

"I'm sorry, Amari. My mind is all over the place. We better get inside the church before the praise team finishes."

"Oh my God, y'all sounded amazing! I like that new director of music, chile. He knows his stuff, and the Negro is fine. I might offer him some milk and cookies now that I'm back in town for a spell. Mmm, mmm, mmm, I love me some sexual chocolate."

All of the Voices of Victory members crowded in the choir lounge laughed at Jerron's dramatics. Every black church choir in America had at least one gay guy among them, and Jerron proudly wore the crown in his choir. There were probably more gay men in Voices of Victory, but he was the only one who had boldly stepped out of the closet.

Jerron had rushed to the lounge immediately after the benediction to greet his fellow choir members. It had been a minute since he'd sung with Voices of Victory because he'd been on the road, acting and singing in Tyler Perry's new stage play. He'd missed his church family, especially his choir buddies. Something exciting was always jumping off in Voices of Victory, and he wanted the latest tea.

"What's been happening, fam?"

"We have a new soloist, and she tore the church up last Sunday," Sister Julia Mae reported. "The gal can blow! She's been in the choir for a while, but we didn't even know she could sing until Brother Dorian got here. He pulled her gift out, and she blessed the church last Sunday."

"Yes, Lord, she did," Joette concurred.

Another soprano agreed. "Brother Dorian helped her stir up her gift."

Jerron didn't miss Amari's sharp eye roll over the compliments for her new competition. She sucked her teeth loud, too. If looks could kill, Atlanta's finest would be on the scene right now investigating a triple homicide, and yellow tape would be all around the choir lounge. The nosy bug had bitten Jerron, so he pushed Amari to the back of his mind. He could chew the fat with her later. At the moment, he wanted the drip-drip on the new lead singer.

"Well, does this new vocal vixen have a name? Who is she? Do tell."

"Her name is Harmony. She sings alto and—"

You could hear an ant piss on cotton when Harmony walked into the choir lounge with Noni playing her shadow. Sister Julia Mae had stopped talking on the spot, which was a clear indication that the songstress everyone had been raving about had entered the room. Jerron's interest piqued to a higher degree. Instinctively, he walked over to Harmony with a smile on his handsome, redbone face.

"Ms. Harmony, Ms. Harmony, I've heard all about you, darling. The word around Light of the World is you've got platinum singing pipes."

"I appreciate the compliment, but who told you that, Jerron?"

"Never mind, my dear. Just know that your choir family thinks you are fabulous."

"Wow! I'm flattered." Harmony smiled and took off her robe. After hanging it on the garment rack, she and Noni left the lounge as quietly as they'd come.

"Talented and humble: that's a recipe for success." Jerron checked out his reflection in the mirror and dusted imaginary dust from the shiny, pink lapels on his designer blazer. He noticed Amari's sour face behind him. The girl looked like she was ready to fight. He spun around dramatically to face her. "May I help you, sugar?"

"Yeah. I think so. You know different kinds of musicians from all over, right?"

"I must admit I do. I've had my share of rendezvous with a few. Why?"

"I need your help. Let me take you to Sunday brunch at Club Rhapsody so we can talk about it."

"Yes, of course. Let me get my purse."

***

Harmony's plan to sleep her Sunday afternoon away flew out the window as soon as she and Dorian arrived at his midtown loft. They didn't even make it to the kitchen to eat the Jamaican food they'd picked up en route to his spot. The bag of spicy Caribbean cuisine and two bottles of ginger beer were on the coffee table, and their discarded clothes were all over the damn place. Dorian's oversized leather recliner was as far as the couple had gotten before they started swapping spit and snatching each other's clothes off until they were butt-ass naked.

Now Harmony was riding Dorian in that recliner, taking in the full length and breadth of his dick every time she arched her back and rolled her wide hips forward. He was guiding her movements and controlling the pace of their coordinating thrusts with his large hands firmly gripping her ass. Harmony's whole left areola and nipple were inside Dorian's mouth, muffling his loud grunts of pleasure. She loved the way he was sucking her nipple and circling the sensitive peak with his tongue.

"Get in touch with your inner freak. She's down in there somewhere."

Noni's words resounded in Harmony's ear, and something inside of her snapped. She felt free and adventurous in the moment, so she followed her body's desire. She eased off of Dorian's lap, missing his dick filling up her walls to capacity already, and reversed her position. With her back to him, she hopped on that big ol' chocolate lightning rod again and went right back to work, thrusting, slipping, and sliding her way to that happy place where only Dorian could take her.

Harmony threw her head back and whimpered when Dorian reached around and cupped her right breast. He fondled the fleshy mound in his palm and teased the nipple until it became rigid. His other hand eased around too, and his middle finger found her clit. When he began strumming it up and down, the dam broke, and Harmony's pussy released a torrential rainfall of her juice all over his dick. Dorian's lap was saturated with sexual moisture, and every time Harmony's ass touched down, it sounded like she was splashing in a puddle of water.

Bass-bottom grunts, feminine coos, and the sound of sweaty flesh slapping against sweaty flesh created sweet music in their love nest, and the pungent scent of wild sex weaved its way through the air. Harmony had never experienced such unrestrained passion and shameless nastiness in her life, but she welcomed both wholeheartedly. Their lovemaking was giving her new life, and she loved the feeling. Just as Noni had predicted, Dorian had opened up his world of sexual pleasure to Harmony, and she'd gladly entered without reservation. How could she ever go back to her life as she knew it before Dorian came along?

Harmony's breath got trapped in her throat when she felt the first spasm of an orgasm creep up on her. The sloshing sound of her dripping pussy as Dorian's dick pumped in and out of it grew louder. She felt his erection expand, stretching her vajayjay to the limit. Her pussy was extra sensitive after fucking all night long and into dawn, so she felt the countless veins in Dorian's dick vibrating against her walls when a fresh stream of warm blood rushed down there. The dick was so damn good. Nah, it was better than good. It was the Eighth Wonder of the World.

Without warning, Dorian stood up, displaying Herculean strength, with his dick still sheathed inside of Harmony's sloppy, wet warmth. His strong arms were secured around her waist as he continued pounding her pussy relentlessly like it was his arch rival. Then, to Harmony's surprise, he turned around to face the recliner without breaking their connection and pushed his kneecaps into the backs of her knees until she fell forward into the kneeling position on the warm leather.

"Dorian, baby," she cried out in a raspy voice with her arms dangling over the back of the recliner.

"You love this dick, don't you? Tell me you love this dick, baby. Tell me."

"Yeah . . . yeah, I love it."

"Then make it rain, baby. Come on and make it rain."

That was all it took for Harmony to launch off into orgasmic orbit, taking Dorian with her.

Chapter Eighteen

Dorian sat up and looked down at Harmony when his cell phone started ringing. She had a post-sex glow that made him want to puff on a Cuban cigar and throw back several shots of tequila. That's how proud he was about thoroughly satisfying her sexual needs. After giving each other a whole lot of loving, they sat on the living room floor in the nude and fed each other lukewarm Jamaican food. Afterward, they took a shower together and retired to his bed for the evening.

When the caller hung up and immediately rang Dorian's number again, he left his bed to answer the phone after peeping at Harmony a second time. He didn't want the phone to wake her up, because she needed to sleep off her physical exertion. It was probably his mother or sister trying to reach him. They were the only people who called him on the regular other than Harmony. When Dorian checked his screen, it was a number with a 312 area code all right, but it didn't belong to his mother or his sister. It was Kyle, a fellow pianist/organist he used to play gigs with on the club scene in the Chi.

"What's up, Kyle? It's been a minute, bruh."

"I know, man. How's it going down there in the A?"

"I'm just making it do what it do."

"I heard that." Kyle laughed. "I think you might be making it do a little too much, because you already got haters down there."

"What the hell you mean, bruh? I've been on my best behavior down here in the A."

"I don't doubt you on that, but something you're doing down there is pissing somebody off. Some dude, a country-ass club promoter from down there, was asking a bunch of questions about you last week at CJ's spot. The nigga was digging deep, but you know how me and my boys operate. If it ain't got nothing to do with making coins, we don't bite. Plus, you're our homie, and we live by the honor code."

"I appreciate that. Good looking out, man. I won—"

"Hold up, bruh. There's more."

"Damn! For real?"

"Yeah. Another dude and some chick from the A reached out to the drummer at your old church today, asking all kinds of questions about why you left Chicago and some other shit."

"And what did Yonk tell them?"

"He told me he didn't say shit because he don't know shit. Then that nigga had the nerve to ask me if I knew why you left Chicago in such a hurry."

"And what did you say?"

"I didn't tell his ass a damn thing. Truth is, I don't know why you left, and if I did, I wouldn't have told him. Anyway, Yonk seemed like he was on some kind of mission. So he told the dude and the chick he would do some snooping around and get back with them."

"I ain't surprised that nigga would hop on some dirty PI shit on me. Yonk don't like me over some mess about his baby mama." Dorian released a sigh in pure frustration. "Anyway, thanks for having my back and reaching out, Kyle. I ain't got nothing but love for you."

"Same here, my man. I'll hit you up again if I hear anything else."

"Yeah, please do that. Later."

"Holla."

Dorian headed to the kitchen in all his naked glory with his head spinning. He needed a stiff drink to process everything Kyle had just told him. Who the hell in Atlanta would be so interested in his life back in Chicago before he moved south, and why? The shit was insane. Reverend Cleveland had cleaned up Dorian's mess before it could hit the streets by demanding that J.P., his assistant pastor, turn over the pictures and video footage of him and Jade in bed together the night they got caught getting busy. There were only six people who knew exactly what happened that night, and they were the two guilty parties, the scorned fiancé, two messy-ass deacons who took pictures and video recorded the bust, and of course, Rev.

There was no way the two deacons had snitched, because Rev had confided in Dorian that they'd been mixed up in financial and sex scandals of their own. Those motherfuckers had gone mute quickly. And the only way J.P. had been allowed to remain assistant pastor at the church was because Rev had forced him and Jade into an agreement to do each other no further harm. Plainly put, they'd called off the wedding together in a joint public statement to the church without answering any questions. Then Jade had sworn not to file assault and battery charges against J.P. for beating the shit out of her before she moved her ass back to Gary, Indiana with her family.

Of course, Dorian had been terminated because he and J.P. couldn't possibly serve at the same church without killing each other. The good thing was even though Reverend Cleveland hadn't had any other choice but to let go of the best director of music and organist his church had ever had, he'd secured him a job elsewhere. But after Dorian's surprise call from Kyle, he was worried about keeping that job, and he didn't even know why.

Who was after him, and what the hell did they want? He hadn't done anybody dirty since he'd moved to Atlanta. He didn't have any male friends yet, and Harmony was the only woman he had been kicking it with. That disaster with Amari didn't count. Or did it?

Dorian removed a cocktail glass from the dish drain and reached behind the microwave for his half bottle of Hennessy Pure White. He poured a generous amount of the liquor into the glass and sat down at the table to sip and think. None of this made sense to him. A brotha was trying to get his life back on track by doing the right thing, yet the devil was busy, using niggas he didn't even know to come after him for reasons unknown. Dorian didn't know what to do. Just when he had found happiness, it seemed like his world was about to be turned upside down again. Only this time, he had much more to lose.

Harmony.

Just thinking about her made him smile, but when he considered that she could get hurt behind his past secrets, he wanted to kill somebody with his bare hands. The last thing he wanted to do was cause her any emotional pain, because she'd already been through enough. She was so sweet and trusting. The girl had already set up residence in his heart, which was foreign to him. He hadn't allowed a woman to get this close to him since his junior year at Morgan State University in Baltimore. And even then, he'd been such a ho dog that he couldn't do right by the woman. So he gave up and embraced his playboy nature, and the rest was history.

"How long have you been awake?" Harmony's arms slid around Dorian's back and shoulders as she kissed his cheek.

"Not long." He reached over and caressed her bare thigh. "How did you sleep?"

"I slept like a baby. Was I snoring?"

Dorian chuckled. "Just a little bit."

"Oh my God, I'm so embarrassed."

"Don't be embarrassed, baby. You snore in perfect E-flat, and it sounds good to me."

Harmony kissed his cheek again. "Quit lying, boy."

"I ain't lying. That's why I want you to spend the night with me. A brotha needs you to snore him to sleep."

"Yeah, I'm sure that's the real reason why you want me to stay with you tonight."

Dorian turned sideways and pulled Harmony onto his lap. "I just want to be with you. Is that okay, or did Papa Luther tell you to have your ass at home when he arrives later tonight after the game?"

"Luther is not my daddy, so I don't have to be anywhere unless I want to. But FYI, because the game doesn't start until eight o'clock, the team won't fly out of Philly until tomorrow morning."

"So you're staying then, right?"

"I'll think about," she purred flirtatiously, and Dorian's dick woke up and tapped her against her ass.

"Girl, don't make me bend you over this table. Keep playing." He eased his hand under her short nightgown and found her pussy hot and juicy.

"Stop it, Dorian!" She hopped up from his lap. "I'm going to take a jasmine and coconut milk bubble bath in your tub that you never use so I can be fresh for kickoff."

"Can I come with you?"

"Ummm, no."

"Please?"

Harmony leaned over and kissed him fully on the mouth. "I'll see you in thirty minutes."

Dorian turned around and watched her ass jiggle and sway as she left the kitchen, laughing at his horny ass. "I'm coming to wash your back."

"I have a brush for that. Goodbye, Doriaaan."

***

“Y’all are some rude-ass ghetto bitches. Don’t y’all see me on the damn phone?”

Joette flipped Amari the bird. “It ain’t like you’re talking business. You’re just over there trying to dig up shit on Dorian.”

“Whatever.” Amari put the phone to her ear again and continued talking.

Joette, LeLe, and Yim were all into the football game. The Falcons were up by two touchdowns, and the players looked like you could reach out and touch them on LeLe’s man’s seventy-two-inch, high-definition flat screen. They had just learned that number 87, the home team’s starting center with the pretty lips, was Harmony’s brother. And according to everything they’d read on the internet, he was single with a net worth of $75 million.

LeLe had a man, and Yim was gay, with several fish dangling from her pole. But Joette was single, so she had her eyes on the prize. She already liked Harmony and thought she was the best singer in the choir hands down. So maybe it was time for them to get to know each other over Sunday brunch or a girls’ night out in the near future.

Amari ended her call and walked back over to the couch to sit between LeLe and Joette. “What were y’all over here screaming and acting a fool for?”

“Check out number 87,” LeLe said. “That nigga is thick and mean looking, but he is pretty. Even Yim wants to give him some.”

Amari’s friends laughed, but she was eyeballing the TV, apparently trying to find number 87.

“There he is! Look at that big, sexy nigga!” Joette licked her lips. “Shit, my pussy done got wet.”

“Damn! He *is* fine. He’s big as hell, so he might break me in half while we’re fucking, but a bitch would die happy.”

All of the ladies laughed and slapped hands.

"I wonder where he hangs out at. Probably someplace ritzy, but I may have to pull up on him soon." Amari grinned before licking her lips.

Joette rolled her eyes to the ceiling. "I don't know where he spends his down time, but I know who can tell me everything I need to know about him."

"Who?" Amari almost broke her neck when she snapped her head around to stare at her BFF.

"Harmony."

"Harmony? How the hell would her fat ass know anything about a nigga who plays for the Falcons?"

"Girl, that's her brother."

"Are you fucking kidding me? Why is she so goddamn lucky? She can sing a little bit, and I know her fat ass is a freak ho because she's fucking Dorian and sucking off his sperm-skeeting ass. And now you're telling me she's got a rich brother? I hate that bitch!"

Joette, LeLe, and Yim stared at Amari like she had lost her fucking mind.

"Girl, you need to stop acting crazy. That girl ain't done nothing to you, and it damn sure ain't her fault that Dorian don't want your ass. Why does it matter who her brother is?" Joette looked at LeLe. "Please roll this bitch a blunt with some of your man's good shit so she can stop spazzing out."

LeLe got up and went to the kitchen, and Yim followed her, leaving the two best friends alone. Joette glared at Amari, and for the first time in the twenty-one years they'd been friends, she realized she was one evil, self-centered, insecure, jealous *bitch*.

Chapter Nineteen

"It looks like you've been gone all weekend."

"Yeah, I was." Harmony continued down the hall toward Luther, pulling her rolling suitcase as he watched her. "Dorian and I went to Savannah and had a good time. Then we watched the game at his place last night. I'm sorry y'all lost. You played a good game, though."

"Thank you."

"What do you want to eat for dinner?"

"I ate already. I stopped by Big Bill's and bought some wings and salad. I got teriyaki wings and a Greek salad with extra feta cheese for you. It's in the fridge."

"Thanks." Harmony stopped directly in front of her brother. "Can we talk, Knee Baby? I mean *really* talk."

"Yeah. What's up?"

"Let me put my suitcase in my room."

Harmony hurried to her bedroom and placed her suitcase on her bed and changed out of her high heels into her comfortable slippers before returning to the hallway. The door to the master suite was open, and she heard the TV playing. When she stepped inside, she found Luther chilling on the love seat. He aimed the remote control at the TV and turned it off after Harmony sat down next to him.

"What's up?"

"We used to be so close, Knee Baby. What happened to us?"

"I don't know. It seems like you changed. One day, everything was all Gucci, and then the next thing I knew, you were all into this Dorian dude, and you started acting funny."

"That's not true. I am still Puddin', your baby sister, who will cut and kill for you. Nothing, especially not a man, will ever change that. But my situation has changed. The day Ham died my whole world crashed, and so did yours. We worked through it, though. It took some time, but we eventually started living again in our new normal without Ham."

"Then you brought Dorian into the mix to try to replace my boy."

Harmony squeezed her brother's knee and met his gaze with sincere eyes. "Ham can never be replaced. He'll always live in my heart, but it's time for me to move on. Ham loved us so much that he would want us to be happy, and right now, Dorian is a part of my happiness."

"You really like ol' dude, huh?"

Harmony smiled. "I really do."

"If y'all are going on trips and shit, I guess you're having sex with him then."

"How come you got to take it there? My sex life is not your business."

"Hell, you used to tell me everything, even about your sex life. Remember when you were sixteen and you told me you were going to give Ham your virginity for his eighteenth birthday present?"

"How could I forget? You showed your ass on me, and then you wanted to fight Ham over *my* decision when he didn't even know anything about it, but I stopped you."

"You blackmailed me. That's what your ass did."

"Hell yeah, I did." Harmony doubled over laughing. "I threatened to tell Mama you had spent the night with Callista Roberts at the Motel 6 in Macon when you were supposed to have been in Warner Robins at a training camp."

"And after all the fussing, cussing, and threats, you still went through with it."

"Yes, I did. I lost my virginity to Ham on his eighteenth birthday, and I've never regretted it."

"You were always stubborn as hell."

"I still am."

The room was quiet for a moment as Harmony thought back to that night and many other memories of the good times she'd shared with her brother and Ham. She was sure Luther was reminiscing about the same thing. They were the gleesome threesome for years until Ham tragically left them.

"Do you love Dorian, Puddin'?"

"It's too early to say for sure, but I think I do. He's so good to me, Knee Baby. I never knew I could laugh so much over small things like a bag of caramel popcorn or twerking in public. He caters to me and makes me feel special. My weight isn't an issue for him. Whenever he looks at me, I feel like a perfect size eight instead of a sixteen. He challenges me musically like no one else ever has. And I've learned things about my body I didn't—"

"That's enough!" Luther shot up from the love seat like it was on fire. "I don't need to hear that shit! Damn, you know how to mess with a nigga's head."

Harmony laughed hysterically. "Sorry."

"I guess now that you and Dorian are all booed up, he'll be making the annual family game trip. This year, y'all are going to the Big Easy with the crew for the Falcons-Saints game."

"Oh shit! I forgot all about that. When is it?"

"It's Sunday after next. Rhema booked flights for everyone to come down that Friday evening, so the kids will only miss one day of school. I rented an eight-bedroom

Victorian mansion at the edge of the French Quarter with a service staff and all the luxuries you can think of."

"You really won't mind if Dorian comes with us?"

"Nah, I don't mind. As long as it'll make you happy, I'm cool. I'll tell Rhema to add him on the flight."

Harmony stood up and gave her brother a hug. "Thank you."

"It ain't no big deal. But don't make me regret giving that nigga a chance. You hear me? If he slips, me and the O'Jays will crush his ass."

Since Luther had finally given Harmony his blessing to date Dorian, she was walking on sunshine. Their once-close brother-sister bond was almost as strong as it used to be. It was like they'd never even had a rift at all.

As a gesture to spread the joy and to get better acquainted with her family before their trip to New Orleans, Dorian had suggested that he and Harmony host a little get-together at his loft for her brothers and their families. She thought it was a dope idea, so she started planning right away. When Friday evening rolled around, Dorian's loft was lit. The moderate-size dwelling was filled to capacity and noisy with children chattering and grown-ups talking shit over good food and strong libations.

A lively game of Spades was in progress with Rhema and Otis playing against Marvin and Dorian. Harmony was too busy making sure everybody had anything they wanted to play cards with her man. But she was having a blast listening to him and Marvin giving Otis the business.

"You seem happy, girl. New love looks good on you."

Harmony turned around and smiled at Noni, who had sneaked up behind her. "I'm beyond happy, girl. I feel like doing a hallelujah dance."

"If you feel like that now, just wait until next Friday when we touch down in the Big Easy with Mama and

Daddy B. I don't think the city will be able to contain all twenty-one of us."

"I know. I'm so excited!"

"What did your mama and daddy say when you told them Dorian was coming?"

"Mama loves him, so she went on and on about how handsome and funny he is."

"What about Daddy B.? What did he have to say?"

"Not much, but he does like Dorian. They clicked over a bottle of Wild Turkey at the game, honey, so I expect them to be just fine when they reunite in New Orleans."

"Y'all set! Y'all set!" Marvin jumped up and slammed his card down on the table. "Get your ass up, punk, and take my pretty sister-in-law with you! Get to stepping, I say! Get to stepping!"

"Oh, Lawd, it's about to be a long night." Noni shook her head at Marvin.

Harmony was laughing so hard that her stomach ached. "Leave it to Marvin to start some shit." In the middle of laughing, she caught Dorian staring at her with a peculiar look in his eyes she couldn't recall seeing before, and it caused the fine hairs on the back of her neck to bristle.

Dorian winked and puckered his lips in a kiss that made Harmony's heart sing. His eyes held hers hostage as seconds ticked by, and she knew at that very moment she was in love with him.

"I saw that, girl." Noni rubbed Harmony's back.

"What did you see?"

"I saw the way Dorian looked at you. Don't try to be cute, heifer. That man is in love with you."

"Dear God, I hope so."

Climbing the stairway to heaven
Climbing the stairway to heaven
And we are going step by step
Together, step by step

"Whooo, chile! Listen to Nat singing that high tenor, y'all. I'm going to have to give him some tonight." Noni raised her fourth glass of wine in the air and waved it back and forth.

Rhema took the wineglass from her and placed it on the bookshelf in the corner of Dorian's music room. "Girl, shut up. You don't need an excuse to fuck that big Negro. You would give him some if he were singing 'Mary Had a Little Lamb.'"

"Don't talk too fast, Rhema, because Otis is killing the lead. You owe him some for singing like that."

"What about you, Puddin'? Don't it turn you on when you hear Dorian singing and playing like that?"

Harmony's face turned fire-engine red when her eyes floated over to the piano, where her man was tickling the ivories and harmonizing with her brothers. "Yeah."

The three sisters-in-law burst into a fit of laughter.

The music suddenly stopped.

"What are y'all over there giggling about?" Marvin asked. "We sound damn good to not have practiced in years. Y'all think y'all can sing better?"

Neither Noni nor Rhema could carry a note, so they didn't respond, but Harmony left her chair in the middle of her girls and sashayed over to the piano.

"I don't want to compete with y'all. Let's sing something together like we used to do back in the day." She caressed Dorian's shoulders. "You got me, boo?"

"Yeah. Just start singing, baby. You know I'll catch you."

"Mmm, 'L.A. proved too much for the man.'"

The Baxter brothers chimed in without any prompting in impeccable three-part harmony on *Midnight Train to Georgia*.

The Gladys Knight and the Pips classic was the first of many oldies but goodies that Harmony and her brothers belted out while Dorian accompanied them on the piano way past midnight. Between songs and lots of alcohol, they talked about growing up, singing, and playing football back home in Gray. Dorian had a few tales to tell too. He talked mostly about his life as the son of a single mom who loved his older sister, Charah, very much, but hated the piano lessons their mother insisted they take. Overall, it was an awesome night of food, fun, and fellowship. Everyone saw it as a preview of the blast they planned to have in New Orleans next weekend.

Chapter Twenty

Harmony entered the master bathroom and opened the shower stall. "Dorian, someone named Kyle is blowing up your phone. Should I answer it if he calls again?"

Fuck! A call from Kyle ain't nothing but bad news.

"Um, nah, nah, I'll hit him back later. I ain't trying to miss the flight, baby. Are you all packed up and ready to roll out?" He poured body wash onto his bath sponge and squeezed it before bending down to scrub his long legs.

"Maybe."

"Harmony, baby, please get your shit together, so we can get out of here and make it to the airport on time."

"I just need to pack my shoes and my toiletries."

"What about lingerie? I know you bought some new pieces when you went shopping with your girls the other day."

"Maybe," she said with a hint of taunting in her voice.

"You know what? Keep saying maybe, girl. I've got something for that smart mouth of yours."

"Promises, promises."

When Harmony closed the shower door, Dorian pressed his back against the tile and inhaled deeply. He had hoped the situation with the two unknown men and the woman who were trying to dig up shit on him for whatever reason had hit a brick wall. But obviously he'd been wrong. Why else would Kyle have called him again?

Dorian stepped out of the shower into a cloud of steam

and grabbed the towel from the hook on the back of the stall door. A million thoughts hit him at once, and none of them were good. His heart told him to come clean with Harmony about everything—why he'd been fired from his former church and the incident with Amari. Secrets like those could be detrimental to a new relationship, but full transparency could explode in a brotha's face too. Women always claimed they wanted a man to be open and honest with them, but most women couldn't handle the truth.

"Dorian, Kyle is calling again!" Harmony called out from the bedroom.

"Let it roll over to voicemail, baby! I'll hit him back when we get to NOLA!"

Dorian didn't understand why this shit was happening now when he and Harmony had just settled into a comfortable routine and all of her brothers were finally on board with their relationship. It had to be karma circling back around to bite him in the ass for the dozens of women he had screwed over in the past. It was a damn shame how many good women he'd smashed and dashed on just because he could. The shit he had done to Jade was the worst stunt he'd ever pulled. His meaningless fling with her had caused her to lose a man who'd truly loved her when the only thing he'd been interested in was a few wild romps between the sheets. A relationship had been ruined and lives turned upside down because of him. Now some unknown bad actors were on a mission to serve him with serious payback.

Tell her, fool! Tell Harmony everything! She'll understand.

Dorian shook his head, mentally defying his conscience. He was too afraid to take the risk of confessing anything to Harmony right now. Their fresh and fragile relationship wouldn't survive it, because the timing was all wrong. The whole gang was about to continue the party they'd started at his spot last weekend. It would be stupid for him to drop the bomb on her in the midst of the festivities or even before it all jumped off. No, he would come clean over dinner Monday evening at his loft after they'd settled back into their regular routine.

"Shit! This is bad. I mean, this is worse than bad if it's true." Kyle ended his call to Dorian without leaving a message and stuffed his phone inside his pocket. "What the hell is this nigga doing that he can't pick up the phone?"

Kyle took a long drag on his cigarette before throwing it to the ground and stomping it out. He was frustrated because he had been trying to reach Dorian for hours with some information he needed to know. Yonk had hit him up earlier, bragging about how he and some so-called minister had the goods on Dorian, and they were about to put him on blast. Kyle couldn't believe how messy church folk could be, especially a musician and a man of the cloth. In short, Yonk had claimed that some pictures and a short video clip of Dorian banging the minister's fiancée had mysteriously appeared from out of nowhere. He hadn't offered any further details, but he was happy about the shit like he was somehow going to benefit from Dorian being exposed.

Kyle checked his watch and then lit another Newport. He had seven minutes before his next set with his band. They were playing at a new club in downtown Chicago that was supposedly owned by a close friend of Stedman Graham's. Someone had even dropped a hint that Mr. Oprah was a silent partner in the business, but Kyle had no idea if that was true, and he didn't give a damn. All he cared about was the coins his band's manager had negotiated for them to receive. It didn't matter to him if Oprah owned the club her-damn-self as long as she paid him and his boys what was due them.

Kyle removed his phone from his pocket and hit the redial button. He had promised to keep Dorian posted on the situation involving Yonk and the three people from Atlanta who were interested in his life in Chicago before he abruptly left. And he was trying his best to keep his word. But he couldn't do shit if Dorian wouldn't pick up his goddamn phone. Kyle smirked and shook his head because he figured his boy was slipping and sliding in some sweet Georgia-peach pussy right about now, and that was why he wasn't taking his calls. The nigga had been known as a womanizer up in the Chi for years, so Kyle wouldn't be the least bit surprised if Dorian was banging some chick and ignoring his calls.

After five rings, he thought it was time to leave a message. "Yo, man, this is Kyle. I need you to get at me ASAP. It don't matter what time. I've got some info you need to know about. Peace."

Harmony picked up Dorian's phone from the end table in the den in the mansion Luther had rented for the family. "Hello?"

She frowned when she looked at the phone's screen and realized it was another missed call from Kyle. For some reason, the guy sure wanted to connect with Dorian. His persistence made Harmony feel some type of way, but she couldn't explain why.

"The limo will be here in five minutes. Are you ready for dinner and dancing?"

Harmony turned around when she heard Dorian's voice. "Yeah, I'm ready."

He had entered the den dressed to the nines in a pair of navy slacks and a white Italian-cut dress shirt with a geometric print, highlighted with splashes of navy and red. To say he looked delicious was an understatement.

Nat, Otis, and Marvin were behind Dorian, looking dapper as well. All four men were nursing cocktail glasses half filled with expensive dark liquor. If Harmony were a betting woman, she would put ten bucks on Remy Martin Extra Fine. That had been the Baxter brothers' signature drink for special occasions since Nat got drafted thirteenth overall into NFL twenty years ago.

Dorian pecked Harmony's lips and reached around and tapped her on the ass. "Go get your girls, baby, so we can get out of here. We're about to tear the Big Easy up!"

"Hell yeah!" Nat raised his glass in the air.

"This town ain't . . . ain't gonna ever be the same after we leave," Otis slurred, confirming he was already tipsy.

"Let me go and check on Marvin Junior and Ilyssia before we leave. Y'all know how Mama and Pops let them eat all kinds of junk food when I ain't around. If either one of them comes down with so much as a tummy ache, Geisel will have my ass back in court, trying to take away my visitation rights."

Marvin's brothers cracked up and nodded because he was right.

"Okay, I'm going to get Noni and Rhema with their slow asses," Harmony finally said. "And you need to call Kyle back, Mr. Hendrix."

"I will."

As Harmony walked down the hall toward the bedrooms, she heard her nephews in their room practicing the song Dorian had drilled them on when they'd first arrived at the mansion and discovered the piano in the formal parlor. They sounded pretty good, and it made her smile. Just as she turned the corner, she came face-to-face with Noni and Rhema.

"Y'all heifers are so slow. The limo is probably outside. What the hell were y'all doing?"

"Markel and Savion were in the rec room fighting over a damn PS4 game, so I had to take off my dress and my heels and beat their bad asses. They make me sick, but I'd rather whip them than let their daddy get ahold of them," Rhema explained.

"And I had to pop my Nuvaring in because alcohol and dancing make Nat horny, so a girl had to protect herself from baby number seven. I hope you popped a Nuvaring or a pill or something too, boo. Your brothers would start a war if you ended up pregnant."

Uh-oh! Dorian and I have been slipping!

When Harmony didn't respond, Noni narrowed her eyes at her. "Puddin', what kind of birth control are you and Dorian using, sweetie?"

"Please tell me you started taking the pill again," Rhema insisted.

"No, I'm not on the pill, but we've been using condoms," she lied. "I'll make an appointment with my gynie first thing Monday morning."

"Ladies, the limo is waiting!" Nat yelled.

Noni rolled her eyes. "Okay, let's go, y'all."

Harmony followed her sisters-in-law back down the hall toward the front door with her stomach twisted in knots.

Chapter Twenty-one

"What's my name, baby girl? Say my goddamn name!"

"Awww, fuck me, Deacon Big Dick! Fuck me!"

The headboard was knocking against the wall so hard and fast that Amari was scared it was going to break, and she hadn't even finished paying it off. And they were giving the mattress springs a hard time with the way they were bucking and bouncing. The sharp squeaking sounded like the springs were crying.

"Say it again! What is my name? What's my name, baby girl? Say it!"

"Deacon Big Dick!" Amari screamed so loud that her throat burned.

Deacon Grady Bell, Sister Virginia Bell's husband, had too much energy tonight. He had probably taken Viagra with a Red Bull again after Amari had told him to stop doing that shit a thousand times. But for a 67-year-old man, he did have a super-sized dick with a slight curve at the end, and he knew how to use it, too. And the best part about his secret hookups with Amari was the financial benefit. It always helped her make it through the month just in case Li'l V's daddy didn't pay child support and business at the salon was slow.

"Grrrrrr! Deacon Big Dick loves this hair pie, baby girl! Grrrrrr!"

Amari was getting tired. Deacon had been riding her for about twenty minutes now, and he didn't seem like he was going to cum anytime soon. It was already late, and he couldn't see all that well to drive at night because of his glaucoma. Plus, Amari's first appointment was a seven o'clock full sew-in. After that, she would have a client every thirty minutes until closing like she did most Saturdays. So she knew she had to do something to make this old man bust a nut so she could send his ass home happy to Sister Bell.

"On top, Deacon Big Dick. Let baby girl get on top and ride the bull."

Amari didn't wait for him to respond. She just pushed against his chest hard with her palms and bucked her hips, flipping him over onto his back. Then she hovered over his sweaty, wrinkled body and eased her pussy down on his dick until her ass cheeks felt his gray pubic hairs underneath her. Then she leaned in at an angle and started rolling her hips forward with a little bounce. The dick was old, but it was still long, thick, and good as it slid in and out of her pussy.

"Aw, shit now!" the deacon shouted and started meeting Amari's thrusts with strong upward strokes. "Aw, shit now, baby girl!"

Amari sped up her pace and added a hip swerve at the end of each bounce when she felt his dick get harder inside of her and his breathing became labored. He was about to cum, and she was relieved.

"Awww, shit!"

Amari's cell phone chimed back-to-back at the same time she felt Deacon Bell release a stream of his seed inside of her. Exhausted, she dismounted him and flopped onto her back next to him with old-ass cum running all down her thighs. There was a heavy, musky odor in the air that made her gag as she struggled to breathe. As they lay there tired as hell, her phone chimed three more times with text-message alerts.

That Red Bull had the good deacon still on one hundred even after fucking Amari raggedy. He got up and went to her en suite bathroom and flipped her toilet seat up without even turning on the light. While he was taking a piss, Amari reached for her cell phone on the nightstand to check her missed messages. The first one was a picture that shocked her shitless. She sat up with her heart racing faster than the speed of sound. There were three more pictures that were equally shocking, but the video clip totally gave her joy. Amari smiled.

"Gotcha, motherfucker."

"Dorian?"

"Yeah, baby." He rolled over in bed to face Harmony and pulled her in so close to him that she could see his eyes even through the darkness the stormy Atlanta weather had caused to cover his bedroom.

"I don't mean to sound whiny or petty, but I need to know who I am to you. If your mom and Charah came to town tomorrow, how would you introduce me to them? Would you say I was just a friend or a special friend or what?'

"You want a label?"

"No. I want the truth."

Dorian ran his index finger across Harmony's high cheekbone and down her jawline to her cleavage. "You're the only woman I'm dealing with right now, and you're very special to me. I think that makes you my lady. Yeah, that's who you are to me. I would introduce you as my lady. How do you feel about that?"

"It's fine as long as it's the truth."

"Oh, it's the truth, baby. Believe that." He kissed her lips softly. "You're my woman, and I better be your man."

Harmony giggled. "If you say you are, you are."

"Cool. Now it's official."

"How do you feel about me?"

"I care very deeply about you, Harmony Baxter. I've never felt this strongly about any other woman in my life the way I feel about you."

"But you don't love me."

Harmony felt Dorian's body tense up, and his even breathing pattern changed to choppy, but he didn't answer her question. His silence was his answer as far as she was concerned.

"It's fine, Dorian. You don't have to say it if it's not true. I appreciate your honesty. But I want you to know I love you."

Harmony moved in even closer to her man and pressed the side of her face against his bare chest. High on the love she had for him, she listened to his heartbeat as it thumped against her cheek until she fell asleep.

Tuesday morning pulled Dorian back to the real world after enjoying a fantastic time in New Orleans with Harmony and her family over the weekend. The Falcons had suffered a humiliating defeat by the Saints, but when Luther joined his family at the mansion in the French Quarter, he was cool and upbeat. Being around the people you cared about could make you forget all about your troubles.

Dorian damn sure had forgotten that three assholes were snooping around in his business while he was having the time of his life with his woman in the Big Easy. And they'd been so tired after returning home Monday afternoon that he had decided to put off telling Harmony about why he'd left Chicago and his mishap with Amari. But now he needed to find out why Kyle had been trying to reach him all weekend. He sat down at his desk in his church office and called him.

"Yo, man, where the hell you been?" Kyle snapped the instant he picked up the phone, skipping a greeting.

"I was down in New Orleans with my girl and her family. What's up?"

"Well, I hope you enjoyed yourself, because all hell done broke loose, bruh."

"Talk to me."

"Yonk is out to stick you, and he's got receipts, man. Dude had told me about some pictures and a video clip of you in bed with some preacher's fiancée, but I didn't believe him until he sent me a picture."

"What the hell? Are you serious?" Dorian had never experienced heart palpitations before, but he was pretty sure his heart had just skipped a few beats.

"Yeah, my man, I have a picture of you and some pretty redbone smashing. And Yonk bragged that he's got a few more just like it plus a fourteen-second video clip of her preacher fiancé busting in on y'all."

"If Yonk sent you that picture, I know the three fools he's been in contact with down here already have all of the pictures and the video."

"No doubt."

"Thanks for the heads-up, Kyle. I'll hit you back later. Right now, I've got some moves to make."

"No problem. Handle your business, man."

Joette burst through the door of Amari's salon showing all thirty-two of her pearly whites. It was a few minutes past noon on Tuesday, so she should've had her ass at work. Amari eyeballed her curiously as she strolled like a runway model toward her station.

"Why ain't you at work?" She pulled the sewing needle through the track covering her client's braided hair.

"I got a promotion and a raise, so I took the rest of the day off to treat myself. I did a little shopping for some new outfits since I'll be up front in the main office now, and I came here so you can hook up my hair. Is Parique available?" Joette looked toward the back of the salon. "I need her to do my nails. I want a new, full set of stilettos."

Amari pursed her lips and gave Joette the side-eye. "You're on the come-up, huh?"

"Yes, I'm making moves. My new title is senior financial intake processor. I love the way that sounds!"

"Yeah, that sounds real important."

"Anyway, my boss wants me to apply for a scholarship the firm awards employees who're students majoring in accounting or business finance, so I picked up an application. God knows I can use the money next semester."

"That's cool, bestie. Congratulations. I'm proud of you."

"Thank you."

The second Joette's ass touched down in the vacant chair in Amari's station, the devil showed up on the scene. It was amazing how evil ideas were birthed from jealousy and hate. Instead of being truly proud of her best friend and happy for her accomplishment, Amari was envious. And on top of that, she saw it as an opportunity to inflict pain on the innocent.

"I think we should go out for dinner and drinks on me tomorrow night to celebrate your promotion and raise. I'll call Yim and LeLe and reserve a table at Club Rhapsody. You should invite your cousin, Gayla, and I'm sure Jerron will want to come. And it'll be the perfect time to reach out to Harmony and ask her to join us."

The suspicious expression on Joette's face didn't faze Amari one bit. "You hate Harmony, so why would you want her to have dinner and drinks with us out of the blue?"

"I've been tripping, girl, and I felt stupid showing my ass the other night. You and Yim were right. I have no reason to dislike Harmony. I believe if I got to know her, we could become friends. But I really want her to hang out with us to help you."

"How will it help me, Mari?"

She gave Joette a wide grin. "It'll give you a chance to connect with Harmony, and maybe she will introduce you to her brother."

"Oh, yeah, I feel you on that." Joette returned Amari's smile. "I'll look up her number in Voices of Victory's directory, give her a call, and invite her to our little get-together. Thanks for looking out, bestie."

No, bestie, thank you, boo.

Chapter Twenty-two

Reverend Cleveland's intercom buzzed while he studied scriptures for this evening's Bible study. "Yes, Sister Finney?"

"Rev, Dorian Hendrix is on line two. Do you have time to talk to him?"

"Sure. Put him through."

"Yes, sir."

Reverend Cleveland picked up on the first ring. "Dorian, how are you, son?"

"I ain't doing so well, Rev."

"What's wrong? Please tell me you haven't gotten mixed up with the wrong woman down there."

"No, sir, that's not it. I'm dating the perfect woman, but I might not have her much longer."

"Explain yourself, son."

"Those pictures and the video clip of Jade and me in bed have somehow come to light."

Rev jerked in his chair. "That's impossible. All of those images and the footage were turned over to me, and I destroyed them myself."

"You may have, but someone has been holding on to a duplicate set, and they landed in the hands of your senior drummer, Yonkerius Tate, and he sent a copy of one of the pictures to a buddy of mine."

"Who would've had copies of that garbage and given them to Brother Tate?"

"I'm not sure, but your drummer is a foul dude, and he needs to be dealt with. Either you check him, or I'll fly up there and do it."

"There's no need for you to come here, son. Stay in place and continue to serve Reverend Holloway and your church down there. I'll handle Brother Tate and whoever gave him the pictures and the video. I don't want you to lose your job."

"I can get another job, Rev. I don't want to lose the young lady I'm dating. I can't replace her."

Rev chuckled. "You really have changed your behavior toward women, huh?"

Dorian's own words about Harmony, and Reverend Cleveland's observation, sucker punched him in the gut. If he hadn't seen the light before this moment, he sure as hell saw it now. He loved Harmony. He was in love with her. Dorian couldn't deny it even if he'd wanted to. The reality of it was scary and unfamiliar, but it was his new truth.

"Yes, sir, I guess I have changed," he mumbled, still in shock.

"Relax and be patient while I get to the bottom of this mess on my end. You take care of that young lady and stay out of trouble down there. I'll be in touch."

"Thanks, Rev. I hope to hear from you soon."

"You will, son. Goodbye."

As Harmony inserted the key Dorian had given her into his front door, her cell phone rang. She was extremely tired and hungry, so all she wanted to do was get inside, relax, and eat some leftover spaghetti. Once she opened the door, she dashed into the den and dropped her briefcase and purse on the sofa. By then, her phone had stopped ringing, but it quickly started again. After digging through her purse, she pulled it out and looked at the screen. Smiling, she pressed the answer icon.

"What's up, Knee Baby?"

"I'm just checking in. Thanks for coming over and cooking for me yesterday. You know how much I love your meatloaf and turnip greens with mashed potatoes."

"That's why I cooked it. I have to make sure you eat well even when I'm not there."

"How's Dorian doing?"

"He's fine. He's at the church preparing the musicians for men's choir rehearsal." Harmony sat down on the sofa and slipped off her boots. "He'll be at the game with me Sunday."

"Cool." When Luther paused, Harmony could tell he had something more to say, so she waited quietly. "I need a favor, Puddin'."

"What's up?"

"Can you meet me at the Mercedes dealership in Buckhead at seven in the morning and drop me off at the gym afterward? I need to drop off my whip for maintenance service. I know it's a lot to ask for so early in the morning before you start your day, but I ain't got nobody else. You know our brothers have kids to take to school and shit."

"I understand. My intern can hold down my first period class until I get there."

"Thank you. I owe you."

"No, you don't, because you would do the same thing for me."

"That's true. Well, I'm about to go play pool with the O'Jays and some teammates at Big Bill's. Thanks again for the food, Puddin'."

"You're welcome. I'll see you in the morning."

"Okay. Bye."

The phone rang again as soon as Harmony ended the call. She didn't recognize the number on the screen, but she decided to answer anyway. "Hello?"

"Hi, Harmony. This is Joette Evans. I'm Amari's friend. I sing soprano in the choir."

"I know you. You're the pretty girl with the long red hair and exotic green eyes."

"Yep, that's me." She laughed. "We're having a little get-together at Club Rhapsody tomorrow evening to celebrate my job promotion, and Amari and I want you to come and hang out with us."

Harmony had already turned down two invitations to spend time with her fellow choir members, so she decided to accept this one. Besides, Dorian would be at the studio practicing with Purity and her nephews tomorrow after work, so a night out with Amari and her crew would give her something to do after leaving her gynecologist's appointment instead of coming home to an empty loft.

"I'll be there."

"Awesome! We have a six o'clock reservation under my name. I can't wait to see you."

"I can't wait either. Thanks for inviting me, and congratulations on your promotion."

"Thank you. I'll see you soon."

Reverend John Paul Jackson opened the envelope Reverend Cleveland had just handed him and read the single document he'd pulled out. He wiped sweat from his brow with a trembling hand before he made eye contact with his boss, who was glaring at him from across his desk.

"You're terminating me, Rev?"

"You better believe I am."

"But why? What did I do?"

Reverend Cleveland opened his middle desk drawer and removed a red folder. He slid it across his desk toward his disgraced former assistant pastor without a word.

Reverend Jackson was sweating more heavily now, and his hand was still shaking as he opened the folder. He flipped through copies of text messages between him and Yonk as well as an agreement he and Jade had signed after the sex scandal. Visibly defeated, he hung his head.

"I fired Dorian on the spot for what he did, but I allowed you to stay because I felt sorry for you, and I understood why you had reacted so drastically to the incident."

"But, Rev—"

"Shut the hell up! You signed that agreement, giving me your word that you had turned over all files of the pictures as well as the video clip to me, but clearly that wasn't the case. You deceived me, J.P., and you gave Brother Tate a license and the evidence to destroy lives. I refuse to have an assistant I can't trust ministering over my flock." He reached over and retrieved the folder and replaced it in the drawer. "You've got one hour to clear out your office before I call the authorities to throw you off the property."

"Rev, please hear me out."

"I don't want to hear anything you have to say. Go find Brother Tate so y'all can fill out applications for new employment together. Good luck finding a church looking for a two-for-one special on wolves in sheep's clothing."

When Dorian entered his bedroom, he immediately inhaled the scent of jasmine rising from Harmony's skin, and he smiled. As he walked closer to the bed, he was able to make out her thick hourglass silhouette under the covers. She was resting peacefully on her stomach and snoring lightly. He had grown accustomed to the soft buzzing sound and her scent in his space. There was no way he could ever go back to a life without her in it because he loved her too much. He leaned over and kissed her cheek and continued to watch her.

On the way home from the church, he'd called and spoken to his mom about everything going on in his life, because he was an emotional mess. He was in love for the first time ever, but there was a possibility he wouldn't be able to fully explore that love if the issues from his past were too much for Harmony to handle. But as only Sheila Hendrix could do for her baby boy, she'd encouraged him to step out on faith and not waste another minute coming clean with the woman he loved. After promising his mom he would follow her advice, he'd hit up Charah with his dilemma, and she'd given him the very same advice their mother had.

Tomorrow would be Dorian's personal day of confession. As soon as Harmony opened her eyes, he would tell her he loved her and then make passionate love to her before sending her off to work smiling. Unfortunately, his evening confession would be tough, and he wasn't sure how it would affect his relationship with his baby. He could only pray that divine intervention would keep him and Harmony together and make their bond stronger at the end of the day.

Dorian,

Sorry I had to leave before you woke up. Luther needed me to meet him at the Mercedes dealership at seven o'clock and take him to the gym afterward. I'll see you at home this evening. Have a great day, and remember I love you.

Harmony

"I love you too, baby."

Dorian folded the letter and kissed it. Then he tucked it inside his sock drawer and headed to the bathroom for a shower.

***

"Do you have any questions, Ms. Baxter?"

Harmony looked down at the pamphlets and two prescriptions in her hand and shook her head. "No."

"Great," Dr. Jaffa said with a smile, caressing her shoulder. "I'll see you next month. Make sure you make an appointment with the receptionist on your way out."

"I will. Thank you, Doctor."

"You're welcome, my dear."

Harmony left the office and headed for the receptionist's counter. She quickly made a follow-up appointment for next month, got her parking ticket validated, and left the building en route to the parking deck. On the elevator ride to the fourth floor, she willed her mind to go completely blank. Harmony didn't want to think about anything or feel anything. All she wanted to do was go home, to her real home, and cry herself to sleep. When she reached her truck, she hopped inside and drove toward the parking attendant's booth. She handed the woman her validated ticket, exited the deck, and maneuvered her way into the evening traffic.

As she made her way toward I-75 North, the dam broke, and tears started spilling from her eyes. She wiped her face with the back of her hand and concentrated on the road. Luther had always been her go-to guy when she needed a shoulder to cry on, but Bobby and Corrine hadn't raised no fool. Calling him now would be catastrophic.

Noni was cooking and doing homework with her kids this time of day, and so was Rhema. The O'Jays couldn't handle this kind of news, so she had no one to talk to at the moment, and maybe that was for the best. The silence gave her time to reflect and think so she could sort things out.

As luck would have it, Harmony's phone rang. She looked at her dashboard display and recognized it as

Joette's number from yesterday. After starting off her day much earlier than usual, and in light of her shocking news, she had forgotten she was supposed to be meeting Amari and her girls for dinner and drinks. Harmony cleared her throat and pressed the button to connect the call.

"Hello?"

"Hey, Harmony, this is Joette. I'm running a little bit late because I had to pick up my cousin and got caught up in traffic. Go ahead and get the party started without me, and mix it up with the rest of the crew over a cocktail. I'll see you soon, okay, girl?"

"Sure. I'll see you soon."

"Okay. Bye."

"Bye."

A glass of wine was exactly what Harmony needed right now, but it damn sure wasn't what the doctor had ordered. However, she was very hungry, and she didn't want to go home anymore because the only thing she would do there was cry. Hanging out with a group of people who didn't share her last name would be a great distraction from her problem.

Chapter Twenty-three

Amari smirked when she spotted Harmony walking toward the table, smiling. She would never admit it, but she was well put together for a fat girl. She had a gorgeous face and pretty hair. Her thickness was stacked just right with a nice set of breasts that sat up high, a snatched waist, and curvy hips. But her most appealing body part was her ass. That thing was music-video perfect, and it had a fan club of its own. And Amari believed Dorian was the president and chief fan.

"Hey, y'all," Harmony greeted Amari, her two girlfriends, and Jerron.

"What's up, Harmony? These are my friends, Yim and LeLe," she introduced, waving her hand at her girls. "And I'm sure you know Jerron."

"It's nice to meet you, Yim and LeLe. How are you, Jerron?"

LeLe smiled. "It's nice to meet you too."

"Same here," Yim replied with a wave.

"I'm great, sweetie," Jerron drawled out dramatically. "I'm just honored to be in the presence of musical greatness."

Amari cringed at his reference to Harmony's voice, but she quickly recovered with a fake smile. "Have a seat and order a cocktail, Harmony. Appetizer platters are on the way."

"I'll have cranberry juice, but I need to go to the little girls' room first."

"Go ahead, darling. I'll give the server your beverage order," Jerron offered.

"Thank you." Harmony remained standing with her clutch bag in her hand.

Amari stood up. "I'll go with you."

The two ladies made their way through the upscale establishment and entered the ladies' room. Harmony went inside a stall while Amari touched up her makeup and hair in the mirror.

"I'm so glad you were able to join us, Harmony."

"Thank you for thinking about me."

"I've always thought you were a nice girl, and we wanted to get to know you better. It's crazy how we didn't know you could sing until Dorian took over the choir."

Harmony exited the stall and joined Amari in front of the mirror. She turned on the water and started washing her hands. "Dorian heard me singing before the first choir rehearsal we had under his direction. Then he kinda coaxed me into learning the lead parts on his song."

"Humph, I hear you, girl. Mr. Hendrix is a smooth talker. That's how he was able to coax me outta my panties just two days after we met."

"Are you serious?"

"Yeah, girl, Dorian ain't shit. He had to leave Chicago because he was running women up there like a pimp." She removed her cell phone from her purse and started scrolling through it even though she noticed tears pooling in Harmony's eyes. "He was fired from his old church because his ass got caught in bed with the assistant pastor's fiancée three weeks before her wedding. Just trifling, I tell you. Check this out." She handed Harmony her phone and watched her swipe through the pictures.

"Oh my God!" She covered her mouth as tears trickled down her cheeks.

Satisfaction swelled inside of Amari when she heard the preacher screaming on the video clip. She felt vindicated after the way Dorian had treated her. It was too bad that Harmony was now a casualty of his bullshit, womanizing ways.

"Wait! Where are you going?" Amari ran after Harmony when she scurried toward the bathroom door, crying and gasping for air. "Are you okay? Harmony, come back!"

Dorian opened his glove compartment and removed the ring box while he waited for the Baxter kids to arrive at the studio. He opened it and grinned at the engagement ring he'd purchased on impulse during his lunch break. Although he and Harmony hadn't been dating very long and he hadn't even told her he loved her yet, buying the ring had felt so right. The fat three-carat princess-cut diamond had called out to him, begging him to take it home to his lady love.

The ring was an exquisite piece of jewelry, just like the woman who would soon wear it on her finger. Dorian didn't care if he and Harmony had only been involved for two months or two seconds. He just wanted to secure his place in her heart and in her life until he took his last breath. There weren't any time limits or term requirements on love. When a man loved a woman—really, really loved a woman the way he loved Harmony—time meant nothing.

Dorian replaced the ring box in the glove compartment and reached for his phone. He wanted to hear Harmony's voice. She had been sleeping when he'd come home last night, and by the time he'd woken up this morning, she'd already left to take her brother to the dealership and then the gym. Dorian was missing her in a bad way. After dialing her number, he waited for her to answer, but the call rolled over to voicemail.

"Baby, where are you? We haven't talked all day. I miss you. Holla at me. I'm at the studio."

Seconds later, Noni pulled up in her big-ass Yukon XL with Li'l Nat, Jabario, and Purity. The kids hopped out and ran toward Dorian's truck. An ice-cold Mercedes G-Class SUV parked in the space next to Noni. O2 and Savion got out and walked over. O2 opened Dorian's passenger side door.

"What's up, Mr. Dorian? Are you ready to practice with us?"

Dorian unbuckled his seat belt. "Man, I was born ready."

Joette looked up from the video on Amari's phone and tossed it on the sofa. All she could see was blood red. The rage bubbling inside of her caused her entire body to shake. She wanted to strangle the shit out of Amari with her bare hands, but she refused to commit murder while her godson was in his room sleeping.

"You are sick! I mean, you are really sick, Mari! I swear to God you are the most evil and jealous bitch on the motherfucking planet! You didn't have to do that to that girl. She ain't ever done anything to you!" Joette picked up her purse from the sofa and rolled her eyes at her so-called best friend. "God don't like ugly. Remember that."

"You're mad because I told that fat-ass bitch the nigga she's fucking with ain't shit? For real, Joette? Somebody needed to tell her before he made a fool outta her! I did her a favor!"

"No, you didn't. You got even. Harmony got the solo and the man, and you couldn't stand it. So you punished her for it. And the saddest part about it is Dorian still doesn't want you. He will never want your crazy ass! Get a clue, bitch!" Joette walked to Amari's front door and grabbed the knob. Then she turned around. "And just so we're clear, we ain't friends anymore."

Luther walked into Harmony's room and flipped on the light switch. She was lying on the bed with her face to the wall. He crossed the room and sat down next to her. "What are you doing here, Puddin'?"

Harmony's cell phone started ringing.

"I was sleeping until you woke me up."

"Girl, quit playing. You know what I mean. We were together this morning, and we spoke on the phone this afternoon, and you didn't mention a damn thing about crashing here tonight. If you had told me, I would've come home earlier so we could've watched movies and knocked back a couple of bottles of wine."

"Dorian was at the studio practicing with the kids, so I decided to hang out with you, but you weren't here. I was tired, and I didn't feel like driving all the way to midtown, so I stayed here. Is that all right with you?"

"You know it is. This is your home too." Luther looked at Harmony's phone ringing on the nightstand. "You ain't gonna answer that?"

"Nope."

He picked up the phone and saw Dorian's face on the screen. He put the phone down. "It's your man."

"So?"

"Oh, *that's* why you're here. There's trouble in paradise."

When Harmony didn't respond or move. Luther reached over her back and effortlessly flipped her over to face him. He noticed her red, swollen eyes and became very concerned.

Harmony snatched away from him and faced the wall again. "I'm tired, Knee Baby. Leave me alone so I can go back to sleep."

"I ain't going no-damn-where until you tell me what's going on. What did that nigga do?"

"Why do you assume he did something?"

"Because I know you, girl. You love hard. The only time you used to wanna hang out with me without Ham back in the day was when he had pissed you off. So what did Dorian do to make you come running to me?"

The cell phone started ringing again.

Harmony sat up. "You were right, Knee Baby! You were right about Dorian! He's a liar and a player, and he doesn't love me! I was so stupid to think he could really want my fat ass! It was all about singing and sex for him! You tried to tell me, but I wouldn't listen! I feel like a damn fool!"

Luther enfolded Harmony in his arms and rocked her. She wasn't his BFF or drinking buddy or roommate anymore. She was his baby sister whom he'd always protected and taken care of. Listening to her sob pitifully as she trembled in his arms broke his heart, but it pissed him off even more. He was seething, and he wanted to tackle Dorian's ass and lay him out flat.

"Hush now, Puddin'. It's gonna be all right. Calm down and tell me what happened."

Harmony's phone continued ringing off the hook.

"He . . . he slept with . . . with Amari before we got together, but he never said a word about it. I was so embarrassed when she told me. And he only moved to Atlanta because he got fired from his old . . . old church for getting caught having sex with the assistant pastor's fiancée. I saw the . . . the pictures and the video tape."

"All of this happened before y'all hooked up," Luther reiterated as he rubbed her back. "Every man has a past, Puddin'." The phone's constant ringing was working on Luther's nerves, but he ignored it while he comforted his sister.

"But he's a liar, Knee Baby, and I can't trust him. Plus, he doesn't even love me. He couldn't say it back when I told him I loved him."

Luther laughed. "All of this can be worked out if you and the man just sit down and talk. Answer your phone and have a conversation with Dorian, Puddin'. No problem is too big to fix when you communicate."

Harmony lifted her head from Luther's chest and locked eyes with him. "I don't know about that." She wiped her eyes with both hands. "I'm pregnant, Knee Baby. Tell me how a conversation is going to fix that."

"What the fuck?" Luther released Harmony and shot up from the bed. He started pacing. "Damn it, Puddin', why didn't you use birth control?"

"I don't know. I hadn't had sex since Ham, so I guess I got caught up."

Luther couldn't handle the phone ringing another second. He snatched it up. "Hello?"

"Luther?"

"Yeah, it's me, and I need to talk to you face-to-face, Mr. Video Man. You thought my sister wouldn't find out about that shit you did in Chicago and your fling with Amari?"

"Um, where is Harmony? I need to talk to her. I can explain everything."

"Nah, don't worry about explaining shit, nigga. The only thing you need to be concerned about is the baby my sister is carrying."

Chapter Twenty-four

"*Baby?* Harmony is pregnant?"

"Yeah, you knocked my baby sister up, nigga, and I ain't happy about it."

"Luther, please let me speak to Harmony. I really need to talk to her right now."

"She don't wanna talk to you, so stop calling her before my brothers and I come over there and kick your ass and burn up all your shit!"

Luther hit Dorian with the click, so he sat there, holding the phone, stunned out of his mind. He jumped up and sprinted around the loft, blowing out the vanilla-scented candles he'd placed everywhere. When he got to his bedroom, he threw a long-sleeved tee over his wife beater before he scattered red rose petals all over the floor when he reached for the ring box he'd placed on top of them in the middle of the bed. He didn't bother changing out of his slides or pajama bottoms. He didn't have time.

The plans he'd made for the evening had been somewhat shattered, but not totally ruined. He raced toward the den, where he found his keys and wallet. He had business to take care of, and no one was going to stop him. No one.

After hanging up on Dorian, Luther couldn't resist the urge to hit up Nat and tell him what was going on with Harmony. The moment the oldest Baxter brother heard the word "pregnant," all hell broke loose. Thirty minutes later, Luther and the O'Jays were gathered in the great room at 10 Sahara Chase.

Marvin accepted a glass of Remy Martin from Luther. "Where's Puddin'?"

"She's sleeping. I had to force her to eat half a bowl of seafood chowder and a few crackers before she took a long soak in the Jacuzzi. She seemed relaxed after that, so she climbed in bed and crashed listening to that 1986 Anita Baker *Rapture* joint."

Otis took a generous swig of his drink and popped his lips. "That's good. She needs to get plenty of rest now for real. I can't believe our baby sister is having a baby, y'all."

"Believe it, bruh. I saw the sonogram, the prenatal vitamins, and the iron tablets," Luther told them. "We oughtta go over to that nigga Dorian's house and kick his goddamn door in and beat the brakes off of him."

"What good would that do?" Nat asked. "Puddin' will still be pregnant and unmarried. And your mug shot would be all over the local, state, and national news tomorrow morning. Did you forget who the hell you are? The league would suspend your ass for sure, all of your endorsement deals would be snatched, and Dorian would sue your drawers off."

After the four brothers sipped their favorite liquor in silence for a few moments, Luther asked, "What are we gonna do, team? What play should we run now? The real star of Team Baxter is emotionally hurt, and I, for one, can't function properly as long as she's down. I was personally responsible for Puddin', but I dropped the damn ball."

"We all dropped the ball," Marvin admitted.

Otis nodded. "True."

"Yeah, we all gave Dorian a fair shot, and he fooled us," Nat confessed.

"I think we—"

The doorbell rang several times, surprising everyone.

"Damn, y'all whipped asses couldn't come over here without reporting to Noni and Rhema?" Marvin looked at Nat and Otis in disgust.

"Noni was sleep when I left, so I didn't tell her shit."

"I told Rhema I was going to the store for some ice cream."

The bell continued ringing nonstop.

Luther placed his half-empty glass on the coffee table and stood up, shaking his head. "Nah, that ain't either one of my sisters-in-law ringing my bell. They both got keys. It must be a security guard passing through on patrol."

He left the great room in his socks and headed toward the front door. A quick glance at the security screen told him who the unexpected visitor was. Luther entered the code on the keypad to disengage the locks and yanked the door open.

"What the hell are you doing at my house?"

"I need to see Harmony, and I ain't leaving until I do." Dorian tried to push his way into the house, but he immediately found out why Luther was one of the highest paid centers in the NFL.

"Nigga, you done tried me!"

Now trapped in a tight body lock, Dorian began to wrestle with Luther. The tussle escalated, and he started yelling, "Harmony! Harmony, baby, I need to talk to you! Harmony!"

Dorian continued calling out even as Luther threw him against the wall, causing pictures and a mirror to crash to the marble floor. Somehow he freed himself from Luther, and they faced off. Dorian faked to his right but charged left. Luther made an attempt to wrap him up, but he missed and slid across the floor in his socks and fell.

Dorian took off running toward the staircase, but he saw the O'Jays advancing in his direction, having emerged from the great room. He went for it, spinning and scrambling right past all three giant-size men who could've easily crushed him if they had been able to catch him.

"Harmony! Harmony!" he shouted as he sprinted up the steps. "Baby, I need to talk to you! Harmony!" Dorian ran down the hall, opening and shutting doors as Harmony's brothers rushed up the steps in hot pursuit.

When he opened the last door on the right, the scent of jasmine told him he had reached his desired destination. He flipped on the light, and Harmony sat straight up in bed. He closed the door and locked it.

"Dorian, how did you get in here? My brothers are going to kill you."

His heart squeezed at the sight of her puffy, red eyes. Dorian could tell she'd been crying, and he knew he was the reason why. But he tucked his emotions in and dragged the bench at the foot of Harmony's bed across the carpet and propped it up against the door as she watched him with wide eyes. Then he found the strength to push an armoire from the corner a few feet and further secured the closed door with the heavy piece of furniture.

Out of breath, Dorian dropped down on the bed next to Harmony. "I fucked up, baby. I fucked up bad, and I'm so sorry. I should've told you about my hookup with Amari, but it happened before we got together, and it ain't like we went all the way."

Harmony's left eyebrow shot up. "What does that mean, Dorian?"

Loud banging and shoving on the door interrupted the conversation before he could respond. "Puddin', open the door, baby!" Nat shouted. "Let us in!"

"I'm gonna kick your ass, Dorian! I swear to God I am!" Luther sounded like he was out for blood.

The banging continued, and so did the yelling and shoving.

Dorian took Harmony's hand into his. "Amari and I didn't have sex, but she did give me head, and that was it. I ain't lying." He touched his heart with his right hand and raised it in the air.

"Why didn't y'all have sex?"

"Because the girl has some serious feminine hygiene issues she needs to deal with." He shook his head. "Something between her legs ain't right."

"Puddin', what's going on in there? Are you all right?" Marvin asked, banging on the door.

"Go away, y'all! I'm fine! I promise I am!" She refocused on Dorian, looking into his eyes. "Tell me about the woman I saw you in the pictures and on the video footage with."

Dorian sighed hard and stroked his mustache with his index finger. "She was engaged to the assistant pastor at the church I had played for since I was sixteen. She had tried to get at me before she hooked up with him, but I wasn't interested. Then two or three months before her wedding, Jade—that's her name—propositioned me. She wanted a farewell-to-bachelorettehood fling."

"And you got involved with her knowing she was engaged?"

"No. We started having sex. I swear it was just sex. Anyway, somehow her man caught on. So he and two deacons busted us one night at the house Jade and her fiancé shared, and they took pictures and recorded us in the act. When they showed the senior pastor the pictures and the clip, he fired me, but because he had known me since I was a kid, he helped me get the job at Light of the World so I could start over fresh down here. Then I met you on my first day on the job, and you changed my life."

"What happened to your promise to always be honest with me, Dorian?"

"I have never lied to you, baby. I just chose not to tell you certain things that had nothing to do with you because I was ashamed."

Harmony sniffed and swiped at her tears. "You hurt me."

"I know, and I'm sorry." He reached out and brushed away a tear with the pad of his thumb. "Please forgive me, because I love you so much and I can't live without you. And my baby will not come into the world without us being married."

"You don't have to pretend that you love me or act like you want to marry me just because I'm pregnant with your child, Dorian. Babies are born to unwed mothers every day, and their fathers are involved in the process. We can coparent our baby as long as you're willing to."

"Girl, I do love you. I just didn't realize it. I knew something strange, a feeling I couldn't explain, had come over me, but it didn't register as love until the day after you asked me how I felt about you. That's when my heart spoke to me, and I accepted the truth." He slid his hand into the pocket of his pajama bottoms. "That's why I bought this on my lunch break today." He showed Harmony the ring box.

Her tears began to fall fast and freely as she stared at it with her bottom lip pinched between her teeth.

"Open it, baby."

Harmony took the ring box from Dorian and opened it. "Oh my God! It's beautiful."

"Just like you." He kissed the tip of her nose. "Let's see if this baby fits." He removed the sparkling, flawless diamond set in platinum from the box and slid it on Harmony's left ring finger when she presented her hand. It fit perfectly. "Harmony Puddin' Baxter, will you make me the happiest cat in the universe and marry me?"

"Yes." She leaned in and kissed his lips.

"Thank God, because I really didn't want to have to move on to plan B."

Harmony giggled and rubbed her palm across Dorian's jawline. "What was your plan B?"

"I was going to hold you hostage in this room until you said yes no matter how many days it would've taken."

"You're crazy."

"I know, baby. I'm crazy for you. You hooked me from day one. And now that we're getting married, I get to spend the rest of my life loving you and making love to you."

"And I'll get to give you all my love too."

"Yeah, baby, and that's a whole lot of loving." Dorian glanced over his shoulder at the door. "You think your brothers are still out there?"

"Are you kidding? Is fat meat greasy?"

"Yep."

"Send the O'Jays home and go to bed, Knee Baby! I'm fine!"

The banging and shoving started all over again. "Open the door, Puddin'!"

"What's going on in there? Open the goddamn door! We ain't playing!"

"Move over, baby." Dorian pulled his tee and wife beater over his head and dropped them on the floor. Then he removed his flannel pajama bottoms. "Let me enjoy this night with you before I have to face Luther in the morning."

Harmony laughed and slid over in the bed and opened her arms to receive her fiancé. "I love you so much, Dorian."

"I love you too, baby."

Epilogue

New Year's Eve

Harmony smiled when she spotted Joette approaching the exquisitely decorated table for two in the center of the stage at the Crystal Chateau. She and Dorian couldn't have picked a more perfect venue for their small and very intimate wedding. The mint, chocolate, and metallic gold color scheme was stunning. The hundreds of white orchids all over the ballroom had released a divine fragrance to enhance the ambience. Chava Simone, their wedding coordinator, had done a marvelous job pulling the ceremony and reception together in such a limited amount of time. Everything was like a fairy tale, and everyone present seemed ecstatic about the nuptials.

"You are the most gorgeous bride ever," Joette gushed when she finally reached Harmony and her handsome groom. "And you are quite handsome in that chocolate tux, Dorian."

"Thank you. It's that Chi-Town swag."

"Thanks for inviting me. I'm so happy we were able to develop a solid friendship after that fiasco with Amari."

"Say no more, girl. You were always nice to me, so it wasn't hard to figure out you had nothing to do with Amari's little ambush in the bathroom at Club Rhapsody that day. Then when you asked to meet with Dorian and me so you could tell your side of the story, I instantly believed you when you laid out the facts."

"But you didn't have to invite me to your wedding."

"Yes, I did. We're friends now, Joette, and friends should always celebrate happy times together."

Seemingly touched, Joette reached over and squeezed Harmony's hand. "Thank you."

"What's going on over here?"

Harmony and Dorian looked at each other and grinned when they saw Luther trekking toward them with his bowtie loose and dangling around his neck as he clutched a bottle of Remy Martin. The expensive alcohol obviously had him buzzing. His unsteady gait, red eyes, and goofy smile were telling signs. But considering that he had footed the entire bill for the wedding, the reception, and even the honeymoon, he deserved to get drunk and turn up even though he had a game in two days.

"Luther, this is my friend from church, Joette Evans. Joette, meet my brother and BFF, Luther Baxter."

"Daaamn!" Luther took hold of Joette's hand with his free one. "Girl, you look delicious enough to eat in a single serving."

Joette giggled and batted her eyes when he lifted her hand to his lips and kissed the back of it softly.

"Come and dance with me so I can get to know you." Luther placed the half-filled liquor bottle on the bride and groom's table with a slight thud. "You like football, girl?"

"I watch it sometimes," Joette replied as she allowed Luther to escort her away from the newlyweds.

Dorian leaned over and placed a warm kiss on Harmony's left temple. "Are you ready to leave and get our honeymoon started, Mrs. Hendrix?"

Smiling because of all the love in her heart for her new husband, Harmony placed her palm on his strong jaw. "Yes, I'm ready, Mr. Hendrix."